Rejecting Destiny:
The Underworlds

A Novel By: Dennis Scheel
dennisscheel.com

Dedicated to: Puma and all the cats, not as lucky as him, who get neglected with not enough love and care.

Thanks to Lindsay for the amazing proofreading, Alex, for the edits, and Jeremy for the suggestions.

This book is a work of fiction. Names, characters, businesses, organizations, places, events, and incidents either are the product of the author's imagination or are used fictitiously. Any resemblance to actual persons, living or dead, events, or locales is entirely coincidental.

Books by Dennis Scheel
NO WAY BACK- THE UNDERWORLDS
TAKEN WITH A DARK DESIRE: THE UNDERWORLDS
REJECTING DESTINY: THE UNDERWORLDS
THE SILVERY PATH: THE UNDERWORLDS

Table of Contents:

Chapter 1- Realizing

The rogue demon, Jack, tiptoed through the forest, glancing about before finally arriving at the large teleportation Gate in a clearing. *After months, I've finally found it.* He ducked into bushes as a man walked by with his dog. Jack peeked back and forth to ensure no one else was around.

Jack raised his palm and Darkness swirled around it. "Sleep," he muttered.

The man slumped down next to his dog.

Jack sidled over to them and peered down at their sleeping forms. A branch cracked in the distance. "Who's there?" He raised his hands and fired a ball of Darkness in the direction of the sound. Squirrels scurried away from the blast. Jack stood alert, but after several minutes of silence, he relaxed.

Damn. Jack shook his head and ambled over to the Gate. He approached the massive structure and ran his hand down one side, stopping when it bumped over the edge of the operating unit. A small smile crossed Jack's lips and he mumbled a quiet chant. A small pulse of Darkness seeped from his hand and enshrouded the main unit.

'Should work now... they'll all think we went the other way,' a voice whispered in his thoughts.

Jack glared at the main unit, watching the Darkness fade. *Denida ruined everything; hunting us, forcing me escape, and all because that twisted Medusa tricked him and killed his son.* Picturing Denida's cocky grin, his eyes glowed red with fury.

Jack scanned 360 degrees, then thrust his arm forward, sending a stream of Dark magic toward the Gate, causing it to light up.

Jack ran through the newly created portal as fast as he could, emerging from another Gate, which powered down as soon he exited it.

Dense woods surrounded Jack like an endless maze.

Most of the Gates are in forested areas. I can't tell where I am...

Jack stalked through the underbrush, pushing branches aside and narrowly avoiding spiderwebs on his pathless trek. When he finally emerged with dead leaf parts and mud all over his boots, he saw a young couple sitting in front of a lake with their lips locked.

Jack approached the couple, but they continued making out with reckless disregard for his presence. "Hey!" Jack yelled.

For a second, the man pulled away from his partner, only to gaze into her eyes before leaning in again to continue their date.

They can't see me. Jack peered around skeptically, seeing fish rippling the lake and hearing birds chirping in the trees. *I'm on Earth, the one place Lucifer can't appear!* Jack laughed hysterically. *I'm finally free to create my own Hell!*

***

Denida sat silently in his Presidential office at headquarters. All the thick curtains were drawn, allowing only faint rays of sunlight to penetrate the room. He sighed, staring into the Darkness. He sighed again, even more heavily.

Denida's vice president, Dan, burst through the door without knocking. "Denny, are you in here?"

"Yes…" Denida didn't move a muscle, instead remaining as still as the rock he had been before Dan entered.

Dan strode over and pulled the big curtains apart, letting daylight flow in, but even with the room illuminated in the bright glow, Denida remained seated in his chair like a statue, absentmindedly marveling at the small cloud of dust sparkling in the sunlight.

Dan sighed. "Daniel's gone. Life goes on…"

"Does it?" Denida shook his head. *How can it? He was my only son…*

Susan paced into the room and stared at Dan and Denida, before tilting her head back to look imploringly at Dan.

Dan sighed and walked out with a shake of his head.

Susan knelt next to Denida and met his eye. "Daniel wouldn't want to see you like this. It's been months since his death; you need to continue living for his sake!"

Denida raised his head and licked his lips. "Maybe you're right." He tried to force a smile but failed. "It's just so hard."

"Let's go see Nina," Susan helped Denida up. "She lost him too, you know. You can grieve this loss together."

We'll see. Denida frowned.

Susan led him to the door, occasionally offering him meek smiles and words of advice. When they were seated in the car waiting for them, Denida finally returned a half-hearted smile. The car lurched into motion and Denida turned his head to the scenery slowly passing by outside. The car's deceleration at the first of several new checkpoints on the road to Dynasty infused him with a sudden sense of weighty impatience. He ground his teeth as he waited to pass through the checkpoint with his identification card clenched tightly in his hand.

Susan rested one hand on Denida's. "Don't worry; Nina will be happy to see you."

I'm not so sure about that… I think I've only spoken to her three times in the last few months and it's never gone well. Denida rubbed his cheek where he could still feel the slap she gave him the day he told her Medusa killed Daniel.

When they finally arrived at Dynasty, Denida's Butler greeted them. The Butler tried avoiding Denida's gaze. "I-"

"Where's Nina?" Denida stared him in the eyes.

The Butler turned his head toward the house. "Daniel's room…"

Not again… Denida nodded solemnly and patted Susan on the shoulder before entering Dynasty. He trudged up the winding stairs to Daniel's room and gently pushed the door to open it wide enough to see into the room.

Nina lay on Daniel's bed with one of his shirts covering her face.

Denida stood in the doorway, just watching her with a tight face and clenched jaw. He lowered his head. *No.* Denida turned and walked back out.

In the foyer downstairs, Susan and the Butler stood talking.

Denida walked into the sitting room, poured himself the most potent drink he could find in the bar cabinet, and swallowed it in a single gulp.

Susan turned towards Denida with wide eyes. "Done already?"

Denida finished another drink. "I couldn't talk to her; it's my fault… Medusa would never…"

Susan rushed over to Denida and squeezed his hand. "No, it's not your fault! Don't think that."

"… but it is!" Nina yelled from the doorway.

Denida jumped up with more energy than he had in a long time and dragged himself toward Nina. He lifted his arms to pull her into his embrace. "Please…"

Nina shoved him away and stepped back. "Don't touch me! Daniel's gone- *forever.*"

"But-"

"No!" Nina held up her hand. "Michelle- no- *Medusa* was here because of *you!*"

"No one could've known she was a demon," Susan came to his defense from across the room.

Nina glared at her.

Lucifer...

Nina spun toward Denida. "Lucifer?" She spat. "He caused this, too! If you didn't have such a colorful past with the *actual* Devil, none of this would've happened." She scrunched up her nose in revulsion at the sight of Denida and stormed out.

"Make sure she's okay; I need to go take care of something..." Denida ordered Susan and rushed out the door. He strode into the forest behind the stables and continued deep into it until he reached the cabin, where Claus had escaped to six months ago.

Denida examined the room. *I can't believe it's come to this.* His eye fell on the kindling in the fireplace, which he lit with a flick of his finger.

Everything's ready. Denida chanted 'Reficul' three times in succession.

A black mist appeared and faded away, revealing Lucifer, who looked around perplexedly, until he noticed Denida. He smiled broadly. "Denny, my boy!"

Denida grumbled. "I'm *not* your boy..."

Lucifer chuckled. "This is the room you caught Claus in, isn't it? How is he?"

"He's fine. We've locked him up this time, seeing as being in your care didn't reform him..." Denida licked his upper lip. "But I didn't want to talk about that. You mentioned that there's a way to keep those dear to me safe from your meddling... and God's?"

Lucifer nodded. "In exchange for a favor, yes."

Of course... Denida's eye widened. "And what would that be?"

Lucifer grinned deviously. "You can enter Heaven freely. Get Heavani and *my* Daniel in the tower and bring them to me!"

Heavani and your son? Denida stood in shock, unsure how he should respond. "The Darkness promised you to..."

Lucifer shrugged. "*Really*? You think the Darkness will ever help me without me killing God, first? I heard from Daniel that you were in Heaven, near Heavani, right, so you know where they are."

Denida sighed. "Yes, but I don't know about this... going to Heaven and all." Denida rubbed his arm uneasily. "Peter watches the Pearly Gates and we're not exactly on good terms, not to mention this is a *kidnapping* scheme." He shook his head.

"Not kidnap," Lucifer insisted. "You'd be bringing them *home*!"

Denida waved his hand dismissively.

"Gabriel never will," Lucifer said. "He's stuck in between God and me, but you-" Lucifer smiled with a hopeful glint in his eye. "You can do it, in exchange for me leaving everyone you know alone forever!"

Denida stumbled into his chair, rubbing his face.

Lucifer sat down in the chair by the fireplace.

"No!" Denida jumped out of his chair.

"I can tell you my story, it might convince you…"

"You want me to trust *your* words?" Denida smirked.

"Not my words, my memories!" Lucifer stared into Denida's eyes.

"Fine," Denida turned his head away and sat down.

"To understand about Heavani and me, you need to see what it was like with God when I first knew him…"

Denida rolled his eyes. "Why?"

"You'll see." Lucifer put his hand on Denida's shoulder and they reappeared in Lucifer's private chamber within his mansion in Hell, the one room where the Darkness couldn't eavesdrop.

Lucifer strolled to the middle of the room and stopped at an old well with ancient inscriptions on the side.

Denida stopped on the other side of the well and glanced into it. "The *'Well of Memory,'* huh?"

Lucifer nodded. "I told you I would show you my memories. At Dynasty, you have a shield against Dark magic, which means I can't show you there, but I can here…"

An image started to form in the well.

Denida stared at Lucifer suspiciously before he focused on the image forming in the water.

***

The suns in the sky baked the ground, as some children ran around playing.

The eldest boy wiped his hand across his forehead, looking up at the two suns, one to the left and the other to the right. Shade was sparse.

The other two boys ran under a tree so tall that even the suns' light couldn't reach everything underneath it.

"Shaddai!" one of the boys yelled and waved his hand, beckoning the one baking in the hot sun.

Shaddai ran over to his friends. "It sure is hot today!" He peered at them, appearing intrigued by something. He turned to see what they were looking at. "For Henna's sake…" Shaddai rolled his eyes.

"It's Odin… he's been told to go somewhere the mother foresaw will be essential to our future."

Shaddai rolled his eyes. "Please! Don't make me laugh, Azal."

Azal shrugged.

"Shaddai, Azal, Gabriel, your parents are looking for you!" one of Shaddai and Azal's neighbors hollered.

"Man," Shaddai threw up his arms.

Shaddai and Azal waved goodbye to Gabriel and walked toward where the prominent families lived.

"You could come with me for a while…" Shaddai glanced nervously at Azal.

Azal jabbed at Shaddai. "Is *somebody* worried?" He grinned.

Azal and Shaddai's fathers came outside and ogled at the boys discontentedly.

"We… were… just…" Shaddai stuttered.

Shaddai's father shushed him. "We're going to see our queen; you two get ready!"

Shaddai and Azal nodded and scurried into their respective houses, next door to each other, to get ready.

"Kids…" Shaddai's father shrugged.

***

Denida sighed and turned away from the well. "I don't think this matters. Why the hell are you showing me three kids in some distant world-" Denida shook his head. "Who is Shaddai, Azal, even …Gabriel, is that God's Gabriel?"

Lucifer chuckled. "Yes. I was not always known as Lucifer; as a child, I was Azal."

Denida wrinkled his nose. "… But it's not Heaven?"

Lucifer shook his head. "Shaddai, Gabriel, and I were from that world. Not Heaven…"

"Gabri-" Denida returned to the well. "That Gabriel *is* Gabriel as a child?" He stared intensely at Lucifer. "Shaddai must be God, then!"

"Do you understand now, why it's important that I show you this here, where no one but us can see?"

Denida scowled. "Yes," he muttered. "You '*Azal,*' Shaddai, and Gabriel visited your queen?"

Lucifer shook his head. "Not Gabriel, only the *high families*, which Shaddai and I belonged to were allowed…"

***

Shaddai, Azal, and their parents entered a ballroom with walls, floors, and even a ceiling, made entirely of glass. Shaddai and Azal's mothers walked over to a crowd of other women to start mingling, while their fathers stood looming over them.

The moon had a cloud surrounding it to restrict its light to a staircase leading up to a second floor. It shone in all the colors of the rainbow and a woman appeared, shining, in the center.

Everyone in the room applauded.

Shaddai's father smacked his son across the head. "Clap!"

Shaddai sighed and peeked over at Azal, as he joined the applause.

The queen descended the stairs until she was surrounded by the women anticipating her. The men, including Odin, stayed back. He stood next to Shaddai's father, applauding her.

"Hi David," Odin patted Shaddai's father.

David smiled. "Why are you here?"

Odin chuckled. "I was selected as a servant to become a god for a world."

"Not just any world," the queen giggled.

Everyone bowed as the queen passed by them.

Shaddai just frowned defiantly.

David slapped him on top of his head. "The Great Mother, Henna is here; bow!"

Henna held up her hand and knelt before Shaddai and smiled. "One day, you might be like Odin. You can be a god yourself." She straightened up and turned her smile to him before facing the crowd with Odin accompanying her.

Shaddai glared at them. "Someday," he said under his breath.

"Go mingle," David instructed Shaddai.

Shaddai took Azal by his hand and stomped off into the crowd.

David ran up and yanked Shaddai back. "Not near the ladies; we're below them. Remember your place!"

Shaddai sighed and nodded, showing Azal a stern face. He led Azal out of the ballroom, then turned and stuck out his tongue at his father's back. "It's a woman's world, why should we be a part of it!"

Azal raised his eyebrows.

Voices sounded down the hall.

Shaddai nodded and his eyes sparkled. "Let's go check it out!" They tiptoed down the hall, finding Odin and Henna.

"We're all your subjects, my Great Mother." Odin bowed down.

Azal and Shaddai giggled.

Henna laid her hand on Odin's head and light emanated from it until it encircled Odin's body.

Odin smiled.

"You're ready." Henna crossed her hands. "Get up, my son. You are a god, now!"

"But, if you don't mind my asking, why have you chosen this little place in the middle of nowhere?" Odin wrinkled his forehead.

"In the Milky Way, I sense something great to come…"

Wow. Azal's eyes lit up. "Let's hurry back to the party," he whispered.

Azal and Shaddai ran back to the party before they were spotted.

***

Henna? Denida squinted his eyes. "You want *me* to believe that a queen you called the Great Mother, could make anyone a god?"

"Yes, *Henna.*"

Denida rolled his eyes. "I think we're done!"

"Wait!" Lucifer yelled.

Denida stormed out the door and, as he stroked his ring, vanished into the air, reappearing at Dynasty, where Susan was still watching Nina.

Nina was tending to her horse, Angel. Susan stood, trying to talk to her, but Nina focused only on Angel.

Denida bit his lip, then returned to Dynasty.

He walked into Dynasty and down the corridors, making his way to the stairs that led to his hidden chamber. He smiled at the maids he passed.

He stopped and checked the hall. *It's clear!* Entering the code for the secret door under the stairs, Denida rushed in and closed the door behind him. He descended the stairs to a concealed room.

"Dan?" Denida peered at the research equipment littered about.

Dan looked up from his microscope. "Denny!" He waved before returning to it.

Denida ran his tongue over his lips. "How's it going? Found anything?"

Dan stood, appalled. "Making a time machine doesn't happen overnight; it took them thirty years in the other Underworld!"

"Didn't you get the report about how they built it?"

Dan sighed. "I did, but it'll still take time. Their report has very few details… no schematics or anything…"

Denida narrowed his eyes. "Do you need the ring?"

Dan shook his head. "It's too soon. I just need time-" He ran his hand across his face. "- if you want me to try this because of what happened to Daniel-"

Denida's eyes flickered dark red. He patted Dan on the shoulder. "I just want to see how it works." He smiled reassuringly, the way he had been taught in Hell. "Just let me know when you get somewhere!"

Denida spun around and climbed the stairs, leaving Dan to his work.

Chapter 2- The Gate

The Colonel arrived on Earth to check on the Special Task Force watching over Denida and Nina's human forms. He stood waiting for the Commander's report.

The Colonel glanced over at the boy Den. "Maybe it's a bad sign his hair's darkening; the Darkness might be up to something again."

The Commander shook his head dismissively. "No demons have been around!"

"Dark magic?"

"On Earth?" The Commander shook his head with a grin.

The Colonel grunted. "Something caused it to go dark."

"In the Underworlds, perhaps?" The Commander wrinkled his forehead.

That can't- The Colonel saluted the Commander and hurried away.

The military in the Underworld was undergoing a thorough examination ever since one of their own had killed the President's son. The Colonel still felt responsible for having allowed the murderer to join his ranks, but everyone knew Denida blamed himself.

When the Colonel entered his office, his fellow soldiers saluted him, but no one would meet his gaze.

He sat down and scanned his messy desk, rubbing his forehead. *Denida.* As if the thought had summoned him, Denida entered the office.

"Colonel," Denida flashed a flicker of a smile.

The Colonel saluted. "Sir, I've got a report from Earth. Something is affecting your human form; his hair's darkening."

Denida wrinkled his forehead. "Darkening?"

"As if Dark magic is affecting him…"

Denida rolled his eye. "Don't worry. I'm sure it's nothing."

But why's he here?

Denida smiled. "I'm here because I want you to check something for me. We know about God, but what about any other gods? Like the ones from Valhalla, where are they? Do they even exist?"

The Colonel scratched his head. "Why now? What does it matter… wouldn't God or the Devil, for that matter have dealt with them?"

Denida insisted, then lazily saluted as he left the Colonel staring in confusion at the door.

****

Denida strolled out of the building. Everyone avoided eye contact as they passed him. "Something you want?" He hissed, baring his teeth in their direction.

"Hi, Denny." Lucifer materialized beside Denida.

"Not you again." Denida continued past him.

Lucifer teleported to sit on the hood of a car in front of Denida. "You might not want to keep walking… or do you want your security guards to notice me?"

Denida stopped and bit his upper lip. "Fine, what do you want?"

"I want you to hear the rest of my story!"

"A tale told by the Devil… you expect me to believe it?" Denida snickered.

"I didn't tell you; *I showed you!*"

Denida stepped closer to Lucifer and stared into his eyes. "I know how the Darkness works. You could have made this up with Magic to convince me to help you get Heavani!"

Lucifer glanced downwards, then nodded.

Denida and Lucifer suddenly appeared in a place surrounded by fire.

Lucifer stood smiling in front of him. "Nothing can kill me. I was born in a world of Gods, same as God and Gabriel-"

Denida rolled his eyes. "You already told me this story!"

"I didn't tell you this," Lucifer smirked.

In front of Lucifer, a dagger lit up with fire engulfing it.

"A dagger?"

Lucifer held up his hand. As he squeezed it into a fist, the fire subsided.

Denida's eye lit up. *Is-*

The dagger flew into Denida's hand. It felt less warm than he imagined. Denida held it, tilting it, gasping, and wondering how it could be. "This material-"

Lucifer grinned and nodded. "The same material as the Gates, as well as your ring."

Denida rubbed the dagger. *He's right; it does feel like my ring…* He peered up. "How?"

Lucifer chuckled. "It's from *our* world. A material only our Great Mother, *Henna* could forge." He grabbed the dagger from Denida's hand and returned it to the fire.

"Why're you showing me this?" Denida squinted his eyes around the room he was in. "Where are we, anyway?"

"You can believe me; I want to show you this. Heavani's too important for lies…" Lucifer smiled broadly. "- but you've never been here before; no one has," he smirked.

Lucifer winked and they found themselves standing in front of the headquarters like they had never left.

Denida scoped out his surroundings, then turned to Lucifer. "Alright, I'll hear more of your tale. I can't guarantee I'll help you, though…"

"You *will* once you understand everything…" Lucifer chuckled and vanished in a dark cloud.

He sure has faith in his story. Denida rolled his eyes. *I can't help but feel uneasy about this.*

Denida sauntered over to his car. His bodyguard jumped up from sitting on the trunk and opened his door, saluting as Denida slid in.

Denida turned to his guard. "Take me to the second Gate, the one in the forest!"

The car drove out to the Gate. It had been a long time since Denida had been there. A little cottage stood nearby in a clearing. The car parked next to the cottage.

Denida stepped out and his eye fell on the cottage. He inhaled deeply. *Back to where Claus and Jack locked Susan up…* He shook his head and turned to walk toward the Gate, but he stopped halfway there and rubbed his glove, which concealed the ring. He gazed down at his hand. *I better make sure it never can be used like that again…*

Denida spun around, and waved his hand forward, sending a gust of wind toward the cottage. It blew hard, increasing in force, until it tore the building asunder.

Denida's guard had raised his gun at the noise, but as he glanced toward Denida, he froze on the spot.

Denida lowered his hand, turned, and smiled at his guard before continuing toward the Gate. He paused suddenly when he was halfway there.

Something's off… "Get over here!" Denida yelled.

The guard drew his weapon and ran to Denida. "Sir?" He surveyed their surroundings with his sidearm raised. "Nobody's here?"

"I feel something…" Denida took off his glove and stroked his hand, while still glaring intently at the Gate. His eye focused on the main unit and ran over to it.

The guard rushed after Denida, still with his handgun at the ready.

There's a different aura about it. Denida knelt, then turned to the guard. "Call the Colonel; the *Scientist* was here. We need to keep this place under constant surveillance!"

The Guard wrinkled. "A scientist?"

Denida shook his head. "Not *a*, *the*! The one who helped Claus with kidnapping Daniel…"

"Daniel-"

"My son!" Denida screamed, his eye full of rage. "You *really* want to say you don't remember? I dare you!" He took a menacing step toward the guard. "He got killed by Medusa… or should I say, Michelle, a person we trusted."

The guard backed away a few steps, but Denida moved faster than he could retreat.

"I'm… sorry," the guard stuttered.

Denida stopped and spat in the dirt. His eye turned from fiery red to its usual blue. "I know. Just get me the Colonel." He waved his hand to dismiss him.

The guard ran back to the car to call the Colonel.

***

As the Colonel arrived, he saw Denida pacing and stopped short. "You found something?" He raised his eyebrows.

Denida ground his teeth. "The Gate's been tampered with. I think it was Jack!"

"Jack? The *Scientist*?" The Colonel spun around. "He's on Earth?"

Denida nodded and led the Colonel over to the Gate.

"He either went to the second Underworld or to Earth?" The Colonel gave a puzzled gaze.

"I'm not sure, but the next world isn't second; it's the third!" Denida shrugged. "I keep telling you, Earth is first, secondly us." Denida turned to the Colonel. "I'm not sure, which one. I'm staying here to see if he comes back through. Can you check with the third world Colonel for me? We need to know if he tampered with this one to throw us off the trail?"

"Why me?"

"The Colonel in the third world, the version of you there… doesn't like me. I want you to contact him to see if Jack went there."

The Colonel gasped. "But isn't Dan handling-"

"Dan's occupied with something else!" Denida patted the Colonel's shoulder. "The Commander will get it set up. Go to the Gate; it's still in the lab! Report any findings to me at my office." He returned to the other soldiers.

***

The Colonel drove to the lab, where the Gate stood, heavily guarded ever since Denida and his son were lost within it.

"Sir!" The guard at the entrance saluted the Colonel and let him through.

Back again… The Colonel sighed as he stepped out of his car and strolled toward the lab.

Inside the lab, it was pitch-black with no one present. Last time the Colonel had been there, it was crowded, with people fluttering about. He flipped the switch, bringing it back to life for the first time in what felt like forever. The Gate stood in the center of the room, illuminated, and whirring quietly.

The Colonel sat down in a chair in front of a set of monitors, which stood beside the Gate. He took off his beret and rubbed his forehead.

I guess I must. The Colonel straightened up and turned on the feed for the android that was in World Three. A soldier appeared on the screen.

The soldier gasped, startled. "Colonel, you um, want to see the version of you in this world?"

The Colonel nodded with a grunt.

The soldier led the android up to a big door. Inside, that world's Colonel sat working at his desk.

"Hello again, Colonel," the Colonel in the home world said. "It's just us, so you may call me John."

The Colonel looked intrigued. "Okay John, what brings you here? It's usually Dan."

John returned to his seat, rubbing his face.

The other Colonel frowned. "What is it?"

"Denida informed me that Dan's busy, so I had to…"

"That Denida," the other Colonel grimaced.

John shook his head sadly. "We fought the Dark Angels together. He's not that bad-"

"He beat me up!"

"He was trying to get farther-" John sighed. "- with Daniel…"

The other Colonel shook his head. "I know, the Gate, but that was then. Why are you calling, now?"

John bit his lip and stared at the screen. "The Scientist… we reason to believe he went through the Gate."

"Dan's watching this one! Jack used the one that connects to you."

The other Colonel scratched his nose. "He's not here. The Gate is under constant security."

Can it be? John's eyes widened. "I've got to go!" He rushed out to his car and drove off.

He parked the car in front of the government building.

The guard at the front entrance saluted him and opened the door.

The Colonel nodded as he continued through it, then to the top of the building, where Denida's office was located.

The secretary was on the phone when the Colonel came in.

The Colonel held up his hand to stop her from getting up, then opened the grand doors into Denida's massive office.

Denida looked up from his desk, nodding at the secretary, who closed the door behind them.

"What's up? Found out anything about *Valhalla*?"

The Colonel stepped up to the desk. "Not Valhalla, just the Gate and Jack."

Denida wrinkled. "What about them?"

The Colonel raised his eyebrows and leaned across Denida's desk. "I just talked to the Colonel of World Three. Jack didn't go there; he's on Earth!"

Denida banged the desk with his fist. "He could truly be on Earth?"

The Colonel nodded.

Chapter 3- Valhalla

Nina sat next to Daniel's grave, located not far away from Dynasty, but still on the grounds where she had the privacy to grieve. She started out, simply gazing down in sorrow, but soon found herself curled up on the ground. *Mommy's here.*

"Nina, stop it!" Dan knelt next to her.

Nina raised her head. "Dan? Why are you here?"

Dan helped her stand and pulled her into his embrace. "What matters is you're not alone!"

Nina squeezed Dan tightly. She held him as close as she could for what felt like an eternity, yet it still was not long enough.

Nina lifted her head and returned to Angel, who was hitched to a nearby tree. She mounted her horse and smiled at Dan. "Thanks." She rode off back toward Dynasty.

She washed her hands after putting Angel back in the stable and peered out into the distance. *Wait, why is Dan at Dynasty, anyway? Is Denny here?*

***

Denida worked out in the gym, welcoming the weariness. *If Jack is on Earth, is my human form safe? Maybe I do need to make a deal with Lucifer!*

A crow flew in from a window, landing on the windowsill, cawing.

Denida turned startled, his eyes filled with hatred. *No, it's just a crow, not like Medusa. She was a sparrow.*

He continued striking at the heavy bag.

"Hello."

Denida jumped back.

An old man with a patch over his eye stood behind him.

"Nice patch; I had one once," Denida smirked. "How can I help you?"

The man moved closer, each step hammering against the floor. "You were looking for me."

Denida squinted his eyes, then shook his head. "I don't think so."

The man lifted his arm and the crow from the window landed on it. "My name's Odin. I lead Valhalla. Are you sure you weren't?" He turned his attention from the crow to Denida.

"Valhalla, from Norse Mythology?" Denida watched in disbelief. *Can it really be?*

Odin smiled tenderly at his crow and nodded. "If you want to see Valhalla, come; I'll take you on Sleipnir."

Denida wrinkled his brow. "Sleipnir?"

"My steed." Odin lifted his arm and the crow flew back out the window.

"A horse?"

Odin stomped on the floor and a majestic giant steed with eight legs appeared in a blue mist.

Denida removed his exercise gloves and sauntered over to Odin. He examined Sleipnir, then turned back to the god. "Alright, I'm game!"

Odin grabbed Denida's hand and lifted him up.

Sleipnir reared up on two legs and set into a gallop, riding through the wall and upwards. It tore through the sky and it wasn't long before Valhalla appeared in front of them.

Denida dismounted, staring curiously at the people gathered around Sleipnir.

A brawny bearded man with a giant hammer hanging from his belt strode up to Denida. "Welcome to Valhalla. I'm Thor!" He wrapped his muscular arms around Denida in a giant embrace.

Odin dismounted from Sleipnir and extended his arm. A scepter appeared in his hand.

Denida licked his lips, remembering this place from the memories the President of the Underworlds had shown him.

"Come!" Odin trudged into a humongous dining hall where a grand throne stood in the middle of the room. He sat down on it and a crow flew in, landing on his shoulder, while another crow already sat on his other shoulder.

The same crow from before… "Why have you brought me here?" Denida asked.

"Your soldier boy was searching for us, so I brought you here to find out why, Denida of the Underworld."

Denida ground his teeth and looked about. A crowd of people filled the room with merry chatter as they enjoyed a grand feast. His eye fell on somebody who reminded him of Claus, standing in the crowd, watching. He turned to Odin. "I just wanted to see if you were real or if the stories were as wrong as the myths of God and Lucifer…"

The crowd started laughing loudly.

Odin glared at them and banged his scepter on the floor, making the ground shake.

The crowd stopped abruptly and silence filled the hall.

Odin sat back down and smiled at Denida. "Now then, you know we exist. Do come back if we can help you with anything else, Denida of the Underworlds."

Is he real? Denida licked his upper lip and smiled. "How do I get home?"

"I'll take him," the man Denida noticed from the crowd advanced through the mob.

Odin rolled his eyes. "Loki, be good."

Loki yanked Denida out with him. When they exited the hall, he turned to face Denida. "The mighty Denida, how I've *anticipated* meeting you!"

Denida raised his eyebrows. "Mighty?"

Loki grinned. "Sure, you were trained by the Devil… the infamous 'Little Evil.'" He chuckled. "You even killed off the mighty Archdemon, Medusa!"

Denida approached Loki. "Just tell me; how do I get back?"

"Odin welcomed you back, so you can come and go with your ring." Loki glanced at Denida's hand. "The President of all the Underworlds did…"

Denida peeked at his hand with the ring and back to Loki. "You knew the President before me?"

"Loki!" Thor yelled from the doorway to the hall.

"I'm coming!" Loki ran to Thor.

Strange people here… Denida stroked his ring and appeared back in the gym. *At least now I know they exist...*

Denida picked up his shirt from the ground. *Loki really reminded me of Claus. Wonder how he's doing?*

Denida told his security guards to take him to the compound. He hadn't been there in a long time. It was supposed to be the special unit's base, but they were on Earth watching his human form. A lot of soldiers were still stationed at the compound for one specific reason; to guard Claus, who was in the very cell he had once used to imprison Daniel.

"Hello." Denida glanced over and greeted the guards, who watched Claus in the dungeon.

Claus lay on his bed, lost in a book.

"How's it going, Claus?" Denida stepped closer to the bars.

Claus raised his head from his book in surprise. "Denny?" He jumped up. "Have you come to let me out?"

"You kidnapped my son. You really think I would be here for that!"

Claus peered down in embarrassment. He suddenly looked up. "You went to Hell and got me because you knew giving me to Lucifer was a mistake!"

Denida rolled his eye. "Your point?"

"A mistake, just like I made one when I took Daniel!"

Denida shook his head and turned. "Still the same old Claus," he muttered.

"Don't go!" Claus yanked at the bars. "If you came here, you must have had a reason."

Denida stopped and turned.

Claus reached after Denida, clutching the bars.

"Someone reminded me of you."

"You can't just leave me here. I need to be free to repay Lucifer or he'll come for me!"

"That won't work." Denida continued out the door, stroking his ring as he left.

He appeared in Lucifer's throne room. *Why did the ring lead me all the way here?*

"I hoped you would return." Lucifer smiled broadly at Denida with wide eyes.

"I'm ready for the rest of your story."

Lucifer grinned. "Great."

"But-" Denida lifted his finger. "If I ever find out you're lying, we're done!"

Lucifer nodded from his throne.

Denida strode over to him. "I'll decide if I'll help you after hearing your story- not before!"

"I would expect nothing less." Lucifer chuckled.

Lucifer stepped forward toward his Well of Memory.

Denida glanced around the room. *Danyel had secret chambers; I wonder if his Master does, too.* He bit his lip. *The dagger Lucifer showed me must be hidden somewhere, but where?* "The Dagger-"

Lucifer shook his head. "All in due time, Denny." He turned to his well. "God-" He shook his head. "- No... Shaddai, I mean, suddenly acted like it wasn't important anymore that Henna ruled."

Denida raised his eyebrows. "I doubt that!"

Lucifer shrugged. "Really. He cared more about the real power he saw Henna grant to Odin..."

Odin. Denida bit his cheek.

***

Azal ran his foot across the dirt as he impatiently waited in front of Gabriel's house.

Gabriel surfaced, then stopped, and stared at Azal. "Only you... where's Shaddai?"

Azal shrugged. "I haven't seen him since that party with Odin..."

Gabriel grunted. "We can just go then!"

Gabriel and Azal headed out and played for the afternoon, entirely forgetting about Shaddai.

Over the following days, neither of them heard from Shaddai, so it became natural for just the two of them to play alone.

Azal kept wanting to explore new places he had never been.

"I don't know," Gabriel mumbled, but grinned as if intrigued by what they might discover.

Late one afternoon, Azal and Gabriel discovered a new place, a town, which had been abandoned and forgotten.

"This looks interesting!" Azal ran forward.

"Azal!" Gabriel yelled.

Azal purposely ignored him and sped forward.

Gabriel sighed and rushed after him. He almost crashed into Azal, who had suddenly stopped, frozen in spot. "Hey, what are you thinking?"

Azal lifted his hand and pointed to a square in the center of the town.

"Is that Shaddai?" Gabriel gasped in disbelief. "All the way out here?"

In the distance, Shaddai stood all alone in the middle of the square, focused on something.

Azal and Gabriel approached Shaddai.

"Shaddai!" Azal yelled shakily.

Shaddai didn't seem to notice them.

What's he so obsessed with? Azal slowed down, unease growing with each step. He frowned at Gabriel.

Azal reached Shaddai.

Shaddai was so engrossed in what he was doing that he didn't appear to notice Azal.

Azal reached for Shaddai's shoulder.

Shaddai jumped.

Azal shook his hands. "It's just us- Azal and Gabriel! What are you doing?"

Shaddai gazed into Azal's eyes. "Henna…"

Azal and Gabriel turned, puzzled, and exchanged a concerned glance. "Henna?" They both asked.

"She granted celestial status to Odin!"

Azal raised his eyebrow. "So? She does for many."

"She's supreme here. Men are nothing, unless she deems them to be chosen ones!"

"Like Odin," Gabriel said.

"Exactly!"

They have to be joking! Azal raised his hands to calm them. "Wait, but only she can-"

"For now," Shaddai insisted.

"That's what you've been up to this entire time?" Azal wrinkled his forehead. "Did you get anywhere?" He gawked at Shaddai. "You didn't, did you?" He rolled his eyes.

"Why only her?" Determined, Shaddai gazed at the two of them. "We don't even know how old she is, where's she from or how she can. No one knows anything about her other than that she's the almighty queen!"

Azal rushed to Shaddai, getting right up in his face. "And you think *you* can change that?"

Shaddai shrugged. "I want to try, at least…"

Azal sighed. "Try," he said, looking doubtful.

"My dad is in her inner circle. I managed to get some of her stuff, but nothing!" Shaddai shrugged his shoulders.

Weird. "What type of stuff?"

Shaddai pointed forward. "Maybe some of her things had some of her powers, but nothing!"

"We'll help, then." Azal peeked at Gabriel, who nodded. "Something's up with her, at least…"

***

Lucifer's eyes filled with regret as he watched Denida. "I never should have helped…"

What does he mean by that?

Lucifer scratched his cheek. "Everything's connected."

Denida raised his eyebrows. "How so? Why shouldn't you?"

"It was best left alone." Lucifer slipped over to his throne.

Only Henna. Denida glared down at his finger with his Underworld ring. "My ring is made of something only she could make, right… like that dagger you showed me?"

"Yes, the same as the Gates," Lucifer said.

Denida nodded. "Well? Are you going to continue? I didn't come here for nothing!"

"Of course," Lucifer smirked. He returned to the well. "Shaddai felt the only way was to find something directly from Henna, not just some small thing she had discarded …"

***

Azal, Shaddai, and Gabriel set off early. Their parents were surprised they were up and about before the two suns were high in the sky.

Shaddai and Azal met outside Shaddai's house, then went to meet Gabriel, who was waiting for them.

"We're really doing this?" Gabriel glanced at his two friends.

Shaddai nodded. "It's the only way… the answer lies inside her castle!"

All three of them walked to the town center, where Henna's mighty estate stood. It was decorated with sparkles and seemed to rise out of the center of their world, where the two suns always shone on the building, never allowing it to sit in complete darkness.

Shaddai rolled his eyes and turned to look at Gabriel.

Azal cleared his throat. "He's-"

"I'll do it myself, then!" Shaddai stormed into the building.

Gabriel and Azal gasped in panic.

"I'll go watch him," Azal ran inside after him.

The inside glimmered just as brilliantly as the outer façade.

Azal stared confusedly down the passageway. *So many doors... where is he?*

He sauntered carefully downward the shimmering hallway. "Shaddai," he whispered repeatedly.

When he reached the end of the first hall, where it forked in several directions, he stopped. *Still nothing. If I were Shaddai- Oh yeah... the chamber where Henna granted Odin his powers!*

Azal turned to orient himself and prepared to run toward the room, but stopped abruptly. *Somebody's coming!* He dashed behind a wall. *One of these doors must open.*

Azal ran back and forth, pulling the handles of each door, but they were all locked. Suddenly, he grabbed a handle that turned at the same moment as the voices he heard reached the corner. He ducked behind a soft cushion in the center of the room.

The voices outside the door grew louder.

Azal put his hands over his mouth to muffle his heavy breathing. The voices passed by the door and sounded lower.

Henna's blessing! Azal ran his hand through his hair, clambered to his feet, and hurried out. He continued upward toward the chamber.

I hope he didn't get caught... Azal nervously checked the corridor, where he heard Henna's voice. He dropped to his knees and crawled forward. The surroundings suddenly changed shape and he saw Henna standing in front of him, smiling. He gaped in shock. Shaddai was standing in the other part of the room.

"Your friend is here. Come and see me tomorrow, Shaddai." Henna snapped her fingers.

Azal found himself outside the building with Shaddai.

He looked about in panic, then back to his friend. "What happened? Did you find anything?"

"Better than that!" Shaddai smirked. "She sees potential in me, as she did with Odin!"

* * *

"You're saying you all went to find something on your queen-"

"Henna chose to show God the way…"

Why do I feel leery about that? Denida ground his teeth.

"We started on our path. There was no going back." Lucifer smiled cautiously.

Denida nodded. "I should get back to the Underworld, but I'll be back."

"You know where to find me." Lucifer chuckled.

Denida nodded and walked out.

Chapter 4- Nina's Discovery

Nina sat on a bench. Sadness covered her like an extra layer of gravity. Even the colors appeared faded as she watched her human side on earth stroke a horse. *We like horses, don't we?* She gave a faint flicker of a smile.

The Commander sat down next to her on the bench. "I thought I would see how you're doing, so how are you?"

Nina grumbled and turned to him. "How can I be good? Daniel's gone!"

The Commander sighed. "Your human side is doing well." He pointed toward the little girl.

Nina smiled at the girl, then peered at the Commander, squeezed his hand, and strolled away.

Nina sauntered down the streets, feeling empty inside, like nothing mattered anymore. She stopped and stared into the sky, then dropped her head. *I should return to Dynasty...*

Nina straightened and her eyes widened. *That's not possible!* She ran around the corner, where she stopped again. Her heart raced and she clenched her fist. *It's her!* She charged toward a girl, her fury making her visible to the humans.

The girl Nina ran toward glared in her direction, her eyes growing wide as Nina knocked her over. "What the hell are you doing?" the girl screamed.

The dogs around the girl growled, catching the attention of two men, who rushed to the girl's rescue before Nina could punch her.

"Michelle!" Nina snarled.

The woman wrinkled and stared blankly. "I don't know who that is. I'm Maia." She cautiously extended her hand.

Nina spat on it. "No, I know who you are!"

"Michelle?" Maia scratched her head. "I swear, I'm not sure who that is…"

The man holding Nina back smiled. "She's just my sister, Maia. Sorry…" He shrugged, let go of Nina, and followed his sister inside.

That can't really be someone else... can it? Nina watched Maia and her brother guide the dogs inside a building.

Nina scurried after them. Inside, Maia fed the animals in the enclosure with the dogs, who all encircled her, some even rubbing up against her. It was clear they knew and liked her.

My horse and the other animals didn't like Michelle, but Maia... she may look like her, but it can't be her! Nina rubbed her forehead. *But how can it be?* "You like pets?"

Maia smiled. "They're awesome. Morton and I are helping with the shelter."

"They sure like you," Nina muttered.

Maia shrugged. "If you treat them right, they treat you right."

Nina waved bye and exited, rubbing her forehead. *Gabriel.*

"I'm already here." Archangel Gabriel sat on a boulder, waving at her.

Nina didn't look at him, instead continuing to hold her hand to her forehead. *How?*

Gabriel peered at her with narrowed eyes. "How what?"

"How can this Maia look so much like Michelle, yet act so completely different!" She raised her eyes to Gabriel.

Gabriel smiled tenderly. "She looks like she could be her twin, I know, but Maia's a half-sister of Michelle's human form; her Father eventually had other children..." He unfolded his wings.

Nina lunged forward and grabbed Gabriel's arm. "Does anyone know about this?"

Gabriel frowned. "No one would care to know."

Nina sighed and her eyes wandered.

"Something the matter?"

"If I brought her back to the Underworlds-"

Gabriel shook his arm. "You can't take a human to the soul realm!"

"Lucifer took Denny's soul..." Nina rested her hand on her cheek.

Gabriel rubbed his hands together. "That was permanent. You can't reverse the process."

Nina grunted and turned back to the building.

"Hi again." Maia smiled and waved as Nina reentered.

Nina leaned over the counter. "I need to go, *Maia*, but I will be back!"

Maia nodded. "We always welcome visitors."

She sure as hell doesn't hold a grudge... Nina spun around. As soon as she was out of sight, she turned invisible to human eyes and returned to the Underworlds.

The Colonel was in the HQ's command center.

"John!"

The Colonel's eyes widened. "Lady Nina? You never call me by my name… is something wrong?"

"Claus! I need to see him. I know Denny has him somewhere! Where is it?"

The Colonel glanced around the room and pulled Nina aside. "The compound, but why do you need to see him?"

"My business!" Nina shoved the Colonel out of the way.

Nina allowed her bodyguards to accompany her. She exhaled heavily as she saw the compound approaching.

"Claus," she insisted before the soldier guarding the compound had a chance to say anything.

The soldier saluted and led her to the dungeon.

Claus tilted his head toward the door when it sprang open. His eyes widened and he sat up straight.

"Interesting, I hoped it was Denida returning, but how nice of you to come!"

"Out!" Nina pointed at the door and scowled at the soldiers, who all saluted and obeyed her command.

"First Denny, now you." Claus frowned. "What does the mighty Lady Nina want?"

She pulled a chair over to the cell and sat down. She glowered across the room. "This is where you kept Daniel, but it suits *you* better!"

Claus rolled his eyes.

Nina bared her teeth. *How dare he mock me!* She lunged toward him, grabbing him through the bars and thrust him into them. "Don't you even try to sully his good memory. Daniel is dead because of you!"

Claus shook his hands frantically. "Not me- Sergeant Michelle!"

Nina released her grip. "Which is why I'm here. When Lucifer brought you to Hell, you said you heard stuff!" She paused and gazed at Claus. "- does that include anything about Michelle?"

Claus scratched his head. "All I heard was that she was an archdemon whom even Lucifer feared. She killed Daniel and all of Jack's demons…"

Nina waved her hand dismissively. "I don't care about that. I want to know about her descendants on Earth."

Claus stopped with pale eyes. "I… don't… know?" he muttered.

No one knows- Gabriel was right! Nina jumped up and ran out the door, ignoring the soldiers waiting outside.

As soon as Nina and her bodyguards arrived back at Dynasty, she continued by herself. She walked inside, stood, and double-checked that no one was around before she opened the secret panel under a set of stairs. After she entered a password and proceeded through the iris and voice scanner, she turned to grab the door, only to find the control pad beeping. She frowned and turned back to it. *What? Denny removed my access?* She slammed the keyboard and tried entering the password again, but the beeping continued. *What's he up to?* She clenched her fists and stormed out to where her bodyguards waited for her.

"Take me to Denida's office!"

She marched into Denida's office. The secretary waved at her as she passed.

So far, so good. Nina hurried behind Denida's computer, where she entered 'Sergeant Michelle,' in the search field. Sweat started dripping from her forehead as she awaited the results in dire suspense.

'Beep.' The computer displayed the results.

She pressed the print button. She heard a sound near the door and ran over to the printer to retrieve the papers, which she hid under her shirt.

The door opened behind her and Denida strolled in with his secretary.

Denida stopped, startled. "Nina?" He stepped toward her.

The computer! "Wait!" Nina waved her arms.

Denida stopped, gawking around the room. "Something the matter?"

"I just-" Nina scratched her forehead. "I just think it's too soon for you to be back at work! It can't be good for you."

Denida shrugged. "Don't worry. Susan's been checking on me periodically..."

"Not enough!" Nina stepped closer to the computer cautiously.

"Besides, we've already got Michelle!"

Got Michelle?

'Yes, she died, remember?' Denida smiled broadly as he spoke that to her thoughts.

Nina stopped, her eyes burning with anger. "You did! *Not we...* I never-" She kicked the computer, knocking it off the desk, disconnecting it.

"We mourned Daniel together, but apparently it didn't help you like it helped me." Denida swiped a tear from his eye before she could notice.

She smacked into Denida and threw a punch that connected with his face. "If you can continue so easily, you do that!" She stomped out.

Nina climbed in her car and took out the folder from beneath her shirt. *Michelle, Medusa... Mara was that her name on Earth?*

She flipped through the pages, examining them thoroughly. *It would have been easier if Denny had made that deal Medusa offered in exchange for Daniel...* She grunted and rubbed her face every few pages. She slammed the last page down on the seat next to her.

There's nothing in here regarding her family on Earth! She ran out of the car to get a cigarette. Her security detail watched her confusedly and she rolled her eyes.

"Nina?" The Colonel stopped in front of her. "What brings you here?"

Nina kicked a can and took the last puff from her cigarette, before discarding the butt, spinning back toward her car.

"Nina!" The Colonel followed and stopped in front of her.

Nina bared her teeth. "Nothing important." She continued past him.

Her security led her to her car. She stared at the Colonel, then shrugged before climbing into the car and driving off.

Nina headed to the stables next to Dynasty to see Angel, where she lowered her head into his mane.

"Hello again, Lady Nina."

Nina spun around with her eyes wide. "Gabriel! Why are you back?"

"You got Denny's papers." Gabriel raised his eyebrows. "Are you convinced, now? No one knows about Maia *or* Morton, for that matter."

Nina grunted and fed Angel a carrot, then faced Gabriel. "Why does it matter to you, anyway- an archangel would *not* care, would he?" Nina clenched her fists tight.

Gabriel cleared his throat.

"Well?" Nina demanded.

Gabriel nodded. "I want you to be happy, but you're not!"

"I repeat, why do you care?" Nina stepped closer to him.

"You're Denny's soul mate…"

Denny again! Nina threw the carrot to the ground. "I'm fine. *Don't* come back!" She snarled and left the stables.

Chapter 5- The Tale Continues

Denida was twiddling his thumbs when Susan entered with the Colonel. *Why are they here?* His eyes shifted between the two of them.

Susan stood at attention near the door, but the Colonel continued to Denida's desk.

"Did you know that Nina came here?"

Denida shrugged. "Sure, she was pissed. She's still trying to get over-"

The Colonel peered back at Susan. "That explains it!" He licked his lips, returning his focus to Denida. "Maybe I should give you my report on your and Nina's human sides, Sir?"

Denida shifted in his chair. "What is it?"

Susan cut in. "They're not moving closer, but rather farther apart. Anyway, Nina was on Earth too, where she talked to the Commander."

This is bad, Nina must find her peace. I hope I can reverse this before seeing her... Denida snapped his fingers. "Leave her!" He stood. "I'm ordering you both, now. She's not to be bothered! If you have nothing else-"

"We do." Susan joined the Colonel. "Claus!"

Denida rolled his eyes. *Not him again.*

The Colonel narrowed his eyes. "You wanted us to leave Nina be, but she's dropped by Claus' cell. We need to move him somewhere else..."

Denida strode over to the bar cabinet and grabbed a drink. "You told her!"

The Colonel cleared his throat.

"From now on, no one, but me is allowed to see him! No exceptions." *I still need to protect everyone from the Darkness, too...* Denida rubbed his ring and gazed at them. "I need to go attend to something." He followed them out of the office.

Denida sighed heavily as he opened his eyes to the feeling of Darkness in the air. *I'll never get used to this...* He stepped toward Lucifer's mansion, then stopped abruptly. "Gabriel," he grunted at the manifestation of Gabriel. He continued past Gabriel into the mansion.

Gabriel followed Denida. "Why are you here... in Hell. I thought you swore never to return?"

Denida smiled discontentedly. "Things change…"

Gabriel wrinkled. "Change, how-"

"Denny," Lucifer trudged out of his chamber, pulled Denida into his embrace, and escorted him inside. He turned to close the door, but before he did, he smirked at his old friend. "Gabriel, I can't see you now. Perhaps next time!"

Denida paced about the room. He tapped his fingers on the Well of Memories.

"Back for more?" Lucifer grinned.

Denida clenched his fists. "You had more you wanted to tell me, didn't you?"

Lucifer smirked as he sauntered over.

Denida tapped his ring on the well. "How did you get the idea to show me?"

Lucifer's smile stagnated. "I heard Daniel telling your story…"

Denida sighed. "Daniel." He shook his head and stared at Lucifer. "Show me then!"

Lucifer lifted his hand over the well. Darkness oozed from his hand and it didn't take long before an image formed. He glared up. "Shaddai was being taught well. He grew more and more distant from both Gabriel and Azal… me, I mean…"

***

Azal stood next to Gabriel, fiddling with his thumbs. He watched Shaddai standing with Henna under the baking suns from across the field.

"What do you think she's teaching him?" Gabriel pouted at his friend.

Azal shook his head. "I wish I knew," he muttered.

Gabriel stood.

"Where are you going?" Azal grabbed Gabriel's arm.

"There's no point in waiting here; they'll be a while…"

Azal's eyes wandered to Shaddai and Henna. "The castle," he smirked. "You're right; they'll be busy, meaning no one is watching it!"

Gabriel shook his head uneasy. "We can't-"

Azal tapped Gabriel's shoulder and ran toward the castle. Gabriel sprinted after him. He caught up to Azal in the lobby of the castle, where Azal stopped.

Azal gazed around in awe. The afternoon twin suns shone through the glass building and the light cut through the floors, refracting and reflecting, shimmering in all colors. *Just like her eyes…*

Azal stepped inside, carefully examining each room he passed.

"If there's something here, wouldn't it be in her chambers up those stairs?"

Azal spun, surprised at Gabriel, who had never even been inside the castle. *Why didn't I think of that… but where… maybe the spot Shaddai showed me!* He snapped his fingers and ran up the stairs.

Gabriel meandered nervously to the door, then followed Azal.

Azal wandered through the rooms of Henna's private chambers, taking in as much as he could without stopping.

"Found anything?" Gabriel whispered.

Azal grunted. *There must be something here!*

Gabriel tilted his head. "Come on! We have to go before she gets back."

Azal marched toward him but suddenly stopped dead in his tracks.

"Az!" Gabriel rushed over to yank at his friend. When Azal remained rooted to the spot, Gabriel turned to look at what he was pointing at. His eyes locked on it, too.

In the room, they could see a shiny dagger impaling the table.

"It's in here!" Henna's voice called.

Gabriel yanked Azal behind a piece of furniture.

Henna gracefully strolled into the room with Shaddai. She sauntered over to the dagger and picked it up, handing it to Shaddai.

Shaddai felt the dagger in his hand and studied it. It was adorned with scriptures and made of a very odd, unfamiliar material. "What's this?"

Henna smiled. "The only thing that can kill a god; Odin, you, even me."

Interesting… Azal stared into Gabriel's eyes.

Shaddai handed the dagger back to Henna. "Why do you have it, then?"

She stabbed it into the desk with a fierce jab. "Backup. I hid the rest throughout the universe. There are seven in all." She raised her eyebrows at Shaddai and her eyes shone with all the colors of the rainbow.

She took Shaddai by the shoulder and guided him out.

Azal stood up, only to be dragged back down by Gabriel. "Wait!" he insisted.

They remained until Azal couldn't stand it any longer and he ran out into the hall with Gabriel close behind. Outside, Azal slowed, but Gabriel kept walking at a brisk pace.

Gabriel didn't slow down until they were back at his house.

Azal grinned. "We really-"

"No!" Gabriel sneered at him. "She's our queen, the one protecting us. Don't even think about it."

"Hey." Shaddai approached with a joyous smile. "What's going on here? You both look profoundly serious."

Azal shook his head. "Nothing at all." He replied with a forced smile.

Shaddai turned to Gabriel, who gazed at the ground. "Gabriel?"

Gabriel sighed. "Azal and I snuck into the castle. We saw the strange dagger…"

Shaddai pulled them into the bush. "You need to forget what you saw!"

"She can die," Azal smirked. "You wanted her gone…"

Shaddai shrugged. "That was before she started teaching me. I know better, now. So should you…" He let go and outstretched his hand. "Together, we can do anything. Are you both still with me?"

Gabriel nodded and grabbed his arm.

Shaddai glared at Azal. "Still with us?"

Azal nodded and shook Shaddai's hand.

***

The image in the well faded. Denida lifted his head. "That dagger you showed me…"

Lucifer nodded.

Denida raised his eyebrows. "It's made of the same material as the Gates."

Lucifer sauntered over to his throne and grunted in affirmation.

Denida's eyes wandered about the room.

"You won't find the dagger, here." Lucifer chuckled. "You think I'm that stupid?"

Denida ground his teeth. "I just thought it would be interesting to see it again…"

Lucifer rubbed his palms. "Tough luck, but be happy; you're the first one to have seen it since…" His eyes turned red.

"Since what?" Denida paced toward Lucifer.

"Not now!" Lucifer snapped his fingers and Denida stood next to the Gate leading into Hell at World Eight of the Underworlds.

'Come back another time and I'll tell you more,' those thoughts rang in Denida's head. His eyes fell on a row of demons watching him warily. His blind right eye flickered red. "Want something?" he hissed.

The demons all turned and scurried away.

Denida scratched his head and clenched his fist with the ring, making him appear back in his office. He unclenched it and grabbed the door handle, only to see Susan waiting outside. She stood when she noticed him.

Denida waved her in. "What is it, Susan? Given that you're here, it must be important?"

Susan saluted him before sitting down. "Claus." She glared at the floor.

Denida straightened up.

She lifted her hand. "I know what you're going to say, but just hear me out!"

Denida shifted in his chair with a grunt.

"Claus tried to seize power, you sent him to Hell. You went back for him to free him from the Devil, but he still kidnapped your son… which eventually led to Michelle killing your son-"

"What're you getting at?" Denida demanded through clenched teeth.

"This," Susan slammed the table. "- you can't trust him! I know you still have him. What'll you do with him? We should finish him off for good!"

Denida tapped his ring on the desk, then smirked at Susan. "You're right!" He came around the table. "We can't trust him." He shook his head. "No one knows that better than you!"

"Why are you agreeing with me?" Susan backed away.

"Because I need to transfer him to a secret spot… where no one will find him and you know him better than anyone!"

"Your idea has one flaw; we don't have a place like that." Susan insisted.

Denida's eyes glowed red. "I do," he smiled.

She wrinkled her brow.

Denida snapped his fingers. "I'll show you!" He rushed out the door. Susan jogged after him, trying to keep up. He ran across the front yard to the Military HQ, where he continued inside to the command center.

Denida faced Susan, who was a little short of breath from the run.

"Why here?" She shrugged.

Denida lifted his hands over the screens and an image appeared.

Men transported ore from massive mine in large, covered trucks. Snow littered the surroundings.

Susan shrugged and leaned over the table. "Why are you showing me this?"

Denida winked as he turned to her. "I had a secret stash there, hidden behind bars, but Claus stole it." He raised his eyebrows. "This is where we can keep Claus. We'll shut down the mine for this. It's in the middle of nowhere with nothing but snow all around…"

"Good idea…" Susan peeked at the image and nodded solemnly.

***

Susan led a handpicked unit to the compound.

The commander of the base stared at her, gaping.

"We're here to escort Claus." Susan handed him a signed document. "Official orders!"

The commander grabbed the papers and rummaged through them.

Susan and her troop marched off toward the dungeon. "Wait!" The commander hurried after them. "Where are you taking him?"

"That's for me to know and you to wonder!" She tore open the dungeon door, Claus sat up.

She nodded to her soldiers, who rushed forward to fasten Claus in chains.

"What-"

Susan strode over to him. "Hi, Claus! Did you miss me?" She didn't try to hide the scorn in her tone.

Claus stared at her as the cars drove off. "What have you convinced Denny to-"

She snapped her fingers in front of him. "Not me; this is *all* Denny's idea!"

Claus watched the others in the car. "Where exactly are you taking me?"

"You'll see soon enough," Susan smirked.

The vehicles sped through the countryside to a military airfield, where a plane waited for them.

Claus clenched his fists. "I don't like this," he murmured.

"Good, you're not supposed to!" Susan yanked him forward by his chains into the plane.

Claus tried to get Susan's attention first, then the soldiers watching him, but everyone refused make eye contact.

"Am I going to an execution?"

Susan grinned and spun to Claus. "Thanks for a laugh, but no, even though I wish you were." She turned back to her colleagues.

"What then!" Claus rattled his chains, making a ruckus.

Susan stood and smacked him across the face with her gun. Claus tumbled back in the seat with his nose bleeding.

He wiped the blood away with the back of his hand. "Such anger. Why do you hate me so much?"

Susan rolled her eyes. "Why wouldn't I!"

Claus wrinkled his forehead.

Susan charged forth and smacked him again. "You imprisoned me. I'll never trust you again!" She spat at Claus.

"That was a long time ago." Claus straightened in his seat. "You should forget-"

Forget? Susan charged him, causing the chair to fall over, dropping Claus with it. Susan pinned him to the ground, punching him with all her might.

Soldiers ran forward to separate them. She picked up her beret and shot Claus a spiteful smirk.

Her soldiers watched him for the duration of the trip, while she kept her distance.

When they landed, Susan smiled at a soldier who stood next to a truck and handed him a bag. "Destroy all evidence that we were here. When done, meet us at the designated spot."

The soldier took the bag and saluted her.

She jumped into the truck and drove it out into the snow along a dirt road.

After a few hours, she arrived next to a fence and guards directed them through.

Susan greeted the General of the base. Soldiers escorted Claus out of the truck. His eyes widened at the sight.

"This is Denny's mine! I took the-"

Susan sneered and marched over to Claus. "Took what? His money?" She patted him on the cheek, which had snowflakes dropping on it. "But we're here to stow something else, now; *you*!"

Chapter 6- Maia

Nina clicked her tongue against her teeth as she stared at Maia, who was playing fetch with the dogs in the kennel's outdoor enclosure. She sauntered over to her. "Hi again, Maia."

Maia sighed and continued to throw balls for the dogs to fetch.

What's wrong with her? Nina squinted. "Is something the matter?"

Maia slammed a ball into the fence. "Just some family things…"

Nina looked at Maia with wide eyes. "If it's affecting you like this, it must be serious. Sometimes it can help to talk to a stranger if you'd like?"

Maia sighed and strolled over to Nina. "Morton's… *missing.*"

Nina frowned. "Missing?"

Maia ran her hand through her dark curly hair. "He's in trouble… he always has been, but it's getting worse as of late." She cracked her knuckles. "The bad people he got involved with… I fear something happened to him!"

"Can someone take over?" Nina straightened up. "Show me where!"

"I guess, but you?" Maia rolled her eyes.

"You'd be surprised what I can do; come on!"

Maia drove Nina into town. She stopped outside of an old dilapidated building.

Nina's gut twisted as she climbed out of the car and Maia started toward the building. Nina peered up at it. *Why is it giving me the creeps?* She shrugged, then followed Maia.

Inside, they were frisked by guards before they were led to the boss.

"Where's Morton?" Maia demanded.

"Haven't seen him. I was coming to see you actually." The boss gloated and leaned back in his chair.

Nina stood back and said nothing. *I don't like this sensation.* Her eyes wandered throughout the room but stopped suddenly. *This can't be- how?* She trudged forward.

"Morton… disappeared?" Maia stuttered.

The boss nodded. "With my dope!"

There are too many here for me to fight all at once; I need to come back later… Nina smiled and grabbed Maia by the shoulder. "We'll find him!" She dragged Maia with her and left the building.

"Wait, what?" Maia objected, but Nina brought her to the car and pushed her into the passenger seat.

Nina sped off, while Maia yelled at her and tried to stop the car.

Nina pulled over and turned to her. "Enough!" She held up her hands.

"Morton… he could be hurt!" Maia shook her head. "We've always protected each other…"

Nina rolled her eyes before turning to Maia with a reassuring smile. "Not now, they don't have him there so nothing you can do. I'll go back and check without you when their boss is alone…"

Maia shook her head and grabbed the car keys. "Not alone, I'm coming, too!" She dangled the keys above her head.

Nina sighed. *She's not gonna give in.* "Fine, you can come." She smiled cautiously.

At night, when the streetlights shone, accompanied only by the moonlight, Nina and Maia viewed the old building from a dark alley. Maia was dressed in non-distinctive clothes, so they wouldn't get spotted.

Nina tilted her head and snuck into the building, but stopped when she noticed guards approaching.

"I've got this," Maia smirked. She came out of hiding and started strolling toward them with her head shaking. "I need… a fix!" She squeezed her left arm.

She's nuts! Nina shook her head.

The two guards peered at each other.

Maia stumbled into the one guard, who grabbed her arm to lift her back up. She nodded violently and headbutted the guard, causing him to fall to the ground.

The other guard grabbed his baton.

Maia spun and kicked the other guard in between his legs, making him crumple to the ground.

The first guard reached for his gun. Maia swept his leg, fell on him and wrapped her legs around his neck, breaking it. She snatched his gun and ran to the second guard, who put his hand on the gun's muzzle, trying to pry it from her grip.

The hand muffled the sound. He fell limp in a bloody pool next to the first guard.

This Maia girl might be even more similar to Michelle than I thought… Nina stood up and raised an eyebrow.

"What? I learned stuff over the years. It was necessary."

"I guess… come on." Nina crept past her into the building. It was dark inside. She heard voices from another room and followed the sounds to where the boss talked with another man while a guard watched.

"Here's the money." The boss accepted a bag.

The man spun and walked out the door.

Nina ducked, pulling Maia down with her.

The guard stopped a few steps past them, glaring back before continuing.

Maia charged. Nina hurried after and yanked her back behind a cabinet.

"What?" Maia hissed.

"We should wait to be sure it's safe." Nina checked to verify that the boss was busy and the soldier didn't return. After a few minutes, Nina flicked her arm.

Maia stormed up to the boss. "Where's my brother!"

Nina sighed and followed her into the room.

The boss glanced between them and shook his head. "I already told you-"

"Don't try it!" Maia slammed the desk, causing him to look up.

The boss stood up with his hands raised. "I'll take you to him…" He carefully stepped forward to another desk. "Let me give you a paper with the address." He reached for a drawer.

"No!" Nina yelled, but it was too late.

The boss pulled a gun from the drawer and shot Maia.

How dare you! Nina's eyes widened in disbelief.

The bullet tore through Maia and lodged itself in the wall. Maia crossed her arms, staring at the boss, as though nothing even happened.

Both the boss and Nina turned to the wall in disbelief.

Nina's expression harshened into a glare, which Maia ignored.

"Morton-" Maia hissed.

Nina slammed the boss into the wall, making him drop his pistol. "Where's her brother? This is your last chance!"

"He went to my boss," he admitted with his face turning red.

Your boss? Wait- that thing I saw! Nina stared at him viciously. "You had graffiti on your wall; I noticed it earlier. 'The Scientist'?"

Maia wrinkled. "The Scientist?"

Nina hushed her. "What does it mean!"

"Just our boss' nickname…"

"Oh, God…" Nina muttered. She loosened her grip in shock.

The man rolled on the ground and grabbed the gun. He glared at the two of them, then aimed at Nina. "Move or I'll kill your friend!"

"Where's Jack?" Rage rose within Nina and she snarled.

"Jack?"

"Your boss," Nina hissed.

He shrugged and started to back out of the room.

"Boss!" a voice yelled from the darkness and racing footsteps grew increasingly louder.

Nina mumbled something and jumped on Maia, pulling her to the floor. They disappeared from sight immediately.

The boss panicked, waving his gun in all directions.

"Was someone here? We heard a woman yelling!"

"They hid somehow... find them!" The boss frantically waved his arms around the room.

Nina snuck out of the building with Maia and they returned to the animal shelter, where Nina lifted the invisibility cloak.

"Who's the Scientist?" Maia stared with determined eyes. "You seemed to know that name."

Of course, she would ask that. Nina scratched her forehead and sat down. "The Scientist, Jack, I'm searching for him. We have unfinished business!"

Maia bit her lip. "But he's not here!"

"He isn't, but your brother may be the key to finding him." Nina's eyes narrowed. "How did those bullets go right through you as if you weren't there?"

Maia bared her teeth. "I'll tell you if you tell me how you made us invisible."

I can't tell her that!

"Well?" Maia raised her eyebrows.

"Magic," Nina muttered. "Now you." She glared piercingly at Maia.

Maia turned and paced about the room, cracking her knuckles. "I can never... die..."

Nina frowned. "What do you mean? From bullets?"

Maia clenched her fist and spun around. "At all! It's my family's curse; I can't die... nor can I be killed. Neither can Morton!"

How is this possible? "O... kay..."

"I know how it sounds, but it has been like this ever since my sister..."

Gabriel was right about Mara? Nina rolled her eyes. "You said it's always been you and Morton. You have a sister, too?"

"Mara. Ever since she died, it's been like this!"

Does that mean Mara was invincible, too? I don't know how her magic can still be active, if not. The fury rose in Nina again and her face twitched.

Maia sighed. "Once upon-"

Nina bolted, slamming the door behind her.

"What just happened?" Maia followed her, but Nina vanished right in front of her.

Nina rushed back to the graveyard next to Dynasty, where her son lay buried. *How could I ever help her sister!* Nina covered her face with her hands, her gut turning at the mere thought of it. She knelt on her son's grave and lowered her head in shame. *Gabriel, come...*

"Thought you didn't want to see me anymore?" Gabriel appeared in a flash of light behind her.

Nina still knelt with her eyes closed. "You knew I would need to see you again, eventually."

Gabriel smiled broadly. "Only when you were ready."

"Mara!" Nina jumped up and stood with her face close to his. "If Maia can survive everything, what about Mara? Is she alive too!" Her face steaming red.

"That matters? They were cursed because of Mara, but if you want them to suffer, rejoice; Morton could be in serious trouble."

Nina rolled her eyes and threw her arms up. "I don't care. It's not like he can die, anyway!"

"Really?" Gabriel put his hand on her shoulder and winked. "Even if Jack has Morton? Jack, who is a demon, and helped with Daniel's abduction, too!"

"Jack still needs to pay up, but how dare you mention Daniel so callously!" Nina pushed him aside and marched off.

"Good luck, Lady Nina."

Maia sat petting dogs in the shelter. They circled around her, wagging their tails. "You're all so innocent…"

"We all are in the beginning, before we lose it with our misdeeds." Nina appeared in front of her. "Stay!" She extended her hand, stopping Maia from getting up. "I think you should specify; how exactly are you and Morton Mara's siblings?"

Maia exhaled a heavy sigh. "I never told anyone this; I'm not even sure why I'm telling you." She glared at Nina and nodded. "She's our sister, but I didn't know of her at first… when Dad was on his deathbed, he wanted Morton and me to see him…"

***

Maia and Morton's mom led them into a room. She kissed their father tenderly on the forehead and squeezed his hand before leaving.

Their father lifted his hand toward his two children. Maia and Morton hurried to the bed and grabbed a hand on each side of the bed. They both forced their smiles, but sorrow lingered in their eyes.

"Don't worry." He smiled at the two of them. "I need to tell you something… before I can rest."

Maia shook her head. "You-"

He squeezed her hand tighter. "Yes, it's time soon."

Morton ripped loose and slammed his fist into the wall.

"Morton," his dad spoke softly. "Listen; it's important!" His voice sounded weak.

Morton grunted, but came back and took his dad's hand. "What?"

Their father licked his lips. "Before I had you both, I was with another woman, with whom I had a daughter…"

Maia lit up. "I have a sister! What's her name? Why haven't I met her?"

Morton glared. "She's not alive, is she?"

Their dad shook his head. "She killed a priest, her mom, and tried to kill others too, all to summon the Dark Arts. We had to kill her."

Maia gasped and released her father's hand. "Why?"

"She believed an old family story about demonic heritage in our ancestry, but whatever Darkness she possessed didn't protect her in the end."

Morton rolled his eyes. "Why does it matter, then? It's over!"

Their dad spat in a bucket. "I met your mom and found a new lease on life. We had you two. All was well-" He watched Maia and Morton's eyes with a sad glare. "She came to see me… *Mara.* As clear as day, she stood before me, with those empty eyes of hers. *'You've got twins now. Know that when you die, you'll see me again.'* It sent a cold chill down my spine."

Maia squeezed her dad's hand. "Don't worry; the Lord will protect you!"

"That's not what worries me…" Her dad stared into her eyes. "Afterward she said, *'your children shall be cursed!'*"

Cursed? The word echoed in Maia's thoughts.

"Always protect each other!" He handed Maia's hand to Morton and slowly slumped into oblivion.

***

Maia glared at Nina. "I didn't understand what that meant until the first time I should have died."

"Died?" Nina frowned.

Maia nodded. "One of the many times Morton did something stupid." She shook her head. "He always has."

"What did he do?" Nina narrowed her eyes concernedly.

"Dad meant everything to Morton, so when he died, Morton went ballistic. He lost his will to live. I had to stop him and I found him where he and Dad always went to watch the sunset."

***

Maia paused for a second as she reached the top of the cliff and looked around frantically. *Morton!* She sprinted toward him, but the rocks were jagged and slowed her down.

Morton stood on the edge of the cliff staring down into the abyss.

"Morton… don't!" Maia reached him, puffing for air.

Morton shook his head. "Dad's really gone."

Maia lifted her arms. "He wouldn't want you-"

Morton spun to face her. "He wouldn't want *me* to follow him? He died. What does any of this matter!" Seagulls flew past them, out across the water. Morton's eyes trailed them. "He believed we were doomed; maybe we are. Let's find out!" He lifted Maia onto his shoulders and jumped.

Maia saw her life flash before her eyes as they plummeted toward the rocks poking through the low tide, but as they reached the ground, it was like time slowed down and set them down, completely unharmed.

What! How's this possible? Maia stood and studied herself, then Morton, but neither of them had as much as a scratch on them.

"What just happened?" She arched her neck up at the cliff, which stood far above them. "We can't have fallen from all the way up there without so much as a bruise?" Her eyes turned to Morton.

"Dad's right. There's a curse on us; we can't die!"

Maia shook her head. "That's not-"

Morton ripped out a dagger and lunged toward her, but the blade flew out of his hand. "Believe me *now*?"

Maia peeked at the dagger. She stepped over to pick it up, tightened her grip, and lowered it to her wrist. A force prevented her from stabbing herself; she couldn't move the blade near her skin. She kept jamming it harder, while holding the knife tightly. Her breathing grew ragged and her hand was shaking with exertion, but despite all her effort, she couldn't get one millimeter closer.

* * *

"Mom died shortly after and we could never have children due to the curse…" Maia gazed at her feet. "It was just us, so we always watched over each other. We were all we had!"

Nina rubbed her face. "Did you ever meet Mara?"

Maia shrugged. "I presumed she was just a witch who Dad imagined seeing, like you… you do magic, after all. Do you know her? Is she alive?"

Nina clicked her teeth with her tongue. "Maybe this leader, Jack, knows; we need to see that boss again to find out where he is- with Morton!"

Maia nodded. "Then let's get him to tell us!"

Chapter 7- Checking on Nina

Dan stared at the strange alloy he had retrieved from the Gate.

I'm missing something here, but what is it? Dan smacked his head into the desk and gazed up at the alloy. His eyes widened and he jumped up to dig through a stack of papers. *In the other Underworld, Claus discovered how to time travel. He used it and got stuck thirty years in the past, but I don't know how they used the alloy to accomplish that!*

Dan lifted a piece above his head to examine it under the light. '*The device from the Gate powered…*' He threw it down and raced to the door.

The Butler watched in confusion as Dan ran out to his car and sped off.

Dan drove to the second Gate, now heavily protected. The guards greeted him. "Dan," one guard saluted him and cleared him to pass the checkpoint.

Guess they remember me from the war with the Dark Angels.

He stepped out of the car near the Gate, which stood in the middle of everything. It was a tall, wide device that seemed incredibly perplexing, even in its inactive state. Dan stopped and stayed still for a second. It had been a while since he'd seen the grand structure in person.

He sighed and continued toward the Gate, arching his neck to gaze at the top of it. He licked his lips and knelt next to the main unit of the Gate. It felt very different from the rest of the device, but Dan knew the material well. He grabbed the unit and removed it from the rest of the Gate.

He returned to his car with it and laid it on the back seat.

As the car reached the checkpoint again, the guard who greeted him peeked in through the window. "Leaving so soon?"

Dan smiled back. "I just needed to check something for Lord Denida."

The guard nodded and tapped the car's roof.

It was starting to get dark when he finally arrived at Dynasty and rain was pouring down, so he hurried inside with the device.

The Butler bumped into him at the front door. "Dan, you're back. What's that you got there?"

Dan smiled faintly and hid the device behind his back. "Just something I need for my research." He pushed past the Butler and rushed down the stairs to the restricted room, where he carefully placed the device on the desk.

Dan stretched his arms, yawned, and sat down, tapping his fingers while he examined it. *It's now or never!* He moved it over to his spectroscope. *Such a unique concentration the alloy has, yet no one knows anything about it...*

The door above the stairs opened. Dan reached for a gun hidden in a compartment under the desk.

"It's just me, Dan." Denida appeared in the light with one hand raised.

Dan let go of the gun with a sigh of relief.

"Anything new?"

Dan shrugged. "You know it takes time."

Denida raised his brow. "I do, but I got a call from the soldiers watching the second Gate; the device disappeared after you visited..." He winked at Dan. "-you wouldn't happen to know where it is?"

Dan marched over to his spectroscope and pointed at the device. "In the other Underworld, they used a main device from the Gates to get the time machine working."

Denida strolled over and laid a hand on it, peering at Dan. "Question is; did you find anything?"

Dan lowered his head. "I only just got back with it."

Denida bit his lip and nodded. "We need to disable the second Gate for now; Jack went through it!"

Dan's eyes widened. "The Scientist is on Earth? And you're not worried?"

"I already have my human form under security." Denida scratched his forehead. "Plus, the Colonel is going there to hunt him down personally!"

Dan frowned. "Why the Colonel and not you?"

"I have something more important to attend to. Let me know if you get anywhere!" Denida ran up the stairs.

More important than capturing the Scientist? What am I missing here?

***

The Colonel saluted the Commander as he arrived with his other soldiers.

"Lady Nina's not here anymore, Sir." The Commander's eyes wandered across the soldiers accompanying the Colonel.

"Nina?" The Colonel sneered. "She's not why I'm here. The Scientist came to this world. We need to find him. Have you heard anything?"

The Commander shook at the very thought.

"We can certainly-" The Colonel froze with wide eyes, as if he had seen a ghost. "Den's hair really darkened fast!"

The Commander spun around. "I already told you about that; you didn't listen."

True, but I still didn't expect it this fast…

"Other than his hair getting even darker, there's no change- no signs of 'the Scientist.'"

The Colonel grunted and approached, kneeling next to the boy. "Still an empty shell."

The Commander peeked at Denida's human side from behind the Colonel. "He doesn't have that blank appearance when he gazes at Nina."

Nina? The Colonel spun. "Where's that girl, anyway… why isn't she here?"

"She's home sick today."

The Colonel frowned. "Do you know where that is?"

The Commander scratched his cheek. "Yes, Sir."

The Colonel tilted his head at his soldiers. "They stay here. You show me where."

The Commander led the Colonel to the farmhouse where Nina lived with her father. They entered silently and continued toward her room.

The Colonel cleared his throat. "You seem to be very comfortable here. Why's that?"

"I was told to-"

"No!" The Colonel lifted his finger. "You wouldn't need to be here to watch her that often, yet you're awfully familiar with the place."

The Commander peeked into the bushes.

"This is a direct *order*, Commander; explain to me how you know this place so well?" The Colonel raised his voice.

The Commander nodded with a grunt. "Nina came to see herself a few times and I followed her."

"But not anymore?"

"No, Sir. She stopped suddenly."

The Colonel glared into the bushes too, now. "If she stopped, something's up," he said under his breath, then turned to the Commander. "I'm placing you in charge. I need to return to the Underworld."

The Colonel headed straight to Dynasty. The guards rushed to salute him and granted him passage, but there was no sign of Nina there.

Angel… Nina's often with her horse. He marched toward the stables, but found no sign of her there, either. He strolled back to Dynasty, his head running amok. *Where is she? Wasn't Susan supposed to be here, too?*

"Colonel!" The Butler ran over.

Oh, Jesus, he's going to wanna talk.

"Denida isn't here."

"I'm not looking for him. I'm searching for Lady Nina. You haven't seen her, have you?"

The Butler shook his head. "She hasn't been here much lately."

"Thanks." The Colonel patted him on the shoulder, then continued to his car.

"Oh yeah, Dan might know."

Wasn't Dan working on something for Denida? The Colonel stopped dead in his tracks. "Dan's here… where?"

"The secret chamber."

The Colonel's eyes widened at the mere mention of that room. Denida had hidden inside it during the hunt for him in the War of the Dark Angels.

He turned and gazed at the monitor concealed behind some books, then proceeded with the fingerprint scanner. An alarm sounded. *I figured Denny would remove me.* He turned to the monitor. "Dan, are-"

The hidden door opened and Dan appeared in the door. "Colonel, what brings you here?"

The Colonel clenched his fist. "Lady Nina. I need to talk-"

Dan opened the door wider. "Come inside."

They descended the stairs. The Colonel noted that all the science equipment was different from the last time he had been there.

"Something's up with Nina."

Dan rubbed his face. "I know. I saw her at Daniel's grave. I suspect the change in her demeanor has to do with losing him…"

The Colonel wrinkled his forehead. "He's dead. She has to have gone somewhere. She can't go to the past-" His eyes sprang open and he pointed at Dan. "Denny told me you're doing something *important* and you're down here where no one can interrupt you… with a crapload of new science equipment."

Dan threw up his arm in a sweeping gesture. "This is nothing." His eyes wandered to his spectroscope.

The Colonel immediately deduced what Dan had been studying. *Oh my god.* He rushed over to Dan's experiment. "Is this a device from a Gate? Why is it here?"

Dan sauntered over. "It's from the second Gate. Denny thought it would be okay to take it because he didn't want the Scientist to come back through anyway."

"What are you doing here?" The Colonel could feel his insides turning as he asked the question, already assuming the worst.

"A time machine… Denny-"

The Colonel slumped down, feeling like his knees couldn't support him any longer. "Denny wants to go back in time…" He took off his beret and buried his face in it.

Dan stood studying him, then moved his hands as if to comfort the Colonel, but stopped midway.

The Colonel raised his head. "That must be where Nina is. She's after the Scientist… on Earth!"

"Nina's on Earth? We have to stop her; it's not safe!" Dan ran toward the door, but stopped suddenly halfway up the stairs. He spun around and casually ambled back down with a smirk across his face. "Denny would rush here if I called."

"Don't let me stop you!"

Dan picked up his cellphone. "Denny, I need to see you-" He winked at the Colonel. "…Alright, see you soon."

After Dan's phone call, they couldn't do anything, but wait. The Colonel paced around the room while Dan continued examinng the device.

"How long has Denida wanted you to do this?"

"Since Daniel's funeral."

"Did you ever come close to figuring it out?"

Dan slammed his fist down. "Neither of you seem to understand that it's not an easy feat; it's a bloody time machine! If it were easy, somebody else would've already made one."

The door above the stairs creaked and footsteps could be heard descending.

The Colonel's hand slipped closer to his sidearm.

Denida came into view. He stopped, flabbergasted at the sight of them. "Colonel?"

The Colonel put on his beret. "Dan told me you've asked him to make a time machine."

Denida sighed. "That's why you called me?"

Dan cleared his throat.

The Colonel approached Denida. "Not exactly… Nina is up to something. She's been acting strangely and she probably wants revenge on the Scientist."

Denida nodded solemnly. "Let her get it, then."

"Sir?" The Colonel frowned. "Don't you want us to stop her?"

Denida waved his hand dismissively. "Aid her all you can and protect her if she needs it! She needs closure." He spun around. "Let me know when you actually make real progress!"

Dan fiddled with his fingers, afraid to make eye contact with the Colonel.

The Colonel clapped his hands. "I guess that's that!"

***

Waste of time! Denida ground his teeth as he strolled out to his car. "Denida, Odin requests your presence!"

Denida stopped and turned to the voice. A very muscular man with a hammer hanging at his side stood in front of him. "Thor?"

Thor clenched his fists, his gaze not wavering.

"Why, what does he want to see me for?"

Thor raised his arm and a sleigh appeared in front of him. "You'll see. Enter!"

Is this a good idea? Well, nothing Lucifer has shown me so far has hinted at them being godawful. Denida rubbed his ring with his thumb and climbed into the sleigh.

Thor whipped the reins and the sleigh lifted off the ground. Denida glared down at Dynasty as they rode away through the skies.

"It's-"

"I can't tell you; only Odin can." Thor gazed straight ahead, not moving a muscle.

The trip to Valhalla went quicker this time. *Maybe Thor's faster than Odin's Sleipnir.*

Thor landed the sleigh and lifted his arms. Denida followed him.

"Odin didn't mind letting you see how to get here…" Thor stopped next to a bench, which stood in the middle of a flower bed. "Wait here. I'll go get Odin." He sauntered off.

An old man with gray hair, but no beard, sat on the bench. He smiled peacefully. *I thought everyone in Valhalla had a beard.*

"I'm not from Valhalla. The name's *Anneh.*" He extended his hand.

Denida shook it, but his eyes glared with suspicion. "How can you read my mind when I'm shielding it?"

Anneh smelled a flower in his hand with a heavy inhale. "Dark magic doesn't work here. You might want to use your ring, instead."

Denida squeezed his hand with the ring. *Of course.*

"Why are you here if you're not from Valhalla?" Anneh tilted his head.

Denida shook his head. "Odin summoned me."

"You're Denida, then." Anneh chuckled.

Denida peered at Anneh, puzzled. "Yes?"

"Sorry about that. Odin invited you so that he could introduce you to me."

Denida ground his teeth. "Why?"

"My time has come and I don't have any children. I must leave my world to someone capable and Odin thought you might be a good choice…"

"As I said, why?"

A crow flew in between them and landed on Odin's shoulder as he appeared next to them.

Anneh stood up. "You led the Underworld revolt against the Dark Angels…"

"Yes, but which world are you from?" Denida stood next to Anneh.

"The most beautiful of worlds, a planet with the most beautiful of creatures…"

"It sounds… nice, but I need to go attend to something, now. Why don't you come see me in the Underworlds sometime?" He shook Anneh's hand. "It was nice to meet you." He turned to Odin and winked. "Always a pleasure to see you, too!"

"Always?" Odin frowned. "You've not been here that many times."

Denida bit his lip. "Your name precedes you. I gotta go." He clenched his fist with the ring, reappearing in his office.

Chapter 8- Getting Jack

Nina nipped at her finger as she pondered. The boss remained surrounded by a group of bodyguards, *four exactly.*

"How can we get close?" Maia whispered.

"I'm thinking," Nina muttered. *There must be a way.* "Wait here. I'm going to try something!" She vanished.

"I really hate it when she does that," Maia grumbled.

Nina ran back to the school, hoping to speak to the Commander, but she stopped at the sight of the many Underworld spirits wearing soldier getup and strolling about. "You have a lot of extra soldiers just to watch Den." She smirked at the Commander.

"They're the Colonel's…"

Nina rubbed her tongue against her teeth. "I came to see you because-"

"The Scientist?"

Nina's eyes widened. "Of course, I need your advice-" She pulled him aside. "If someone were to have security with them at all times, how would you get to them?"

"Why, what does that have to do with finding the Scientist?" The Commander sounded concerned.

"Can you help me or not?" Nina crossed her arms.

'You usually just take them out of the equation, first… '

"Okay," Nina remarked at the Commander's thought.

He flapped his hands dismissively. "Denny always liked to distract them instead, though."

That could work too- I am a spirit in this world, after all. "Thanks." Nina ecstatically sped away.

The Commander sighed as he peeked over at his soldiers.

Maia dozed off in the car. Her head rested on the window.

"Maia, rise and shine!" Nina shook Maia, startling her.

"No," she groaned. "Why'd you wake me up? Sleep's the one place I can find peace…"

"Because I might have found a way." Nina chuckled.

Maia's eyes widened. "How?"

She can't know. "The magic you saw me do…"

Maia slammed the dashboard. "Yes! Let's do this."

Nina vanished from sight and marched toward the boss and his bodyguards. She slid in between them, examining their surroundings.

She yanked the door open, slamming it into the wall.

They all turned with raised guns. Two of the bodyguards approached carefully.

"No one's here?" one of them said, sounding like he didn't believe his own words.

The door banged shut between them, causing everyone to wave their weapons around frantically with trembling hands.

Nina blew air into one of the guard's ears and ducked.

The guard spun around, firing until his gun was empty, then threw it down. "I'm outta here!" He ran away as fast as he could.

"Will you all relax?" the boss hissed. "No one's here!"

The remaining three guards stared at each other.

"I mean it! You checked and nobody-" He grabbed his pants, which had been pulled down while he talked.

The guards gawked at him without uttering a word.

"Maybe we should aid the boss." One of the bodyguards stepped closer and froze. His foot was stuck on something. He yanked it, making him lose his balance and stumble into the others.

"Your shoelaces, you idiot!" another of the bodyguards yelled and helped the first one untie them.

The boss lifted his foot, only to stumble over something. His eyes widened as he looked around.

"Told you!" The three bodyguards approached and helped him up.

"This is… so strange," the boss muttered.

"Here, keep a gun at the ready." One guard handed the boss a sidearm. The gun suddenly slid out of the guard's hand, floating in the air in front of them, where it started tilting around. The men ducked rapidly to avoid it.

"Eh nah, no way. I quit!" The man who handed him the gun left in a hurry.

The last two glared at each other before accompanying him.

"Jesus Christ!" the boss moaned as the gun clattered to the ground.

Maia rushed up to him from across the road, where she sneered at the boss. "Miss me?"

The boss bared his teeth. "Not you!"

Nina surfaced in front of him. "Yes, us." She grabbed the boss off his feet and slammed him against the wall. "You saw what I can do, so now you're going to tell me where the Scientist is or you're next!"

The boss tried to wrestle free, but Nina just increased her grip and squeezed her hand around his throat. "Do not!" Her eyes filled with the hatred she felt for Jack.

"I… can't," he stuttered. "The Scientist will kill me."

He will? Nina kneed the boss and slammed him back into the wall. "What the hell do you think I'll do if you don't tell me?"

He shook his head. "It's not the same!" He gazed into Nina's eyes and his own filled with terror. "He can use Dark magic."

Nina loosened her grip. *He's using Dark magic here. How's that possible with no backing from the Devil?*

The boss ripped free and bolted into the building behind them.

Maia shoved Nina. "What the hell! You let him go!"

What? Nina blinked at Maia, then back at the building. "Never!" She turned invisible and trudged in after him.

The boss didn't stop until he reached his office, where he locked the door and retrieved a gun from his desk. He cocked the gun and aimed it at the door.

Nina knelt next to him. "Hiding from sight is Dark magic, too."

The boss spun around, shooting his wall to smithereens.

She reappeared behind him. The light flickered off. She winked and threw the boss through the doorway.

The boss crawled backward, trying to escape.

"You can run, but you can't hide," Nina giggled.

Maia entered the room, noticed Nina, and rolled her eyes. "I'm not even gonna ask, but where is he?"

Nina waved her hand across the room. "Somewhere in all this darkness."

"So, you lost him?"

Nina chuckled, then stepped forth and tapped Maia on the shoulder. "Far from." Her boot cracked on the rubble covering the floor with each passing step. "I know Jack well, you know. Your boss- he does not know the real heavy Dark Arts." She raised her eyebrows. "His name says it all; *Scientist.* He was just a Scientist. I, however, am not…"

"What exactly *are* you?" Maia interrupted. "You came from nowhere. I don't even know much about you. All I know for sure is that you've got a personal thing with the Scientist, but other than that, I know nothing."

The personal thing… that could work! "The Darkness wants Jack because he betrayed the Devil!" Nina turned toward Maia with a dark glare.

"Jesus," Maia stuttered. "Darkness… is… a thing?"

"Not just a being, an individual."

"Alright." The boss waved his arms. "I'll tell you."

***

Nina and Maia climbed into a cab headed to the address the boss gave them. The cab drove up to a gated entrance to a fancy neighborhood and parked.

The driver turned to them. "We're here."

Nina gazed out the window. *Here?* "Are you sure?"

"It's the address you gave me."

Maia reached past Nina, paid the taxi fare, and exited the car.

Nina detected an ominous change in the air instantly. "He's here; I can feel it!" She nodded to agree with her own words. *Here, at last! I wonder how Denny is doing- no, no time for that!* Nina's eyes shone with the viciousness she felt.

Maia cracked her knuckles and fiddled with her fingers, but being so close to revenge made Nina nervous.

"Can it really be here?" Nina reluctantly followed Maia, who marched to the front gate, where several guards stood.

"Hey, I need to see your boss!" Maia yelled demandingly.

The guards readied their weapons. The one in front shook his head. "No way, José!"

Nina stepped in front of Maia. "Yes, José. We need to see *Jack* on the double."

The guards peered at each other.

"Now!" Nina commanded.

"I'll take them." A man all dressed in black stepped through the guards' formation from the other side of the gate.

The guard in front instructed them to lower their guns. "The boss will take you to the Master!"

Master? If he walks like a soldier and cracks like a soldier, he must be a soldier. Nina peeked back as they walked through the gate. The air within felt denser, forcing her to grab at her throat. *Dark magic is very concentrated here.*

The man led them into a room, where several other men, armed to the teeth, watched their every move. He knocked on a glamorous door. "They're here!" he yelled.

They? Nina took a step back, but another man with a gun already stood there. He pushed her forward into the room.

Nina noticed Jack in the center right away.

"Long time no see." Jack sneered. "Missed me that much?"

Nina peeked back at the door.

"There's no escape. I was expecting you… both of you, actually." Jack lifted his hand and a dark cloud encircled Nina and Maia. "Just to be sure you won't get any ideas."

"Enough of this nonsense. Where's Morton!" Maia raised her voice.

Jack frowned. "Morton, that's right." He flicked his finger. Two armed men exited through a door in the back.

"What-"

The two men came back, dragging Morton by his arms.

Maia ran up to him. "Morton, are you okay?" Morton's eyes were pale and lifeless. He didn't respond.

Maia spun to face Jack. "What have you done to him!"

"Isn't *heroin* nice? He wanted to be free, never to feel again, so I granted his wish."

"You drugged him?" Maia charged Jack, but the man who brought them in stopped her. He twisted her arm.

"Heroin doesn't make him free!" Nina bared her teeth. "He just doesn't-"

"Feel? Care about anything I do?" Jack gloated. "Jackpot, you've got it!" He sauntered over and lifted Morton's head. "So fascinating. Medusa's own siblings..." Jack taunted while staring at Nina. "- yet, you came here with the sister of the demon who killed your only son. How can you live with yourself?"

Nina pushed against the cloud around her to no avail. She built up all her energy and charged Jack, but still nothing. "Whatever it takes to get to you! Why do you care? You worked with Medusa."

Jack strolled over to Nina's side. "Only as a necessity," He stopped just outside the cloud. "-she tried to kill me!"

Nina sighed. "Morton's hooked. If that's what you were after, then let us go."

Jack leered with a vicious grin. "I had to escape the Underworlds because of you! I'm far from done; I'm just getting started." He clapped his hands and two armed men approached from behind him. "Take them away... all three of them."

The two men grabbed Maia and Morton and dragged them away.

Nina retreated as far back as she could from the man who brought them there.

He marched toward her.

Nina felt the cloud growing denser. "Don't come near me!"

He ignored her and walked into the cloud, where Nina kicked him in the crotch and elbowed him with all her might. He fell to the ground in agony.

Nina grabbed his sidearm and ran out of the cloud, but at the edge, she could go no farther. *What the hell?*

The man struggled to his feet and extended his arm. "You can't escape... no spirit can."

Nina cocked the gun at him. "Maybe not, but this one can shoot your brains out."

He shrugged. "Nina… may I call you Nina?"

"Why would you?"

He held his fingertips to his throat. "My name's Jerry. I work with Jack. I'm supposed to bring you somewhere, nothing more."

Nina lowered the gun, but rapidly raised it again. "You get me out of here!"

"I can't; only Jack can control the cloud."

Jack, of course. "Jack!" Nina hollered at the top of her lungs.

A dark cloud lifted her and squeezed her tight, until she could hardly breathe. The gun fell from her hand as she grasped at her throat for air.

Jerry picked up the gun and the dark cloud released her. She fell to the ground with a bump. Jack shook his head, waved a hand, and two other guards pulled her up.

Jerry escorted Nina out, leading her to a truck where Maia and Morton already sat tied up.

They bound Nina next to them.

Nina gazed at her rope. "It's different from the other two."

"Magic restraints!" Jerry yelled as he jumped into the front of the truck.

Maia watched Nina with sad eyes. "They're taking us to an abandoned island It allegedly has some sort of shield is on it."

"A magic barrier," Nina muttered under her breath as the truck lurched into motion.

"Why did you want to see *Jack*?"

Nina rolled her head back. "Medusa… Mara, as you know her, kidnapped my son… and killed him." Her tongue clicked against her teeth. "-my husband killed your sister for it. Jack worked with her; I don't believe he should get away…" She lowered her head.

Maia nudged Nina with her leg, bringing her to lift her head with a glare. "We don't care… Mara's the one who cursed Morton and me, so we don't have any love for her."

The vehicle came to an abrupt halt at a pier. Jerry came around to the back. "It's time." He let the other guards lead them, while Nina could feel his eyes burning into her back.

The island they were going to was only fifteen minutes by speedboat. It had no buildings on it, nothing but forests.

Nina felt the same thick air she had in the house. *Wonder if the Devil knows about this?*

The soldiers dragged them off the boat and onto the shore, then marched back to the ship and pushed it so that it was just offshore.

Jerry raised his arm and their restraints vanished.

"I thought you couldn't do magic?" Nina clenched her fists.

"I guess I lied." Jerry turned and the speedboat took off.

Nina could see the pier on the other shore in the distance.
So close, yet so far.

Chapter 9- Shaddai's Plan

Denida arrived in Hell, but the mansion had moved. *Not this again.* He rubbed his ring and marched into the Darkness. Everyone jumped out of his way as he strolled through Hell, knowing exactly where he was going. Eventually, he stopped in front of the mansion on the far side of Hell. *Wonder if this is how the chambers in his palace work?*

The demon watching the entrance stared intently at him, retreating when Denida approached.

Denida teleported to right in front of the demon before he vanished. "Why are you running?" He lifted his arm and the front doors burst open.

"Denny, you're back." Lucifer stepped out with a broad smile. He put his arm around Denida and led him inside.

Denida clenched his fist.

"How about I show you more?" Lucifer leered from beside the Well of Memories.

Denida sauntered over. "The mansion always moves; do the chambers stay the same?"

Lucifer's eyes flickered with a faint glow of fire. "Why do you ask that?"

"Just wondered," Denida licked his lips. "- well, do they?" He raised one eyebrow.

Lucifer shrugged. "Sometimes they do." He turned back to the well. "Shall we?"

Denida rubbed his hands together. "Let's."

"Shaddai continued being taught while Henna sent more and more Gods throughout the galaxies. She kept passing him by, which only made Shaddai keep trying to learn more hoping to get noticed."

Denida chuckled. "Did it work?"

Lucifer smirked. "- but when Henna announced Odin was coming to see her, Shaddai saw who her favorite always was, and always would be…"

The water in the well started to bubble and grew dark until an image formed.

***

Azal watched Shaddai pace back and forth under the two suns. "Maybe-"

Shaddai stomped over to Azal's side. "No, don't even start!" He clenched his fist as if ready to strike.

"Odin's here." Gabriel came running up to them as if from a raging fire.

Shaddai dashed toward Henna's castle. Gabriel and Azal hurried after.

Henna greeted Odin with a tight embrace. A big man with a hammer accompanied Odin. They both followed Henna inside.

Shaddai jabbed his fist into Azal's side. "We need to hear what they're talking about!" He yanked Azal with him.

When the three of them reached the castle, Shaddai turned to Gabriel. "Make sure no one enters while we're in there." He tapped Azal's shoulder and followed inside.

Shaddai headed straight to Henna's conference chamber.

When they reached it, Henna sat on a throne with Odin and the man with the hammer standing opposite her.

"Everything's proceeding as planned in the galaxy you wanted, but are you certain about this?" Odin scratched his thick beard.

Henna raised herself from her throne and took Odin's hand. "I had a vision; that little planet will be the essential in the future. One day, it will be the epicenter of destiny; *mark my words.*"

"She's just talking business," Azal whispered. "- is this really important?"

Shaddai hushed Azal. He stared at her holding Odin's hand tenderly. "Why does she like him so much?" He bared his teeth.

"I wanted you here to inform you that I'm sending others to your galaxy."

Odin turned to her. "Others?"

"Zeus, you'll like him, amongst a few others I'm sending." Henna intertwined her fingers. "Furthermore, I want you to protect something…" Henna's hand started to glow and a dagger surfaced in it. She placed it in his hand and closed his fingers around it. "I trust you, and *only* you, with it!"

Shaddai fled outside, running past Gabriel.

Gabriel turned confusedly to Azal, who came up behind him. "What happened? Why does Shaddai look mad?

Azal shrugged. "I wish I knew…"

Azal saw Shaddai sitting next to his house when he returned home. He frowned and moved toward Shaddai, who sat grumbling to himself until he noticed Azal.

Shaddai's father, David, trudged toward them. "You're not ready yet?"

Shaddai glared bewilderedly at Azal. "Ready for what?"

David sighed. "That mother of yours didn't tell you?" He rolled his eyes. "So be it. Queen Henna has a visitor and we are to attend a gathering at her castle tonight for a new appointment... a god named Zeus..." He led Shaddai into the house. "Always making me do all the work."

My dad probably wants me to get ready, too... Azal strolled inside his own house, where his father waited for him, as anticipated.

When evening fell, the high society gathered at the castle, led by the ladies with the men in their shadow, as always.

Azal smiled at Shaddai. "Nice, we won't be noticed."

Shaddai clenched his fist. "She just wants to show off her latest creation and Odin..."

"Odin is just accompanying her ..."

Shaddai shook his head. "She was never this cozy with me! Will she ever treat me like that or am I destined to be treated like you *forever*?"

"Me?" Azal gasped, confused.

"As all men are here... servants!"

The crowd started clapping as Henna descended the stairs. She greeted Odin at the bottom, where he stood beside the man with the hammer.

"This is my son, Milady. His name's Thor, a lightning God!" Odin radiated pride.

Henna smiled at Thor and waved to a man, who sauntered over. "This is Odin and Thor." She squeezed the man's shoulder as he nodded in reply.

"Greetings, my name's Zeus." The man shook their hands.

Shaddai slammed his fist into the table, making everything on the table clang. Azal dragged him from the table and out of the room. "Are you nuts?" He turned and raised his voice when they stood alone in the hall.

Shaddai bared his teeth. "They're so comfortable together."

"You'll never be Odin... or Zeus for that matter," Azal insisted.

Shaddai tightened his fist, looking into his friend's eyes, before he exhaled deeply. "You're right!"

"Yes, and-"

Shaddai wandered back into the ballroom, Azal hurried after him.

Shaddai darted through the crowd, turning around, and scanning all the faces until he spotted his father. "Dad, where's Henna?"

David frowned and pointed up the stairs. "She's in her private chambers with Odin, Thor, and the new guy."

Shaddai bolted to the stairway, ready to climb it, but Azal stopped in front of it and shook his head. "They'll see us!"

Shaddai peered around the room. His facial expressions kept changing. After a while, he threw his hand up. "Fine, but we're missing something important."

Azal shrugged. "Maybe so, but if you ever want her to trust you too, you can't!"

Shaddai tore through the crowd and plopped down next to his father.

An hour passed before anything happened. Shaddai kept tapping the table impatiently, annoying Azal, but finally, Henna and her male companions returned, David stood with Azal and applauded her return.

Shaddai raised his head to look at them. "Figures," he muttered. "It's done… another god…" He swallowed his drink.

Gabriel knocked at Azal's door in the morning. Azal appeared with a sorrowful face.

"Something wrong?" Gabriel asked.

"We were at a gathering at the queen's castle. I just have a bad feeling deep down in my gut…"

Gabriel tilted his head toward Shaddai's house.

"Don't!" Azal reached for Gabriel's arm, but it was too late; Gabriel was already on his way to the house. He dashed after him and caught up to him in the garden, where Gabriel had stopped.

Gabriel tilted his head forward. "He's over there."

They approached and Shaddai tore at his hair.

"Is everything alright?" Gabriel's voice clearly showed his concern for his friend.

Shaddai stumbled to his feet. "I need to win her trust. I see now that this is going to take a long time." He grabbed his friends by the shoulders and drew them into a huddle. "- but I have a plan to end everything here for good," he whispered. "- are you both with me?"

"What plan?" Azal sounded as doubtful as he felt.

"Gain her trust as Odin has… she'll have to make me a god in that *special* world of hers…"

* * *

Denida watched as the image faded from the well. He bit his lip and tilted his head toward Lucifer.

Lucifer smirked wickedly. "It was the beginning of the end when Shaddai decided that…"

"Well?" Denida threw up his arms.

Lucifer strode over to Denida and grabbed his shoulder. "Not yet, my dear Denny. When the time's right."

Denida suddenly materialized next to the Gate in Hell.

Crap, he did it again! Denida squeezed his fist and traveled back to his lobby outside his office. He unclenched his hands and moved his ring around, smiling at his secretary, as he strolled past her.

She jumped to her feet to block the door. "Hang on; someone's been waiting for you!"

Waiting? Denida glanced to the other side of the room, where Anneh sat reading a newspaper. He stepped closer to Anneh. "Anneh was your name, right?"

Anneh looked up with a smile. "That's right; you asked me to come see you."

Denida's eye lit up. "Of course, follow me." He beckoned with his hand and entered his office.

"Nice room…" Anneh glared across it. "This was once Danyel, the Dark Angel's, right?"

Denida nodded. "You're well-informed, but we should discuss your business with me. You wanted someone else to lead your planet?" Denida shut his eyes and let a deep breath out. "But I never intended to become a leader; it just happened here, within this one Underworld." Denida paused skeptically. "Why do you even ask about *Danyel?*"

Anneh grinned. "Because I believe you are the only one destined to lead my world!"

Denida ground his teeth. "I don't know about that. I-"

"Just consider it; leadership is inside of you…"

Denida scratched his forehead. "It just fell into my lap."

"You may want to look into uniting the Underworlds. You know, like they once were…"

"Why?" Denida rolled his eyes.

"It took only one President to lead them all before; it might be *you* this time." Anneh winked.

"That's silly," Denida scoffed. "I should go check on Dan…" He guided Anneh toward the door.

"Aren't you curious to see if you could, let alone how those worlds are doing?"

"No," Denida declared coldly.

"Even if I tell you what I heard?"

Denida spun around. "Heard about what?"

"They say there's trouble brewing in the Underworlds…"

Denida grunted. "Trouble? What trouble? I haven't heard anything about this."

"Perhaps *Dan* has been too occupied to inform you?" Anneh's eyes widened. "When Daniel, your son died, the Darkness began its descent onto your worlds…"

"No…" Denida shook his head in disbelief and stopped at the door. *He has a point, though. I should make sure everything's okay…* "I'm going!" He tore the door open to find Lucifer standing there. Anneh and Lucifer stood face-to-face. Their eyes locked like the air had suddenly turned to ice.

Lucifer watched Anneh with each step.

"Remember what I said…" Anneh waved as he stepped out of the office.

Lucifer shoved Denida into his office and slammed the door. "How do you know that man?"

"Maybe I should ask you that question?" Denida raised his eyebrows. Lucifer's eyes flared red.

Denida shrugged. "I verified Odin was real. That's a friend of his…"

"A friend of Odin's…" Lucifer maintained his red eyes as he glared at Denida.

"If you want to play Devil, knock yourself out, but I have to go see Dan." Denida marched toward the door.

"I'm here to tell you the rest…"

Denida stopped at the door, his hand resting on the handle. "Really… so soon?"

Lucifer laid hold of Denida's hand. "Time is of the essence."

Yet again, they stood outside Lucifer's private chamber with the Well of Memory.

Denida tilted his head around the hallway and the demon who always guarded the front entrance scurried away.

Lucifer stood in front of his chamber. "Coming?"

Denida glared back down the hallway. "What's so important?"

Lucifer closed the door, with only Denida inside with him, and rubbed his palms. "What I want to show you took place a long time after the last memory you saw…" He held his hand over the well, making Darkness encircle it. The well bubbled and he stared into Denida's eyes. "Shaddai did everything he could to appease Henna. He was determined…"

***

Azal and Gabriel ran playing under the twin suns. They came to a stop under a tree in the shade.

"Too hot," Gabriel huffed, running his hand across his forehead, wiping away the sweat.

Azal grinned. "The heat never bothers me; I embrace it!"

"Gabriel and Azal, isn't it?" Henna sat under the trunk, gazing up at them.

"Yes, I'm-"

Azal pushed Gabriel behind him. "Mighty queen, what an honor to see you." He smiled tenderly.

She glanced at Gabriel and back at Azal. "Is something the matter?"

Azal shook his head rapidly. "Aren't you teaching Shaddai something?"

Henna stood up. "Not today. What Shaddai's doing today doesn't require my assistance. You are his two confidants, right?" Her eyes stole a look. "Yes, including you, Gabriel?" She smiled softly at him.

This is not going to end well… "We need to be on our way." Azal yanked Gabriel up. He and Gabriel hurried away.

Henna smiled after them.

Azal guided Gabriel to a spot they all knew, the one place no one would find them. He carefully scoped out the surroundings before he turned to Gabriel. "You can *never* tell her anything!"

"She seemed nice."

Azal rolled his eyes and a small flicker of red appeared as he slapped Gabriel across his face. "She's never nice. She always has an agenda; this is no different!"

Gabriel stepped back with his hand planted on his cheek. He stared at Azal in shock.

Azal kicked the ground. "I'm sorry, okay? It wasn't on purpose."

"It's fine." Gabriel lowered his arm. "Why don't we head home?"

Azal nodded.

It was late in the day when they arrived. Shaddai stood outside Gabriel's door, waiting for them.

"Shaddai." Gabriel sprinted toward his friend as soon as he noticed him.

Shaddai frowned. "What happened to your face?"

Gabriel shrugged. "Nothing important."

"Know what's important?" Shaddai bared his teeth as he stared at them. "Henna's starting to question me. She met with you, didn't she?"

"Yes," Gabriel admitted, making Azal roll his eyes.

"I could tell; it didn't change her suspicions…" Azal shrugged.

Shaddai approached Azal and put his hand on his shoulder. "- I need you, my friend, to convince her…"

Azal grunted and clenched his fist. "Even if I wanted to… I don't know where she is at this hour!"

"I do." Shaddai leaned in with a wicked grin. He grabbed Azal's hand and dragged him down the road. He led Azal to the majestic garden that stood next to Henna's castle. It was filled with colors as far as the eye could see.

"She has a special place at the center of the garden that she adores." Shaddai tilted his head forward.

"Why aren't you leading me the rest of the way?" Azal frowned.

"Henna can sense anyone in her garden; it's an extension of her. Go!"

Azal took a step into the garden. Even with just one foot inside, everything felt different. He could feel the change at his core. He glared back at Shaddai, who nodded for him to continue. Azal stepped completely into the garden.

So peaceful and soothing in here… Azal arched his neck in disbelief at the birds flying between the trees above. He sauntered along, watching in amazement, and noticing the fauna surrounding him. *You'd never guess all this was here from seeing the outside…*

'*That you wouldn't.*' Those words crept into his thoughts as clearly as his own, yet it was someone else. *But whose?*

Henna appeared out of thin air in front of Azal, startling him. "It was always intended to only be for me." She smiled wide, her rainbow eyes shining. "- but since you're here, I wanted to ask you something about Shaddai."

"Yes?" Azal tried to sound confused to the best of his ability.

"Is your friend a good child… is he *loyal*? Or should I distrust him?"

Azal threw up his arm. "Of course, he's a good friend."

"So, he has always been loyal to you?"

What a strange question. "I guess?"

Henna smiled broadly and pulled Azal into her embrace. "Thank you, my child."

With a flash, Azal stood back inside his house. *What just happened? How did I get here?*

He rushed to Shaddai's house.

"Azal?" David waved at him.

"Where's Shaddai?"

"He went to see Queen Henna."

Azal sped toward the castle, stopping abruptly. "Gabriel, why are you here?"

Gabriel raised his eyebrows. "Shaddai's in there with the queen…"

Again. Azal stood next to his friend and watched the castle.

Gabriel shook his head. "Not in there," He turned to the garden and pointed. "- in there…"

"He went in by himself?"

"Nope; Henna took him…"

"But only she's allowed in there," Azal whispered under his breath.

They sat outside the castle for what felt like an eternity, but finally, Shaddai came strolling out of the garden.

Shaddai sneered as Azal and Gabriel ran over to him. "Come." He walked rapidly toward the abandoned settlement.

Shaddai stopped and spun to face them as soon as they were away from any prying eyes. His eyes widened as if he just had been given the greatest gift. "It worked. Thanks, Azal."

"Don't… celebrate… before it… works," Azal huffed.

Shaddai chuckled. "I'm not-" He lifted a cloth from under his shirt, grinning as he unfolded it, revealing one of Henna's daggers.

"How-" Azal gasped with Gabriel eyeing it, just as stunned.

"She trusts me, now. She feels one of the daggers should remain here." He lowered his voice in a mocking tone. "-with a trusted one…"

***

Denida grunted. "You promised to show me the rest?"

Lucifer smirked. "You'll get the rest in time!" He sauntered back to his throne.

Denida bared his teeth. "Fine." He rushed out of the throne room and exited the mansion, where the demon who always stood guard, waited.

The demon's eyes grew wide at the sight of him. *"Little Evil,"* he muttered.

Little- that's right; he was here back when Lucifer helped me find Mara… He shook his head and continued, while the demon watched his every step. He clenched his fist to appear back at Dynasty. *Dan!* He hurried toward the main house and headed straight to the secret room.

"Dan!" he yelled while running down the stairs.

Dan raised his head from his spectroscope. "Denny? Something wrong?"

Denida waved his fingers toward Dan. "Come on; I need you."

Dan stood up, frowning. "Why, what for?"

"We need to check on the Underworlds. Maybe it's time to get them to work together again." Denida raised his ring to his lips. "It might help you get over your struggle with the time machine!"

Dan fell back in his chair. "So, we're going to the Gate? We shouldn't leave Nina alone here."

Denida ground his teeth and shook his head. "We can't travel to the other Underworlds with the Gates; we're using my ring!" He licked his lips. "As for Nina, don't worry… she needs time. I'll talk to her once the time machine works!"

Chapter 10- Getting Off the Island

I'm not calling Denny. There has to be a way out of here! Nina ran to the edge of the island, only to slam into a magical barrier. She tried changing to her nonphysical soul form, but it yielded the same result.

She trotted over to Maia, who sat on the beach, sifting her fingers through the sand. "Throw me off the island!"

Maia glared up. "What are you-"

Nina yanked her up and dragged her out to the water.

Maia resisted and stopped at the shoreline. "This is nuts! I'm not-"

Nina released Maia's arm and sighed. "You're right; The barrier's too strong."

Maia threw up her arms and turned to go back to the beach.

"-but *you* might be able to leave. I can't because I'm not human, so the magic barrier prevents me!"

Maia's forehead wrinkled as much as it could. "Not… human?"

"I come from another dimension… where only souls reside…"

Maia fell to her knees. "That's how he knew you!" She pointed at Nina. "And Mara… the Darkness! It was real, not just in her head." Her head dropped.

Nina stepped out of the water and fell to her knees. "Mara *killed* my son." Her voice resounded with the insurmountable pain of a mother still in agony. "-you looked exactly like her, so I wanted you *dead*, but I learned you're nothing like her…" She locked eyes with Maia.

"Mara caused nothing but pain." Maia spat on the dirt next to her and stormed into the ocean. She kept on going with the water rising all around her. Suddenly, she stopped walking.

Nina squinted her eyes and gazed out at her. "What's the matter?"

Maia trudged through the sea back to Nina. "I can't… something prevents me, too…"

"A magic seal that works on both of you," a voice echoed.

Nina spun in the direction of the voice with wide eyes. *Jack!* She bared her teeth and charged.

Jerry jumped in front of Jack. He grabbed Nina by the throat and lifted her off the ground. She tried to free herself from him, but Jerry's hold on her was too strong. He marched back to the sand where he released his grip, making her collapse to her knees in the sand.

"There's so much!" Morton ran over and grabbed a bundle of drugs from a man next to Jack.

"No!" Maia ran to her brother, but he was already snorting some heroin.

"You can't stop it, my dear," Jack chuckled.

"How did you even get here?" Nina glared at Jack, who laughed.

"Magic, Nina. Dark magic can do more than you think." Jack lifted his hand and slowly spun around.

So you think. Nina jumped up. "No, that's not… you all can't do magic!"

"Really?" Jack spun around in a circle, making the leaves to fly up between Nina and him.

No, he doesn't! Nina pushed through the crimson wall, but it was so thick that she couldn't break through it.

Jack chuckled and disappeared into the forest behind him. His leaves subsided after several minutes.

Nina rubbed her face and ran back to the beach. Maia was tending to Morton. She poked Maia's shoulder. "Come on; we gotta go, now!"

Maia shook her head. "I can't go with Morton like this!" She stroked his sweaty forehead.

Nina rolled her eyes. "Forget you, then." She sped back toward where she last saw Jack. Nina slowed down as she neared the forest, checking her surroundings with an elevated sense of caution.

There! A bunch of leaves lay scattered in a pile on the ground. She examined them, picking them up smelling them. *The same sensation of Darkness as in the Underworlds.*

She sauntered forward, where she found footprints in the dirt and followed them deeper into the forest.

The trail suddenly ended in front of a thicket.

Nina's tongue clicked against her teeth. *Why have they stopped here?* She pulled the shrubs aside, revealing a hidden entrance. *At last… magic, my ass!* She grabbed at the handle, but it was locked. She kicked and slammed the door. *This isn't going to work…*

She backed out of the shrubs and arched her neck. A small ray of sunlight shone through the trees, concentrated in a beam just next to a precariously angled mirror. A bird landed on a branch, weighing it down enough to allow the light to hit the mirror, sending a beam to the door, causing it to flick green for a second. The bird took flight and the beam disappeared, making the door turn red.

Of course, but how am I going to get up there? She licked her lips as she pondered that conundrum. *I'm a spirit in this world!* A smile appeared on her face and she flashed upward to the branch. The sun lit the mirror, making the door beep green. She shifted her position to look at the door, making the branch move with her, covering the light again, and causing the door to turn off again.

Nina jammed her fist into the tree, making a bird on another branch flap its wings.

She leaned over the branch and whistled to get the bird's attention.

The bird blinked at her and flew off, leaving her alone, making her sigh.

Creak.

What's that sound? She stretched her arms to check under her for the source of the sound. The branch she was lying on had an ominous crack in it.

Crap. The branch broke, and she tumbled down through the other twigs into a bush under the tree.

She moaned as she tried to stand. *Guess spirits can feel pain too...*

'Beep.'

Her attention flew to the sound in the direction of the door and back to the tree. *The light's back.* She jumped up and raced to the door.

Nina grabbed the handle and tore it open, her eyes full of anticipation. The room was bare, except for a set of stairs leading into a basement. A faint light from below beckoned Nina forward. She descended the stairs. When she reached the middle step, Jerry turned around and their eyes met for a moment.

Jerry charged forward, but Nina vanished after a few steps. "One of our prisoners has escaped!"

Another man appeared at the bottom of the stairs. "Who escaped?"

"Nina's here… help me find her before she gets away! She used a concealment spell." Jerry felt with his arms as he climbed the stairs.

The man started doing the same from the bottom of the steps.

Jerry arrived at the top without finding anything. He spun around. The other man reached the step from which Jerry had started. Jerry waved for the man to close the gap between them. They readied their guns.

"Are we checking outside? The door didn't even open." The man frowned.

"She's a spirit; maybe she found a way through it!" Jerry ran outside, his gun raised.

The man stayed inside, where he peeked back down the stairs, before shrugging and following Jerry.

Nina jumped down from a beam in the ceiling and dashed down the stairs. She raced along the corridor, past the soldiers.

They shivered as she ran past. "Did you feel a draft?" one asked.

Nina finally came to another set of stairs and climbed them. When she exited, she was back on the grounds of Jack's mansion. She marched away but stopped after a few steps to face the tunnel.

I'm sorry Maia. I'll be back for you; I promise! She ran forward, invisible to the guards. Suddenly, she jumped down behind a bush with a thud.

Jack stared at the bush. "Did you hear that?" he asked his waiter.

"Jack!" Jerry ran up to him, huffing and puffing.

Jack shot him a disgusted look. "Jack? I'm *the Scientist!*"

"Nina's… gone," Jerry sighed.

Jack's face grew cold. "Gone? What do you mean gone? The island has a shield preventing her from leaving!"

Jerry shook his head. "She was in the tunnel…"

Jack's knuckles whitened around his fork.

The waiter poured him a drink. Jack grabbed ahold of the waiter's hand and jammed the fork into it over and over, until it was no longer recognizable.

Jack, covered with the waiter's blood, handed the bloody fork to one of his guards. "Clean this mess up!" He put his arms on Jerry's shoulder and stared into his eyes, making Jerry sweat.

"Do… *not…* let… her… escape," Jack said slowly and smiled, squeezing Jerry's shoulder. "If you don't get her back, consider your life forfeited!" He took a handkerchief from the table and wiped Jerry's sweat off his forehead. "Look how nice I can be and remember I can be just as vicious!" He sat back down, tossing out the drink, and poured himself a new one. He put on his shades as he leaned back in his chair. "Just so you know, no, I'm not kidding."

Jerry nodded frantically and ran to the other guards.

A dark cloud appeared above the ground. Several figures that had been invisible before, appeared.

This is bad… With an unnerving stare, Nina watched her body as it started to become visible.

A guard grabbed one of the uncloaked figures. "What do we do with it?"

Jerry bared his teeth as he gazed toward Jack. "Take all of them to the island!"

I need to get out of here, but how? Nina looked around in a panic for something- anything. *Gabriel!* "Gabriel, I need you," she whispered in as low a voice as she could, while the guards drew closer to her. Nothing happened; it was as if she never said the words.

"Gotcha!" Jerry grabbed her.

"Gabriel!" she screamed as loud as she could. Everyone stared at her, even Jack from where he was. "- I *really* need you!"

Jack smirked. "Nina! This is Earth, not the Underworlds. He can't just appear because you're asking him to." He waved his thumb up. "Nice work, Jerry!"

It was all pointless... Nina could feel the despair within her rising.

"That look!" Jack applauded. "So priceless... just like Daniel's when he was kidnapped."

Nina stared at him viciously. She kneed Jerry and grabbed his gun, firing at Jack.

Jack's glass exploded into a million pieces and he ducked behind a pillar.

The guards all returned fire and the glass near her shattered. Several shards sliced hit her cheek.

"Ouch!" Nina grabbed her cheek and returned fire while she fled.

Jack charged after her, noticing small drops of blood next to some footprints. He indicated for his guards to duck as he led in pursuit of Nina, following her prints in the dirt. Nothing could be heard but the birds singing overhead.

They led down some stairs to a door.

Jack's face twisted into a broad smile. "The cellar. There's no way out. Get ready!" He yanked the door open and everyone stormed inside, guns at the ready.

Nina jumped down from a tree on the other side of the courtyard, running out of the yard proudly.

A gunshot fired behind her and the dirt by her foot puffed into the air.

Jerry... Nina froze, fiddling with her fingers rapidly, as she turned around. She exhaled slowly, then jumped backward in a windmill motion.

Jerry pulled the trigger again, causing Jack and the others to come running to the sound. "She's over there." He tilted his head toward a flowerbed. "Nina, we have you surrounded," He spat. "- come out!" He pulled the hammer back, pointing the gun at the flowers.

Jack snapped his fingers and pointed at Jerry, shaking his head with an intense look.

Nina surrendered, standing up and holding her arms above her head. The other guards grabbed the gun hanging from her finger, then pulled her up.

Jack ambled over and pinched her cheek with the blood streaking down it. "Clever girl, shame it didn't work!" He sauntered over to Jerry, who smiled broadly. "Feeling smug?" He grabbed Jerry and kneed him, before hitting him with his fist as hard as he could, spattering blood onto the flowers.

"Why?" Jerry wiped the blood away with his palm, glaring at Jack with shock written all over his face.

"Never- *ever* kill her. If she dies, she'll be sent back to Denida."

Intriguing...

The guards led her to the tunnel, where other spirits were surrounded as well. Nina gasped, holding her hands over her mouth.

"Don't stop... move it!" one of the guards shook his head and shoved her into the crowd with the other souls.

Nina fell to her knees and a hand reached down for her. She grabbed it and got pulled up.

"Commander- how?" Her face pale and confused.

"I realized something was up, so I came looking for you..."

Nina sighed. "... and now we're both caught."

The Commander watched the guards. "For now, but we'll find a way out!"

"Take them back, already!" Jack yelled.

The guards guided them down the tunnel. The Commander slowed down, whispering to the others around him. The chatter began to spread throughout the crowd of souls marching.

"Shut up!" A guard pointed his gun toward them.

"Charge!" the Commander commanded.

The souls all spread out in a coordinated maneuver, attacking the guards with bare hands and hidden knives.

Nina stared in puzzlement. She turned to the Commander as the last guard fell to the ground. "They're not your-"

"The Task Force," the Commander smirked. "Think I would go alone? We just needed a place where we could overpower them without being noticed."

Nina giggled and rubbed her forehead. "We have to go through Jack's underground tunnel. The island has a shield..."

The Commander nodded. "I'm already aware of this. We're waiting until the cloud lifts, then we're gone."

They grabbed the guards' guns and ventured back toward the exit, where they waited for the cloud to dissipate from the grounds.

Nina paced back and forth in the tunnel, anxiously glaring out.

"You should relax, Lady Nina." The Commander smiled at her.

Nina rapidly shook her head.

"We'll be out of here soon..."

Nina halted defiantly and turned to the Commander. "We can't leave!"

They all peered at each other.

"Denny isn't here, making me your commanding officer, no?"

"I guess?" The Commander shrugged.

"- and I'm telling you!"

They all stared at the Commander, who stood up and sighed. He suddenly tapped his foot and saluted Nina. "Attention!"

The soldiers followed suit.

"How may we serve you, Ma'am?" The Commander asked in a harsh tone.

"Jack has to die," Nina bared her teeth.

Chapter 11- Revisiting

Denida and Dan arrived in front of a tall building with the Underworld symbol embedded on top.

"Amazing!" Dan strolled around the courtyard. He ran his fingers through his hair, pointed to the forest on the other side of the road, and snapped his fingers. "The Gate's over there!"

Denida was too intent on getting into the building to pay attention to what Dan said.

Dan ran to catch up with Denida at the reception desk. "I know the way; come." Dan led the way through the building to the upper floors.

He must remember the way from when he drove the robots there...

The top floor crawled with soldiers. Dan stopped abruptly.

Denida continued halfway down the corridor before he noticed. He sighed and returned to his friend. "Something wrong?" he asked as he drew closer and saw Dan watching the soldiers pacing about the floor.

"There have never been soldiers this close to the Colonel's office..."

He's right. Denida waved his hand. "Come on." He marched to the end of the hallway with Dan close behind and stopped in front of two guards.

"Dan?" One of the guards frowned.

Dan shrugged and smiled.

The guard nodded and opened the twin doors behind him.

The Colonel stood hunched over a table surrounded by soldiers. He turned to the door and narrowed his eyes as Denida marched into the room and he charged forward.

Denida lifted his hand to stop the Colonel.

The Colonel ignored it and bumped into Dan. Denida teleported to the other side of the room evasively.

"Relax, Colonel. We're here to help." Denida held up his arms.

The Colonel bared his teeth. "Really? Last time you were here, you sure didn't!" He pulled his sidearm.

Denida clenched his fist.

The Colonel squeezed the trigger and emptied the magazine. All the bullets bounced off Denida. "Quit hiding behind your magic and face me like a man!"

Denida shook his head. "I'm sorry, I don't think so. I've learned that isn't constructive, but I didn't have a choice last time…" He shrugged as he strolled closer to the Colonel, waving his hand at the soldiers at the table. "-why do you have so many soldiers here, anyway? Is everything okay?"

The Colonel raised an eyebrow and returned to the table, ignoring Denida.

"They just keep coming," a soldier declared.

"We shoot them with everything we've got, but nothing seems to work…" Another shoulder's slumped.

"Their bodies are so weird, but they must have a weak point!" The soldier next to Denida scrutinized a photo in his hand.

Interesting. Denida arched his neck to look at it. *Demons… here?* Grabbing the picture as soon as the soldier put it down, he studied it and nipped his upper lip. He pushed through the crowd to the Colonel, who squinted his eyes disgustly.

"I can help," Denida insisted.

The Colonel rolled his eyes and smirked. "Really?"

Denida handed the picture to the Colonel. "I know how to kill them."

The Colonel stared into Denida's eyes with an intensity he recognized from the Colonel in his own world.

"How?" The Colonel asked reluctantly.

"They're just demons… I've dealt with their kind before." Denida peeked back at Dan, then at the Colonel again. "I need all the Underworlds to stand together as one, united! If my plan works, will you join me?"

"Affirmative! I want them gone by any means necessary, but how can we achieve that?" The Colonel bared his teeth and his eyes didn't waver.

"Their eyes… shoot them in the eye and they go down." Denida winked.

The soldiers gawked at each other and started to mumble amongst themselves.

Denida grabbed the Colonel's arm. "You know about me from Dan and I know about this; trust me."

"Silence!" the Colonel yelled and exhaled deeply. "Tell them to try it!"

"Sir?" a soldier sounded confused.

"That's an order, Soldier."

The soldiers vacated the office, leaving only the Colonel, Denida, and Dan to resume their tense reunion.

Dan sauntered through the office, examining the bookcase and everything else in the room.

The Colonel scowled, tapping his leg with his fist.

Denida froze, watching the Colonel's every move.

The Colonel's eyes wandered to Dan, then to Denida's arms.

"A lot has changed," Denida dropped his arms.

"Maybe for you, but not for me!" The Colonel charged Denida, swinging his fist.

Denida deflected with his hands. The Colonel hit him in the back with a roundhouse kick and Denida dropped to his knees.

The Colonel followed up with a succession of kicks, but Denida rolled to the side, then jumped to his feet, but the Colonel pursued him.

"Sorry, I'm over here, now." Denida raised his eyebrows.

The Colonel clenched his fists and swung a haymaker.

Denida's nose gushed blood as he dodged the Colonel's next strike, which shattered a flowerpot.

The Colonel spun to face Denida. "Fight me!"

Denida wiped away the blood. "That's not what I'm here for."

Soldiers burst through the doors, panting.

The Colonel lost focus on Denida and approached his soldiers with concern written across his face. "What's the matter?"

"It... worked," the two soldiers said in unison.

"What do you mean it worked?" The Colonel peered at Denida, who winked.

"They're falling one by one when we shoot them in the eye as... as-" the soldier pointed at Denida. "- as he said, Sir."

Denida sauntered over to the Colonel and patted his shoulder. "I believe it's time for you to honor your part of the deal, Colonel?"

The Colonel lifted his finger. He turned his attention to his soldiers. "Are they all gone?"

"We're still dispatching them, Sir."

"Dismissed." The Colonel saluted. He turned to Denida with a wide grin. "We're not done yet, are we." He swept Denida's leg and slammed his fist down.

Denida gripped the Colonel's fist tightly.

"Jesus!" Dan slammed the table. "Stop it already. You want the demons gone, don't you? Denida can help!"

The Colonel glared at Denida for a second before nodding and offering his hand to aid Denida to his feet.

Denida smiled at Dan. *'I knew bringing you along was a good idea,'* he spoke into Dan's thoughts.

Lucifer suddenly materialized behind Dan. "Denny," he scowled. "-you're not in your own world."

Dan jumped away from Lucifer, cowering behind Denida.

The Colonel raised his gun. "Who are you? How did you get in here?"

"I'm the Devil," Lucifer smirked.

Denida put his hand on the Colonel's gun and stepped forward. "My world? You're the one who doesn't belong here, Luci."

"I'm only here for you; we should-"

"No," Denida insisted. "If you want any chance of me seeing the rest of *your tale*, you leave, *now!*" Denida clenched his fist and scowled at Lucifer, a tint of red within his bad eye.

Lucifer lifted his hand and dissipated into smoke.

Dan jumped in front of Denida. "What's going on… why were you being so cozy with Lucifer?"

"How I keep him at bay…"

A knock sounded at the door. "Enter!" the Colonel hollered.

A soldier saluted. "They're gone, Sir! The last of them ran away…"

The Colonel chuckled and gazed at Denida. "Dan and John were right. I would never have imagined anyone would even think of talking to the Devil like that, but you did. He listened and his last demons left, too!" He marched over and extended his hand to Denida. "We'll follow you anywhere, anytime."

Denida smiled and winked as he shook the Colonel's hand, then turned and took Dan's hand. He clenched his other fist and teleported them to a Gate on a hilltop.

"Are you sure this is going to help? I'm still drawing a blank." Dan sighed.

"Have faith; I'm sure it will."

Dan grunted, then scurried around the Gate, examining every piece of it. "This is the world Danyel fled to."

Not that name again… "That's in the past. Let's go see the Colonel of this world." Denida strolled down the hilltop toward the castle. He trotted ahead with Dan walking behind him, swiveling to examine every nook and cranny they passed.

Denida stopped and glanced back after Dan, who was still at the other end of the road, and rolled his eyes. He trudged up to Dan, who stood with his eyes fixed on something.

"Dan!" Denida nudged his friend.

Dan sighed and tilted his head forward.

Is that? Denida stepped forward and entered an old pub. It was almost pitch-black inside.

"Praise to the Darkness," the barkeep greeted him. "What can I help you with today?"

Denida grimaced. "Your clothes-"

The barkeep smiled. "Just like the mighty Danyel."

Mighty? I must have missed that memo! Denida and Dan glared at each other.

"Thanks for coming to Danyel's Tavern." The barkeep poured another customer a drink.

Danyel's Tavern? Denida spun around and swiftly jumped over the counter, grabbed the barkeep, and slammed him into the wall, knocking down bottles. "Why is this called Danyel's Tavern and why are you dressed like the former Dark Angel?"

"Because he's the greatest?" The barkeep's eyes glowed with admiration.

"… You mean he *was*. In case you haven't heard, Danyel was *killed*." Denida tightened his grip.

"Was he really?" the barkeep sneered.

The barkeep's grin made Denida uneasy. He released the barkeep and marched out.

Dan ran after him. "What just happened?"

Denida shrugged, increasing his speed toward the castle.

The rest of the way, Dan still glanced around, fascinated by everything they passed, but all his attempts to get Denida to talk proved fruitless.

They finally reached the castle, which now had soldiers patrolling the grounds, and barbed wire surrounding it.

Dan sauntered over. "I need to-"

"Denida!" The guard pushed past Dan and led him inside the castle.

Dan followed behind them as they walked. The guard led them directly to a massive chamber, where the Colonel sat at a desk.

The Colonel jumped to his feet and sprinted over to Denida. He pulled back a chair for him.

Dan frowned. "What's going on here? Why are you all so excited to see Denny?"

The Colonel poured a drink and handed it to Denida.

The guard smiled broadly. Denida put the drink down on the table. "Dan's got a point; why are you being so nice?"

The Colonel sighed and pushed everyone else out of the room, shutting the door behind them.

Dan and Denida exchanged a glance.

"We have grown since the Dark Angel, Danyel-" The Colonel squeezed his hands tight. "- but Darkness seems to be back. Rumors say Danyel's still around-"

"No," Denida shook his head. "I killed him myself, in Hell."

"There's a movement for Danyel…" the Colonel insisted.

That bar… Denida ground his teeth. "No… I won't accept that!" He put his hand on Dan's shoulder. "You stay here."

Denida yanked the door open and disappeared into the air.

He resurfaced in front of the tavern, examining his surroundings, before turning the knob and marching inside.

The barkeep frowned as faced Denida. "Back again?"

"…Danyel…"

"Oh, you changed your mind?"

Denida's eyes wandered around the room, then turned back to the barkeep. "Everyone here is a follower of… Danyel?" He felt his gut turn inside-out as he repeated that name.

The barkeep chuckled deviously. "Of course, you're with likeminded individuals." He poured Denida a drink. "So, what's your name, Mister?"

Denida sat down in front of his drink, took a sip and put it back on the table. He straightened up and watched the other patrons in the tavern. He faced the barkeep and sneered. "My name's Denida!" he said with a raised voice. The chatter died down as everyone turned to him.

The barkeep stared. "Denida… the one-"

"-the one who ended Danyel once and for all." Denida stood back up. "Plus, I know *real* Dark magic." He lifted his hand. A dark cloud formed around it and a fire ran across the floor, drawing a pentagram, which forced all of the costumers to scatter, unable to touch it.

"What… are… you doing?" the barkeep stuttered.

Denida strolled into the circle, despite the blaze. He clenched his fist with the ring and a dark aura surrounded his hand. His right eye flickered red. "You summoned Darkness, here?" Denida questioned what he could sense inside the Darkness. "A strong demon? An *archdemon*?" He opened his eyes with bewilderment. "Who? Danyel?"

The barkeep shrugged. "I don't-"

Denida held up his finger. "I've been to Hell; I can sense when I'm being played, so be very careful with your words…"

The barkeep exhaled heavily. "…Yes, Danyel."

Denida projected to the barkeep and slammed the man's head down on the desk. He held it there. "That's impossible; I ripped out his heart. I *know* he's dead!"

"I've *seen* him!"

Denida released the barkeep, grinding his teeth so hard it could be heard throughout the tavern. *How is that possible? Is he lying? I never saw through Mara, so I might've lost my gift. Has Lucifer been playing me?*

The barkeep just smirked at him.

Only one way to find out… Denida swept the barkeep's legs and grabbed ahold of his temples. The barkeep's memories flashed through Denida's mind. He found the one he needed. *The barkeep met a dark figure, a demon.* The face he saw made Denida release the barkeep and fall to his knees. *But… how?*

"Told you," the barkeep gloated.

Denida rubbed his forehead and flicked his fingers. The pentagram vanished and he sat down behind the counter, burying his head in his hands. "Give me a drink."

He recalled that destined day in Hell when Lucifer wanted him to become dark again, so he let him kill Danyel. Denida ripped his heart out to destroy his soul. *It was Danyel; I'm sure of it, but no one can survive that... I must see Lucifer. There's no other way!*

Denida clenched his fist, appearing in front of the mansion, which was still guarded by a demon. He paid the demon no mind and rushed inside the mansion. Lifting his arm in a forward motion, he thrust open the doors to Lucifer's throne room.

"Lucifer!" he yelled.

The doors slammed shut behind Denida and Lucifer appeared in a dark cloud in front of him. "Denny, my child."

"*Danyel!*" Denida pointed at Lucifer's throne. "You sat there and watched me rip out Danyel's heart... or is my memory wrong? Is he dead or not!"

Lucifer stepped up to embrace him tenderly, but Denida stopped him with a raised hand.

"He's gone; don't worry." Lucifer smiled so broadly that it reached his eyes. "- but since you're here, let's continue the tale..."

"I saw him..."

Lucifer shrugged. "... There are many demons who look like him..."

Denida grunted. "What's next?"

"Shaddai's wish being granted," Lucifer rubbed his hands together.

Chapter 12- The Last of Henna

Azal paced in the garden next to the Henna's castle, never taking his eyes off the entrance.

Shaddai stepped out.

Azal stopped dead in his tracks and licked his lips.

Behind Shaddai, Henna surfaced, patted Shaddai on the shoulder, and headed toward her castle.

Azal followed Shaddai, keeping his distance until Shaddai was far enough away that he felt certain Henna couldn't hear.

"What happened?" He darted in front of Shaddai, who smiled vividly. Azal frowned. "What have I missed?"

"Go get Gabriel and meet me at our spot." Shaddai walked away with his excitement still intact.

Azal hurried to find Gabriel and they strode to the abandoned settlement that had become their meeting place.

"What's the rush?" Gabriel asked.

Azal shook his head. "I don't know, just what Shaddai asked…"

When they reached the settlement, Shaddai sat at the center of town the square, waiting for them. He stood with the same exuberant smile Azal saw earlier.

"Why are you so happy?" A knot turned inside Azal.

Shaddai raised his arms. "The time has arrived at last; it's what I've been waiting for!"

Azal and Gabriel exchanged a confused look.

"What are you on about?" Azal demanded.

"It has been my goal all along," Shaddai smirked, "- for Henna to make me a god!"

"She will?" Gabriel's voice sounded surprised.

"She'll gather the high society tonight to announce her next god… me!" Joy filled Shaddai's face.

Azal frowned. "Know where you will go?"

"She wants to appoint more Gods to this world like she has Odin. I must join him there…"

I have a terrible feeling it won't go as smoothly as he thinks… Azal hugged Shaddai to congratulate him. "Let's return home."

Gabriel departed when they reached his house; Azal and Shaddai continued to their homes.

Azal peered at Shaddai as they ventured; he still wore the same broad smile. "You know, it might not all go as you expect it… keep realistic expect-"

Shaddai jabbed him hard. "What in Shaddai's name are you talking about! This is what I am destined to; she suspects *nothing!*"

Azal sighed, but nodded in agreement.

When they arrived home, David awaited their return to inform them about tonight. David lifted his finger. "… but tonight will be different; you're expected to arrive before everyone else-" He turned his attention to Azal. "-same goes for you!"

Azal frowned. "Why me? It's about Shaddai, not me."

David shrugged. "That is what I've been instructed to tell you." He entered the house with his son.

Azal rubbed his face and turned to his own home, where he prepared to see Henna in the evening, but he had to hurry since they were told to be there early.

He wandered over to Shaddai's house when he finished to pick him up.

David answered the door. "He's not ready yet; his mom is… just come in." He showed him inside.

Shaddai's mom was showering him with attention, making him shift on his feet uneasily. "Azal's here; I gotta go."

His mom hugged him tightly. "My little baby's all grown up!"

Shaddai rolled his eyes.

"We have to see Queen Henna…" Azal tried to say.

Shaddai's mother nodded and squeezed her son's cheek tenderly. "Go make me proud."

Shaddai hurried out with Azal. "Thank the Goddess, she's done." He strolled toward the castle.

"Excited?" Azal gazed at Shaddai, who nodded back.

The air felt different to Azal somehow. "I just can't shake the feeling; this is…" He sighed. "We shouldn't do this!"

Shaddai brushed him off. "You're being silly; come on." He increased his pace.

A lady waited for them at the castle. She greeted them and showed them inside.

Shaddai peered around the room, confused. "I've never been in this room before."

"For good reason," the lady smiled.

Azal suddenly appeared in Henna's garden. Panicky, he spun around. *Henna…* He pressed a hand to his chest and drew in a few heavy breaths to ease his racing heartbeat.

"That's right," Henna stood in front of him.

"… but why?" Azal scratched his forehead.

"Shaddai's not as ready as Odin; he requires assistance." Henna smiled with eyes every color of the rainbow. "Will you help me? Go with him on his journey?"

"Journey?" Azal cleared his throat, unsure what to say.

"He has a different path ahead than Odin…" Henna blinked with her warm rainbow eyes.

Azal cleared his throat.

"You're unsure, maybe?" She frowned.

Azal shook his head. "It's not that… I just don't think he needs me."

"If you're sure," Henna smiled.

"I am; I would rather stay here with Gabriel…"

"Alright." Henna patted Azal on the shoulder. "It's your choice."

In a blink of an eye, Azal appeared back in the room with Shaddai.

"If you say so," Shaddai mumbled wearily. "Where's Queen Henna, aren't we here to meet her?"

Have I moved in time? It's as if I never left?

"Shaddai, welcome!" Henna appeared, embraced Shaddai, and smiled at Azal. "How nice of you, Azal, to accompany your friend. You should aid him tonight; it shall be a big night for him."

Azal glanced at her cautiously.

Shaddai hugged Azal. "Don't worry, my friend," he whispered and followed Henna out.

As the evening wore on, the hall started to fill with attendees as it so often had. Azal's eyes kept wandering toward the staircase to Henna's private chambers.

"Azal!" David waved and approached with Shaddai's mother. "Where's Shaddai?"

Azal sighed heavily. "I haven't seen him since I brought him…" He glared back at the stairs.

The stairs lit up, and Henna came into view with Shaddai following behind her, glowing with pride as he descended the stairs with Henna.

"Shaddai's the next who's *destined* to be a god," Henna introduced Shaddai to the ladies gathering.

Shaddai's mother gloated as if it were her own accomplishment. "My son; I sure did well."

Henna patted Shaddai on the shoulder. "It's time."

Shaddai smiled and followed Henna back up the stairs.

Guess he'll finally get what he wants, but why do I have this ominous feeling? Azal sat down next to David. "Congratulations on your son."

David grunted. "One more person in the family above me…"

Azal gazed into the crowd, where he noticed Shaddai's mom at the center of attention now. "She sure got popular thanks to Shaddai…"

"The mothers always do." David swallowed his drink.

The hours that followed felt agonizing to Azal; he kept stealing looks toward the staircase, but no one appeared.

Then light suddenly appeared at the top of the staircase, Shaddai descended the stairs with Henna behind him, his eyes cold as ice as he smiled at the spectators.

Azal's eyes widened. *He's in front…*

"Meet my new god, *Shaddai*!" Henna smiled.

Shaddai waved at the ladies, who surrounded him.

Azal frowned, the knot in his gut tightening.

Shaddai walked up to his dad, greeting everyone he passed. His one hand hung at his side, squeezing his fist tighter and tighter.

He kissed David on the cheek. "Thank you, Father." His eyes stared into Azal's. "- come with me a second." He marched out the door with Azal hurrying after him.

"What's going on?" Azal shrugged his shoulders.

"Henna tricked me!" Shaddai slammed his fist into the wall, with such an immense force that the wall rumbled to its core.

Azal hushed. "Be careful with the noise; how did she trick you? Aren't you a god now?"

Shaddai bared his teeth. "I guess; I'm leaving tomorrow for a new world, a small insignificant one to test *how I do*," he growled scornfully. "- not one as *important* as Odin's…"

"But you're still a god." Azal pointed out.

Shaddai unclenched his fist. "I guess."

"Make the most of it. Prove how wrong Henna is!"

As the morning dawned, Shaddai met with Azal and Gabriel, responding listlessly.

"Look at the bright side." Gabriel raised his eyebrows. "We tricked her into making you a god who can surpass her one day!"

It was the first time Shaddai showed any real feedback; his eyes lit up with a sparkle. "You're right! I'll prove it to her." He patted Gabriel on the shoulder. "When I return, I'll be back with news to wow her!" He jumped up, ran toward home, while waving bye.

***

Denida scratched his head. "This can't end well," he muttered under his breath.

Lucifer leered over the well. "You're right…"

"Since you're done; there were some rumors about Danyel-"

Lucifer snapped his fingers. "I'm not done yet; you're here. It's time to finish my story with Shaddai's return. It took a long time; Odin often visited. Gabriel and I grew closer by ourselves. We forgot all about Shaddai, until…" Lucifer's eyes glowed with Darkness as he spoke those words.

***

Azal and Gabriel laughed loudly, then gazed up as an entity flew toward Henna's castle.

"One of her gods is here to see her. Odin again?" Gabriel frowned.

Azal shook his head and pointed his hand up into the sky. "It didn't stop at her castle; it went further. Did it go to our spot?"

They both scurried toward their secret place.

Azal stopped suddenly, making Gabriel bump into him.

"Hey," Gabriel moaned.

Azal raised his finger straight ahead, where a figure stood with light encircling him.

The man folded his hands together and the light subsided.

"Shaddai?" Azal glared.

"I'm back." Shaddai smiled and surveyed the area. "This place looks different."

Gabriel darted forward to hug him, but Azal was too surprised to move. "A lot has changed; you've been away for a long time…"

Shaddai nodded. "I've changed, too."

Gabriel smiled. "How's it being a god?"

Shaddai winked. "It's more work than anything; I'm lucky Queen Henna summoned me here."

He's been summoned? Azal glared suspiciously. "You'd better go see her; I'll take you!"

"I don't need a chaperone!" Shaddai sounded repulsed by the idea.

Azal shook his head. "That's not why; things have changed around here."

Shaddai threw his hands up in the air. "What a strange thing to keep saying. But fine; let's go."

Shaddai had a different expression now. "You have changed the stuff in our spot, I see?"

Azal came back to attention. "Just trying to make it cozier; it's just Gabriel and me now, after all."

"I know." Shaddai put his hand on Azal's shoulder and smiled, warmth emanating from his palm.

Azal swallowed and returned an uncertain smile and continued toward the castle. "She's in the garden at this hour, which is why I'm taking you. She won't mind me entering." He steered into the garden next to the castle.

Shaddai paused, taken aback. "You, how come? No one's allowed in?"

Azal spun. "I told you, things have changed." He tilted his head and smiled.

Shaddai grunted as he followed Azal.

Inside the garden, Azal led Shaddai directly to Henna.

Shaddai kneeled and bowed to Henna. "You've summoned me, my queen."

Henna inhaled deeply and brushed her fingers along a leaf next to her. "You're surprised? I sent you to lead a world and you have yet to bring me an update on your progress!"

"They're not easy, getting them-"

"Maybe it's not them that's the problem; maybe it's *you*. My test for you has proven this much." Henna approached Shaddai. "- the dagger I entrusted with you; I'd like it back!"

Shaddai's eyes widened. "But-"

"Unless you want me to remove your God status too?" Henna extended her arm.

"I left it in my world, but here..." Shaddai held his palms together. A flash appeared around them and the dagger appeared in his hand.

"Thank you." Henna closed her fingers around the dagger, causing it to vanish from her hand. "You're excused, go fulfill your destiny." She locked eyes with Azal.

'How you must regret not going with him... lead him back out,' she said into Azal's mind and returned to her flowers.

Azal pulled Shaddai to his feet and guided him out of the garden.

Shaddai kept glaring back in Henna's direction, but Azal was adamant about leading him out.

"Curses!" Shaddai yelled when they came outside of the garden. He shoved Azal away.

Azal raised his hands. "Relax; I'm just doing what I'm told."

Shaddai bared his teeth and clenched his fist, making magic swirl around it.

"Maybe you can regain her trust in your test with time..."

Shaddai unclenched his fist. "No, I can't; there's only one way." He stared into Azal's eyes, sending a cold chill down Azal's spine. "Get Gabriel ready; you both will be invited to tonight's gathering at the castle. I need to do something first; I'll see you there!" He tapped Azal's shoulder and vaporized.

Azal shook himself to clear the sick sensation within him and marched back to Gabriel.

Gabriel frowned with the entirety of his face. "But I'm not a part of the high society?"

"From what Shaddai told me, I guess he has a say since the party is to commemorate his visit."

Gabriel waved, seeming to accept that answer and hurried home to prepare.

Azal arched his neck. In the sky above him, a small flicker of a star shone between the two setting suns. *A star during the daytime, how's that possible? What does it mean?*

"I'm ready." Gabriel jumped out of the house. "Is something wrong?" He frowned.

"It's nothing!" Azal shook his head and set off for the castle.

By the time they arrived, several members of the higher society were already present. Gabriel gaped at the sight. "Wow," he murmured.

Azal rolled his eyes, focusing on the stairs. "Go mingle; I need to go check something." He raced to the stairs, then stopped to look around, before he climbed them, confident no one would notice him.

Upstairs he ran straight to the room he and Shaddai had seen a dagger in all those years ago. Oddly, he didn't feel an urge to check anywhere else.

Inside the room, Shaddai and Henna stood opposite each other.

"You sent Odin there, Zeus too; why not me?"

Henna smiled. "You're not ready."

"Ready for what? A world with several gods?"

"It shall be the center of the universe one day; someday you'll understand…"

Shaddai clenched his fist. "Then send me there, too. I'll prove to you I can do it."

Henna's eyes glowed with faint rainbow colors. "No, that's not where you belong. Your destiny is different."

"Different?" Shaddai hissed. "Wrong; I'll do this my way!" The dagger from before appeared in his hand. He stabbed Henna, causing the very world to rumble as she dropped to her knees. The colors on the walls and floors began to fade.

"No," she winced in disbelief. She grabbed hold of the dagger. But it flew away from her, landing across the room, causing her to hold the wound tightly as more blood gushed out.

Shaddai ran after the dagger.

"Shaddai, stop!" Azal rushed to Henna's side; he met her sorrowful eyes that burned into his core.

Shaddai chuckled as he fiddled with the dagger in his palm. "Want to allow me, yet?"

"You… will… never… have… Earth," she stuttered.

"Really?" Shaddai grinned, he teleported in front of her, thrusting the dagger into her heart.

Her rainbow eyes stared straight at him as she grabbed tightly around his hands, clutching the dagger. "You don't realize what you've done, my child."

Shaddai tried to yank himself free, but her grip was firm. Even his magic was too weak against her grasp.

"This world will die with me; everyone living here shall perish, including your father, David."

"I… don't… care," Shaddai hissed. "At least you'll be no more!" He glared at Henna coldly.

"You chose this destiny, Shaddai." She gawked intently into his eyes. "One day, it will reach you and all who follow you; Gabriel and Azal, too-those who shall follow you won't do so forever."

"We should get you help…" Azal insisted.

"The dagger's made of the only material that can kill us; it's too late…" Henna grinned at Shaddai. "Hear my last testament of what shall be; all the wrongs you have done shall come to a reckoning by a child. A child with powers unlike any other…" She buried her nails into Shaddai's hands. "-in this child's youthful years, he'll set everything right, all that I could not." The rainbow colors in her eyes became stronger before they faded slowly and finally glazed over. Her hands fell as her body slumped to the ground.

Shaddai grabbed his hand and rubbed it where her nails had sunk into him.

Her body vanished as if it had never been there, leaving the dagger with a bloody stain behind. The light from the twin suns started to fade.

Shaddai picked the dagger up.

"Gabriel," Azal sprinted down the stairs, but stopped halfway. His eyes widened in shock; underneath, Gabriel stood all alone, but everyone from the high society was gone.

Azal descended cautiously, anxiously peeking about, hoping to find somebody, but no one came into view. "Where's everyone? What happened here?"

Gabriel scratched his forehead. "Everyone just vanished. It's my first time here. I thought it was intentional?"

"It's not…"

"Gabriel." Shaddai sauntered down the stairs.

"Everyone vanished; only Gabriel's left." The worry Azal felt sounded clearly in his voice. "Outside?"

Shaddai ran out the door to find that the crowd which always surrounded Henna's castle was nowhere to be seen, it was all empty. No sign of life, *nothing*. The light from the two suns dimmed rapidly. "We need to leave; now!" He spun and grabbed Gabriel and Azal. They flew into the sky.

***

"Shad- I mean, God killed his own Goddess?" Denida didn't try to hide his scorn.

"His heart darkened…"

"This is this legend you mentioned that God frets?"

Lucifer nodded.

"But I'm not a child anymore."

Lucifer raised an eyebrow. "You are on Earth…"

Denida shook his head. "That's…" He gasped. "- I need to go see Dan…" He teleported away.

Chapter 13- Finding Nina

The soldiers the Colonel sent to Earth saluted him when he arrived. "At ease, where's the Commander, Private?"

"You don't know?"

The Colonel's eyes widened. "Don't be sassy, Private. Where?"

The soldier saluted his Colonel. "He left with the Special Task Force, Sir!"

Left with? The Colonel dismissed the soldier and strolled over to the boy Den. *What would you consider more important than watching Denida's human form?* He leaned back on a bench and sighed.

"Hello, Colonel." Gabriel appeared sitting next to him in a flash.

"Archangel Gabriel?" The Colonel felt weary. "Why're you here?"

"I like it here; young Den has a soothing sort of innocence, doesn't he?" Gabriel smiled.

The Colonel shrugged. "I guess."

"How's Lady Nina, by the way? I heard the Commander saw her?"

The Colonel rubbed his hands together. *Nina and the Commander?*

Gabriel patted the Colonel on the knee. "I won't keep you; I know you need to be somewhere." In a flash, Gabriel disappeared.

The Colonel narrowed his eyes at the light. "But how can I possibly know where they went?" He scratched his head.

"Sir?" A soldier saluted him. "I think they went to see the younger Nina after Lady Nina showed up."

"Here, where?"

The soldier led him over to the spot Lady Nina had stood with the Commander.

The Colonel knelt to examine the dirt for footsteps. He followed the trail, but after a few steps their tracks ended. With a shout, the Colonel slammed a tree next to him so hard birds flew off squawking.

There's only one person who can track them... with magic...

He paraded into Denida's office and saluted the secretary. "Inform Denida; I'm here, Ma'am!"

The secretary cleared her throat. "That will be hard with him not being here, Sir. He said he would be out with Dan for a while."

The Colonel grunted and leaned over the desk. "I need to leave him something personal; may I?" He tilted his head toward the door to Denida's office.

The secretary sighed. "Only because it's you…"

The Colonel smiled and stepped inside Denida's office, closing the door behind him.

His eyes wandered across the room, uneasy with the thought of being alone in the office. The Colonel's eyes fell on Denida's desk. He approached it and carefully sat down. A framed picture stood on the center of the table, one of Denida and Nina together with their son Daniel, standing between them. The Colonel dropped his head and sighed.

He pulled his chair closer to the desk and rummaged through the drawers. *I know Denny; he'll have a note of it…* He stopped dead in his tracks, his eyes locked on the picture.

'Colonel?' it sounded from the intercom, causing the Colonel to fall from the chair, his face covered with cold sweat.

The doors sprang open, and the secretary burst into the room. "You didn't answer the intercom; is everything okay?" Her eyes widened. "What're you doing on the floor?"

"I just tripped." The Colonel stood and brushed himself off. "Can I borrow a pen and paper?"

The secretary departed, only to return a minute later with a notepad and pen. She handed them to the Colonel and stood smiling at him.

The Colonel raised his eyebrows. "You'll excuse me a second…"

"Oh," the secretary blushed, perplexed. "I'll be outside." She hurried out and closed the doors behind her.

The Colonel spun around and grabbed the frame, turning it around, checking its back. *It might be this!*

The Colonel removed the picture from the frame, placing it aside and examining the inside of it, but there was nothing else in it. He put the frame down irritably and glared at the picture, which he picked up and turned around, revealing another one on the back. *The old mines?* He fiddled with the picture to return it to the frame and slammed it down on the desk. It stood with the front facing out into the room.

The Colonel stormed past the secretary without saying anything.

He set off toward the closest airbase where the guards granted him passage without hesitation. The Colonel greeted the base's commander. "Prepare a jet; I need to go somewhere."

"Let me gather some troops-"

"Negative, Sir. I need to go to this place by myself; it's classified."

The commander saluted and ordered someone to escort the Colonel to the plane.

The Colonel climbed into the cockpit and strapped himself in beside the pilot. "Mind if I join you? No one else is here, after all."

As they flew through the clouds, the pilot glanced over at the Colonel. "Sir, what do you need in the North?"

The Colonel stared at him blankly. "It's on a need to know basis. Just take me there."

The pilot muttered something incoherent, but the Colonel paid it no mind.

As the plane approached the airfield, all covered in white, the Colonel peered out the window. *There sure is a lot of snow...*

"Hang on tight; it might be a rough descent." The plane sank down toward the airfield, rumbling as it descended.

Concerned, the Colonel turned to the pilot, then back to his window.

The pilot struggled with the plane; the rumbling intensified.

The Colonel grabbed the handle on his side. "I'll help." He pulled the handle further back. Their combined strength stabilized the plane, and it set down with a light bump. The plane skidded slightly on the tarmac before coming to a stop.

"Thanks, keep up... the good work." The Colonel smiled and exited; the pilot followed him.

They stopped dead in their tracks. The building next to the tarmac was blown to smithereens. Snow covered the rubble.

The Colonel carefully exited the plane, only to pause yet again. The wreckage of an airplane crash lingered next to the building.

Someone must really want them both destroyed... "I need you to take me further; unload the truck."

The pilot nodded. It didn't take long before he drove out the snow cat. "Ready for you, Sir."

The Colonel nodded and climbed in.

They drove through the snow in the direction the Colonel instructed.

After a while, the pilot widened his eyes and eased off the gas, then glared at Colonel. "Are you sure you want to do this?"

The Colonel snapped his fingers and pointed forward. "Drive!"

The pilot grunted but set it back in motion and slowed down as they drew nearer. There was a checkpoint at a new barbed wire fence and motion sensors all around the mines.

The Colonel stepped out of the car and saluted the guard. "Bring me your commanding officer."

A man with a uniform covered in medals and achievements marched toward them. "I'm the General in charge here. What can I do for you?"

General? The Colonel straightened and saluted. "Sir!"

The General saluted back without changing his stone-cold glare. "What can I do for you?"

"Susan; she's here, Sir?"

"What about her?"

The Colonel clenched his fist, sighed and released it. "I need to talk to her; I'm an old friend. She's here with Claus, correct?"

The snow creaked under the General's feet as he tilted his foot slightly. "I'm not at liberty to say."

"You're not? Even to the Colonel directly under *Denida*?" The Colonel met the General's empty eyes.

"Let them through!" the General yelled and spun around, leading them.

The Colonel followed a few steps behind as the General guided him inside the mine, which had sensors at every turn. Soldiers armed to the teeth passed them several times.

The General halted and raised his eyebrows. "It's in here." He saluted the Colonel. "-let me know if you, on behalf of Lord Denida, require more." He stomped off.

The Colonel gazed at the door, freezing for a second before he grabbed the handle and walked inside. It was a dungeon and even more armed guards were the first thing he noticed. At the center of the room, he saw a locked cell with Claus lying on a bed.

"Colonel?" Susan got up from her chair with a shocked expression. "Why are you here?"

The Colonel sauntered closer to the cell. "You have Claus away from prying eyes…" He peered back at Susan. "The Commander went searching for Nina; I think Claus can help me find them."

"Searching? Nina's gone?" Susan looked worried.

"No one has seen her for a while… maybe Claus would know where since-" The Colonel paused. "- she's after the Scientist on Earth…"

"The Scientist!" Susan screamed, startling Claus, making him fall out of his bunk bed. "He doesn't know a rat's ass!"

"Colonel? What's going on here?" Claus grinned. "Trouble in paradise?"

"He might be able to sense where the Commander is with his Dark Arts or have heard something when he was in Hell." the Colonel insisted.

"He knows nothing about Nina, the Scientist, nor Earth. He can't even use Dark Arts!"

Claus rattled the bars. "Wrong!" he yelled. "I was in Hell; I can perform Dark Arts when not under a spell," he moaned.

The Colonel's eyes widened. "Then tell me; can you help me find Lady Nina?"

Claus peered at Susan. "I guess not... I wouldn't know where she went."

Susan chortled and sat back down. "Told you."

Have I come all this way for nothing- wait, magic! "Dark magic; you can sense a person's spirit energy?"

Claus shrugged. "I guess, so what?"

The Colonel spun to Susan. "He can help Nina, your *friend*. You have to help me."

Susan scowled. "Denida instructed me-"

"Denny's not here; he went somewhere with Dan." The Colonel winked at Susan. "You can come and watch Claus' every step; if he tries to escape, you've got a good excuse to finish him off."

Susan picked at her lips for a moment, before running over to the cell and putting Claus in handcuffs with his hands behind his back. She tightened them and double-checked they were secure.

Claus made a face. "I'll show you. You can trust me."

Susan ignored Claus and dragged him out to the Colonel. "Let's go."

At last! The Colonel trudged forward and led them to where the pilot was parked. Every soldier they passed watched them with suspicious eyes.

The pilot came over to open the vehicle's doors but froze when he noticed Claus in handcuffs.

Susan brushed past him and shoved Claus into the vehicle.

"Take us back to the plane, Soldier!" The Colonel climbed into the front seat.

The pilot looked down at his feet before he joined them in the car.

Claus twiddled his thumbs behind his back. "You could let me be cuffed in the front, you know?"

Susan grabbed his face and leaned into his ear. "Never; I still don't trust you," she whispered before pushing him back into the seat.

Susan yanked Claus from the car when they arrived back at the airstrip and forced him down on his knees in the cold snow while the pilot refueled the jet.

"Nina was last seen talking with the Commander where he watched over Denida's human form." The Colonel glanced at Claus. "- on Earth."

Susan grunted and pulled Claus up when the pilot had finished. She pushed him forward into the plane.

"You really want us to take *Claus* to Earth?" Susan scowled at Claus, who deliberately avoided any eye contact with her.

"I believe we should, yes. Denida used magic to track Medusa once," the Colonel insisted. "I'm hoping Claus can do the same..."

Susan rolled her eyes. "I still don't know; I don't trust him!"

The Colonel raised his brow. "Then trust me, instead."

Susan opened her mouth, ready to object, but closed it without uttering a word. Biting her lip, she nodded solemnly.

When the plane skidded on the tarmac, Susan turned to the Colonel. "We should go by Denida's office just to be sure."

The Colonel shook his head. "I've already been there!"

Susan clenched her fist. "I insist!"

The Colonel inhaled deeply and peered at Claus. "If it's what it'll take to get you to go…"

At the headquarters, the secretary confirmed there still wasn't any sign of Denida.

"See, I told you," the Colonel winked.

"Fine!" Susan retorted. "Let's just go to Earth!"

Claus sneered at the sight of the boy, Den.

"Claus!" Susan yelled, distracting him.

They followed the Colonel to the spot where Nina's trail ended.

"There's no trace of her beyond this point; can you follow them by magic?" His eyes glinted hopefully.

Claus lifted his arms with a smirk in Susan's direction. "I need my hands free for this."

Susan's eyes narrowed and she stepped toward Claus, turning him around forcefully and unlocking his cuffs. "Go ahead, then; *wow* us!"

Claus sat down on one leg and put his hands flat on the ground. A small flicker of fire surrounded Claus' hands and a pentagram took shape from amongst the flames. After a moment, Claus raised his head as if he saw something in the distance. "Follow me," Claus muttered in a low voice. He stepped carefully as if he were following a trail, still glowing with the dark aura as he continued.

Susan's hand hovered near her sidearm as she followed.

Claus suddenly stopped in front of an old building. "She went in there…"

The Colonel nodded. "Watch him while I go check." He bolted across the street and entered the building, seeing nothing until his eyes adjusted to the darkness. As the Colonel's eyes took in the room, two buffed guys came up from behind him. He spun around, only to have them pass through him and continue farther on. The Colonel shook his head. *Jesus, how I hate being in soul form here on Earth…* He scurried after them.

The two walked into an office where a man sat surrounded by guards.

The guards frisked the two men and confiscated a bag one of them was holding. A guard sifted through it. "It's safe," the guard gestured for the men to approach the man behind the desk.

One of the men placed the bag on the desk. The other one stayed behind, glancing nervously at the guards. "It's all here, Boss."

The boss grabbed the bag without moving his eyes from the man, then turned his attention to its content. He nodded and waved his hand.

The guards pushed them out of the office.

The Colonel ran his eyes through the room. *They're not here; where could-* His focus locked on some graffiti on the wall. He took another step, then another steadily drawing nearer. *'The Scientist.'* A chill ran down the Colonel's spine. He gazed at the office and squinted his eyes before charging toward the office.

The guards stood laughing with each other, distracted.

The Colonel grabbed the two guards' sidearms while they joked with each other.

"Your guns!" the boss yelled.

The guards grabbed the hovering guns out of the Colonel's hands.

Not good, I won't be able to avoid all the bullets! The Colonel shifted on his feet, making the floorboard creak, then he dropped to the floor.

The soldiers started to fire.

Guards surrounded the boss, who clutched his own gun desperately, while the others frantically waved their weapons in every direction.

The Colonel jumped up and sprinted after them.

The Colonel chased the mob out of the building. Susan frowned at them and ran over to him, leaving Claus behind.

"We have to stop them! That man knows something about 'The Scientist,'" the Colonel huffed.

"How?"

Claus chanted behind them.

Susan turned to him. "What's he doing?" Her frown intensified.

Darkness surrounded Claus. As his chanting continued, the Darkness deepened, until the two guards tossed their handguns aside with loud moans and grabbed their arms. Claus snickered and raised his eyebrows. A gust of wind sent both the guards flying into the wall behind them, knocking them out.

"You're welcome." He smirked at Susan and the Colonel.

Susan clenched her fist. "You could've done that without your hands!"

The Colonel strode past Susan, revealing himself to the boss.

"Not again." The boss' eyes filled with terror.

Again? The Colonel paused, leering back at Susan. "Why do you say *again…* who did this before?"

"Nina… could do… stuff," the boss stuttered in a screechy voice.

The Colonel grabbed the boss and jammed him onto the hood of a car. "Where is she now?"

"There's no need to be aggressive!"

The Colonel nodded. "Oh yes, there is. 'The Scientist' was written in graffiti on the wall!"

The boss licked his lips, peeking at the two of them. "Again," he muttered.

"What? Speak up!" The Colonel slapped the boss' cheek.

The boss tried to wriggle free, but after a few tries, he gave up. "My boss is nicknamed 'the Scientist,' Nina was very intrigued by that too..."

The Colonel grabbed the boss' head and squeezed it tightly with his fingertips. "She went to him, didn't she? Where!"

"Colonel!" Susan yelled behind him.

The Colonel released his captive and rubbed his face.

"I can use magic," Claus grinned.

The boss' eyes widened with fear. "No, not that! I'll tell you... Anything but that!"

Chapter 14- Reuniting

Susan watched Claus' every move, hovering over him.

"You can relax; I won't misbehave…"

Not again… The Colonel turned to Susan and Claus. "At ease, Susan. He helped us when we needed him to."

Susan clenched her fist so tight her knuckles turned white. "As you command, Sir."

"He's moving." The Colonel jumped up and set out in pursuit of the guy they were following.

Susan yanked Claus along.

They lingered a short distance behind the car as it made its rounds, picking up bags from various places throughout the city before pulling into a driveway at a grand, heavily guarded mansion.

"Wait!" Claus stopped suddenly, digging his heels in to hinder Susan's attempts to push him. "There's Dark magic in there…" His eyes widened in terror.

Susan rolled her eyes and dragged him by the chains. "You're coming; like it or not!"

The sweat ran down Claus' cheek as he shook his head frantically.

"Why are *you* so scared?" The Colonel approached them.

"That Darkness is as heavy as in Hell; there's real evil in there."

The Colonel rubbed his eyes and turned to the building. *In there?* He knelt beside Claus. "Don't you want to show Denida you've changed?"

Claus stumbled to his feet. "Yes, and I will!" He tilted his head toward Susan. "I'm ready."

They sauntered forward.

The guard patted the other guard next to him as they approached and both guards raised their guns. "Freeze!"

How can they see us in our soul forms on Earth?

Susan and the Colonel gazed at each other in disbelief.

"No, it's not possible," Susan whispered.

No way we're stopping here! The Colonel spun toward one of the guards and kicked his leg, grabbing the gun.

The other guard ran over and kicked the firearm out of the Colonel's reach.

The Colonel jumped to his feet, only to be overpowered by the first guard, who tackled him from behind. The guard in front aimed his gun at the Colonel's eye. "Make a move; I dare you!"

The guards held the Colonel, Claus, and Susan at gunpoint and instructed them to enter the mansion.

Claus' eyes widened. "There's a Dark magic cloud here," He tilted his head. "- to detect spirits, maybe?"

"Claus!" a familiar voice shouted. "How nice to see you again." Jack clapped his hands with a joyful sneer and used the cloth he held to wipe some blood from his hands. "Don't worry; it's not mine. I was just toying with someone worthless!"

Claus' face turned cold. "You sold me out to *Lucifer*!" His eyes flared red, but swiftly reverted to their normal blue.

"You expected to use magic against *me*? *In my own domain*?" Jack walked closer, poked his chest, and raised his arms wide. "Lucifer can't set foot on Earth, which makes it mine!" He snapped his fingers and a man appeared. "Jerry; take them to the island."

Jerry waved his hand, and the guards followed behind him, pushing the Colonel and the others forward with their guns. "Not much point using the boat, as Nina already found the other way. We'll use the tunnel."

The Colonel walked ahead of Susan, slight movements of his head, showing he was inspecting their surroundings. Susan focused on Claus.

Jerry stopped next to an entry into a tunnel, spinning around with a maniacal smile. "Time for your prison stay." He smirked as Claus passed him inside of the tunnel and strolled away.

The Colonel crept into the tunnel after Claus.

"The light's out." A guard reached for a flashlight mounted on the wall next to the entrance. He shrugged at the other guard before gesturing for them to move down into the tunnel.

The guard with the flashlight led the way, lighting up a path.

The flashlight suddenly flew from the guard's hand and banged against the ceiling before landing with a resounding clang, casting light into their faces.

"Stay here!" The other guard darted forward from behind them to pick up the flashlight. He waved his gun around in 360 degrees with the flashlight in his other hand. "He's gone, but how?" He turned to the Colonel and the others. "Come on, we're-"

The Commander appeared behind the guard, grabbing his head and snapping his neck. "Colonel, Sir, welcome." He saluted the Colonel.

Several soldiers stepped forward, saluting the Colonel, whose focus remained locked on the Commander. "Is Lady Nina with you, Commander?" He returned the salute.

The Commander stepped aside, revealing Nina.

"Why are you here with her?" The Colonel eyed the Commander. "- near the Scientist, of all people!"

"Sir, we came to rescue her, but then she ordered us to finish off the Scientist!"

Nina sighed heavily. "Denny wouldn't just-" Her mouth hung open and she gritted her teeth, staring at Claus. "You!" She charged Claus, shoving him to the floor, her hands squeezing around his neck.

The Colonel grabbed Nina, and pulled her back kicking and screaming.

"No, he kidnapped Daniel... my son would still be alive if it weren't for him!"

Susan gloated, her eyes on Claus. She grabbed Nina's arm and pulled her back far enough that the others couldn't hear. "We can't kill him… yet. We might need him to get Jack; but I am watching him like a hawk, don't worry!"

Nina glared disgruntled at Claus. "Alright…"

"Enough of this nonsense. I'm the commanding officer now," the Colonel asserted. "We're leaving!"

"We can't; they have magic, which makes us visible." Claus shrugged.

The Colonel sighed. "There's no other choice, but to sneak past them."

The Colonel led them back toward the exit of the tunnel, Nina glanced back before following.

The Colonel snuck a quick look outside from the tunnel's opening. He saw Jerry talking to Jack and turned to face the Commander. "We'll only get one chance. Once they notice we're free, all hell will break loose." He gestured with lowered hands. "Stay low!" He tilted his head and they started to crawl out from one hiding spot to the next. The Colonel smiled at Nina. "I need to keep you safe; you stay close to me."

The Commander led the way and carefully snuck past the guards patrolling the area. He paused behind a bush, close to Jack and Jerry. The Colonel and Nina crept up to him, as he watched Jack.

"I know Nina wants him dead, but not now. We're leaving first," the Colonel whispered with a stern authoritative look.

"How?" Nina frowned.

The Colonel peered back at the soldiers and crawled up next to the Commander to watch Jack and Jerry. "I've got an idea," he muttered.

Nina frowned in worry. "No, they know magic; we can't!"

"Makes it more of a challenge." the Colonel smiled.

"Shouldn't the guards be back, yet?" Jerry stared in the direction of the tunnel.

Jack waved his hand. "Who cares?"

Jerry grunted. "I'll go check." He gestured for two guards to accompany him. The Colonel snuck after them, watching for a chance to strike.

He marches like a soldier... "We should be careful when following him... let's keep our distance." The Colonel decreased his pace, but as soon as Jerry entered the tunnel, they caught up to him.

Nina put her hand on the door handle. "Remember; he knows magic!"

The Colonel nodded and proceeded inside.

Jerry and his guards were halfway down the tunnel with several flashlights. They stopped and hovered over the corpses of the other guards.

"Their necks are broken." Jerry readied his sidearm and waved his flashlight around. "Only a professional could do this; stay alert. They could still be here." He threw out his arm and the tunnel lit up. His eyes wandered back and forth while he stepped farther, cold sweat dripping from his forehead.

The Colonel stepped back as Jerry looked behind him.

"Is the door open?" Jerry turned to one of his guards. "Go check!"

The guard ran toward the door and slammed it open.

The Commander grabbed the guard by the neck, but the guard wrapped his hand around the Commander's arms and threw him off. He grabbed his own sidearm.

Nina used a roundhouse kick to knock the gun from the guard's hand, forcing him to retreat back into the tunnel.

"They're out there!" the guard yelled as he ran.

Jerry and the other guard aimed their guns at the door.

Jerry frowned at the guard. "Are you sure?"

The two guards marched with their guns aimed at the door with Jerry just behind them.

"Freeze!" The guards commanded in unison, aiming their guns at the Commander.

"There are *more* of you?" The Commander raised his arms.

"Of course," one of the guards gloated.

"Same here." The Commander raised his brow with a broad smile.

The Commander's troops jumped out from hiding and swarmed the guards.

Jerry charged through the door, cocking his weapon.

"Jerry!"

Jerry turned at the sound of Nina's voice, but the Colonel slammed Jerry's hand into the doorway, causing the gun to fall from his grip. In response, Jerry rammed his body forward, knocking the Colonel backward into the tunnel and clenched his other fist. Darkness circled around it, growing denser with each passing second.

Nina knelt and started muttering.

What's she doing?

A cloud circled above Jerry, blocking out the light.

The Colonel charged Jerry, but his legs suddenly stopped working, rooting him to the spot no matter how hard he tried to break free.

Jerry winked at him as he raised his arm and the black cloud encircled the Colonel.

"Nina, get down!" The Colonel waved his arms in Nina's direction, but he froze in confusion when he couldn't see her. *Where is she?*

Nina appeared behind Jerry and grabbed him by the throat, ending his spell casting.

The cloud above the Colonel dissipated, his legs felt light again. *I can move!* He dashed to Nina.

Jerry elbowed Nina and broke free, grabbing her throat and squeezing it with all his might, Nina grew pale and her eyes rolled upwards.

The Colonel jumped on Jerry's back with his arms around Jerry's neck.

Jerry released Nina to jab at the Colonel. When the Colonel dodged his maneuver, Jerry slammed his back into the wall, but the Colonel dug his heels in and pressed down on Jerry's shoulders, making Jerry stagger to his knees.

The Colonel wiped the sweat off his forehead and glared at Nina. "How'd you do that?"

"The Warlock taught me an invisibility spell I used to watch Michelle once…" Nina helped the Colonel to his feet.

The Colonel turned to Jerry. "What now?"

"The island." Nina met the Colonel's eyes. "It has a magic shield around it, but Jerry could…" She sounded confused by her own words.

The Colonel ordered his troops to grab Jerry. "Only one way to find out if he can!" He tilted his head at Nina. "Take us to the island, please."

Nina peered over at Jerry and sighed before leading them through the tunnel, with half the Commander's soldiers making sure they weren't being followed and the others focused on what lay ahead.

Nina shrugged when they reached the other exit. "We're here…"

The Colonel grabbed his gun and smacked Jerry across the face with it, causing blood to gush on the ground. He aimed the gun at Jerry's eye. "Want to watch the bullet coming, or will you help us escape?"

"You-"

A branch creaked, causing everyone to focus on the sound.

Someone's here? The Colonel charged forth toward the sound in between the trees and yanked a boy out, holding him tightly by his arm. He threw the boy on the ground. "Who are you!"

"It's *Morton*," Nina helped Morton back to his feet.

Morton jittered frantically.

"What's wrong with him?"

"Maia… will wonder… where I am." Morton trembled.

"Maia?" The Colonel turned to Nina with a confused look. "Who's Maia?"

"His sister…" Nina avoided the Colonel's eyes.

She's hiding something… The Colonel patted Morton's shoulder. "Take me to your sister."

The Colonel handed his gun to the Commander. "Watch him." He stared Nina down while he followed Morton.

Morton guided the Colonel through the forest to the beach, where there was a small campsite around the distinct orange glow of a campfire. A girl sat hunched over the fire.

The Colonel scratched his head. *What's so special about her?*

Morton scooted over to hug Maia, who turned to greet him.

The Colonel fell backward.

"Unreal, isn't it?" Nina helped the Colonel to his feet.

The Colonel tightened his fist and reached for his gun, but it was gone. *Crap- I gave it to the Commander.*

Nina grabbed the Colonel's arm. "It's *not* Michelle, just her sister."

The Colonel widened his stare, still locked on Maia.

"Our primary goal is getting out of here; we can come back for them afterwards… she suffered so much thanks to her sister." Nina's voice filled with sorrow. "We need to regroup first; she'll be safe here with Morton."

The Colonel glanced at Maia and Morton once more before turning back with Nina, returning to the other soldiers.

"What was it?" The Commander raised his head.

"Don't worry about it. Is Jerry ready to do as planned?"

"I'll do it," Jerry groaned with a vicious glare.

The Colonel marched behind Jerry, so close his breath raised the hairs on Jerry's neck.

Claus accelerated his pace to walk next to Jerry. "How did Jack find you?"

Jerry smiled. "We share a desire for power!"

"You'll both lose, though. I used to work with Jack until he betrayed me; he'll double-cross you too…"

"How will that make Jack lose?"

"Lucifer will stop at nothing. Eventually, he'll find him, if someone doesn't kill him first…"

Susan sped up to yank Claus back.

Jerry turned his head.

"Don't try anything," the Colonel hissed as they exited the tunnel.

They marched to the front of the compound and climbed inside some parked vehicles.

The Colonel sat in the driver's seat in the front car with Jerry in the passenger's seat. He concealed his gun under a blanket and set the vehicle in motion with his other hand.

They drove to the entrance of the compound. Throughout the drive, Jerry peeked over at the Colonel, then away again only to glance back after a few seconds.

"What?" the Colonel hissed after a few awkward iterations.

"Claus," Jerry said carefully.

"What about him? Susan will watch him."

"How did he know Jack?"

The Colonel turned his gaze to Jerry with a glow in his eyes. "Same way as you, *Jerry*; Jack used you both. Claus was handed over to the Devil, though…"

"But he's here?" Jerry insisted.

"Denida wanted him back to help find his son, but it was too late…" The Colonel tightened his grip on the wheel.

The Colonel slowed down as they approached the checkpoint.

"Don't!" Jerry rolled down his window and waved at the guards. "Move it; open the Gate!"

The guards did as they were instructed.

Jerry chuckled at the Colonel.

"Good job!" The Colonel winked. "We'll set you free soon."

Jerry shook his head, narrowing his eyes and they darkened with rage. "You want my help, don't you? I'll help you finish Jack off before he betrays me like he did Claus!"

Nina will like this development…

Chapter 15- The Status of the Past

When Denida returned, Dan sat in the Colonel's couch, hunched over with the Colonel next to him. "That's interesting, how-"

"Dan?" Denida licked his lips. "What are you doing?"

Dan sprang up and shook his head. "Nothing, I just wanted to ask how things were going."

Denida smiled in approval.

"Have you stopped them?" The Colonel's eyes widened.

Denida bit his lip. "A demon *is* seeing them, but it's not Danyel; it can't be!" He leaned over the desk. "Want me to end this?" He raised his eyebrows.

"How?" The Colonel asked with a screechy, almost doubtful voice.

He raised his ring, magic swirled around his fingers. "I wanted to see if all the Underworlds could be united again. Allow me to show you what I can do…"

"Affirmative," the Colonel said.

Denida turned to Dan and whispered. "Make him one of those machines that can detect magic while I'm gone."

Dan had a look of puzzlement. "How would I make that?"

Denida held out his hand and a device magically appeared in his palm. "Duplicate this; the Dark Angels used it in the olden days."

"Where… are you going?" Dan grabbed the device, examining it with intrigue.

Denida's eyes flickered red. "I need to check in on the barkeep who's been summoning this archdemon…"

The barkeep was pouring a drink for a customer when Denida burst through the door.

"You again?" The barkeep sighed. "I thought we saw the last of you."

Denida chortled. "Because I saw an archdemon? Do you know how many of those I met?" He leaned over the counter. "- I even killed one…"

The barkeep chortled. "Medusa, yes. I know all about you, 'Little Evil.'" He pulled out a shotgun and loaded it, aiming it at Denida. "Leave; you're not welcome here!"

Denida sat there stunned, opening his mouth to say something, but no words came out. *How can he know that… yet not be scared?* He stood up and raised his arms. "Don't… do… anything, you'll… regret!"

"Like this?" The barkeep snickered and fired the gun.

Denida unprepared, couldn't counter it; the blast pushed him into the wall. The shot stung, but the ring swiftly healed the wounds. "You wish to mock me?" Denida bared his teeth. "-fine, we'll tango then." He grabbed a bottle from the table and stumbled to the middle of the room and smashed it on the floor. "You might all want to pay attention to this." He inhaled slowly and stared at the barkeep. "Reficul, Reficul, Reficul."

A dark cloud formed and flew through the room, carrying a malicious sensation. It flowed out a window, then tore back in and centered in a dense spot in the middle of the room, where a figure appeared with Darkness surrounding him. A malevolent aura enveloped the room.

"Lucifer," Denida smirked at the crowd with his arms crossed.

"Denny?" Lucifer glanced across the many faces in the bar, now filled with real fear.

"An archdemon was here." Denida turned to Lucifer.

"Your point?"

"They insist it's Danyel!" Denida moved closer to Lucifer and stared intently at him. *'Plus, you may not want to anger me if you still want my aid with Heavani,'* he spoke into Lucifer's thoughts.

"Danyel…" Lucifer gazed out into the room in front of him, then spun to Denida. "You killed him yourself!"

"Yet these people think he's still here!" Denida winked at the barkeep. "Don't you?"

"I do," the barkeep agreed in a low voice.

"Lookalikes…" Lucifer shrugged. "Is this why you called me? Because of a doppelganger."

"Why would a demon give the credit to someone else!"

Lucifer scanned the room with a vicious death stare, filling the room with dread. "Don't call me for this nonsense!" Lucifer's eyes flared red.

'Don't forget you need to do me a favor, if you want your family safe,' Lucifer's thoughts spoke into Denida's mind.

"You're no longer needed here!" Lucifer pushed his arm forward, throwing Denida backward out of the bar.

Denida clenched his fist and slammed it into the ground, rooting himself so that the magic couldn't pull him any farther. He stopped just outside the door, jumped to his feet, stared at Lucifer and his eyes flickered red with rage as he marched toward the door.

The door slammed shut and a thick dark mist shrouded Denida. "Lucifer!" he screamed and lifted his arm, clenching his fist. Light emanated from his fist, thinning out the dark haze. Some demons appeared and encircled him. Most of them focused on strengthening the Dark aura, while two charged Denida.

Denida pushed his fist forward, grabbing the first demon, flinging him into the others casting the Darkness spell, ending it instantly. The last one crawled behind Denida and jumped out, throwing a ball of Darkness straight into his face.

Denida lost his balance and fell, but swiftly got back up and started to throw light spells toward the demons. They dodged left and right to avoid them before returning fireballs toward Denida.

Denida rolled and slammed his fist with the ring into the ground, creating a silvery glow that vaporized all the demons. The light thinned out the Darkness until it was gone. He wiped the sweat from his forehead and took a deep breath before he stood up.

Denida turned to the building. His jaw dropped; the entire building had vanished with Lucifer and everyone in it.

No, he doesn't! Denida's eyes flared a murky red as he squeezed his hand. He appeared in Hell at the spot where Lucifer's mansion last was, but it had moved again. He ran his finger over his ring.

'Go here,' the ring spoke into Denida's thoughts and an image of a specific location in Hell appeared in his mind. Denida spun around and marched toward it with determination.

When he approached, he froze, realizing something wasn't quite right. *Where's the demon guarding it?* He shrugged and proceeded inside. He marched straight to Lucifer's chamber, where he grabbed the handle, ready to turn it when he heard a voice from inside.

"Master; you need to hear me out-"

"Silence!" Lucifer yelled. "Do not disobey me; the Underworlds are a no-go zone!"

Underworlds? Denida tore the door open. "What about the Underworlds!"

Lucifer snapped his fingers, causing the demon to vanish. "I just informed him that all demons are forbidden from entering your world." He smiled gently.

"Did you learn that smile from Henna?" Denida scowled. "Where are all the people from the pub?"

Lucifer glanced at him before turning to stride over to the well. "Let's continue. Shaddai, Gabriel and I-"

"No, we're done!" Denida spun around and stomped out the door in a rage.

Denida resurfaced outside the Colonel's office where Dan still tinkered with the advice. The guards let him through. He waved. "Have you finished duplicating it, yet?"

Dan nodded. "The Dark Angels were clever; you've got to give them that, but yes, I figured it out." He handed Denida the old device. "The Colonel is downstairs, setting up the new one. You've dealt with the people at the pub?"

Denida ground his teeth. "Let's just go see the Colonel." The device vanished from his hand.

Guards had to accompany them, as not even Dan himself was allowed to enter. When they arrived, the Colonel stood, peering over the device.

"Colonel." Denida saluted him.

The Colonel turned to face them. "Darkness vanished from where the pub was... and here you are..."

"They won't bother you again." Denida lowered his head.

Dan glared curiously at Denida.

"You did it; we've got a deal then!" The Colonel tapped his feet together and shook Denida's hand.

Denida smiled with glee and grabbed Dan, embracing him. He clenched his other hand and they reappeared next to another Gate in another Underworld.

Wonder if they have some more info that can be useful to Dan in regards to the time machine, seen as they had one first? Denida stole a peek at Dan, before stepping out of the Gate with Dan following behind. They encountered a thick, misty haze that they could barely see through.

Not here too... "We need to get to the castle!"

The haze grew denser the farther they trudged through it. Denida paused, laying his hand on Dan's shoulder.

"What?" Dan whispered.

Denida squinted his eyes, attempting to see through the dense fog. *'Somebody's there.'* He spoke into Dan's thoughts and lifted his hand, creating light to thin the cloud, revealing demons gathering in front of them. He swiftly lowered his hand, ending the spell.

"What was that?" One of the demon's stepped toward them and pointed. "There was something bright just a minute ago; did you see it?"

The other demons gawked in Denida's direction, before returning to their chitchat. "Nobody's there!"

The first demon shrugged and continued through the haze.

Denida threw his hands around Dan and his ring flickered as he muttered a spell, and they became invisible.

The demon searched the crowd, stopping next to where Denida stood. "Maybe they're right," he muttered.

Dan's face paled as he stared at the demon.

The demon clapped his hands together and turned back to the others.

Denida loosened his grip on Dan and took a long detour around the demons, staying near Dan as they trekked to the castle. Contrary to what he had hoped, the Darkness didn't lift around the castle. *Why is there Darkness here? Did it take over?*

Demons strolled across the courtyard.

"They look like they belong here." Dan peered at Denida.

"Not for long!" Denida murmured.

Black-hooded men swarmed Dan and Denida, pulling them into a barn on the side of the castle, where they were thrown into the hay.

Denida reared up and clenched his fist, ready to strike.

The Colonel stepped in between Denida and the men. "Hello again, Denida."

"Colonel?" Denida frowned. "Why are you here?"

"There are demons here; we have to be!"

"We?" Denida glanced around the room. "You mean your troops?"

"No, not them." A young girl burst through the troops, who cleared the way for her. She lowered her hood, revealing Nina's younger face. Her smile lit up her eyes. "It's been a long time."

Denida ground his teeth. "Where's the President?"

Nina tilted her head back and approached Denida, who knelt in front of her. "The demons caught him!"

"Then let's arm up, free him, and end this dark reign!" Denida glared viciously.

Dan stepped in between Denida and Nina. "Why don't we just use the time machine that's in this world?"

"Because the President disabled it after the debacle with Claus," the Colonel remarked from the barn door, where he stood watch.

***

Denida followed as the Colonel snuck through the dark courtyard, where several demons patrolled, using the haze for cover. He paused every few steps to ensure their path was still clear. When he reached the front door to the castle, he sighed and turned to his soldiers. "When we open this, it will make a noise, alerting the demons, so think fast!"

"No need to open it; follow me." Denida clenched his fist and stepped forward, phasing through the closed door.

Everyone gasped.

"Magic." Dan shrugged, stepping through the door behind Denida. The rest followed suit.

Denida put his ring to his mouth and nipped it with his lips. *Really, up there?* He turned to the Colonel. "They're holding him in the throne room."

"Good to hear; let's rumble. Colonel, follow me!" Nina clenched her fist and charged forward.

Denida glared in disbelief.

The Colonel gestured for his troops to block Nina.

Nina glared with eyes that could kill, but then her eyes widened as she trudged back to the Colonel. "You're right; I need a gun first!" She extended her hand with a smile.

"Sorry, but no, not arming a civilian with no training. *We* are trained in this and we will handle this, not you!"

"Forget you, I will handle it myself, armed or not!" Nina spun around.

"I said no!" The Colonel grabbed her. "I know how headstrong you are, but there's a difference between being brave and plain reckless." He yanked her behind him and marched forward. "Stay behind us," he commanded.

Denida scratched his forehead with a tender smile. *It's just like back home... Nina's always determined... I miss her so much.*

"Denny, shall we follow them?" Dan stood baffled. "Is something the matter?

"It's nothing!" Denida pushed Dan forward.

Nina grumbled while she trudged behind the other soldiers with eyes brimming with fury, ready to strike, but no demons appeared on the way to the chamber.

"It's in there," the Colonel whispered.

"You're right; I can feel Darkness in there," Denida nodded.

Nina tiptoed to a backpack one of the soldiers had put on the floor. She glared back at the Colonel and Denida and grabbed a rifle while no one was looking. "Good, let's do this!" Nina charged forward and Denida reached for her swiftly, but her was too late; she pushed forward and slammed through the door. She aimed the gun and fired; the kickback knocked her back off her feet.

Demons swarmed Nina and tore the rifle from her.

"Let her go!" The Colonel stormed through the door with his soldiers.

A demon flicked his fingers. Nina became enveloped in Darkness and floated off the floor. "Lower your weapons or she's dead!"

The Colonel gritted his teeth. "You won't hurt a civilian!" He ran toward Nina. Demons swarmed him before he reached her. He drew his side arm and starting to shoot the ones charging him. The Colonel soon ran out of bullets and they overwhelmed him.

Denida clenched his fist, only to get swarmed by several demons, too. "No, you don't!" Another demon slammed Denida into a wall before shoving him into the room with the rest of the demons.

I need to help the Colonel! Before Denida could spin around, he gasped at the sight of the President lying on the floor in a bloody pool. He peered at the lead demon in the middle of the room with spite in his red eyes. "You're gonna pay for that!"

"Doubt it." The demon chortled.

Denida's eyes darkened with rage. He bared his teeth until they were as dark as coal. "My price is death!" He charged forward as demons appeared from the Darkness. He ripped hearts from their torsos, but soon there were so many slamming him with Dark magic, that he no longer could keep up.

The boss casually strolled forward while the other demons held Denida down. His eyes reddened with glee.

Denida tried to wrestle free, but that only caused the demons to tighten their grip.

"Time to die," the boss demon gloated and Darkness floated around his hand.

He's going to rip my heart out! Denida's eyes widened with panic. He clenched them and muttered a chant, creating a Dark Cone to form around him and the demons holding him, keeping the boss demon out.

"You have Darkness within you, me likey!"

The demons restraining Denida gasped at the sight of the cone, loosening their grip for a second.

Denida felt the change and yanked free, thrusting both his hands forward into the demons' chests.

"I don't care," Denida hissed and extended his arm, shattering the cone.

The boss demon raised his finger, waving it. "Sorry, but bye," he clenched his hand and Darkness enveloped Denida, throwing him outside the castle to the courtyard, where several other demons started to swarm him.

Denida paused for a second to reorient himself. *No, Nina... I can't go through what happened with Daniel again!* He slammed his fist with his ring into his open palm, creating a bright silvery light, which fully illuminated the grounds, vaporizing all the demons charging at him. He stood up, only to fall back to his knees, tired after using the ring's magic.

Denida teleported back to the Colonel. He felt his heart sink down into his stomach as he noticed the Colonel on the floor with his heart laying next to his body. He knelt next to him. *If only I'd been here...* He ran his fingers over the Colonel's eyes to close his eyelids.

"Time to make them pay!" Denida stormed through the door.

Where did they go? He searched through the room and his eyes fell to the dead body of the President and he sighed deeply. *Wait, Dan... he couldn't have gone to the time machine, could he?*

'Yes,' the ring whispered.

Denida rushed to the door and teleported to the time machine, remembering it vividly.

"It needs a part of the Gate, but I'm telling you, I don't know more than that." Dan tried his best to insist, but his voice clearly trembled.

The boss demon leered at Dan. "I want this time machine to work. The President said he destroyed his findings. You better figure it out, unless you wish to join him!"

Another demon dragged Nina over next to Dan. "You wanted the girl?"

"I did!" The boss demon yanked her closer and shoved her to the floor. "Use her to help or you both die here."

Nina bared her teeth. "I don't know anything, no one does!"

"Really?" the boss demon mocked and lifted her off the ground by the throat. "Then there's no reason to keep you alive, is there?"

Nina kicked the demon in the stomach repeatedly with all her might, making him thrust her into the wall and form a fireball.

"Wait!" Dan ran up, waving his hands. "Don't hurt her! I'll do it; I'll find a way."

The boss demon lowered his arm, gloating, Nina slumped to the floor, unconscious. "Then do it!"

Dan turned to the device, rubbing his face.

Denida crawled around the perimeter of the room, slowly drawing near enough to hear. He snuck over to Nina who was knocked out, pulling her behind a desk, where the boss demon couldn't see her.

Denida lifted her head and examined her face; she was a younger version, but still the Nina he remembered from the time he first met her back in his home world, with the same face as the one he loved, the one he hadn't been able to embrace since Daniel's death. He put his hand over her eyes and she woke from her slumber. "Hi." Denida smiled tenderly.

Nina tried to spring up with the same fury in her eyes that Denida remembered from his own Nina as of late.

Denida put his hand over her mouth, hushing her and lowering her back to the floor. "I need to take care of this demon with magic. You get Dan to safety; can you do that?"

Nina nodded her head, her eyes still locked on Denida as he stood.

The boss demon paced throughout the room, impatiently waiting. "Got anything, yet?"

"I... need to find... out how... first," Dan stuttered.

The boss demon kicked a metal trashcan, causing a deafening clang to reverberate throughout the room. "Fine," he hissed. His eyes widened as a small shadow appeared behind him. He spun and quickly reacted to Denida charging him, thrusting a fireball forth, slamming Denida with it. "We've got company!" he hollered and demons burst through the door and Dan flung the guns forward and started firing on the demons.

Denida felt the burn from the fireball on his skin, but he also knew that he had no time to let it faze him, so he jumped up and threw a dark ball toward the demon while his burnt skin recovered with the help of the ring.

The boss demon jumped to the side and turned to shoot Darkness toward where Nina lay, but she was gone. He was hammered by incoming balls of Darkness, which almost made him fall to his knees. Remaining on his feet, the demon swiftly spun around and sent a barrage of fireballs back, hitting the wall. In the midst of the chaos, Denida vanished. He ran to the time machine, but Dan was gone too. "Dammit," he moaned.

"Don't worry, I'm still here!" Denida appeared in front of the boss demon, letting his invisibility cloak lift as he thrust his hand into the demon's gut and ripped its heart out in one swift motion. All the demons swarming Dan and Nina vanished in a blink of an eye and the Darkness lifted.

The soldiers started to twitch and stretch as they came to.

Nina approached Denida. "Thank you for your help. Why have you returned, though?"

"He wants to unite all the Underworlds. I, however, want to inspect this," Dan said, ecstatically examining the time machine.

Nina sighed. "The President died. There's no one left to unite this world with the others. The Colonel, maybe?" Nina turned her head to the soldiers.

Denida shook his head. "I'm afraid not. I found his body…"

Nina gasped, holding her hand to her mouth. "Dead… he can't be! Are you certain?"

Denida looked at the floorboards. "I swear; I saw it myself!"

Nina lowered her hand. "Just like the President…"

"He was a soldier, Nina, aware of the risks…"

Nina turned to face Denida. "This is what happens!" She lifted her finger at the Colonel's body. "He's dead, just like the President! I don't want to die too," she growled and stomped out past Denida.

Dan scratched his cheek. "What do we do now?"

Nina, you're always so headstrong… Denida rolled his eyes. "We're not done here. Follow me."

* * *

Nina felt tears running down her cheek. *I have to get away from here.* Feeling her legs turn to bricks, she slumped down on a bench, burying her face in her hands.

"Miss, everything alright?" A uniformed man stood in front of the bench, watching her with concerned eyes.

Nina's eyes ran across the uniform. *A soldier… of course, we can't let this ever happening again!* "Take me to your barracks!"

The soldier stepped back. "Why would our barracks interest a kid like you?"

"The Colonel deserves a proper burial…"

The soldier squinted at her. "I'm not sure what you're talking about, but sure, I guess I'll take you." The soldier helped Nina to her feet.

When they arrived at the barracks, he led her to his commanding officer.

"Private, who's this civilian?"

The soldier glared at Nina. "I'm not sure; maybe this little girl needs help finding her parents or something, Sir?"

Nina stepped in front of the soldier. "I *knew* the President!"

"What do you mean knew?"

"He's dead. So is the Colonel who oversaw his security." She lowered her gaze. "Are you in charge here?"

The commander saluted her. "Yes, I'm Lieutenant Colonel Anderson."

Nina bared her teeth. "The demons have been eliminated. We need to be prepared if they send more our way!"

"More?" The Lt. Col. flicked his fingers impatiently.

"Yes," Nina snarled. "We need to do it before they return. Time's a-wasting."

The Lt. Col. glared at Nina for a long moment. "What makes you think that's going to happen?"

Nina stepped forward with certainty and clenched her fist. "Lieutenant Colonel, I believe it is your duty as a soldier to keep this world safe. Are you really going to risk letting anyone else die when you and your troops can prevent it just by being prepared?"

The Lt. Col. looked Nina over in silence before nodding. "You make a good point! Thanks for informing us; I'll see to it that we're ready if they come back." The Lt. Col. saluted her and turned to his soldiers.

Nina paced around the barracks.

"Hi again." Anderson waved at Nina. "We are ready if the demons return. Can we take you somewhere… to your parents, maybe?

Nina let out a sigh. "The President watched over me…"

"I see…" Anderson cleared his throat. "You… you wanted to help arrange the Colonel's funeral?"

"A funeral for him and the President, yes…"

Anderson gave a flicker of a smile. "Then let's." He strolled with Nina back to the command center.

Nina's eyes fell on Dan leering at some equipment.

"You; stop!" Anderson charged forward and yanked Dan back.

"Wait!" Nina hurried in between Dan and Anderson. "That's just Dan; he helped fight off the demons."

Anderson grunted and released his grip.

Denida tapped his ring against a desk. "You made some new friends, Nina."

"I had to; we can't ever have those demons returning!"

"We got rid of them once… if they dare to return, we will do it again." Denida winked. "More importantly; you're here in the command center. This is the most dangerous place to be if they return…"

Nina waved her hand. "You got a point?"

"The President saw you as his daughter, showing you how to lead this world…"

Nina heaved. "Why does that matter?"

"He's right, Nina. You've more than proven you'd make a strong leader." Dan nudged Nina. "Ms. President!"

Nina glared around the room. *The President did teach me a lot…*

"Furthermore," Denida pushed himself up by his knuckles. "- my world knows a lot about demons, too. We fought them a number of times."

Nina just stared at Denida as he approached her.

Denida put out his hand. "United we stand mightier; we can prevent them from ever coming back."

Nina turned to look at Anderson, then back to Denida. She smiled and shook his hand. "United, yes. We will be stronger together."

Dan walked over to Denida with a defeated expression. "Shall we continue. There's nothing left to do here…"

"Until next time… Nina." Denida gazed at her longingly, before teleporting to the next Underworld.

Chapter 16- Mark

The teleport brought them to another Gate. A little boy gazed up at them from the Gate. "Lord Denida?" he said, sounding as if he doubted himself.

Denida waved back. "Hi, Mark."

"Mark? The one who was second-in-command?" Dan frowned. "We're in the world where another version of Claus used magic to control the adults!"

Denida nodded solemnly. "For seventy years, correct." He turned to Mark. "How's the General? I have to see him; can you take us?"

"He'll be ecstatic to see you." Mark ran on ahead. "Follow me," he yelled.

Dan gazed at everything he passed on the way, as he had everywhere else.

The General stood in the town square. His eyes widened as Mark approached with Denida and Dan behind him.

"Denny?" He sauntered over to them, looking perplexed. "Claus is dead; what brings you here?"

Dan focused on the dirt. Denida stepped in front of him. "General, it's been a long time. How's your world now that the adults are free?"

The General clenched his fist tightly. "They still carry contempt for their children deep in their hearts, even though it was Claus who manipulated those kids to subdue us…"

"What about you?" Denida turned to face Mark.

"*Me?*" Mark scratched his forehead.

"You had a high rank under Claus while he was in charge, no?"

Mark shrugged. "I guess, but I told you how to track and catch Claus. Plus, I served under the General to clean up the aftermath; I *earned* my place!"

Denida raised his brow. "Might be what we need-" He spun back to the General. "- make all the kids earn their trust again…"

The General shook his head. "Dark magic is forbidden here anyway; they never could do anything like they did before!"

Denida sighed. "They need to prove they can't. None of them even pose a threat because they don't know advanced Dark magic."

The General slammed his fist into a barren tree trunk next to him. "I told you; none of them can use Dark-"

Denida lifted his hand above his head and clenched it. A cloud manifested above him and swirled until it grew dark.

Everyone screamed in terror and rushed inside, scattering at the mere sight of it.

Denida peeked at the General and tightened his fist as if choking the air from the spell, causing it to subside instantly. "As you can see, Dark magic can still be used." He turned and lowered his arm. "None of the children know advanced Arts; Claus would never have endangered himself by allowing anyone to use stronger magic."

Chatter grew throughout the crowd as everyone warily emerged from hiding. The General and Mark exchanged a nervous look.

Denida lifted a finger as the General was about to step toward Denida. "Wait!"

"For what?" the General spat out the words.

The adults who had gathered together stared at the children before whispering amongst themselves.

"Allow me!" A big man with scars littered across his face took a few significant steps toward the crowd of kids.

"Not gonna go well," the General sprinted forward, but Denida muttered a chant, causing the General to freeze on the spot. "We have to stop them; this won't end well!"

"Trust me." Denida patted the General's shoulder reassuringly.

The man with the scars stopped in front of the kids, gazing across them. His face tightened as he glared back at the other adults, seeing hatred in their eyes. Turning back to the children, all with fear and distress on their faces. He dropped to his knees and hugged the child in front of him as tightly as he could. "I'm sorry for not believing you." He started to sob uncontrollably.

The other adults watched for a moment in stoic trepidation before they all ran to their children and embraced them, too.

Denida nodded at Mark. "Don't you want to go see your family, too?"

"My family… my mom's dead and my father…" Mark lowered his head.

"Your dad, what?" Dan insisted.

Mark kicked a stone on the ground. "He doesn't know who I am…"

"But you know him?" Denida narrowed his eyes. "You could go see him, now."

Mark shook his head rapidly. "I know, but I can't!" He ran into the dining hall behind them.

Denida followed with Dan and the General close behind.

"Impressive how you've led them since Denida's first visit!" Dan sounded ecstatic.

Denida turned to Mark with a broad smile. "Everyone is turning to the future; yours could be with your father. Don't you wish to meet him?"

Mark clenched his fist. "I *have* met him," he hissed.

Denida frowned. "But-"

"No, I'm not telling him and that's final!" Mark charged out.

"Why's he so against it?" Denida scratched his head, puzzled.

The General shrugged. "We all lost loved ones in the time Claus ruled..."

"You too?" Dan's eyes widened.

"Yes, my wife, Isabella, and I were separated by force. I never saw her again. She died before I could..."

Denida's bit his lip. "How long were you apart before Isabella passed?"

"It was years... Claus wanted to keep us as far apart as possible."

Years? Could it be? "Dan, stay with the General." Denida raced out. It didn't take him long to locate Mark.

Mark glanced at Denida. "You again? Why do you even care?"

"You always knew how to protect yourself, even when Claus reigned, almost like the son of a *soldier*..." Denida leered at Mark.

Mark ruffled through his hair. "You have no idea..."

Denida knelt next to Mark. "What happened to your mom?"

Mark sighed. "Mom died when I was little..."

"Isabella..." Denida nodded.

Mark sighed.

"I thought so." Denida stood up and lifted his arm. "Why not come back with me?" He smiled with such tender eyes that Mark could only agree.

"You came a long way to accept it, haven't you?" Denida turned to Mark outside the dining hall.

"I'm not ready to tell him."

Denida nodded. "There are some things we're never ready for." He patted Mark on the shoulder and sauntered inside. "Dan, come here a second." They walked over to the other end of the room, across from the General.

"What's up?"

Denida raised his hand. "Just stay here for a sec." He stared across the room at the General.

Mark strolled in, stopping at the entrance and looked from the General to Denida before approaching the General. "Sir?" He saluted him.

"At ease." The General gazed through him, displeased. "Why did you run off? You really should go see your father; I know you're stronger than this!"

Mark looked down; a faint smile appearing on his face. "You think so?"

"I *know* so; you've proven yourself since Claus' reign."

Mark rubbed his nose and raised his head. "I did it for one specific person."

The General narrowed his eyes with a frown.

"My dad; I needed him to see who I was…"

The General shrugged. "Of course-"

"My mom, Isabella, always told me stories of my father, how he wasn't bad…"

"Isabella," The General gasped as the name hung in the air. His eyes wandered about before he bolted away from Mark, who turned toward Denida in shock.

Like father, like son… Denida rolled his eyes and chased after him. He found the General outside, tearing at his hair. Denida couldn't help but chuckle.

The General turned to him abruptly with bewildered eyes. "What's so funny?"

"… You and Mark did the same thing," Denida smiled vividly.

The General clenched both his fists in front of Denida's face, but when Denida didn't move a muscle, he slammed one of them into the wall behind him.

… And now he acts as the Colonel… "Why are you out here?"

The General rubbed his hands together. "*Isabella*; can that really be true?"

"You're asking a question you already know the answer to, General."

The General let his arms fall to his side in defeat and leaned against the wall. "What do I do then; I know how to fight… not how to be a dad."

"I know a little bit about fatherhood; you learn as you go…"

"Oh yeah, your son… *Daniel*, is that his name?"

Denida lowered his head. "Yes, it *was*…"

The General shook his hands. "Sorry, I forgot… I didn't-"

"Forget about it," Denida lifted his head. "- but don't make my mistake. Talk to him before it's too late."

The General rubbed his palms together. "You never told me what exactly happened; he was kidnapped… then died? What exactly happened?"

Denida snorted.

"It might help to talk about it?"

Denida shook his head. "It's not important."

"I insist. I really think you could use someone to talk to."

Denida arched his neck. "Fine, but only because I think it'll help you in your own situation." Denida plopped down on the grass. "Claus…" Denida twisted his mouth at the name. As he told the story of Daniel's kidnapping and death, he ripped grass up by the roots, tossing it into the air for the wind to carry away.

He finished his tale by shredding the last handful of grass as if it were Michelle's neck.

The General stood up. "Do you feel better? You still seem to be suffering…"

Denida stood and took a few shaky steps before he stopped, allowing a sense of tranquility to begin to soothe him for the first time since his loss. "As I said, don't be like me, regretting what you can't change."

"Yes, I understand." The General returned to the dining hall.

Denida arched his neck. *I sincerely hope Dan finds a way with the time machine. I have to bring our son back to Nina…*

When he returned to the dining hall, he discovered the General and Mark holding each other in a tight embrace. Warmth filled Denida for the first time since Daniel died.

The General and Mark approached, their faces glowing with joy.

"Denida, you never said why you're here?"

Dan and Denida shared a glance.

"I'm trying to unite all the Underworlds together as one," Denida said.

The General blinked. "You've got one more world then." He dragged Denida to the far side of the room. "You need to give yourself a chance to mourn, or grief will devour you; it almost did with Isabella for me…"

Denida tightened his jaw. "And how did you get past that?"

"Allow yourself a chance to cry and mourn what's lost."

Dan can still make it; that's why I'm bringing him… "I see. Dan!" He sprinted to Dan. "Thank you, General!"

Dan waved, but was abruptly interrupted when Denida suddenly teleported him to another world.

Dan didn't glance at the Gate, but rather at the bottom of the hilltop on which it stood, where spellcasting battles raged. Balls of fire and gusts of wind flashed across the field. One competent repelled several balls with a shield covering his fist, only to launch a huge one back.

"Wow," Dan gasped. "This is the world with the Warlock, isn't it?"

Denida joined Dan and licked his lips apprehensively. "It is. They are only practicing now…" He cleared his throat. "We need to go see her at the Holy Lands."

Dan kept gazing at the maelstrom of magic wreaking havoc on the field as if Denida hadn't spoken.

After a moment, Denida tapped Dan on the shoulder before leading him through the town toward the holy grounds. People pointed fingers and chattered amongst themselves as they passed; a number of them even paid attention to Dan.

When they reached the entrance, the guards greeted them with admiration and hastily let them through.

"Why are we getting so much reverence?" Dan tilted his head to Denida.

"Because you look exactly like me!" A man who looked just like Dan chuckled. "- that, and you're with the mighty Denida…"

Dan stopped and his eyes widened as he gasped at the sight of himself.

The other Dan hugged Denida. "The Warlock and the High Sorcerer are expecting you; come!" He brought them to the center of the grounds where the Warlock and Sorcerer waited, as if having anticipated their arrival.

"Two Dans," the Warlock grinned. "What brings you here?"

Denida stepped up to the High Sorcerer. "Well met, Your Honor. A wise President once united all the Underworlds. I strongly believe it's time to return to that state of peace."

The Sorcerer scratched his temple. "The President was an amazing man. You think you can be just as good?"

Denida smiled confidently and extended his flat hand. An image formed in front of him. Depicting the President of all the Underworlds hovering as a spirit, nodding at Denida. "I left it here, in the real world, in a place only you would be able to find, and only when you were ready. Your soul needed to mature until you could handle what's in this box."

"The Ring," the High Sorcerer remarked and exchanged a glance with the Warlock.

Denida nodded. "He chose me to wield it… and if that's not all-" He nipped his lip. "Lucifer and God's goddess had a vision, prophesying that I'd come as a chosen one."

"Dan," The Sorcerer commanded.

Dan looked perplexed. "Yes, Sir?"

The High Sorcerer shook his head. "Not you; the other Dan. Escort Denida and your namesake out, while the Warlock and I discuss something."

Something? Denida glared suspiciously at the Warlock and the Sorcerer.

"I'll take you to see how Susan's preparing for our next Magical Championship. The other Dan nudged them out the door, while Denida kept peering back.

"We will make it work." Susan grunted.

"Susan." Dan waved his hands ecstatically.

Susan spun around and ran her tongue across her teeth. "Hi, Dan… and Denida. You won in our last Magical Championship; what a godsend!"

Denida frowned his forehead. "Why is that?"

"Our host suddenly fell ill and can't officiate. A former winner is a real blessing."

Denida cleared his throat. "We don't have-"

Dan yanked Denida back and leaned in, whispering into his ear. "The Warlock and the Sorcerer wanted to talk alone; maybe if they witness us helping out, it might convince them to help us."

He has a point. "I'll help," he smiled at Susan.

Susan grinned. "Let's get you ready for the fight!"

"Wait." Denida took a step back. "What fight?"

"To begin the ceremony at the Holy Lands, of course."

Denida grunted and peered back at Dan, irritably. *Just look at what you've gotten me into this time.* "Aright."

Susan presented Denida with a colorful cloak to wear, which made him stand out when he took his place in the middle of the room. All eyes were on him as the participants stood in anticipation.

Denida stroked his ring with his thumb and extended it upwards. A silvery light appeared around his hand. "Welcome to the Magical Championship at the Holy Lands!" He turned his sight across the crowd. "-Where one of you will be the last one standing and have your deepest desire granted by the High Sorcerer."

Applause radiated from the crowd, deafening the room.

The High Sorcerer and the Warlock appeared behind Denida.

"Let the games begin!" The High Sorcerer stepped in between Denida and the Warlock, taking one of their hands in each of his own, raising them. The magic surrounding Denida's hand ceased to exist as soon as the Sorcerer touched Denida.

The Warlock lay her hand on Denida's shoulder and nudged him toward the Sorcerer's chamber with Dan awkwardly following behind them.

They want to talk to me already? I haven't even done anything helpful, yet.

The Warlock leaned against the High Sorcerer chair. The Sorcerer looked up at her with a smile.

"Denida," The High Sorcerer said without moving his eyes from the Warlock. "I see you can use the powers of the Ring of the Underworlds."

"I needed-"

The High Sorcerer turned to Denida and lifted his finger. "The Warlock and I discussed this. The forbidden Dark magic you hold…"

I have a bad feeling about this! Denida shifted at his feet, feeling an unrest growing within his stomach.

The Warlock leaned in and whispered something to the High Sorcerer, making him hum in agreement.

"- yet you didn't use this. You used the magic of the ring instead... Maybe the Warlock is right about you. Whether she is or not, I am willing to join you." The Sorcerer clenched his fist. "But be aware, abuse my trust and we will end our unity... for good!"

Denida nodded and stepped closed to extend his hand, hopefully.

The Sorcerer's glared at the Warlock. "I do hope you're right!" He shook Denida's hand.

To the next world! "Come on, Dan."

Chapter 17- A Deal

Denida's eyes flickered red. *Back here again... wish I could see Nina instead.* He sighed, shaking his head. *No, I need to do this first; it's not worth bringing Daniel back if the world isn't safe for him.*

Dan frowned in worry. "Something the matter?"

"This will be a challenge, but maybe it shall inspire me! There are no leaders in this world, just a good side and a bad one, which is led by the Scientist's twin."

"*The Gatekeeper*, I remember." Dan nodded. "Why don't we visit the person who helped us here before? The *Colonel* had a version of himself in this world; he operated an inn, I think?"

Denida sighed slightly and headed off toward the inn, pausing after a few steps. *Something feels off.* He dismissed the thoughts and continued.

When they arrived at the inn, it became evident that this world's Colonel still waited tables, just as Denida remembered.

Denida and Dan sat down at a table and waited for the Colonel's approach. Denida buried his head in a menu card.

"Welcome, how may I help you today?" The Innkeeper gave a tired smile, which faded abruptly as Denida met his eyes. "Not you again! Do you realize the shitstorm your last visit brought?"

Denida squinted his eyes. "The Gatekeeper replaced Claus; how does that impact you?"

"The Gatekeeper has taken over most of this world. The light you see is fading with each passing day!"

Denida's eyes widened and he ran to the door. "Oh... my... god..." He rubbed his forehead and turned to the Innkeeper. "They didn't just settle for the Darkness. They came all the way to this side of the world..."

"Yes..." The Innkeeper lowered his head.

"-and you just accepted it!" Denida raised his voice.

The Innkeeper turned away from Denida. "Do let me know if I can get you anything."

Denida chuckled. *Just like our Colonel not to accept it!* He followed the Innkeeper, who ignored him completely.

Denida eventually stopped dead in his tracks when he reached the backroom. "Dan?"

Dan ran to Denida. "I'm here!"

Denida shook his head. "Not you-" He gently pushed Dan forward, so he could see the man wearing a black robe, standing next to the Innkeeper.

Dan gasped. "How's this possible... a version of me *here*?"

The man in the rope lowered his hood, revealing a dirty face full of scars. "My name's *Naphtali*. How are you?"

Naphtali? What a strange name. "You're attempting to fight back against the Gate-"

Naphtali swiftly put a hand over Denida's mouth. "Don't say the name; there are demons everywhere you look."

Denida stepped back and bit his lip. "Dan, go talk with the Innkeeper for a second. Naphtali and I need to have a chat..."

Naphtali wrinkled his forehead in puzzlement, but said nothing while Dan and the Innkeeper strolled out.

Denida's smile intensified as soon as they were alone. "Your eyes... there's Darkness in them; you're a demon, aren't you?"

"Former..."

Ex-demon? Denida frowned. "You can't just stop being a demon."

"True, but I was only in Hell for a short time. I was able to escape thanks to someone's mercy..."

Can it be? Denida felt a chill creep down his spine. "The Dark Angels in Hell?" He was almost afraid to speak those words.

Naphtali nodded. "It was a long time ago; a group of seven young demons helped other newcomers in Hell-"

"- to escape, yes. Danyel, Ignacio, Nicklas, Mia, Jan, Pedro, and-" Denida's eyes met Naphtali. "-and their leader, Denida."

Naphtali agreed. "'Little Evil,' as they called him. He had discovered a way and it worked!"

"That was a long time ago..."

"What do you mean?" Naphtali scratched his head.

"I never introduced myself, did I?" Denida's eyes glowed red as he reached out his hand. "My name's Denida."

"Denida?" Naphtali muttered in disbelief.

"What is it you're after here, Naphtali- you got away from Hell, yet you remain so close?"

"We must stop the Darkness here! It has grown too much." Beads of cold sweat formed on Naphtali's forehead as he spoke.

"If I were to help you remove them from this world, would you join me in leading it?"

Naphtali lit up. "Of course, I'll do anything for you!"

Denida patted Naphtali on the shoulder before exiting. He stopped next to Dan. "Make sure Naphtali stays safe while I'm away, old friend." He sprinted to the door, where a pair of demons entered.

No way! Denida punched his arm forward, sending the pair flying backward, out of the inn. He sauntered after them.

The air grew dense and a dark cloud appeared above the demons as they scrambled to their feet.

"You think you're something special because you can use wind magic?" one of them screamed and thrust a fiery spell at Denida.

Denida pointed his finger forward, extinguishing the spell in the air.

The infuriated demons cried out in dismay and charged Denida.

Denida clenched his fist and slammed it into the ground, forming a magic cone around him.

The demons pressed forward undeterred, slamming into the cone.

They stood and lifted their arms, circling the cone while chanting. A pentagram appeared in the sky above the cone. The air around the cone grew denser.

"You can't break it," Denida taunted.

"Dark magic is stronger here," one gloated triumphantly.

Denida tilted his head and noticed the pentagram in the sky getting stronger until it shattered the cone.

The two demons swarmed Denida. One of them grabbed his arms and the other punched him with fire, causing Denida to wince in agony.

The demon delivering the blows sneered as Darkness encircled his hand. "Time to say goodbye!"

Naphtali shot an energy ball toward them, knocking both the demons and Denida off their feet.

Denida grabbed one of the demons, using him as a shield against the fiery balls his ally threw at him. He pushed the demons charred body into the combatant, still using him as a shield.

The demon sent a dark cloud that vaporized everything in its path.

Denida shoved the demon he held into the cloud and rolled to the side to dodge it himself.

The demon combatant stood alone, grinning. "Serves you right messing with Darkness," he smirked.

Denida materialized in front of the demon with a wicked grin. "One down, one to go!" He swiftly jabbed his hand into the demon in front of him.

He tore the heart from the demon's body with menacing eyes. He held the heart out in front of the demon, who followed its every move with wide, pleading eyes.

Denida squeezed the heart tightly. Blood dripped as the demon took his last breath and fell to the ground.

Naphtali helped Denida up. "Nice work!"

"You too; thanks for the help. I know Dan will be safe with you."

Naphtali smiled faintly. "The least I can do…"

"Good to hear. I need to attend to something." Denida walked farther into the world toward the Gate. He didn't want to use the ring, as he wanted to experience the change for himself. *It feels just like Hell…*

It hadn't just increased in Darkness like the last time. Instead, it was now filled with a malicious atmosphere.

Denida paused, grinding his teeth as he stood with several demons in front of him. *I need to look like the rest of them…* His eye fell on an old building. *Lucifer's…* He rubbed his forehead before continuing toward it.

As soon as he stepped through the door, he found Lucifer sitting with an expectant look on his face, like he'd been waiting for Denida.

"Déjà vu time," Lucifer said with a broad smile.

Denida trudged over and pulled up a chair. "You want to waste my time or are you going to tell me the rest of your tale?"

Lucifer's smile turned into a frown. "Here?"

"Darkness has taken over this place, no? It sure does feel like Hell, so you should be able to show me while we're here!"

"That's-"

Denida lifted his hands. "I can't hear your story if I have to deal with this, too- or rather I don't *want* to."

He leaned in toward Lucifer. "How do you suggest we solve this standstill, huh?"

"You want this world? No problem." Lucifer's eyes glowed. "Follow me!" He led the way to the Gate. All the demons they passed cleared out of the way and knelt.

When they arrived at the giant structure holding the Gate, the guards opened the doors before they were even close. Lucifer didn't waver.

The Gatekeeper jumped up from his seat as soon as they entered his chamber. "Master! How can I serve you?" He lowered his head.

Denida kept his distance behind Lucifer.

Lucifer leaned down to the Gatekeeper's ear. "Where's your brother, *the Scientist?*" he whispered while gazing at him with eyes as cold as ice.

Red lights lit up all around the room, illuminating the room with a crimson glow.

Lucifer shed his human shape and appeared in his demonic form as he hovered above the Gatekeeper. "This is the last time I'll ask."

The Gatekeeper cringed with horrified eyes. "I haven't talked to him since he was-"

A pentagram formed around the Gatekeeper and a magic cone surfaced around it.

"Wait!" The Gatekeeper lifted his trembling hands. "The last time I heard from him was when he worked with Medusa; I have no idea where he is!"

Denida cleared his throat. "I do."

"Ask him, then," the Gatekeeper pointed at Denida.

Lucifer appeared right in front of Denida with fire raging in his eyes. "Where is the *traitor*, then. Do you have him?" The room suddenly started to grow even more ominous.

The Darkness here is prevalent! Denida clenched his fist. "Earth; the Colonel is searching for him on Earth."

Lucifer became more enraged at the news. He charged the Gatekeeper, who ran in the other direction.

A cone stopped the Gatekeeper in his track. Frightened, he spun around to find Lucifer right in front of him, sneering.

Darkness filled the cone so no one from outside could see, including Denida. A loud, agonized scream echoed from within the cone, followed by a thump and utter silence for several minutes.

"Lucifer?" Denida's voice screeched.

The cone suddenly vaporized and the dark cloud dissipated.

"Denny." Lucifer appeared where the cone had been. "The demons in this world are no more; all you have to do is hear the rest of my story, for better or worse!"

Denida shrugged. "But how can I honestly consider helping you just because I'm hearing your tale?"

"You'll consider it, not for me, but for Heavani. I know you remember her; I'll be waiting…" Lucifer vanished with the last traces of the dark cloud.

Denida strode over to where the cone had been. He knelt and raked his fingers through a powdery remnant, which was the only sign that it had been there at all. *Just like with Medusa…* He threw the ashes down and rushed out the door. The building was deserted, so he continued outside. *There's no one around.*

Denida squinted his eyes and lifted his arm. The sun shone as brightly as it had on any typical day; the Darkness in the air was gone like it had never been there.

This place looks incredible without the Darkness!

Denida sauntered back to the inn, but paused frequently to marvel at various sights he encountered along the way. When he finally arrived at it, the Innkeeper had set up outdoor seating. *It feels so different now, even here…* "Enjoying the sunshine?"

The Innkeeper turned with glowing eyes. "It feels great!"

"They're gone?" Naphtali asked cautiously.

Denida raised his arms high. "This world is now yours, again." He turned to the Innkeeper. "You'll assist Naphtali, I hope?"

The Innkeeper frowned. "Me?"

Denida squeezed the Innkeeper's shoulder and nodded.

He tilted his head at Dan.

Dan followed Denida. "Time for us to leave?"

Denida lowered his head while nipping a llt his upper lip. "Not you; I need to go take care of something. I want you to help them reestablish order here."

Dan snorted. "I can't help them!"

"Yes, you can. You helped establish order when *the Dark Angels* fell in our world."

"But this is a different world," Dan insisted.

Denida hugged Dan. "They need guidance, and I trust *only* you!"

"Fine." Dan threw up his arms and went back to Naphtali.

That will keep him occupied while I go see Lucifer…

Denida teleported inside of Lucifer's throne room.

Lucifer turned away from a conversation with the demon guarding the front of the mansion. He waved his hand at the demon. "We'll talk later." The demon transformed into a crow and flew out a window in the back of the room.

"Why is he always here?"

"That demon is just my protection." Lucifer's eyes had a faint red glow.

Denida ran his tongue against the back of his mouth. "Anyway-" He sauntered over to the Well of Memory. "You wanted to continue showing me?"

"Yes…" Lucifer's tone contained a trace of melancholy. "After destroying Henna, Shaddai brought Gabriel and me back to the world where he was God…"

"And…" Denida gaped at Lucifer.

"We didn't feel at home there, especially Shaddai…"

Chapter 18- God and Lucifer

"They seem very primitive," Azal gazed down at the unknown species running about on the planet below him. "How is it possible we can do all this here? Henna never made Gabriel or me a god."

Shaddai chuckled. "Maybe she was never as powerful as we all thought!"

Was she just saying that? Azal turned around. "Wait! That's not possible; you still have more abilities than both Gabriel and I combined. Maybe the world we come from…" Azal pondered with his gaze locked on his fingers. "- maybe what we did to Henna was a bad thing, after all? Her prophecy…"

Shaddai shook his head and buried it in his hands. "She was just upset that her time was up!" He grabbed the blood-stained dagger and held it where Azal could see. "This was hers; she created her own downfall."

Azal's eyes widened and he rushed over to grab the dagger.

"Why are you so intrigued by this thing?"

The blood turned rainbow colors… Azal raised his head, baffled. "Henna said this material could kill us all; why would she have spread seven of them across the universe? She created these…"

Shaddai snatched the dagger back from Azal. He rubbed the shaft and tilted it, inspecting it from every angle before he blew on it and it vanished. "Don't worry; it's over, now and we're safe here- forever!"

"Shaddai! Azal!" Gabriel ran over to them.

"Yeah?" Shaddai lifted his brow, puzzled.

"I saw a stone on fire in the sky- it's coming this way!"

"A stone?" Shaddai turned to witness what Gabriel had seen. "No," he uttered.

Azal hurried over to him. "What?" He gasped at the sight of a huge meteor hurtling toward the planet below. "You have to stop it; it'll destroy your world."

Shaddai lowered his head. "I'm not sure I can…"

"But you have to try!" Azal raised his voice.

Shaddai sighed and turned his attention to the approaching meteor.

Azal and Gabriel shared a concerned gaze before they turned to it too, awaiting the inevitable impact.

The meteor tore through the sky without slowing down at all. Azal watched Shaddai, whose forehead started to ooze sweat. Shaddai squinted his eyes to no avail.

Azal felt the heat of the meteor approaching. It hurtled past them into the atmosphere of the planet below and slammed into the surface with a deafening bang, setting the atmosphere of the planet ablaze.

"We can't stay here," Gabriel broke the silence after staring down at the surface in silence. "Maybe we can go back to our world?"

"Never!" Azal yelled. "If any of the gods come back and see us there, they'll know we killed Henna." He shook his head. "We can never go back; it's not an option!"

"Well, this world's dying; we can't stay here…" Gabriel peeked at the menacing blaze below.

"Perhaps we *should* return." Shaddai grabbed Azal's hand. "Everyone was gone; if anyone returned, they would never find out what happened…" His sight focused on the ongoing destruction below. "But perhaps Henna was right that I wasn't ready… oh well." He shrugged. "The world here's gone." He chortled. "Let's go!"

He doesn't feel bad about this? Azal and Gabriel gazed at each other.

Shaddai tightened his fist. "We can't do anything to help them; we have to put ourselves first!"

Azal nodded sadly and waved at Gabriel. They strolled over to Shaddai.

Shaddai picked them up and took flight, abandoning the planet and his duties as a watchful god, never to return. "We'll be back home, soon. I know the way like the back of my hand!" he yelled to the other two as he flew through the sky.

After several days of nonstop flight, Shaddai suddenly slowed down. Azal opened his mouth to speak, but then Shaddai continued flying at a faster pace, entering the atmosphere. *We must be here.*

Shaddai unfolded his arms.

Azal scanned 360 degrees. "This isn't home; where are we?"

Shaddai ran a hand through his hair. "I had to set us down on this barren rock. I can't find our home planet; it's like it's gone."

Shaddai's eyes finally reflected the sorrow Azal had expected to see when the planet Shaddai had watched over was destroyed.

"We can never return… at all!" Shaddai plopped down on the rock. "We've got nowhere to go."

He sighed heavily.

Gabriel knelt. "We'll just have to find somewhere else!"

***

The image in the well faded. Denida looked up at Lucifer, noticing a forlorn expression on his face.

"I'm sorry," Lucifer whispered before clearing his throat. "That planet was our home and, at that moment, we really thought it was gone."

Denida wrinkled his brow. "It wasn't?"

"No," Lucifer shook his head. "Henna had lied. We just didn't know it at the time, so we really thought we had to find somewhere else to call home."

Lucifer held his hand on the well and the image of Shaddai, Azal, and Gabriel on that desolate rock formed in the well.

***

Shaddai pushed Gabriel to the side and got up. "No!" he roared and stormed off.

Azal helped Gabriel up. "Just leave him be."

Gabriel nodded and gazed at the sky. "You really think our world is gone for good?"

Azal closed his eyes and lowered his head. "One thing is certain; destroyed or not, we're not welcome-"

"Azal, Gabriel; I know where we can go!" Shaddai ran back to them with a smile across his face.

Azal lifted his brow. "Where?"

"Henna always spoke of this one world; it's a special place she sent her favorite gods. It's in the Milky Way Galaxy."

"That's… very… far," Gabriel stuttered.

"Henna believed the very future of the universe resided there-"

"Exactly," Azal interrupted. "Odin and Zeus are there; they'll know something is wrong if we just show up unannounced!"

Shaddai grinned openly at that remark. "Trust me; it'll be fine." He spread his arms as if preparing for an embrace.

Azal and Gabriel joined Shaddai, who blew air on them both, causing them to doze off.

Azal's eyelids fluttered, adjusting to the dark, but all he could see were stars rapidly passing them by. *Why am I awake? We're still going.* His eyes searched the small range of vision allotted to him. He found it fascinating, a new frontier. *Will we meet Odin again, I wonder?*

The stars faded as Shaddai traveled through a dust cloud containing some flying debris. Azal dozed off again.

Azal awoke when he was suddenly slammed down. He quickly surveyed his surroundings in confusion.

Gabriel! Shaddai ran over to his friend, who was just as puzzled as he was. It took Shaddai a second for him to get his bearings.

"Where's Shaddai?" Gabriel sounded worried.

Azal scanned the sandy terrain, hoping to find Shaddai, but he couldn't detect any trace of him. There was nothing but sand as far as the eye could see. Standing up, Azal began to wander a short distance, examining the ground with each purposeful step. A hole appeared in front of him.

"Curse Henna," Shaddai's groan echoed from deep within it.

Azal sped to the edge of the pit, finding that it was profoundly deep. Shaddai was still struggling to his feet at the bottom. "What are you doing down there?"

"You think I'm down here on purpose?" Shaddai hissed and jumped out. "I saw Odin's boy near the planet they all are watching, lost my focus, and crashed into some debris, which is why we're all here in this dump."

Azal sighed. "Why are we here if they're not supposed to see us?"

Shaddai chuckled deviously as he led the way back to Gabriel. When they met up with their friend, Shaddai spun to face them both. "You wanted to know why we're here?" He glowed with pride.

Azal shrugged. "I-"

Shaddai raised his hand and a hole appeared in front of him.

Gabriel nodded and jumped into the hole and vanished.

Azal's eyes widened. He took a step back and bit his lip. "Alright…" He leapt in after Shaddai and found himself standing on a soft cushion-like surface and knelt to touch it with his hands. He noticed Gabriel gasping. "Something wrong?"

Gabriel lifted his hand. "Behind you."

Azal turned to see Shaddai approaching. A large device stood behind Shaddai, illuminating the nothingness around it. "In Henna's name, what's that?" He rushed forward to examine it. "Shaddai!" he screamed. "Come over here."

Shaddai marveled at the mysterious device. His eyes remained fixed on it as circled it, slowly making his way over to Azal. "What's so intriguing?"

"This." Azal stepped aside, revealing the center of the massive device, which was made from a different material than the rest of it.

Shaddai knelt. "Can it really be?" The dagger materialized and he held it up next to the unique material. "It's made of the same alloy... did Henna put this here?" He stared back at Azal, their eyes filled with bewilderment.

***

"The Gate to the Underworlds, right?" Denida met Lucifer's eyes.

Lucifer nodded. "We were all taken aback to discover that Henna somehow made that device and left it there, of all places. Did she know it would be vital, or…" He raised his eyebrows. "Either way, we decided to stay to see if anyone would come. We figured Odin or Zeus might use it, but no one showed up. After some time, Shaddai decided we might as well stay, so we created a new home…"

Denida grabbed the tip of the well as he leaned over it. "You're finally at the part about Heavani?"

Lucifer shook his head solemnly. "Not yet…"

Denida threw his arms up and marched toward the door, but after a few steps, he paused and turned. "- but I know that he's bad!"

"You only know the beginning about where Shaddai, Gabriel, and I came from, only…"

Denida ground his teeth as he returned to the well. "What's next, then?"

Lucifer's eyes had a red flicker. "We built a new home, because it was just the three of us, it started to feel lonely in no time. Shaddai sent me out to try to persuade others. He gave us extra powers to help with that as well."

***

Azal wandered through a jungle on Earth. *It feels so different here…* He froze in place at a rumbling sound dead ahead. The leaves in the trees overhead shook. He tilted his head upward. A giant creature stood above Azal, eating fruit hanging from the tree. Azal felt a warmth within.

"Hey, Azal."

Azal frantically spun around to the sound to see who it was, but no one was there. He glanced around.

'Creek.'

He turned toward the sound, but it was just a crow sitting in a nearby tree. It flew off the branch and flapped its wings, creating a gust of wind.

Azal squinted his eyes and put his hand over his face.

The wind condensed and in a flash, it vanished with the bird. Odin appeared in its place, looking noticeably older and wearing a patch over one of his eyes.

"You've gotten old!" Azal widened his eyes.

Odin chuckled. "Time passes differently here on Earth." He bared his palm. "Why are you here, Azal?"

How should I phrase this?

"However, you'd like to." Odin smiled reassuringly.

Azal gawked. "You can read my thoughts?"

"Everyone Henna granted divinity can do that." Odin lifted his left arm and two crows landed on his sleeve. "You wanted to tell me why you're here?" He petted the two crows.

"Sorry, yes." Azal was taken aback at the sight of the crows. "Shaddai, Gabriel, and I have found a place where you might feel at home-"

"No." The crows flew off Odin's arm and he turned his focus to Azal. "I already have a place of my own; *Valhalla*."

"As you wish." Azal kicked the ground.

Odin put his hand on Azal's shoulder; it felt like a warm sensation. "You have a long journey ahead of you, '*Azal*,' just as Henna said. It was nice seeing you." After another brief flash, a crow flew from the spot Odin had stood, circled the trees above, then disappeared.

It didn't take long for Azal to rush back to their place in the Underworlds. Shaddai had constructed a wall that separated their home from Henna's strange device.

Gabriel sat within the border, right next to the entrance, when he saw Azal fly inside. He frowned and hurried after. Azal didn't stop until he reached Shaddai. "I met Odin; he's already made a place of his own!" he yelled, startling Shaddai.

Shaddai turned, rubbing his shin. "I see."

"You never told me you can read our minds. Also, I have a feeling he knows about Henna…"

Both Shaddai and Gabriel approached Azal.

"How?" Shaddai yelled.

"Just something he said."

Shaddai shrugged. "Nobody can join us then; maybe we'll just have to make some followers ourselves." Shaddai licked his lips.

"You want to play God, Shaddai?" Azal smirked.

Shaddai peered intently at Azal. "Henna made me a god, so I am one-" He stopped mid-sentence, staring into the air as if he realized something. "-no, no, no." He shook his head rapidly. "Not a god, I'm the *supreme God* of all the rest. I'll be known as *God* from now on!" He snapped his fingers and darted away.

Gabriel peered over at his friend. "There's something else, isn't there?"

Azal sighed. "Yes, Odin said something else; '*You have a long journey ahead of you.*' I can't shake the feeling that he meant something dire with that…" Azal tightened his fist and turned to Gabriel. "I should change my name too, but to what?"

Gabriel shrugged. "Whatever you change it to, won't change who you are."

Azal rolled his eyes and returned to the entrance to keep watch.

Gabriel puffed heavily as he ran up to Azal.

Azal looked at Gabriel. "Gabe, want to be one guard duty instead?

Gabriel shook his head and pulled Azal to his feet. "'God' wants to show us something." He guided Azal back to the center, where God waited for them.

God raised his arms above his head. "The time has come for me to show you the *first* to join us here in this haven- no *Heaven*." He stepped aside, revealing a person standing behind him. "Meet Saint Peter, who'll protect our Pearly Gates!"

Azal frowned. "Pearly what?"

"Peter, meet my friend, Gabriel, and my other friend, my brightest Morning Star-"

"That's it," Azal tapped Gabriel's shoulder. "Morning Star; Lucifer is my name!"

Gabriel ignored the outburst and greeted Peter. "Let me show you to the entrance." He took Peter's hand and led him to it.

"You've *made* someone?" Lucifer puffed at God. "How?"

"Gods can create life; I'm just exercising what Henna taught me."

Lucifer rolled his eyes. "You're going to do it again?"

God smirked. "Let's see how he does first, does, first. And, just to be clear, it's Lucifer, now... no more Azal?"

"You changed from Shaddai to God. We both need a new beginning..."

God nodded. "That we do. From here on out, it's God and his Morning Star, Lucifer in Heaven..."

***

Denida growled as the image faded. "I never did like Saint Peter..."

Lucifer shrugged. "The first one is never perfect. God made more after. He created Archangel Michael next."

Denida's grunt morphed into a smile, and he snapped his fingers. "This one, on the other hand, is perfect!" Denida tapped his ring on the side of the well. "I need to head back to Dan."

Lucifer straightened up. "What is it you're doing in the other Underworlds?"

"Assuring our robots are well; don't concern yourself with that. I'll be back." Denida rubbed his ring and he reappeared back at the Inn, but it was barren. Dan and the Innkeeper were gone.

Where is everyone? Denida strolled outside, but there was no sign of them there, either. He rubbed his ring as he searched around.

'The second Gate.'

Denida wrinkled his brow. *Really? Okay, I'll try...* He tightened his hand and teleported to the front of the building that contained the second Gate. The spot seemed strange to Denida now that it was liberated from the Darkness. He sighed as he approached the building.

As soon as he entered the door, he encountered a guard.

"How can I help you, Mister?"

"Da- I mean, is Naphtali here?" Denida felt wary asking that.

"Yes, but who are you?" The guard hand hovered next to his sidearm.

He held up his hands. "Denida, the President of another Underworld. He knows me!"

"It's okay." Dan appeared and waved his hand.

The guard nodded and stepped aside.

"What's going on; why are you all here?"

Dan led Denida into the room Denida remembered from the time with the Gatekeeper.

Naphtali noticed Denida from where he stood speaking. "Our savior is back." He started clapping and everyone in the room joined in the round of applause.

"Dan prepared you?"

Naphtali pointed at Dan. "This boy of yours is awesome!"

Denida winked and held up his thumb. "In that case, we need to continue. I look forward to working with you." He patted Naphtali's shoulder.

Dan walked faster to catch up with Denida. "We're going back home?"

Denida stopped and turned to Dan. "That's right; you never saw anything past this point."

"Um, not exactly." Dan blushed with an embarrassed expression. "We tried the next one; Hell. Lucifer stopped us there."

"He won't this time." Denida took Dan's hand in his and they vanished from that world.

Denida and Dan reappeared in a very different world than the last ones. The Gate stood on a barren ground, with nothing else anywhere in the vicinity.

Dan scratched his head. "This is the Wild West world you told me about, right? The one after Heaven and Hell?"

Denida gazed over the horizon. "I went through a lot in this world…"

Dan smiled. "Let's go to town. I presume you know where that is?"

"It's near," Denida chuckled.

Dan followed after Denida. It didn't take more than a few minutes before they spotted a town in front of them.

Already? Denida shook his head in disbelief. "This can't be! Wasn't it farther away?"

"Maybe you just remember wrong!" Dan yelled as he continued. "Come on, I am curious about this one!"

The town was dead silent and the streets were empty, but the lack of tumbleweeds implied that the town hadn't been abandoned, yet.

Denida's eyes wandered across the barren street and to the buildings lining it. He could see people inside each building before they hurried to close the curtains.

"Something's off with this world too," Dan turned to Denida, but realized his friend was already halfway down the road. He hurried up and reached Denida at an intersection.

Denida stood, shaking his head. "Why is everyone indoors?" Where is everybody?" he hissed and clenched his fist.

"Maybe Lucifer took over this world too," Dan suggested.

Denida rolled his eyes. "Not pos-" He paused and spun back to Dan. "Whipboy and Lars!" He grabbed Dan and yanked him along.

"Whipboy? Somebody's actually named that?" Dan laughed.

"Yes, a demon…"

Dan's smile faded.

Denida stepped out into the plains, where he approached some wild horses munching on grass. He slowly approached them, remaining mindful of each step, while still making calming sounds with his tongue.

The horses neighed and shifted uneasily when they noticed Denida. He paused and glared at Dan before turning back and tightening his fist. A light encircling it.

The horses seemed entranced by the light, calming down despite Denida steadily drawing closer.

Denida picked two of them and used the light to lead them back to Dan.

"You're not expecting *me* to ride that thing, are you?" Dan stepped back.

Denida stroked the horse. "Dan, it's just a horse."

Dan retreated farther. "No way; I'm not getting on that thing. I've heard horror stories about people who've been thrown off horses." He waved his hands. "- plus, they're wild!"

Denida rolled his eyes and let one horse escape the trance, while staying focused on the other by his side. Denida mounted the horse and stretched his hand out to Dan. "Come on; I'll keep you safe." He winked with a grin.

Dan grumbled, but took hold of Denida's hand.

Denida pulled him up on the horse behind him and set it into a gallop with a soft squeeze of his legs. Dan held Denida's waist tightly as the horse picked up its pace.

Denida rode the horse around all nearby settlements, but eventually, he slowed down next to an old farm in the middle of nowhere. Its field expanded to the horizon in every direction. He dismounted the horse carefully, walking with small, evenly paced steps.

"Hey, don't forget about me!" Dan yelled before Denida wandered too far.

Denida turned back to help Dan down.

Dan cleared his throat. "Where are we?"

Denida lowered his head. "This is where a friend who saved me lives. I have to know if he's safe…"

"Saved you from what?" Dan raised his brow.

"Escaping from this world and Lucifer with Daniel." Denida continued past Dan, stopping after a few steps. His eyes widened at the tall, wooden fence surrounding the property. "What happened here?"

Denida increased his pace toward the entrance. He didn't even slow down when he reached the gate; he just extended his arm and the gate flew off its hinges. Denida stormed through the entrance with fiery eyes, prepared to kill if he saw anything wrong.

The building was falling apart, but an old man still sat on the porch, shooting at cans. He wore old clothes, filled with holes.

Denida stopped as the first shot landed, knocking down a can sitting on top of a boulder. "Robert is that you?" he called out, trying to be louder than the bullets.

The old man lowered his rifle and turned to Denida. Warmth appeared in his eyes. He threw down the gun and ran to Denida, embracing him in a tender hug. "So great to see you again, but it's dangerous here, now…" He scanned the field and pushed them inside his house.

"Robert, what-"

Robert shushed him as he closed the curtains.

Denida squinted his eyes. "Who are you hiding from, let alone have a wall for?" He glanced at Dan. "What happened here?"

Robert breathed heavily as he turned to Denida. "Whipboy has ended all order here, exterminated anyone who had anything to do with the law- as you might remember, I was a lawman once!"

Whipboy! Ice ran down Denida's back. "His boss, Lars, is he still here?"

Robert grumbled and nodded.

"I knew something was wrong here," Denida snorted and tightened his fist so hard that it made the sound of cracking bones.

Dan grew as jittery as Robert.

"Why are you back, Denny… and who's this; it's not your boy, *Daniel?*" Robert peeked out the curtain.

Denida wandered across the room, rubbing his face.

"I'm Dan, nice to meet you. I'm one of Denny's old friends from his Underworld." Dan shook Robert's hand.

"I'm trying to bring all the Underworlds back together; this is the last one, seeing as I already lead the one on Earth." Denida forced a smile.

Robert shrugged. "Lars rules everything here. Everyone fears Whipboy; it's just not possible!"

"I tried to beat them once; I can, and will, succeed this time!" Denida had a red flicker in his eyes as he uttered those words.

"Um…" Dan stepped forward. "- are you *sure* that's a good idea?"

Denida clenched both his fists. "They're here because of Lucifer. Demons don't belong here! Am I sure?" He bit his lip. "By Hen- I mean… yes, I'm certain!"

Denida stormed out the door with Dan watching him go, staring into the air where Denida had been. "Hen? Who's that," Dan muttered.

Robert scurried after as if Dan hadn't spoken, grabbing Denida by the arm. "Don't do this; you barely escaped with Daniel!"

Denida smiled and rubbed Robert's cheek before slapping it. "Daniel's not here, anymore; Whipboy and Lars won't be here either!" He cracked his fingers and teleported away.

Denida reappeared in front of a fortress with a lot of armed men patrolling the grounds around it.

Back yet again… Denida marched up to the entrance, where two guards stood, teasing each other.

The two guards turned with a smirk on their faces.

"You don't belong here; go away," one guard sneered and waved his hand indifferently.

"Really," Denida sniggered. "Neither do you." He lunged forward and jabbed his hand into the guard's torso, watching his smile fade in an instant.

The other guard reached for his gun, but Denida flung the first guard around, blocking the bullets with the corpse.

Denida flung the dead body forward, slamming it into the other guard. The guard's gun fell from his grip.

The guard rolled on the floor before turning to Denida. He rushed after him into the building.

Denida was about to take a step, when a bullet hit his leg. He dropped to his knees, the pain so intense that it made his eyes water, especially his bad one.

"You think you can trespass here and survive?" The guard grinned mockingly.

Denida screamed with an agonizing roar. He held his ring over his leg, healing the wound. The room grew a murky, dark red color, while his eyes glinted.

The guard lifted his gun in front of him. The weapon started to glow red as if it were on fire. "Ouch!" He dropped it and grabbed his hand, blowing air on it.

"Where are Lars and Whipboy?"

The guard shrugged. "If you're after them, you're out of luck."

Denida narrowed his eyes. "In that case…"

"Wait!" The guard waved his arms. "They're at an even safer area than here. A fortress…"

"Where is it?"

The guard lowered his head. "Maybe I shouldn't say; they'll kill me…"

Denida yanked him off his feet with excessive force and held the guard up by his throat.

"What do you think I'll do? Make out with you?" Denida's eyes wandered to his leg and back. "You may have shot me, but you saw that I know how to kill a soul…"

The guard swallowed, but didn't say anything. The cold sweat on his forehead dripped. "No." He shook his head stubbornly.

Denida threw the guard to the floor and jumped on top of him. "Won't tell me? I have other ways to find out!" He put his hands on the guard's temples, causing guard's memories to flash through his head. "Thanks," Denida whispered before ripping out the guard's heart. He stood and sauntered to the entrance, where he paused to peek at the guard lying on the floor. Denida clenched his fist so tightly that his knuckles turned white, a fire appeared, surrounding his hand, and he lifted it in the direction of the room. "Fire," Denida muttered.

The building burst ablaze as Denida vanished.

He reappeared at Robert's house, but it was deserted. Both Dan and Robert had vanished.

Where are they? Denida strolled through the rooms, looking for any sign of life, but nothing appeared.

'Clank.'

Denida ran outside to the sound, only to find Dan and Robert working on the patio. He sighed loudly. "For heaven's sake!"

Robert and Dan turned to Denida, startled. Both their faces showed genuine concern.

"Before you ask, Whipboy and Lars were not where I thought they'd be, but I know where they are now!" Denida bared his teeth.

The news didn't ease the worry on their faces; it only reinforced it. "Maybe, it's best to forget it," Robert suggested cautiously.

"Never!" Denida insisted, banging his fist on his leg. "They… don't… belong… here." He focused on stabilizing his breathing.

Robert cleared his throat. "Where then?"

"Hell-" Denida spat on the ground. "They've built a fortress at the second Gate!"

Chapter 19- A Chance to get Jack

Nina sat twiddling her thumbs, trying not to glare at Claus, which proved difficult.

The Colonel walked through the door, pulling up a chair next to Nina. "Are you okay? You sure you're ready for this?"

Definitely, let's find out what this 'Jerry' wants to tell us! Nina raised her head and smiled faintly, nodding.

The Colonel patted Susan on the shoulder. "Watch Claus; we'll be back!"

"Yes, Sir!" Susan aimed her gun in Claus' direction.

Nina followed in silence. From the Colonel's stiffness, she knew he disagreed with her desire.

When they entered the room, the Commander was playing cards with Jerry. "Winning?" she sneered.

The Commander scratched his neck. "Not really, he's-"

"You wanted to help us?" The Colonel stepped in front of Jerry. "Can you?" He wrinkled his forehead.

"I'm the second-in-command, Jack trusts me unconditionally!"

The Colonel chuckled. "In other words, you'll take his role after we dispose of him?"

Jerry folded his hands and straightened in his chair. "One man's loss is another man's gain." He wiggled his eyebrows.

The aggressive approach won't work here. Nina took a seat next to Jerry and made her best pair of innocent puppy eyes. "We need you, Jerry." She lifted her hand and put it on top of his. "Won't you help us?"

Jerry knocked on the table with his knuckles. "Isn't that sweet of you to ask, Missy! There's only one problem; I'm not doing it for you, but for number one; me!" He turned to the Commander. "Can you finish him off or not?"

"We'll take care of him, don't worry," the Colonel insisted.

Jerry clicked his tongue against his teeth. "Not just take care of him, destroy his very soul. Do you know how?" He raised his voice. "You need to rip his damn heart out!"

"We will," Nina grimaced.

"How?" The Commander shuffled the cards.

Jerry slammed the table with both of his palms and smiled. "First, you need to understand Jack's very core, his fear for his former master, *Lucifer*."

Intrigued, the Colonel pulled up a chair and sat down. "Why would Jack still fear him?"

"Jack betrayed Lucifer; betraying the Devil has one punishment; death."

Nina shook her head. "That's not possible; he feels secure here."

Jerry chuckled. "The lady's right; Jack likes it here because Lucifer can never physically appear on Earth. Only his demons can. God himself ensured that… which is why Jack made his *paradise* here, where Lucifer can't reach him."

He'll regret feeling safe; I can do just as much damage as Denny! Nina stood and bared her teeth. She approached Jerry and knelt to whisper in his ear. "Don't you worry; I want him dead, no matter the cost."

Jerry nodded. "In that case, I'll set him up for you!" He rose and extended his hand to Nina.

She shook it.

"I'll inform you when I'm ready." Jerry marched out of the room, not meeting anyone else's eyes.

In the following days, Nina grew more impatient; she hated waiting, but there was no other way. *We're so close, yet so far away…* If they fought the Scientist without Jerry, he would be too strong. *We have to consider Maia and Morton's safety, as well.*

Nina kicked the ground. She stood outside, puffing on a cigarette. Claus sat on a bench with Susan hovering over him. She strolled over toward them. "Susan, what's going on?" Nina tried to hide the contempt she felt for Claus.

Susan turned her focus away from Claus for a second. "Airing this one…" Her sight returned to Claus.

Nina grimaced and sat down next to Claus, staring at him without uttering a word. She ran her fingers against each other.

"Something I can help you with, Lady Nina?" Claus raised his eyebrows.

Nina sighed heavily. "You're here because you want to be free, correct?"

Claus shook his head. "I want to prove myself…"

"… It would be a miracle for you to get your freedom by proving yourself, but you *won't* be able to do it," Susan hissed.

Claus shrugged. "The Scientist betrayed me too, you know."

"In exchange for Michelle," Nina retorted.

Susan patted Claus' shoulder. "Time to go back inside!"

Claus waved at Nina and stood.

As soon as he was out of earshot, Susan hunched over next to Nina. "Don't even think it; he can't help."

The Colonel strolled past them, approaching Nina. "Jerry called; he's ready!"

"Finally." Nina rushed to her feet.

The Colonel gathered everyone even Claus, much to Susan's discontent. "Sir! I must object."

"He knows Dark magic; it might prove useful." The Colonel pushed past her with Claus.

Susan frowned with dissent, but nodded. "Alright, but I'll be watching him like a hawk." Susan yanking him into the car's backseat.

They drove toward the spot Jerry's designated rendezvous spot. When they pulled up with the cars, Jerry sat on the hood of his own vehicle, waiting for them with a cigarette in hand.

Nina trudged out.

Jerry discarded his cigarette butt and stepped on it before sauntering over to Nina.

Nina greeted him with an anxious smile, but she shone with anticipation.

"You seem happy," Jerry smirked. He lifted his hands and slowly started taking off his very white gloves, which inexplicably stood out and captured everyone's complete focus. Jerry's hands appeared to be moving in slow-motion as he removed them.

Nina clapped her hands together; they were coated with cold sweat. "Anyway, how do we kill him?"

The Colonel cleared his throat behind her.

"Aren't the rest coming out?" Jerry looked past Nina, the Commander, and the Colonel.

"Negative," the Colonel affirmed sternly.

Jerry rubbed his nose. "Alright. Well the thing is-"

"No!" Nina jabbed Jerry. "Don't even start with the excuses; you promised you would help."

Jerry took a few steps back and held up his hands. "I know, but you see, I changed my mind; I'll help Jack instead…"

Jack? Nina spun around to inspect their surroundings, hoping she was wrong, but she saw it clearly now. "Ambush!" she screamed.

Jerry chortled and raised his gun at Nina.

Everything happened so fast; Nina didn't have time to stake a step. She felt paralyzed, staring in disbelief.

The Colonel yanked her down and pulled her behind the vehicle.

The first bullet narrowly missed her and struck the car. Jerry followed it up with a barrage of shots, as if the first one had been a warning.

The Commander jumped out of the car and waved his hand at them before returning fire. As soon as they climbed back in the car, they drove away at top speed, but it didn't take long before cars met them from the other direction with more guns blazing.

The Commander swerved onto a dirt road and the other cars gave chase.

"We don't have any more bullets." The Colonel clenched his fists. "I don't know how we're gonna get away."

"We disperse." The Commander made a sharp turn through the woods, speeding through the trees. "Jump!"

Everyone jumped from the vehicle and it smashed into a tree. They scurried away from the site.

Their pursuers hurried to check the wrecked car.

"They're gone; spread out! They have to be here." A man waved his hand to signal the others with him.

As they started their search, the Colonel sank into the grass, lying flat on his stomach. "We need to be careful."

The Commander crawled on his elbows and knees. "Should we make a run for it?" he whispered.

The Colonel squinted his eyes, pondering the suggestion. "Negative. We'll take them out one by one; keep Nina safe while the rest of us take care of them…" He motioned for the rest of his soldiers to follow him.

Concern sat like a stone in Nina's stomach as the Commander shimmied over to her, still staying as close to the ground as possible. "Can we really beat them? I doubt Jack would have amateurs working for him."

The Commander stroked Nina's shoulder. "Don't worry," he whispered.

I'm not so sure… Nina pushed the Commander's hand away and sighed as she followed him. A machine gun sounded, and she spun to watch.

The soldiers swarmed the pursuers from every angle, trying to overpower them.

"We'll get a lot of extra firepower from them," the Commander remarked behind Nina.

"If it goes well," she whispered anxiously.

The Colonel snuck up behind the last one and grabbed him, causing the man to drop his gun and reach for the Colonel's arm. The Colonel threw him toward a tree and grabbed the weapon he had dropped, aiming it at the guy's head, ready to squeeze the trigger.

The distinct rumbling of a car's engine approached. The man charged the Colonel.

The Colonel fell to his knees. As the man ran toward him, the Colonel grabbed the man's arms and flipped him, covering the man's mouth with one hand and holding the gun to his temple with the other. "Hush! Make a peep and you're dead."

The car stopped in front of the wrecked vehicle. Jerry stepped out of the car, accompanied by Jack. Jerry analyzed the scene. "Maybe our men are still searching for them?"

Jack grunted. "I hope so… for your sake. Remember what I said; no one here can save you. Fail me and you'll *suffer*!"

Jerry fiddled with his fingers, then darted over to check the wrecked car. Finding nothing useful, he inspected the vehicle his allies left behind. He rubbed the sweat from his forehead and snapped his fingers. "It's a humongous forest; they'll never escape. We'll find them, it'll take time, but we will!"

Jack glanced at Jerry scornfully before passing him. "Take our other car with the rest, *if* you do find them…" He turned to face Jerry. - if they're still alive!" He left in the car they arrived in, leaving Jerry behind with only a few men.

Jerry! Nina bared her teeth and prepared to charge him when she felt the Colonel's hand on her shoulder.

The Colonel shook his head without uttering a word.

Nina kicked the dirt and lowered her head with a low sigh. "Fine; I won't."

Jerry stepped cautiously amongst the trees and strolled a short distance before he turned to his remaining guards, who were still with him. "Anything?"

"Nothing," one man affirmed from farther away.

Jerry turned to the other guy hopefully, but he dropped his eyes and threw up his arms. "Forget this."

"But Sir, if we don't find them, the Scientist won't be happy!" One of the men rushed in front of Jerry with urgency on his face.

Jerry approached the man, focusing on him intently.

The man licked his lips and opened his mouth to say something, but closed it again without saying anything.

Jerry slapped the man's cheek. "Yeah, go find them! Call me when you find them, dead or alive. I'm taking the car." He shoved past the man and climbed into the car that had been left by the first set of pursuers and sped off.

"We can take two," the Colonel winked at the Commander and tilted his head at them.

The Colonel and the Commander carefully crept forward toward the last two men, while Nina watched the other guy the Colonel had left alive.

She aimed the gun at the guy's left eye. "Make *one* wrong move, little one…" Nina squeezed the grip on the gun tightly.

"My name's James! Now that you know it, think about what you're-"

Nina jammed her gun into James' cheek.

"What… do… you want… with me?" James' voice stuttered.

Nina peeked back to see the Colonel and the Commander helping each other to lure the last one into a trap. She narrowed her eyes and smiled coldly. "I want something useful, or perhaps I should just finish you now, like your companions?"

A single gunshot sounded in the distance. James' eyes widened. Nina squinted and started squeezing the trigger.

"Wait!" James screamed with sweat rolling down into his eyes, causing him to blink uncontrollably.

Nina wiped his eyes with her sleeve but kept the gun aimed straight at him. "Yes?"

The Colonel walked up behind Nina. "The Commander's collecting the guns; the problem is that there's no way to escape, now. Our car is wrecked and that Jerry guy just left in the last working car…"

"I can help with that." James lifted his finger.

Nina spun back and pointed the gun in James' face, anger written across her own face.

James buried his head in his hands. "Wait, I know where there's a car you can use!"

Nina and the Colonel turned to each other and Nina nodded to him. She yanked James to his feet. "Take us there."

James sighed and directed them forward as the Commander joined them. Nina held her gun so close that the barrel touched his back. He said nothing, just trudged onward, while his face dampened with sweat. Eventually, they reached an old barn hidden within some bushes. James cleared the leaves and pulled open the barn's heavy door with the Commander's help.

An old white truck coated in gray dust stood inside the barn.

Nina strolled over to the vehicle and peeked through the window. "Does this piece of junk even work?" She glanced back.

James nodded and pointed his finger. "The key's in the glove compartment; go ahead and check."

The Commander opened the door on the passenger side and examined the glove box. "Found it!" He lifted his head out of the car. "They're full of dust, though…"

"The dust means no one will remember about it!" The Colonel lifted the bag that held the guns the Commander had acquired during the skirmish. He marched over and threw them into the car. "Get the windows cleaned and let's get out of here before anyone finds us."

The Commander searched through the barn, digging through drawers and compartments of toolboxes until he found an old rag. He ran back to the car and started wiping the windshield as the Colonel climbed into the vehicle and tried turning it on, but the engine wouldn't start.

As soon as it sounded like it might run, it died down almost instantly. The Colonel peeked over with a disapproving sigh. "Are you sure it has gas?"

James pointed at the gauge. "Try again," he insisted.

The Colonel rolled his eyes but turned the key in the ignition one last time. His eyes widened as it started. He waved his hand. "Come on."

Nina hurried to push James into the truck and the Commander followed. As soon as they were inside, the Colonel set the old vehicle in motion and drove off onto a dirt road running past the barn.

Nina ran her fingers through her long white hair.

"Maybe we should talk to Denny," the Colonel peered back at Nina through the rearview mirror.

Nina slammed her fist into the back of the Colonel's seat. "Never; I won't be able to finish this with Jack; Denny will think it's *too dangerous*," she hissed, baring her teeth.

The Colonel said nothing, choosing to focus on the road instead. He drove out of the forest in the old truck. When they left the woods, he turned onto a highway, but after just a few minutes of driving, the car started to give out and the engine stopped, forcing the Colonel to park on the side of the road. He pressed down to turn it back on, but nothing. The Colonel turned the key to no avail. He kept trying, but it yielded the same result.

"What's wrong with it!" The Colonel slammed the wheel.

"Maybe it was too old after all, Sir." The Commander rubbed his forehead.

The Colonel glared at the Commander annoyedly. He breathed deeply like he was about to yell, but closed his eyes and exhaled without uttering a word. "We escaped from the forest, at least…"

"Open the hood; let me check there." The Commander stepped out of the car, where he poked through the engine compartment before strolling to the back and checking for a jerry can. He stepped back and ran his hand through his hair, slamming the top of the trunk, and walked in front of the side window where he hunched over. "There is no spare fuel. The fuel gauge must be broken; I think we're stuck here…"

The Colonel squinted his eyes at Nina. "Watch him!" He exited the car to talk with the Commander.

The Commander wet his lips. "Sir?"

The Colonel pushed the Commander a few steps away from the car. "We can't-" The Colonel stopped mid-sentence; his mouth hung open as his eyes followed a vehicle braking hard.

The Commander reached for his sidearm, but the Colonel stopped him with his hand and shook his head.

"At ease, Soldier."

Susan jumped out of the vehicle and saluted the Colonel. "Sir, is everything okay?"

"We were tricked." The Colonel bared his teeth. "- but it's not over; we have one of theirs."

Chapter 20- A Second Chance

Susan wants to keep Claus apart from James. The Colonel kept their captive, James, in another room, as far away from Claus as possible. To acknowledge Susan's distrust, the Colonel allowed Susan to keep watch over Claus, while appointing the Commander to watch over their new prisoner in his dimly lit room.

The Commander wasn't joking; it sure is dark in here! The Colonel tried to adjust his eyes, which didn't help much, so he spun to grab a candle and lit it before returning. The Colonel sauntered over to the table where James sat hunched over, snoring.

"He's sleeping." The Commander stood with his shoulder leaning up against the wall behind James, startling the Colonel.

"Not anymore." The Colonel slammed his fist onto the desk and smacked a candle off the table.

James lurched awake and almost fell out of his chair in surprise.

"How do we get to the Scientist? Talk or else." The Colonel clenched his fist around the back of the chair.

James kept his head lowered as he rubbed his eyes. "You need to get him when he's in his private chambers; there's minimal security there…"

His private chambers? The Colonel frowned. "Where are they?"

James raised his head. "All I know is that it's on the top floor of the estate. Only a few of his most-trusted cohorts are allowed entry."

"Lady Nina might get her wish then; this doesn't sound unrealistic," the Commander punched his fist into his other hand.

The Colonel hushed him with a stern gaze.

"Sir. I just mean-"

The Colonel grumbled and stood. "There are no guarantees in life, Commander… especially with a demon…" He left the room. *Wonder where Nina is?*

The corridor was pitch-black, but a small flicker of light shone out from under a door at the other end. The Colonel strolled down the hallway, pausing momentarily to listen to a faint chatter from within the room. He opened the door, revealing Susan and Nina talking in a corner, while Claus was lying at the far end of the room, shackled to a bed.

The Colonel cleared his throat. "Nina, we found a way."

Nina spun around with her eyes fixed on the Colonel.

Susan saluted. "Sir! Am I coming, too?"

The Colonel shook his head. "Negative, Susan; keep an eye on Claus."

The Commander, his unit, the Colonel, and Nina all prepared for a massive chaotic showdown in Jack's homestead. If James kept his word, that is.

They drove to Jack's mansion, but parked off his property so that they wouldn't be detected. Despite Nina's initial protests, they allowed James to lead the way.

I hope trusting him this much isn't a mistake... The Colonel brought up the rear.

They all followed close. James continued farther to a damp cellar. He peeked back nervously before pulling a tapestry aside, revealing a secret entrance. "This is as far as I can go..." His voice trembled.

Nina grunted. "You did well, thank you."

"Are you sure it's fine letting him leave before we-"

"We don't need him anymore..." Nina stared intently at the Colonel.

The Colonel stepped aside, and James scurried away.

The Colonel bared his teeth before turning to continue further into the house. As soon as he reached the next floor, he heard the Commander whisper. *'Hide,'* making him jump back through the doorway.

Two armed guards nodded to Jerry, ended their conversation, and started toward the Colonel and the others.

The Colonel moved his hand to his sidearm.

"Hold it!" Jerry approached and snapped his fingers. "Not that way; you're to watch from the outside!"

One of the guards tapped the other on the shoulder and they walked the other way.

The Colonel exhaled heavily.

"Is somebody there?" Jerry spun toward the door. His eyes narrowed as he reached for his gun.

"Jerry, the Scientist is calling for you!" a loud yell came.

Jerry clenched his jaw and looked toward the door one last time before turning the other way.

That was close... The Colonel stepped out from hiding. "Let's follow him; he's seeing Jack!" He waved his hand and his allies carefully snuck in pursuit of Jerry, wary of their surroundings, except for Nina, who rushed ahead.

"Freeze!" The two guards from before chased her.

The Colonel and Commander charged at the guards, grabbing them from behind and squeezing their necks until they fell lifeless.

The Colonel flicked his fingers at his soldiers. "Stash them in the cellar." He ran after Nina with their other allies, catching up to her outside of Jack's private chambers

"I prepared… plan…" Jack's voice echoed in the distance when they arrived on the upper floor. "I set… meeting…"

"Wait, Sir," Jerry said in a loud voice. "We're using Dark magic on them?"

"Yes," Jack's voice affirmed.

"But won't using so much concentrated Dark magic catch the Devil's attention?"

"I don't care!" Jack shouted. "Lucifer will *never* be able appear here on Earth."

Jerry paced across the room, stopping close to the door, causing his voice to be heard more easily. "He can send Archdemons after you…"

The Colonel crept close enough to peek into the doorway. He saw Jerry kneeling before Jack, who sat in a majestic throne, similar to the one *Danyel, the Dark Angel,* used. He motioned for them to hide. "I have a hunch we need to hear this," he whispered.

Jack chuckled softly. "He has yet to send any. If he does-" He patted Jerry on the shoulder. "I'll deal with them. I've got this; don't worry!"

Jerry sighed heavily before he lifted his head and frowned. "I'll set up the meeting." He spun and hurried out the door.

The others all ducked rapidly and watched as Jack loped down the corridor.

"It's time," Nina hissed and tiptoed with all the others following.

Jack stood hunched over a minibar, where he poured himself a drink. A board creaked under Nina's foot. Jack tilted his head and tossed back the drink before sitting down. "Nina, I'm guessing?"

The Colonel sidestepped to the window to inspect their surroundings. His eyes fell on the fire escape. "This could work if needed," he muttered.

Nina pointed her gun in Jack's face. "Damn straight! The reckoning has come!"

"The reckoning?" Jack grinned and poured himself another drink, eyeing Nina all the while. "What for, Maia and Morton?"

Nina slapped Jack's cheek and blood splattered on the floor. "Daniel!"

Jack spat some blood on the ground and turned to Nina. "Daniel's dead, shouldn't you be more worried about the living," he smirked.

"The living? Is that a threat?"

"How much do you care about, say, Maia and Morton?"

"Not nearly as much as I do my son… and you took him from me!"

Jack scoffed. "I didn't kill him. Medusa-" He bared his teeth. "- who tried to kill me too, did!"

Nina pushed the gun into Jack's eye socket. "Well, she's not here anymore, is she? Besides, she only managed to achieve everything she did because you enabled her!" She yanked him over to the Commander, whose eyes met Jack's for a second. She pushed Jack down on his knees. "Commander, give me your army knife." She demanded, holding out her open hand expectantly.

The Commander's eyes met the Colonel's for a moment.

"Commander!" Nina shouted in a determinedly tone.

The Commander turned to her, startled. He started unwrapping the cloth on the knife when Nina became impatient and tore it from his hands. The Commander's muscles tensed and he started lifting his hand.

The Colonel stepped up to the Commander. "Stand down, Soldier," he whispered. "Denida wanted her to achieve peace; we are here to help her by whatever means…"

Nina ripped off the cloth and threw it on the floor.

Jack lifted his hands above his head. "You really think you can kill me that easily?"

Flames encircled Jack, intensifying until the entire room was illuminated by a tall, unruly fire, which prevented anyone from getting closer to him.

"I'm untouchable!" Jack smirked.

Nina turned to one of the soldiers and yanked the gun from his grip. "We'll see about that!" Her teeth shut tight as she squinted her eyes at Jack.

"No," Jerry stormed over from across the room. He drew his gun, firing as he ran. A bullet grazed Nina's left arm and her weapon clattered to the floor.

The Colonel picked up Nina's gun and fired at Jerry, the bullet hitting Jerry's forehead. He fell to the floor.

"No!" Jack charged from his circle, bursting through the flames. He grabbed Jerry in a tight embrace. "You can't; Lucifer can find his soul because he wasn't shot in the eye." He gazed in horror at the lifeless body in front of him, his eyes darkening as he stood up and turned to face the others. "You killed…" He bared his teeth. "I'll never go back to Hell, but maybe you should." Fire enclosed his body from head to toe.

The Colonel aimed and repeatedly fired at the flames with everyone following suit, but the bullets bounced off Jack's fiery exterior.

Jack chuckled. "I told you; I'm untouchable!" He pushed both his arms forward, sending a stream of flames toward the Colonel and his allies.

Everyone dispersed to hide behind whatever they could find, but Jack didn't stop. He flung dark balls of energy at the furniture they were hiding behind, shattering their cover.

The Commander's men scurried about, desperately seeking safety.

"We need to leave!" The Colonel yelled.

"You want to leave my party?" Jack smirked. He clenched his fist and sent a fierce energy ball toward the Colonel.

The Colonel ducked. The ball shattered the wall behind him, creating a passageway to the outside world. Several guards stood outside and stared up at the house in shock before rushing toward it.

"Perfect; we're using the fire escape!" The Colonel led his soldiers down the rickety black stairs. His other companions stayed in hiding, waiting for an opportunity to follow the Colonel.

"We're coming, Boss!" loud trampling approached.

Nina sighed heavily and stood up.

Jack paused to shoot and glanced at her. "Giving up?"

She gestured behind herself with her hand, indicating to the Commander that it was safe to guide the rest out. "You don't wish to hurt Denida's soulmate, do you?"

***

Jack raised his brow. "*Soulmate*, really? "You have been apart so much, even now... I bet Denida doesn't even know where you are." He reached for his switchblade and tilted it before his eyes. "... Not if I rip out your heart!"

Nina shifted cautiously on her feet. "We're connected in the Underworlds, just like we are here on Earth!"

"Really?" Jack gloated. "How are you connected here on Earth? Young Den never talks with young Nina... How is that a connection?"

"Our souls are connected; they will intertwine on Earth in due time!"

Jack snickered and grinned maniacally. "Not if I were to kill you here, my dear Lady Nina."

"You won't." Nina returned the same predatory smile before she vanished.

She can use magic, here? The hole; she must have gone through there! Jack ran over to the hole in the wall to see the Commander's troop descending the fire escape.

The guards ran into the room with their guns raised. "Where are they, Boss?"

"Down there; after them!"

They rushed to the fire escape in hot pursuit, leaving Jack glaring around the room, perplexed about what just happened.

"Soul forms can't be used here! This must be... a cloaking spell?" he muttered.

'*Yes,*' a low voice said.

"Where are you!" Jack threw fireballs in every direction, finishing the destruction of the room.

***

Nina had left as soon as she'd spoken, heading to the hall where the Colonel stood waiting for her. She let the magic subside and revealed herself.

"Ready to go?"

"For now," Nina said with a glow in her eyes.

Shots sounded in the distance, a telltale sign that their allies had encountered a setback. The Colonel stayed vigilant as he and Nina followed the sound of gunshots.

Suddenly, the Colonel grabbed Nina's arm and dragged her to safety behind a tree. The courtyard they had been approaching was now a massive battleground with Jack's guards firing recklessly across the expanse at a target too far away to see with a brief glance.

The Colonel peeked at what the guards were aiming at, using his arm to keep Nina back while he surveyed the scene.

"We have to save them!" Nina started toward them, but the Colonel grabbed her and dragged her down.

"We need a plan, first." He searched his surroundings, hoping to find something that would help give him an idea.

"The Commander is fighting them on one end…"

The Colonel rolled his eyes and turned to Nina. "Your point?"

"We can attack, too; lock them in a pincer!" Nina winked.

A pincer… The Colonel stared into the air for a second before he turned his eyes to Nina again. He nodded and examined his sidearm to count how many bullets he had left. Afterward, he sighed. "It's not going to be enough to make a pincer…" He rubbed his forehead.

"We need something else then," Nina insisted.

He shook his head and stared at his pistol. "We should have brought Claus; magic could have helped…"

Nina had a glow in her eyes.

The Colonel frowned wearily. "What…"

She rubbed her hands together gleefully. "Trust me," she said in a low, creepy voice.

I've got a bad feeling… The Colonel watched Nina, who had spaced out. "What are you doing?" He knelt close to her and rested his hand on her shoulder, but she didn't move a muscle, still appearing dazed.

Suddenly she turned her focus to him. "All done!"

"What's all done?"

The tall fence behind the Commander flew off its hinges with a thunderous bang. Everyone in the courtyard turned toward the sound. Behind the fallen fence and rising dust, Claus came into view. "Miss me?" He chortled, clenching his fist and blowing into it.

Clouds formed above them. The more he blew into his hand, the darker they grew. Within seconds, the clouds were so dense that it was difficult the breathe. The guards scattered, trying to run inside. The heavy air caused them to pass out before they could reach the house. Claus raised his head. His eyes widened as Jack marched toward them.

"Claus," he sneered.

"This is Dark magic, advanced too!" Claus taunted.

Jack peered at the cloud above them; his eyes widened. "I... see.... that is... really... advanced," he stuttered and turned his head to Claus, licking his lips. "You learn that in Hell or something?"

"Lucifer," Claus scoffed at him.

"The Devil?" Jack frowned with a worried glare. "You were only in Hell a short time; why would Lucifer teach *you,* of all people?"

"Lucifer had a plan for the future. He said he would grant me freedom in exchange for a favor…"

"Lucifer, the man with the horns?"

Claus shrugged. "He didn't exactly appear like that, just a Dark being in a cloud with a cold stare…"

Jack gave a high chortle. "The one thing Medusa taught me was who was in charge of Hell, and it *wasn't* Lucifer." His eyes turned dark, as wind started to swirl around him. "Time to die, Claus!"

"We need to leave, now." The Colonel raced toward the Commander. Behind him, strange dark shapes appeared, devouring every living thing they approached, including Jack's own guards.

Nina gasped at the sight and hurried after the Colonel so fast that she almost stumbled a few times. The other soldiers followed swiftly.

"Susan, come on," the Colonel waved his arms at her.

Susan tried to pull Claus with her, but he ground his feet into the dirt, adamant about staying.

"I have to stop them from following…" Claus raised his arms above his head, creating a portal. Nearly as soon as the portal appeared, demons filed out of it and stormed Jack and the shapes. Claus spun and hurried away with Susan. "They'll be too occupied to follow us…"

Susan grunted. Her eyes darkened with suspicion until she shook her head and ran with the rest of the group, as if the evil's pursuit still posed a threat. was still in pursuit of them. When they reached the cars, the Colonel grabbed Susan's arm. "How did you get here?"

Susan turned to the Colonel. "Nina; she told me in my thoughts that you needed Claus' help…" She clenched her fist. "- but I'm even more convinced, now!"

"About?" The Colonel frowned.

"Claus," Susan shrugged. "He just used strong Dark magic that-"

"To save you all," Claus insisted.

Susan turned with her teeth bared. "- this time!"

"Colonel!" the Commander yelled. "We gotta go!"

The Colonel yanked the cardoor open and pushed Claus in. "Susan, now! That'll have to be a talk for another time!"

As soon as they sat down, Susan hit the gas, and they raced away.

Claus peeked back to see the dark cloud he made gradually shrinking as they drove farther away.

Chapter 21- An Offer

Denida grabbed a bag for supplies, ignoring Robert's disapproving frown. "You really shouldn't go there."

Denida continued with his pack.

"They're more dangerous than when you were here with your son!"

My son... Denida slammed the bag on the table. "So am I! A lot has changed since then..."

"Then be smart and stay away from there!"

Denida zipped up the bag and slung it over his shoulder. "I think what you fail to understand is that *I lost Daniel!* All I can do now, is make damn sure that the demons don't hurt anyone else!" He stomped past him.

Robert pursued him outside. "The little boy I met when you first came here all those years ago... that boy is still within you."

"He's hiding in a long-forgotten place, but keep an eye on Dan for *him,* will you?" *Time for the second Gate!* Denida set the horse into a gallop. It was a long ride, and the road brought many sad memories. Try as he might to avoid thinking about it, he couldn't help but remember the last time he was in that world, heading for the second Gate. *With Daniel...*

As dusk fell, Denida arrived at long last, but the area surrounding the Gate was completely different from what he remembered it being like. Agonized screams echoed from within the grounds.

Denida's horse halted and pulled back with a nervous whinny, not wanting to continue toward the grounds. The birds in the sky cut their circles short to avoid flying overhead. His horse would not obey, so Denida dismounted and the horse galloped the other way.

He sighed as he arched his neck to gaze at the clouds above. *What could be in there that makes all the animals want to avoid it?* Denida tightened his fist and made himself invisible. He sauntered into the dusk and paused as he stepped within the walls. *This feels Dark, like in Hell...* Within the dusk, there was a clear, malicious force that could only be one thing: *the Darkness! I need to see Lucifer and hear the rest of his tale...* Denida squinted to peer through the thick mist, from which he noticed a demon approaching. He shook his head. *No way, Lucifer it is...*

Denida spun around and disappeared, reappearing in Hell a moment later, which didn't feel any different. He followed the ring's directions to Lucifer's mansion.

The demon guarding the mansion transformed and scurried away as soon as Denida came into view.

How long is that demon going to avoid me? Denida rolled his eyes, but didn't give it another thought. He continued inside the mansion and paused in the Hall, where he stood nipping at his upper lip. *That dagger Lucifer had... I wonder if one of the doors leads-*

"Denny." Lucifer manifested right in front of him with his arms raised. "You're back for more!"

Denida lifted his hand. "Shall we?"

Lucifer led the way into his chamber with Denida trailing after him. Denida couldn't help peeking around the hall all the while.

The doors slammed shut behind them as they entered.

"God made more angels; he insisted that they were *just* angels, unlike us. He called me and Gabriel *archangels*." Lucifer leered over the well. "We were never to talk about Odin or our old world. God, Gabriel, and I would be the only ones who knew about our past from then on."

"But? You're showing me your story, so something must have happened!" Denida stopped on the other side of the well.

Lucifer lifted his hand, which was surrounded by Darkness, over the well, causing the water to steam and bubble. He withdrew his hand and an image formed in the well.

***

Lucifer and Gabriel goofed around as they often did, when they noticed a flash from the other side of the Pearly Gates. They hustled to it, only to find Peter standing in front of Odin nervously.

"Gabriel and Azal, I'm here to see Shaddai!"

Peter turned to Gabriel with a frown. "I don't know anyone by that name..."

Lucifer cleared his throat. "I'll handle this." He stepped forward, only to have Gabriel block his path.

"You're not planning on taking him to..." Gabriel tilted his head with intent eyes.

"I am!" Lucifer led Odin to God's home inside Heaven as swiftly as he could.

As soon as they entered, God's attention focused on Lucifer and Odin and he rushed over to greet them. "Odin, welcome, my old friend."

Odin looked around the room before returning a greeting. "Hello, Shaddai-"

"No." God held up his hand. "I go by God here; I'm not Shaddai anymore. Azal calls himself Lucifer now, too."

Odin shrugged. "You've made some changes since Henna..."

God lowered his head. "Such a shame what happened to her... is that why you're here... because you want to join us?"

"*You?*" Odin scorned. "Henna isn't as gone as you seem to think. Her will remains here because she still has... unresolved affairs."

Lucifer and God exchanged a glance.

"She still talks to you? What has she said?" Lucifer asked cautiously.

Odin turned to Lucifer and Lucifer wondered how a god could lose an eye.

"You shouldn't have followed Shaddai," Odin condemned and turned to God.

Does he know? Lucifer felt a chill.

"My name's God, I said," God hissed. "Why are you here then, if not to join Heaven?"

"...To see if Henna was right..."

God charged Odin, but a scepter appeared in a flash out of nowhere, blocking him.

"I'm not as simple a mark as Henna was; I've come prepared," Odin smirked. "This is an offer, *Shaddai*. I urge you to take it before it's too late..." He glanced over at Lucifer. "Azal, it's always a pleasure." He spun around and paced out.

"Can Henna really still be around?"

God shrugged. "I doubt it, but no one ever knew her origins."

"I should check to make sure he really left..." Lucifer jogged out, accompanied by God. They found Odin chatting with Gabriel.

"You're still here? You're not welcome here," God hissed.

Odin waved. "Consider what I said." He stepped over to a horse with eight legs and stroked its mane. "Time to go, Sleipnir." He mounted it and rode off into the distance.

"Who was that?" Peter frowned.

"Should we tell him?" Lucifer scratched his head. "He *is* guarding our Gates..."

God gazed at Lucifer, then at Gabriel, and back at Lucifer before he nodded. "Lucifer, stay to watch over the Pearly Gates." He guided Peter outside of Heaven with Gabriel accompanying them to the old relic, which had a remnant of Henna's material on it.

How can we possibly make amends to Queen Henna? Lucifer sighed.

It didn't take long before God and the others returned.

"Lucifer, you're not to venture alone outside of Heaven anymore; it's not safe. Bring Gabriel with you from now on!" God continued past him, clearly not expecting a reply.

Peter smiled at Lucifer. "Don't worry; I'll keep Heaven safe from anyone wanting to avenge what you all did!"

Lucifer clenched his fist and stalked toward Peter, ready to strike.

Gabriel jumped in front of Lucifer just before he reached Peter. "Lucifer, why don't you show me the world below."

"Go on; I've got this," Peter gloated.

"Lucifer." Gabriel pinched Lucifer's arm and stared.

That's an intense look... "Alright, Gabriel."

Lucifer descended to Earth to scope it out with Gabriel by his side.

"The creatures who live here tend to gather here..." Lucifer pointed.

"I think God is more concerned by the queen and Odin, but this planet is neat. Is this the one she always insisted was of great importance?"

Oh yeah, she did... wonder why that is? Lucifer turned with an empty look and nodded.

"Interesting," Gabriel muttered as he gazed at the greenery in front of them. "Those creatures are the reason?"

Lucifer snorted, unable to keep a straight face. "She was always right, but for all the time I've watched these things, they've done almost nothing except hunt each other..."

"Luci..." Gabriel sat down on a boulder. "Did she really die or could she be with Odin?"

Lucifer peered up at the sky, watching giant creatures flying overhead.

Gabriel became jittery and began to stand up.

"Shaddai stabbed her. I remember her blood and dying gaze, as clear as day..."

Gabriel tapped the boulder with his fingers. "Maybe her spirit still lingers here, wanting vengeance... what is the deal Odin offered, anyway?"

"I don't know. Shaddai threw him out before he could say."

Gabriel stood up. "Then why don't *we* find out what this offer is?"

We? "How? I don't know where Odin is."

A sound of a horse stomping its hoof reverberated from behind them and they turned toward the sound.

"Azal and Gabriel, you wanted to see me?" Odin descended from his horse.

Lucifer and Gabriel exchanged a glance.

"Fine," Lucifer whispered and turned his attention to Odin. "What exactly is the deal you wanted to offer to Shaddai?"

Odin's eyes glowed. "Asking that puts you on the right path. You killed *Henna*. There's only one way to repent; Shaddai must relinquish his divine magic."

Gabriel lowered his head. "He'll never agree to that..."

Odin softly laid his hand on Gabriel's shoulder. "Maybe you can convince him. If you don't, Henna's fury will fall upon both of you, too..."

Gabriel staggered. His knees almost gave out and he grabbed Lucifer's arm before falling to the ground. "Why *us*? How's that even fair? I didn't even know she died until after the fact! And Lucifer only witnessed it-"

"Life wasn't fair when '*God*' killed her. If he rejects the offer, her vengeance will be unleashed, so if both of you-" He squinted his eyes between Lucifer and Gabriel. "- want to live, you'll assure that he takes the offer!" Odin jumped on his horse. "I expect good tidings from you." The horse ascended into the clouds.

Gabriel dropped down on his boulder with a blank face.

Lucifer kicked and slammed a tree, making fruit drop from its branches. "Cursed Henna," he hissed.

"Maybe we should… at least attempt…"

Lucifer turned with a low sigh. "You know what he'll say! He'll never…"

"Maybe he'll surprise us. We'll never know if we don't try… or am I wrong?"

"Fine, we'll try, but I'd better do the talking. You probably shouldn't say anything…"

They returned to Heaven, which now had even more people swarming within it.

"More servants," Lucifer scoffed as he strolled toward God's chamber.

They both gawked at the sight that met them; a massive throne on a golden pedestal towered over everything from the center of the room.

"What-"

"- is that?" Lucifer finished the sentence.

"Like my throne? I can see all of Heaven from up there," God gloated, walking up to them. " How did the trip go?"

"Well," Gabriel started.

Lucifer lay his hand on Gabriel's shoulder and stepped forward. "Odin appeared again. He told us why you should take his deal… and what *exactly* the deal is!"

God frowned. "Well?"

"Henna wants you to relinquish your divine powers for her to forgive-"

"Never!"

"If we don't, Odin said Henna will avenge her death by killing all of us; you, Gabriel, and me." Lucifer glanced at Gabriel.

God's eyes darkened. "What can Odin do? He's a god, like me, but I'm still stronger than him and destined for more than he'll ever know. I say, let him come! Besides, I already made more '*angels*' to stop anyone from getting in. You'll be safe; I'll protect you both."

"But he knows stuff he shouldn't!"

God stared at Lucifer, not saying anything for what felt forever, before turning and marching out. Lucifer followed as God stomped straight to Peter.

"No one is to enter under any circumstances. Am I clear?" God's eyes were a little less dark, but they still had a different aura about them. He spun to face Lucifer. "You, my trusted friend…" He put his arms on Lucifer's shoulders. "- are to help him. No one leaves Heaven in the foreseeable future!"

***

The image faded from the well and the water settled down.

Denida raised his head. "Yes? Why are you stopping?"

"I assumed this would be a good time for a break. You usually need to attend to matters in your Underworld?"

"That's an *Ass*-sumption! I have more time for you, now." Denida leaned over the well. "What happened with Odin, next? I presume when God didn't agree to take the deal, a confrontation happened?"

Lucifer chortled. "That's putting it mildly…" He lifted his hand over the well and the image in the water returned.

***

Lucifer sat at the Pearly Gates with Gabriel and Peter, gawking. *I wonder how Odin will take the news…* As he finished the thought, an eight-legged horse came into view. *Odin.* "Gabriel, go get God." He waved his hand.

Gabriel sped into Heaven, while Lucifer stepped forward to greet Odin.

Odin descended from the horse, extending his arm, and a scepter appeared in his hand.

Lucifer peeked into Heaven, but there was no sign of God yet, so smiled at Odin meekly. "Welcome."

"Azal, I need to see your *God*, who will hopefully bring good tidings."

"You shall, but-"

Odin slammed his scepter into the clouds below him, causing them to tremble. "I'm but a messenger for my queen- *your* queen, too. I… demand… an… answer!"

"Then, I'll give you one." God appeared with Gabriel cowering behind him.

Odin turned with a hopeful gaze.

"Henna's dead." God's eyes darkened. "- and you're not welcome here, ever!"

Odin lowered his head. "She thought you would say this, so-"

"She didn't think *anything*; she's no longer. She was never anything but a pathetic queen, who died by my hand. Her blood is on *my hands* and I am *proud* of it!" God raised his voice. "If you're smart, you'll leave before you face a similar fate!"

"Smart?" Odin scratched his beard. "Perhaps not, but I'm loyal, which you should have been, but alright. Seeing as you've made up your mind, I'll leave." He climbed on his horse and tilted his chin to Lucifer. "Azal, remember what I said…" His horse jetted through the clouds.

"We won't suffer, will we?"

"Don't worry," God patted Lucifer on the back.

Lucifer couldn't help but feel uneasiness creep into his core. He peered back at the spot where Odin had been. "I hope you're right…"

God smiled and returned to Heaven. Nothing happened in the following days. Despite them expecting it, neither Odin nor his followers made any effort to contact them.

Maybe God was right. Lucifer started to feel at ease. He sauntered through Heaven, until angels speeding toward God's chamber pushed him aside.

Lucifer rolled his eyes. *He won't like you all just going in.*

A second later, Gabriel grabbed his arm, huffing and puffing, trying to breathe.

Lucifer yanked his arm free. "Watch it, Gabriel!"

Gabriel wiped the sweat from his forehead, peering in the direction of the Pearly Gates. "I'm sorry, old friend." He grabbed Lucifer's arm again and suddenly kneed him in the stomach and yanked him with him, sprinting in the same direction as the angels. Just like the other angels, Gabriel burst in without asking permission. He slammed the door shut behind him.

The faces throughout the room glared nervously at each other.

"It won't affect us!" God yelled insistently.

"*It won't?* What-"

A rumble echoed through the room. The ground of clouds shook as if there were an earthquake ripping through it.

Lucifer's eyes widened and he sauntered over to God's side. He stared into his eyes before he approached the throne where God could see all of Heaven and the planet below. He gasped at the sight which met him. *It's happening again… here?*

A gigantic meteor hurtled past Heaven toward Earth with fantastic speed. Lucifer could not help but watch as it streaked toward the planet below, where he had been so many times.

The meteor increased in speed until it slammed into the planet below them. *This is remarkably similar to what happened in God's other world…* The impact caused debris to break from the planet and fly into its orbit. Even Heaven shook at its core.

"It's going to reach us!" Lucifer screamed.

"Not possible," God smirked and held up his hand. The very same dagger that killed Henna appeared in his grasp. He muttered something and made a swiping motion with the blade. A bright light appeared, emanating from the knife, spreading until it encompassed them, then all of Heaven and beyond, repelling the flames as it grew.

Lucifer met God's eyes for a moment before God lowered his arm and the dagger vanished. '*We need to talk,*' he spoke to God's mind.

God winked. '*I know.*'

Lucifer peered at the planet below them, which was now covered in nothing but flames and a rising dust cloud. *Maybe Henna is wrong about this world being vital for the future...*

'*She's not; she destroyed this like she did my last world. It's her master plan,*' God's thoughts said.

* * *

"Wait!" Denida slammed the water with his fist. "Your queen made the meteor kill the dinosaurs on Earth?" Denida frowned, not trying to hide his disbelief.

"If you doubt me, why not ask Gabriel?"

Why didn't I think of that! Denida bit his upper lip and spun around. He squeezed his hand tightly and vanished from sight. He resurfaced outside of Heaven's Pearly Gates.

Saint Peter bared his teeth at the sight of him. "Denida," he hissed.

Denida pushed through the crowd in front of him to make his way to where Peter stood. "I need to see Gabriel."

Peter clenched his fist while his eyes wandered through the crowd watching him. A smile appeared on his face. "You'll have to wait your turn, *Denida,*" he smirked.

"No need, I'll take him." Archangel Michael appeared from within Heaven.

Denida sneered as he walked past Peter, who watched his every move as he entered Heaven with Michael.

"Nice to see you, Denny." Michael gave the same warm smile Denida remembered. Michael led Denida through Heaven toward God's chamber.

Denida couldn't keep himself from gaping like Dan had in every world they passed through. *How it has truly changed since what Lucifer showed me, yet it still hasn't... if those memories are true.*

Inside, Gabriel stood in front of God. They stopped talking as soon as Denida entered.

Michael cleared his throat. "Denida wanted to see Gabriel."

"I'm in an audience-"

God shook his hand. "We're done; go ahead."

Gabriel nodded and marched over to lead Denida out. "Why are you here? You usually just summon me."

Denida shook his head. "This is too important!"

Gabriel folded his hands. "How so? What can I help you with?"

Denida scanned the area. His eyes fell on Heavani's tower, which soared into the clouds. *Wonder how Heavani is?*

'She's fine,' Gabriel spoke in Denida's mind. *'- but I have a feeling that's not why you're here.'*

Denida lowered his head. "It's not," he said under his breath. He raised his head and stared at Gabriel. *"Henna!"*

Terror grew in Gabriel's eyes like nothing Denida ever witnessed. He took a step back, his eyes watering as he peered around them nervously. "Come," he commanded, grabbing Denida, disappearing from Heaven, and reappearing back at Dynasty, where he turned to face Denida. "How do you know that name?"

Denida wrinkled his forehead. "You know it, don't you?"

"Of course, I know *Queen Henna!*" Gabriel yelled. "- but how… do… you?"

"Lucifer…"

Gabriel sighed heavily. "He should not have told you about her…"

"She caused the destruction of the dinosaurs?"

Gabriel lowered his head in shame. "Seems so, but how much has he told you?"

Denida shrugged. "Nothing much following that…"

Gabriel nodded, put his hands on Denida's shoulders. "Whatever you know, best to keep it to yourself. Promise me you will?"

"You confirmed it, now. I've got no reason-"

"No excuses… *promise!* It's vital, Denida!" Gabriel's gaze was intense and his eyes locked with Denida's in desperation.

"Fine." Denida felt uneasy. "I'll try…"

Gabriel stared at him for a moment and nodded.

Chapter 22- Lars

Denida wore a bandana over his face to avoid any unsought attention inside the Darkness. He approached the demons keeping watch over a wall surrounding the Gate. *Wonder how I'll get past them?* He slowed down, taking leisurely short steps while pondering how to solve that enigma.

Demons passed him with ease, given his pace, and the guards started to notice him.

Denida drew in a deep breath and increased his pace, stopping at the wall around the second Gate, where there was a line of demons waiting to enter through a well-guarded opening. He scanned his surroundings, trying to come up with an idea, *any* idea. *I'm still blank...*

"You're too low-level for a demon!" The guard jabbed his fist inside of a demon's body and ripped out its still-beating heart. He shredded it and threw it to the ground. With a flick of his fingers, a crowd of demons dragged the body away.

Denida's eyes sparkled. *I know what'll work!*

The man in front of him was granted passage and Denida was next in line.

"We only allow-"

"Top demons, such as an archdemon; I know." Denida's eyes, which were all the guards could see of his face, flickered a murky red. "You really doubt that I'm one? Would you like me to show you?" He chuckled sadistically.

The guard shook his head rapidly and jumped aside. "Please." He gestured his hand for Denida to enter.

Denida stepped through the gap in the stonewall. The Darkness in the air felt even denser inside the perimeter.

Time to find them! He marched forward, examining everything he passed. The enclosure was brimming with demons, so he kept his red eyes active.

Denida stopped when he reached the Gate, which stood in the center of the enclosure, as everything had been built around it. It towered into the sky and had more demons guarding it than perimeter's entrance.

Denida lowered his head and rubbed his forehead. *Daniel…* The crack of a whip sounded behind him, causing him to turn his head.

Whipboy stood whipping a man, who was covered in welts. Blood ran down his back, but he still tried crawling away. Whipboy lashed the man more aggressively. Eventually, he succumbed to the pain and collapsed into the dirt.

"That's no fun." Whipboy grinned. His eyes narrowed, and he whipped the ground. "Red Eyes, have we met?" He sauntered up to Denida.

"I'm an old friend of your boss."

Whipboy raised his eyebrows. "You know Lars?"

"Yes." Denida turned to face Whipboy. "- and you're Whipboy. Your name precedes you."

"Oh? I'm intrigued!" Whipboy's eyes brimmed with the same anticipation as a young child's.

"You're the one who killed Sheriff Mick and the rest of the law."

Whipboy blushed, throwing his hands up. "Half true, I only killed some of them. Lars killed off Sheriff Mick when Lucifer visited, searching for Denida."

What! "I see… speaking of which, I need to see Lars. You wouldn't happen to know where he is?" Denida smirked.

"Nope." Whipboy slashed the whip into the ground. "Probably at the mansion overseeing everything. Lars leaves us to do the grunt work nowadays." He pointed his finger up at a hilltop, which had an estate on top it.

Denida turned his head. *That's new…* "Thank you, Whipboy." He waved and ventured up the hill.

"Until next time." Whipboy waved back before turning to the man groveling on the ground and starting to show signs of life again.

Don't you worry; we shall meet again… after Lars. Rage burned in Denida. He clenched his fist so tightly that his knuckles turned white. *Mick, my old friend, Lars will pay for this!*

As he climbed the hilltop, Denida encountered fewer demons, but the ones he passed were users of advanced Dark Arts.

"Halt!" A demon pounded the ground with a pitchforked spear, causing the entrance to the hilltop in front of Denida to light ablaze.

Denida paused and turned his head to the demon. "Did you want something?"

"I doubt you can continue without talking to me," the demon gloated.

"Are you sure about that?" Denida flicked his fingers and the fire was snuffed out in an instant.

The man squeezed his spear tightly, gasped, and licked his lips.

Denida stared at the guard in front of him with his eyes burning red.

The man stepped back and knelt. "I'm sorry; please pass!"

Denida grunted and continued up the hill, letting the red in his eyes vanish, instead avoiding eye contact with any demons who passed by.

After a long climb, he finally reached the top, where he found a grand estate. *Very unbecoming of an old western world, but here it is, in all its... glory.* The Darkness up there was so thick that it blocked out any light from the sky, let alone anything from below.

Denida marched up to the front door, which was unguarded, much to Denida's amazement. He paused outside the door, not touching its handle. *Is this a trap? Guess there's only one way to find out...* He grabbed the handle and opened the heavy door. Within, the only light in the room emanated from red candles lining the corridor.

"Welcome, how may we help you?" A demon appeared before him. *There's not much Dark magic coming from him. He can't be a high demon!* "Who are you?"

The man dropped to one knee. "I serve Master Lars."

A measly servant! Denida chortled and gestured for him to rise. "I'm here to see your master!"

The man guided him to a set of chairs, where several other demons sat awaiting an audience with Lars. "Wait here; I'll call for you when it's your turn."

Denida sat on an empty seat in between two demons, one of which sat as cold as stone, while the other kept tapping his foot.

"This is taking too long," the impatient one with the restless foot bit his finger.

"Then you'll be happy; you're up," the man who guided Denida appeared next to the impatient demon.

"Finally!" He jumped up and followed the servant.

Denida glared around the room. None of the demons acknowledged each other as they awaited their turn. No one even looked at the demons standing up to meet with Lars. A few more arrived after Denida, but the waiting room continued to grow less crowded as time wore on. Denida's wait felt eternal. *I've got to be patient. This is the only way... and Lars must pay!*

"Sir, it's your turn," the servant approached to Denida.

Finally. Glee filled Denida's heart. *Wait, I'm like that demon who was impatient earlier...*

"Sir?" The servant frowned.

Denida nodded. "Sorry, I'm coming." He followed the man, who led him down a corridor lit with the same red candles as the first hallway.

At the end of the corridor, the man turned. "This elevator will take you to Lars- your bandana, please?" He held out his hand.

"My- why?"

"You know him, right? If that's the case, why would you need to hide your face?"

He's got a valid point... Denida nodded and began to remove the bandana, ensuring that his eyes glowed red as he handed it to the demon.

The servant smiled and opened the door. Denida strolled into the elevator and the door closed. A number on a screen near the elevator door started incrementing as the elevator ascended, but it didn't take long for dusk to set through the elevator, making it hard to see the count.

The elevator came to such an abrupt halt that Denida could feel it jostle him. A beep sounded and the door opened. He stepped out into a room with a vibe very reminiscent of the maliciousness plaguing Hell.

"*Howdy mowdy!*" Lars sat on a throne, raising a glass to welcome him.

Denida said nothing, just lifted his hand and waved, while taking short steps toward him.

"How may I-"

"Lucifer," Denida said in a deep voice.

The very mention of the name made Lars' eyes widen. He put the glass down and fell to the floor, kneeling subserviently. "What does the Dark Prince desire?"

Denida paused, his red eyes gazing intently at Lars, making him sweat. "... This was the last world Lucifer saw Denida in before he returned to his homeworld..."

"Denida? You mean 'Little Evil?'"

"*Sheriff* Denida! He was the law here, once." Denida clenched his fist.

"I'm well-aware! Is he important to the Dark Lord?"

Denida took a step forward. "What about Sheriff Mick? Whipboy says you took care of him."

Lars wiped his forehead as the cold sweat almost reached his eyes. "The Dark Lord wanted them gone-"

"Gone? How did you accomplish this?"

"I shot him... in the eye... before torching the village..."

The red in Denida's eyes turned to charcoal. He warped forward, slamming Lars against the wall. "You *killed* his soul?"

"I... I... thought it was... best," Lars stuttered. "Why does the Dark Lord care? It was so long ago..."

Denida threw Lars to the floor and clenched his fist, making the room light up. "He doesn't; I'm the one who cares!"

Lars peered around the room confusedly. "You? Are you an archdemon or something?"

Denida leered at Lars. "Your *Little Evil* is back!"

Lars bolted toward the elevator.

Denida rolled his eyes and folded his hands together, appearing in front of the elevator. "Sorry, Lars… we're not done, yet." He pushed his arm forward, sending Lars flying back across the room, slamming him into his throne.

Denida casually strolled toward Lars, lifting his finger. "You did something bad to a dear friend of mine!"

"I'm not a weakling!" Lars slammed his fist into the ground, creating a cone around him.

Denida stopped outside of the cone, where he rubbed his forehead. "This will only delay your punishment. I can wait!"

Lars stepped in front of him and stood opposite him, with only the cone's wall between them. "I'm not done, yet. Lucifer wanted you," he gloated.

Denida shook his head. "You'll regret this."

"I doubt it!" Lars stepped back. "Reficul, Reficul, Reficul," he chanted.

A cloud formed next to Lars, its Darkness filling the cone. It faded within a second and Lucifer appeared next to Lars.

"You called?"

Lars fell to his knees and bowed. "Welcome, Master! The one you desired… I present him to you!"

Lucifer frowned. "You summoned me to talk in code? You'd better tell me why I'm here or get ready to face my wrath!"

"Wait!" Lars lifted his hands. "'Little Evil.'" He pointed at Denida.

Denida winked. "Miss me, Luci?"

Lucifer drew in a deep breath. "I'm guessing you want them gone from this world, too?"

"What I want-" Denida smirked. "… or what *you* want… I wonder which is most vital?" He raised his eyebrows.

"My Lord?" Lars stepped back, his eyes wandering back and forth from Denida to Lucifer.

"When you're done with him, I'll be expecting you!" Lucifer lifted his hands and the cone vaporized. "Goodbye, Lars." He vanished into a dark cloud and disappeared with it.

"Guess Darkness is useless to you, now," Denida gloated.

As if in protest, Lars lifted his fist. Darkness encircled it, forming a vortex in front of him, from which several demons emerged. "Kill him!"

The demons charged Denida, who raised his ring, sending a beam of light in the demons' direction, vaporizing them. The light continued into the portal, devouring it completely.

"That's the best you've got? Disappointing!" Denida stormed forward.

"Wait!" Lars held up his finger with wide eyes. "Step closer and I'll be forced to use my last ace, which you won't like!"

"You will die shortly, Lars. If you've got an ace, I suggest you to use it, but there's no saving you!"

"As you wish." Lars smiled broadly. "Time to meet your demise, *Little Evil*." He grabbed a knife from a hilt on his belt and slashed his palm. Clutching his fist, he raised his knuckles high above his head. "Whippy, I call ye forth!"

As the first drop of blood spilled on the floor, Whipboy appeared with his foot covering it, still clutching his blood-soaked whip. "My, my, this looks intriguing."

"Denida-"

Whipboy struck the ground near Denida's feet with his whip. "That's who you are..." He strolled across the room toward Denida, his whip trailing behind him. "I've always had an inkling about you, ever since we met with your son."

"I wanted to-"

"What you *want* matters not," Whipboy sniggered.

"Not what I meant." Denida rolled his eyes. "I meant; I intended to kill you *after* Lars!"

Whipboy started laughing and shook his head as if to stop himself.

"Since you insist," Denida winked and raised his fist. A dark shade emanated from it, tearing across the room to create a shield.

"It will only stop us for now, but your death will cancel the spell."

Denida shrugged. "I'm counting on it."

"Then you shouldn't have cast it! I summoned Whipboy, not to kill you for me, but to *assist* me in killing you." Lars stood next to Whipboy, whom he stroked on the shoulder. "Let's finish off the mighty 'Little Evil.'"

Wicked glee appeared in Whipboy's eyes as he lashed the whip in Denida's direction.

Denida rolled on the floor, but the slashes continued coming, breaking everything they struck.

Lars aided Whipboy by attacking with dark energy, shattering anything Denida tried using as cover.

The whip struck Denida's back, vaporizing his shirt under the lash. The pain was agonizing. Denida gritted his teeth. Another slash made contact with his legs and he collapsed.

I must... Denida started raising his hand, but the strikes kept coming, which brought his fingers to uncurl with each slash.

Whipboy grabbed his hand. "My, my, intriguing." He removed the ring from Denida's hand.

Denida groaned louder as the ring's power that boosted his own was taken from him.

Whipboy turned to Lars. "Isn't this the magic ring Lucifer wanted?"

Lars took the ring and held it up to the light. "It is, but Lucifer seems to be in cahoots with Denida nowadays."

"So what?" Whipboy smirked. "It can be a good bargaining chip if we ever need it."

"You… can't… use," Denida stuttered from the floor, extending his arm, desperately trying to reach it.

"We know we can't use it!" Lars shrieked and pulled Denida from the floor.

"We can't?" Whipboy shuddered. "Wait, what's that!" He reached for a creased object peeking out of Denida's shirt pocket. He unfolded it to reveal a picture of Denida standing beside Nina, who cradled an infant in her arms. He showed it to Lars. "Looks like he has a family we can pay a visit to…"

Lars shook Denida. "Where are they?" He grabbed the photo and flashed it in front of Denida.

"That… I forgot… I had that," Denida inhaled deeply.

"I said, where are they!" Lars clenched his nails around Denida's throat.

Denida gritted his teeth and shut his eyes.

Lars threw him to the floor and grabbed the picture. tearing it apart. "Enough of this!" He glared down at the ring with renewed focus. "The magic in that ring chooses one master and it has *never* been a user of the Dark Arts…"

"Wrong!" Whipboy roared. "Denida was a demon!"

"Was…" Denida staggered to his feet, but Lars kicked him back to the floor. He glared at the two demons. "It decides based on what lies deep within your… heart." He coughed up blood on Lars' carpet. *Nina…*

"For the Darkness' sake!" Lars threw up his hands.

Darkness' sake? Henna! "Want to know why Lucifer wanted… to protect me?"

Whipboy raised his whip, ready to strike. Before he slashed it, Lars grabbed his arm.

"Sure, why would the Prince of Darkness protect you? Trying to get you back in the fold?"

Denida shook his head. "He gave that up in favor of another motive…"

Lars lowered his hand. "Now I'm interested. What could that other motive possibly be?"

"Well…" Denida attempted to stand.

Whipboy kicked him back down and lashed his whip next to Denida. "Talk. You're not getting up!"

"Henna!"

Whipboy shared a confused look with Lars before he turned back to Denida. "Who's that?"

"The goddess, who prophesized about me," Denida gloated. "The child more powerful than-"

Whipboy started laughing until he managed to stop himself. *"You?"* he mocked. "You are *nothing* without your ring." He leered at Denida. "Let's just kill him!" Whipboy tilted his head at Lars. "I'll tear out his heart and you can have his so-called powers, Lars."

Lars tossed the ring into the air and grabbed it with his other hand, putting it on his finger immediately. "Let's see." He clenched his fist tightly, standing still for several minutes, peering at the ring.

Whipboy slashed his whip around Denida, making him squirm to avoid it.

"Nope, it doesn't work for me. In that case…" Lars marched up to Denida, tapping Whipboy's shoulder as he passed. Lars' eyes were blank, but grew with Darkness as Denida stared into them. He sneered and started kicking Denida in the groin and stomach.

Denida was too weak to fight, though he didn't stop trying.

Lars' rage ended with a final kick to Denida's face, causing blood to spatter the walls. "You should have killed me off right away." Lars ran his hand over his cheek and turned to step away, only to spin, run back, and assault Denida with one last kick.

"Had your fun?" Whipboy raised his brow. "What do we do with him, now?"

Lars paced over to his desk and withdrew a glove from a drawer. "First, I will assure the ring stays safe on me… with no one being the wiser!" He put on the gloves. "Secondly, lock him up. The mighty 'Little Evil' can scare off any demons messing with us… plus, we can always rejoice in beating him up whenever we want!"

"Good idea!" Whipboy saluted gloatingly and carried Denida away.

Chapter 23- Mission to Save Denida

Dan disassembled a revolver and laid it out on the table in front of him.

Fascinating! Dan picked up a part and examined it closely by candlelight. *So simple, yet so advanced...*

Robert walked over to the window to peep out. He grunted in displeasure and returned to his seat at the table.

"Something the matter?" Dan scratched his head, but didn't take his eyes off his work.

"I don't like it; Denny's been gone a while."

Dan shrugged and finally spared Robert a glance. "He can handle himself... he always has!" He resumed focusing on the pieces in front of him.

Robert grabbed a pack of cigarettes, lit one, and took a deep puff.

Dan coughed and wiped his hand through the big cloud of smoke wafting through the air.

"Don't like smoke, huh?"

No," Dan coughed. "Where I'm from, you can't smoke inside most buildings!"

Robert's eyes grew round. "You're kidding!"

Dan shook his head and returned to his work.

Robert's eyes narrowed. "What are you doing with that gun?"

"Improving it." Dan started to reassemble it.

"By taking it apart?"

"Adding stuff to it, too," Dan smirked. He continued to piece it together. Picking it up, he sauntered over to Robert and handed him the revolver. "All done!"

Robert glared at it nervously before taking it for inspection. "Why's it have a second barrel?"

Dan winked. "It shoots two bullets simultaneously!"

"Two? How's that useful?"

"If the first doesn't kill the target, the second will!" Dan pointed his thumb back over his shoulder. "Come on; let's test it out." Dan pushed Robert outside onto the porch. The evening sun was setting in the distance, leaving a dim streak of light shining over the field, stretching over the horizon. Dan tilted his head toward the barrels.

Robert grunted, but stepped to the edge of the patio and aimed.

"It's a beautiful night tonight." Gabriel appeared next to Dan.

Dan nipped at his lip. "Gabriel, why are you here?"

"I just wanted to see how you're doing. I see Denny isn't here… shouldn't he be back by now?"

Denny? "Do you know something we don't?" Dan raised his voice.

Gabriel lifted his hand. Everything around him and Dan froze in time. "I'm an archangel, Dan. I never do things for no reason; I never have and I never will." He patted Dan on the shoulder. "I believe Robert knows where the second Gate is. Don't you wish to examine it?" He smiled tenderly.

"This is awesome!" Robert yelled ecstatically.

The world started to come alive again. In an instant, Gabriel vanished as if he had never been there at all.

Robert handed Dan the revolver. "You're right."

Dan grabbed it, still dazed. He examined the gun absentmindedly before raising his head. "Let's go see Denny. The second Gate… you know where it is, right?"

"I… don't… think…" Robert stepped back.

"Something's up; I can *feel* it. I bet you do, too… But if you won't help me, I'll find someone who will!" Dan clenched his fist.

Robert grinned. "No, Denny would never forgive me…" He trudged inside the house.

Is he going to help me or not? Dan frowned, but didn't follow. *Should I check on-*

Robert trudged back outside, carrying two saddles. "Come on." He marched toward the barn.

Saddles? Oh no… "Wait!" Dan hurried after him. He caught up with him inside the barn, where Robert prepared two horses for departure. "I can't… ride those." Dan pointed a weak, jittery finger at the horses.

Robert paid him no mind. He just continued saddling the horses and adjusting their bridles and reins. When they were ready, he turned to Dan and extended his hand. "Shall I help you up?"

"No, no…" Dan shook his hands. "Not… that."

"Okay, we're not going after Denny, then." He lowered his hands and started to unbuckle one of the satchels.

"No!" Dan rushed forward and hoisted himself up onto the saddle. "O-kay… how do I…"

"Not that hard, just follow my lead." Robert nudged Dan up onto the back of the horse and handed him the reins.

"Is this saddle gonna keep me from falling off?" His eyes widened.

Robert chuckled. "It's seventy percent safe… give or take." He set his horse in motion.

"That's still thirty percent unsafe!" Dan's horse started following.

Robert slowed down on a hilltop, from which he could scope out the area. "It's down there, but you can't see it because of that thick air around it. Are you sure you want to go inside that Darkness?" He gestured toward the dark cloud that shrouded the valley in front of them.

"We have to; Denny's in there…"

"In that case, we need to find a way inside, other than through the front. Let's circle it…"

"I'll wait here!" Dan jumped down from his horse and crouched.

Robert grumbled, but with a shake of his head, he gently squeezed the horse's sides with his heels to bring it to a slow trot, and started to ride around the dark cloud, while Dan watched the front of the cloud intently.

A lot of people passed through the Darkness under Dan's watch. Each time someone emerged from it, their red eyes and demonic features gradually became less pronounced until they were in a human form.

Dan licked his lips. *I wonder if only demons come here?*

"I've got something." Robert trudged up to Dan, gently leading his horse with the reins.

"Why aren't you on…" Dan pointed at Robert's horse.

"We're better off going the rest of the way on foot." Robert tilted his head upward. "I found a place where the cloud is weaker, so the magic isn't as strong…"

"How can you tell the magic is weak?" Dan frowned.

"We had to learn that sort of thing in this world; Darkness reigns here." Robert led Dan around the cloud, staying low to the ground as he circled it, leering back every few paces.

Dan squinted his eyes as they drew closer to the back of the cloud, noticing that it was a shad of grey, not nearly as thick as it was from other angles. *That looks weaker, for sure!* When Robert stepped forward, Dan tensed. "You think it's safe?" Dan shifted his watering eyes toward Robert.

"Safe or not, I'm going regardless. You can stay out here if you wish!"

Dan grabbed Robert's arm, stopping him from proceeding into the Darkness. "I thought you didn't believe me?"

Robert lifted a revolver Dan had modified. "I still don't, but I have to go, just in case. One must always do what's right!" He pushed past Dan and entered the Darkness.

Dan stood stunned, his eyes wide with an empty gaze at the hole in the otherwise impenetrable Darkness. *Screw it*! He stormed through it. It was nearly pitch-dark inside, as the sun's light couldn't penetrate the cloud. Massive fires in the road lit the ground and caused Dan to gasp.

"Took you long enough." Robert stood leaning against a boulder. He lazily lifted his hand to gesture toward the fires. "Good news is you're gonna get used to smoke, now."

"This… the Darkness is so thick…"

Robert simply nodded. "If Denny had taken care of everything, it would be gone. Something must have happened…"

Dan rubbed his hands together. "Yes, but how do we find him?"

Robert lifted his revolver, pointing it at the hilltop. "There's some sort of building up there. I'd wager that's where the leaders are!" He started jogging.

Dan hurried after him, but kept his head down, avoiding eye contact with any passersby. He suddenly halted and raised his head to take in the sight of a massive structure. *The Gate!* He stared and rubbed his mouth.

Robert noticed Dan's hesitation and returned to check on him, only to see what Dan's eyes were locked on.

Robert reached for Dan's neck and pulled him close. *"Not now!"* He grabbed his arm, yanking him forward.

"Halt!" A demon stepped forth on the hilltop and held his arm out to his side. "Only demons who wield advanced Dark Arts are allowed past here."

Dan nodded, swiftly turning to descend the hill, but Robert stepped in front of him.

"We've been summoned- for Denida!" Robert didn't waiver, his eyes pinning the demon. Even when the demon approached him, his stare remained unyielding, the malice increasing in concentration with each passing second.

"Call Whipboy," the demon said to his fellow guard, without taking his eyes off Robert.

"We can't; he's torturing someone. If you want to interrupt that, be my guest…"

The demon glared at his accomplice and stepped back. "Let him know I need to see him!" He turned to Robert. "Let's go see Denida- I'll take you!"

Dan lifted his head so that his eyes met Robert's for a short moment. Robert shoved him forward after the demon.

The demon guided them to the cliff. The Darkness grew denser with each step.

"Make sure he can't see you struggling to breathe," Robert whispered. "Demons are supposed to breathe just fine up here!"

Dan scratched his nose, breathing in heavily behind his hand.

The demon didn't seem to take notice. He plodded along, still ascending the hill.

Robert followed in front of Dan, breathing more casually.

Dan gazed at Robert, then glanced back. *He's done this before, but I wonder if we'll get there before this whip guy returns...*

The demon reached the top of the hill, where a grand mansion stood, but he turned away from the house, walking down a rugged dirt road.

At the end of the road, Dan's eyes widened at the sight of something he recognized. *A magic barrier!*

In a cone, the only place on the hilltop that was not covered by dark mist, Denida lay on the ground, covered in bruises and soaked with blood.

"He's out cold," Robert said.

The demon smirked. "Looks like Whipboy had his fun with Little Evil, but couldn't do too much. Lars wants him alive for some reason..."

Dan stood frozen, unable to wrench his eyes from the bloody mess that was his friend. *How?* He sighed. "We're not done with him!" He stepped closer to the cone as Denida groaned in agony.

"More fun with 'Little Evil,' sure!" The demon charged into the cone and lifted Denida off the ground. "Missed us?" he sneered.

Robert moved behind the demon. "Maybe we ought to take it from here?"

The demon slammed Denida to the ground. "No, I'm not leaving you until Whipboy confirms that he wanted you here!"

Robert smiled faintly. "Probably time, then." He reached for the revolver under his coat.

The demon mumbled something and lifted his hand.

The gun glowed red and the heat burnt Robert's hand. He dropped the weapon and the leaves around it caught ablaze.

The demon charged Robert, knocking him off his feet. He kicked Robert in the groin, each kick landing harder than the last.

Dan rushed to Denida, trying to pull him to his feet.

"Going somewhere?" the demon turned to face them.

Dan glanced over at the revolver.

"Try it; I dare you!"

"It won't... help," Denida stuttered, still trying to stand. "Only... his heart," Denida raised his hand, but stopped, grimacing in agony.

"Isn't he smart?" the demon raised his brow. "Want to listen to him, or..."

"Shooting your eye would kill you, too," Dan peered over at the revolver contemplatively before turning to help Denida to his feet.

"Such a disappointment." The demon shook his head while continuing forward.

Dan tried to pull Denida backward with him, which proved difficult. The demon reached them swiftly.

The demon pushed Dan away and threw him to the ground, causing Denida to lose his footing and drop to his knees.

Denida started a chant as fast as he could. Darkness encircled his hand.

The demon squeezed Denida's throat more tightly and lifted him off the ground, ending the chant.

"Not fast enough," the demon gloated and squeezed tightly, as Denida tried to wrestle loose.

Robert ran over, his face indicative of the pain, and grabbed the revolver. He raised the weapon, loaded it, and took aim at the demon.

'*Click*,' he pulled back the hammer.

The demon tilted his head when he heard the sound, but he kept his grip on Denida.

The revolver fired the dual rounds Dan had prepared. They blasted into the demon, making him drop Denida. It propelled the demon out of the cone, shattering the shield, and slamming him into a tree.

Denida clutched his throat, coughing and gasping for air.

Dan rushed over to Denida.

Denida took charge, using Dan as support to hobble over to the tree, where the demon lay sprawled out on the ground at its trunk. When they reached him, Denida dropped to his knees to check if there was any sign of life. "He's dead, so I can't get his power, *dammit!*"

"Power?" Dan tilted his head to the side perplexedly.

Denida held up his hand, which had an untanned circular mark where his ring had been. "Lars took it with Whipboy's help …"

Whipboy! Dan's eyes widened. He spun to Robert. "We have to leave before Whipboy comes back!"

Robert lowered his head. "Getting out won't be as easy, seeing as we're not demons."

"Maybe not, but we have a demon here. If you accompany him, the guards won't pay us any mind," Denida winked and his face started to transform into that of a demon. "I can… still… do this!"

Robert peeked over at Dan and blinked before turning his attention back to Denida. "That is very… unsettling, seeing you like that…"

"You knew I was a demon, once…"

Robert exhaled deeply. "Yeah once, not anymore!"

Denida shrugged. "Once you are one, it will always be within you…" He shook his head. "I don't like it any more than you do, but it's the only way out…" Denida tightened his fists. "Let's go." He took significant, heavy steps forward with Robert and Dan following.

Robert hid the revolver under his shirt.

"Rob… ert." Denida raised his hand. "Stay behind me. I need to look like I'm in charge in order to get you out of here."

Dan shifted uncomfortably on his feet. *He always wanted to forget his time as a demon, but now it might save him…*

Denida gazed over at Dan and their eyes met. *'Times have changed, my friend. I need to do this. I don't have much strength… without the ring,'* Denida spoke in Dan's thoughts before turning his head and continuing farther down the path back to the mansion.

Dan peered nervously at the demons they passed along the way, but, as Denida said, the demons didn't even acknowledge them.

Denida ventured down the hill. At the bottom, the other demon guarding the grounds still stood at his post, checking everyone coming and going from the mansion.

"He's dead," Denida stated as soon as he was within earshot of the demon.

The demon looked at Denida dumbfoundedly. "Who's dead?"

Denida squeezed his hand tight and turned to the demon with dark red eyes. "The demon who's supposed to be here *with you!*" He stepped closer and tilted his head toward Dan. "Look at that scared kid. Want to know why he's scared? Because I'm taking him to Whipboy." He sighed and bared his teeth. "Go deal with the other guard's body before I lose my patience!"

The demon stared at Dan's terrified face before rushing up the hill.

Denida patted Dan's shoulder. "First time you being scared has been a benefit to us," he chuckled.

"I know where we can get out easily," Robert ran forward and led them the rest of the way to the spot they entered from.

"Thank god," Dan emerged from the Darkness, drawing in a deep breath of fresh air.

Denida's eyes darkened as he turned to Dan.

"What?"

Denida shook his head. "Nothing, let's just go…"

"Go where?" Dan shrugged. "Without the ring, we can't return to our world. Heck, the Gate home is in there!" He pointed back to the dark cloud they just emerged from.

"We're going to my place. Denida needs time to recover…" Robert led the way to their horses. He helped Dan mount one and climbed on the other, extending his hand to Denida. "You're not strong enough, yet."

Denida sighed and grabbed Robert's hand, allowing Robert to pull him up, and the horses set off.

It didn't take long before Robert pulled the reins of the horse to stop it in its tracks. Denida almost fell off at the sudden stop, but grabbed ahold of Robert in the nick of time.

Robert tilted his head forward. "Demons…"

Dan jumped off his horse and hid in the bushes. Denida, on the other hand, stayed near Robert, squinting.

Denida slowly dismounted from the horse and crouched. "That's Whipboy!"

No, he's not going there... Dan leapt from the bush and ran to Denida, who was now scurrying forward. "Robert!" he yelled as he hurried after Denida. He jumped on Denida's back, tackling him.

Robert gazed into the distance. Whipboy and his allies were still far away. He continued outside the bushes, where he helped Denida back to his feet.

Denida pushed him off, refusing his help. "I can take care of myself!"

"But you can't handle him..."

Denida exhaled heavily. "I know," he hissed with his head down, not meeting Robert or Dan's eyes. He kept staring at the demons as Whipboy and the others galloped off into the distance until they were out of sight. "... Let's go..." He ground his teeth and followed Robert back to his horse.

When they arrived at the farm, Robert and Dan helped Denida inside and lowered him onto a bed. Robert fetched a bowl of water and a rag and started to clean up some of Denida's dried blood. "Dan, get me some whiskey. I need to clean these wounds, next!"

Dan hurried into the other room and returned a few minutes later with a bottle, which he handed to Robert.

Robert dampened the rag and started cleaning the wounds.

Denida let out a loud groan, which was followed by another more contained grunt, but he clearly felt it, judging by his grimaces.

Dan backed out and closed the door behind him. *He's free, at least...* He rubbed his palms.

Dan paced back and forth outside the room for what felt like forever, but eventually, Robert appeared in the doorway with the bowl in hand.

"This will be a long recovery and they'll be searching for him, so we have to be careful..." Robert placed the bowl on a table and hunched over it, running his hand through his hair.

Dan gasped. "How-"

"Dan!" Denida yelled. "I need... you." He coughed.

Robert ran in and wiped his mouth, spattering the rag with blood.

Denida pushed Robert's hand aside. "The first Gate in this world, the one that lets people enter from Heaven, I need you to get the device from it!"

What? Dan scratched his head. "Why?"

Denida turned to Robert. "I need to explain something to Dan and he might need a drink afterwards. Can you go get him one?"

Robert handed Dan the rag and left the room to get a drink.

"Dan." Denida pushed himself upright with evident difficulty. "Listen to me; the Gate's main devices are more powerful than we first thought."

"I know." Dan sat on the bed. "The young Claus used it to lock a world with magic for seventy years…"

Denida raised his eyebrows. "I now know who made the Gates and it wasn't Lucifer or God, nothing like that-" He inhaled deeply. "Henna, God and Lucifer's goddess, made it from a material only she could forge. My ring was forged from the same material!"

Robert came back with a glass. He lifted it with a smile. "Did you want it?"

Dan nodded, grabbed the glass, and swallowed it one fell swoop. Placing the glass aside, he turned to Denida. "Why are you telling me this… why is it important now?"

"My ring is gone!" Denida bared his teeth. "Lars has it, but he can't use it. Maybe- since the ring is the same material…" He dropped back on the pillow and shook his head. "I don't know. I was hoping, I guess…"

"Maybe it's not such a crazy idea, after all." Dan licked his lips. "I'll go."

Chapter 24- The Ring

Dan was in the middle of preparing his horse when Robert entered the barn.

Robert frowned with disapproval and continued over to Dan, handing him a map. "I've marked the Gate on here, but I must encourage you to abandon this idea. It's ludicrous!"

Dan folded the paper and shoved it into his pocket. "Maybe so, but I have to try if we ever want to return home." He mounted his horse.

"Will you be alright on your own?"

Dan shrugged. "I doubt anyone will be at this Gate, so it'll be fine." He set his horse into a trot and headed for the first Gate. The sun baked high in the sky, causing Dan to sweat immensely. *One hand won't support me; I have to hold on!* Dan closed his eyes and, awkwardly shifted his shoulder to quickly wipe some sweat off his face.

When he opened his eyes again, the sight that met Dan startled him. He pulled the reins, bringing his horse to a standstill.

As he passed the mountain, several demons in the distance came into view.. They rode by on horses, heading in the same direction as Dan.

Dan sat on his horse, frozen in place for what felt like forever. He stayed like that until the demons disappeared in the distance. He clenched his shaking fists around the reins. *I can't fail Denny!* He sighed and let up on the reins, holding them more naturally, and set his horse back in motion, pursuing the demons from a safe distance. Despite expecting them to turn away from his intended path, they kept riding toward the Gate.

As he drew nearer, he saw the demons dismount in front of a small group of demons waiting for them outside some tents set up beside the Gate.

Why are they here at the Gate that leads back to Heaven? Dan sighed. *I have to do whatever I can for Denny...* He drew in a deep breath and crawled as close as he could while staying out of sight.

Two demons marched over to the bush Dan hid behind, making him crouch lower.

The two demons unbuckled their trousers and started peeing.

Crap, crap, crap... Dan closed his eyes tight.

"Why does Whipboy care so much about *this* Gate, anyway?'"

Whipboy? Dan opened his eyes and peeked up at them.

"Didn't you hear? 'Little Evil' escaped. There are only two exits he could've used; the Gate at the camp and this one!"

"No one escapes Whipboy!" The demon shook, which caused Dan to squeeze his eyelids shut again as the pee sprayed.

"I didn't know he got away," the other demon said.

The demon grabbed his necklace and lifted it. "The Darkness will assure that we catch him!"

The other demon threw up his hand. "You rely on that necklace way too much; We make our own luck."

They returned to the other demons at the camp.

Dan glared down at the bush they had peed on. Most of it didn't reach him, but some did. *How am I gonna-* A smile surfaced on his lips as he sniffed himself. *I smell like a demon... this could work.* He rose to his feet, licked his lips, and inhaled as deeply as he could. With a renewed sense of confidence, he ventured toward the Gate and the demons.

The demon sitting closest raised his head, scratched his nose, and lowered his head again.

Dan swallowed as he approached, but the demon didn't look back up as he passed. He increased his pace with his eyes focused on the ancient Gate standing in between the tents. Dan stopped in front of it and arched his neck to see it towering high into the clouds.

"What are you doing?" The demon with the necklace marched up to him.

Dan's gut churned.

The demon examined him with dark eyes.

"Whipboy," Dan said perplexedly.

"Whippy- what about him?" The demon frowned.

Yeah, what about him? "He wanted the device from the Gate, just in case Den- 'Little Evil,' I mean, tries to leave through this one!"

The demon glanced at the Gate. "What about us? Are we to go back with you?"

"No," Dan said rapidly. "- you are to stay here in case he shows up…"

The demon shrugged his shoulders. "Makes sense." He walked over to the Gate and retrieved the device, which he handed to Dan. "If he returns, we'll catch him! Come on; I'll follow you back."

Dan marched forward with the demon just behind him. He clutched the device tightly, feeling like he knew it so well in his heart, and yet, still not at all. *I'm so close!* Dan's guts churned with each passing step, just waiting for the situation to go sour.

Dan's eyes wandered in every direction as he passed through the camp and he scratched his forehead. "I'm not sure… why… we are at this Gate, since they are one way…"

The demon grunted. "You do know that Dark magic can reverse the process so you can return to Heaven through it, don't you?" His eyes ogled Dan suspiciously.

"Forgot about that…" Dan spun around and glared sternly at the demon. "Set up a surveillance perimeter, now! I can take it from here."

The demon's eyes widened briefly before his cold stare returned. "I don't-"

"You don't, *what*?" Dan mocked him. "Neither Whipboy nor Lars will like that reply." Dan leaned in uncomfortably close. "Want me to inform them anyway?"

The demon glanced back at the others.

"Well?" Dan demanded.

The demon turned back to Dan while rubbing his necklace.

"Do it for the Darkness," Dan smiled wickedly.

The demon chuckled. "I shall." He hurried back to the camp.

It worked! Time to leave before they suspect anything… Dan spun around and returned to his horse, which was grazing where he'd left it. The horse stopped eating as Dan approached, stepping back.

The scent… Dan's eyes scoped the area and fell on some sand. He knelt and smeared it on his pants to cloak the stench of urine. Hoping it was enough, he approached the horse casually, put the device in the horse's satchel, and mounted the horse. Before he left, he peered back toward the camp.

Sorry… He spurred the horse and galloped away, his relief making him more comfortable in riding.

When Dan arrived at the farm, the sun was setting.

"Halt!"

The sound of someone cocking a rifle clicked behind Dan. He stopped the horse with a tug on the reins and raised his arms. "It's just me… I mean, it's just Dan!"

Robert emerged from the dusk and lowered his gun. "Did you find what Denny wanted?"

Dan's eyes glowed. "I didn't just find it; I've got it!"

"We must stay vigilant." Robert opened the gate into the farm, only to seal the entrance again once Dan was inside. He followed Dan into the farmhouse.

"How is he?"

Robert shrugged. "His recovery is moving along, but it'll take time."

Dan took the device out of the satchel when they were back inside the barn.

"That's the vital part? It doesn't look like much of anything." Robert led the horse into a stall.

Good point, can Denny really extract magic from it? Claus needed the full Gate to do it... Then again, another world made a time machine just from this...

When Denida woke up in his bed, Dan sat on a chair opposite him, waiting for him to wake up.

"Dan?" Denida rapidly pushed himself up in the bed. "You're back already? Did you... find it?"

Dan lowered his head to conceal his blush and sat down on the bed next to Denida. "You mean *this*?" He lifted the device from under the bed. "However-" Dan licked his lips. "While we know this part is powerful, can it really be used just like your ring?"

Denida glared disapprovingly. "No, but we need to try to get away..."

He has a point...

Denida rested his hand on it and his eyes filled with relief. "I'm impressed that you managed to get this!" He lifted it close to his head as he mumbled something under his breath. The candles lighting the room turned a murky red, casting a crimson light throughout the room.

Dan backed away from the bed, staring at his friend, who gripped the device tightly. The bed's immediate surroundings turned darker than the rest of the room, but the device itself didn't change color, despite Denida continuing to chant, causing the area around to bed to grow so dim that Dan had trouble seeing the bed in front of him.

"Dammit!" Denida threw it to the floor. The Darkness in the room vanished as soon as he stopped his chant.

"Not going to work?" Dan peeked at the device timidly.

Denida collapsed on the bed, burying his head in his hands. "I just don't know how we can get back, now..."

Dan knelt and delicately picked up the device. "Why don't you take some time?" He backed out of the room and closed the door behind him. He placed the device on a desk and hunched over it.

It's exactly the same as the main unit from the Gate in our world... how is that possible?

Robert grunted. "Maybe you ought to stay focused on things that actually matter. We need to stay mindful; the demons are searching for Denida... vigorously!" He rolled his eyes. "Superstitious beliefs won't aid us here."

Superstition? Dan's eyes wandered. *That demon believed profoundly in his... necklace... like a ring!* He turned to Robert. "Do you have something-" Dan lowered his head.

Robert frowned. "Do I have something of what?"

"A mine! I need mining tools... you have those in this world, right?" Dan wrinkled his forehead.

Robert rolled his eyes. "Of course!"

"Where?" Dan demanded.

"The mountains you passed on the way to the first Gate. There's a mine there. Why does it-"

Dan scooped up the device and dashed inside the barn. He saddled a horse and strolled behind some old items, hiding the device behind them. Dan confidently mounted the horse and galloped off.

The mountain stood only half the distance to the Gate. He turned uphill, hoping he would find the mine Robert mentioned.

A rumble sounded and Dan saw several men pointing to where dust billowed out of a hole in the rock. Dan rode over to them.

"Hold it." A man aimed a pistol at Dan. "Who are you, Stranger?"

Dan licked his lips. "Are you the foreman of the mine?"

"Who's asking?" He raised his pistol.

"A friend of Sheriff Denida and Sheriff Robert... do you remember them?"

The man lowered his gun, staying silent as he gazed around thoughtfully. "Come with me; the others can take care of your horse."

He strolled to a wooden house not far from the mine.

"Want a drink, Mister? You never said your name."

"Dan, and no, thank you."

"Well, I do!" He poured himself a drink and consumed it one gulp. "Denida and Robert... I've not heard their names in a long time. No one dares to utter them, but you just did..." He put down his glass and poured himself another drink. "- which means; either you are not from here, you're reckless, or this is important. Which one is it?"

Dan sauntered over to the man, who gulped down his second drink. "Maybe all three! I'm not from this world, but I need a tool from the mine to make something to help me fight Lars-" He shrugged casually. "I guess that makes me reckless, as you said. And helping Denida fight a demon *is* important!"

"What exactly is it that you need?"

Dan ran a hand through his hair. "I've got an item, a stone-like material, which I need to cut through. It's just extremely durable..."

The man fiddled with the glass in his hand. "I'm not sure I have something like-"

"I need it! I can't just-"

The man held up his free hand, the one without the glass. "*I don't*, but I think I know who might." He put his drink down. "His name's Henry. You can find him higher up on the mountain; just follow the path."

"Can he really help?" Dan muttered.

"Trust me; he's your guy!"

Henry is a very Western name... can't be a demon. Dan nodded solemnly and ventured out to his horse. He proceeded up the mountain, following the path as he was advised.

The mountain grew more vibrant as he ascended. Brightly colored flowers lined the path and expanded out across the mountain, creating a rocky, but somehow, still soft meadow. Birds chirped loudly as they flitted about. Dan tilted his head toward the roar of a waterfall ahead of him.

I gotta see this! He led his horse to a tree, dismounted, and hitched it before walking through the trees.

Wow. Dan leaned forward to look down the mountain as the water flowed down the waterfall's crevice. *I never thought there'd be something like this here!*

"Pretty, isn't it?"

Dan spun around in shock, only to see a man in front of him. He could not tell if the man was young or old, so he narrowed his eyes, but it didn't help. "Henry, perhaps?"

"I am... but my friends just call me '*Hen*.'"

Hen... "Sure." Dan hustled after the man, who carried a bundle of firewood into the cottage behind him.

Henry put the logs down next to the fireplace.

Dan knocked on the doorframe, staying outside.

"What can I help you with, Mister?"

"I need to make something, so I need a way to separate a very harsh material!"

"Which? Stone, iron, gold?"

Dan cleared his throat. "None of those... this material is even more durable than those."

"More?" Henry raised his eyebrows and turned to Dan. "What is it?"

Dan lowered his head. "You wouldn't know it..."

Henry peered into Dan's eyes. "If you want my help, I'll need to see whatever it is."

See it? But he's a stranger! Dan raised his head and started to step back.

Henry reached for Dan's hand. "I'm the best; trust me." He smiled broadly. His eyes glowed with rainbow tenderness.

"Okay, Hen." Dan nodded, strangely at ease in Henry's presence.

When Dan and Henry arrived at the farmhouse, it was nighttime, so no one noticed them coming. Dan dismounted his horse and boarded it in its stall.

"This way." Dan led Henry to the back of the barn, where he dug through the pile of junk until he pulled out the device. He turned to Henry and handed it to him. "I need some of this material."

Henry glanced at the device, turning it over and stroking it with his fingertips. "But how big a piece; what do you need it for?"

Dan lowered his head and kicked a stone on the ground.

"If you want my help, you're going to have to tell me!"

Dan sighed and raised his head. "Denida; do you know the name?"

"Denida… you mean the former Sheriff? I heard about him! His inhuman speed is legendary."

Dan raised his eyebrows with a wink. "About that. Denida was that fast because of the Dark magic he learned, but times have changed." He rubbed his forehead and leaned up against the stall. The horse Dan rode stuck out its head and brushed up against him. "His ring is gone!" Dan threw his hands up, then patted the horse.

Henry's eyes narrowed. "Ring?"

"The Ring of the Underworlds was made of the same material. It strengthened his magic, so I thought if I could make a necklace or something with this, then maybe…"

"Interesting." Henry examined the device.

"It's funny, you know. Denida's son, Daniel, was killed when the demons attempted to get this ring, yet now Lucifer doesn't even realize they finally have it!"

"Is he alright?" Henry peered up from the device. "Denida, I mean."

Dan sighed. "Denida's fine, I guess. He's recovering, but we can't leave. Without the ring, he's too weak. They overpowered him, so we're stuck here…"

"They?"

"Lars and Whipboy," Dan said with contemptibly.

"Can I see your friend, this legendary Denida?"

Dan ground his teeth. "I don't-"

Henry grabbed Dan's hand and squeezed it, smiling broadly. "Please?"

Dan inhaled deeply. "Fine, but make it quick!" He headed into the main building and led the way to the room Denida was in. Robert sat in the chair with his cowboy hat pulled over his eyes, snoring. Farther inside the room, Denida lay sleeping in the bed.

Robert shifted in the char, rubbed his nose, and then continued snoring.

"Denida," Henry whispered, his eyes glowing.

"Yes, you saw him. Now, let's go!" Dan turned nervously to Robert.

Henry glanced once more at Denida before following Dan out.

Dan closed the door carefully behind them and tiptoed out of the building.

"He'll be fine." Henry stowed the device in his horse's satchel.

"Wait, you can't-"

Henry turned and slung his arm around Dan's shoulders. "Trust me- I can't make the necklace without my tools, which are too heavy to transport. I'll bring it to you soon." He smirked and patted Dan on the back before he spun around and jumped on his horse.

Dan gazed after Henry, arching his neck up to peer at the moon. *I hope I didn't just make a mistake...*

Chapter 25- In Hiding

Dan sat at the table in the barn, modifying more guns. The desk in front of him was littered with an assortment of revolver parts, but in between them, he had a clear view of the window and noticed Denida coming outside with Robert's help. Dan jumped to his feet and ran out of the barn, waving and hollering.

"Keep your shorts on. I'm just starting." Denida sat down on the porch, rubbing his legs. "Any progress with the device?"

Dan cleared his throat. "I… I'm working on it; separating material from it isn't easy!"

Denida grunted. ""I understand that it's hard, but we really need it before Lars' demons find us."

Dan nodded and frowned before turning back toward the barn. *It's been a day… I wonder if Henry will ever return? Maybe I ought to tell Denida…* He glanced back in the direction of the house. Denida met his gaze and waved. Dan promptly returned a wave with a smile before fleeing to the barn.

Over the following days, Dan kept to himself, locked up in the barn for long hours. He kept himself occupied with modifying more guns in secrecy. *I have to do something, anything to help and can't tell Denida I'm not working with that material.* Meanwhile, Denida continued to regain his strength. It was just a matter of time before he would inquire about the device again.

"Dan!" Robert screamed, galloping into the barn. He dismounted his horse with his rifle raised. "They found us."

They? The terror in Dan's gut filled it with acid. "You don't mean… the demons?"

"They'll be here soon. Let's go."

"Wait!" Dan rushed back to the desk, grabbed a modified revolver, and returned to Robert.

"Don't you need to bring that device thing you were working on?"

Dan sighed. "Don't worry about that; we need to get to Denida before it's too late!"

Robert and Dan dashed across the yard to the house, only to be surrounded by demons on horseback.

Dan lifted the revolver and swiftly loaded it, feeling his heart pounding hard in his chest.

The cloud above them darkened.

"Denida… where is he?" a deep voice asked from the cloud above.

"Never!" Dan lifted his gun at the sky.

The cloud above them thickened, blocking out the moonlight and stars. The demons dismounted and started to approach.

Dan tried to aim, but the night's veil was so thick that he couldn't see two steps in front of him.

Red eyes approached, swirling around in the darkness. Dan tried to follow them, but they moved too fast. He raised his twin revolver, aimed, and fired. The spark lit up the darkness directly in front of him for a second. It wasn't enough, so he paused and fired another shot, proving that there weren't any demons directly ahead of him. Dan ran out into the field as fast as his legs could carry him.

"Hello, Dan. What a hurry you're in…" Henry leaned up against a big oak tree in a clearing.

Dan spun and gawked with pale, glazed eyes. *No demons chasing me?* He rushed over to face Henry. "Hen? Why are you here?"

Henry smirked and raised his arm. He unclenched his fist, revealing a piece of jewelry. "I thought I should bring you this."

Dan hurried over to Henry and carefully picked up the necklace. It had a silver chain with a pendant dangling from the center, adorned with the UW symbol. The mysterious material coated the emblem, just like it did the device.

I don't believe it! Dan raised his head to Henry, his expression betraying his shock. "I thought you would never come… this is… incredible!"

"I'm not done; I have more." Henry smiled gleefully.

More?

Henry extended his other hand, revealing the device, which appeared unaltered.

Dan paused, almost afraid to touch it.

"You don't want it?"

Dan grabbed it as soon as Henry said those words. "How? This necklace is quite bulky. How did you extract so much and still keep the device perfectly intact?"

"Where there's a will, there's a way." Henry chuckled. "Or, in this case, a kiln to melt it down. Keep that in mind; it might help you someday…" He winked. "Anyway, don't you need to go see someone… you seemed to be in a hurry?" His eyes glowed brightly with all the colors of the rainbow.

What strange eyes... A loud scream came from behind him. *Denny!* "Thanks!" Dan hustled back to the farmhouse.

The demons had dragged Denida out of the house and were beating him viciously. A bloody pool formed under him as the demons kicked him repeatedly.

Denida clenched his fist and a dark cloud started to form around it.

"Nope." A demon grabbed it and cracked Denida's fingers, laughing deviously.

"Denny!" Dan ran to his friend. He dropped the device in the dirt and pulled Denida up. "Use this necklace," he whispered, forcing it into Denida's hand.

The demons yanked Dan away.

Denida glared down at the necklace. He lowered his head and affixed it around his neck, using his bruised hand. He grimaced and gritted his teeth against the pain.

"Wait." Dan crawled backward. "You don't... want to... do this," he stuttered.

The demons surrounded Dan, closing in, forcing Dan to continue his retreat, soaked in sweat.

"Aren't you forgetting about me?" Denida stood behind them with glee resounding in his voice.

The demons turned around.

Denida's eyes darkened with a red glow as he charged at them, jabbing his hands through their bodies like knives through butter, and ripping their hearts out.

One demon grabbed Denida's hand before it reached him. Another put his arm around Dan's neck and began choking him.

Denida radiated with a bright aura, which vaporized the demons around him.

Dan fell to his knees and clutched his throat. "What just happened to them?"

Denida lightly laid ahold of the necklace's UW pendant. "Magic..." He approached to help Dan to his feet.

Robert sped to them with the guns. "We need to prepare before others come!"

Denida patted Robert's shoulder. "Don't worry."

"How can you *not* worry? The demons almost killed you this time; they might *actually* succeed next time!" Robert shouted.

Denida scratched his forehead. "I doubt it. Besides, I intend to take care of them, first... and get my ring back."

No, you don't! Dan jumped in front of Denida. "You need us! The last time you confronted them by yourself, everything fell apart."

Denida embraced Dan, who shut his eyes. Next thing Dan knew, Denida had vanished.

Dan opened his eyes and glanced around frantically, stunned. *He's gone...*

***

Denida strode into the dusk wearing a cloak, which concealed his face and the necklace. *The time has come to finish them and set this right!* He continued farther, turning at the trail leading up the hill.

"You," the demon standing guard on the hill stepped in front of him. "Show me your face! Knowing advanced Dark Arts isn't enough to get you through, anymore."

He'll regret this! Denida stopped, lowered his head, and removed his hood. The necklace fortified his Dark magic, so when he dropped the hood to reveal his demonic face, Denida's red eyes burned like wildfires.

The demon dropped to his knees reverently. "Archdemon, welcome. Go ahead." His arm raised with his head still bowed.

He thinks I'm an archdemon? Denida laid a hand on his necklace for a moment before lowering it and continuing up the hill. He hesitated and stopped after a few steps. "Lars; where's he?"

"The Master isn't here. He's searching for Deni- I mean, 'Little Evil.'" The demon kept his head down as he answered.

Denida turned back to the demon. "Where exactly is he?"

"Whipboy informed him that Denida was hiding with the former Sheriff Robert, who-"

Denida yanked the demon off his feet, holding him above the ground. *"Where?"* he demanded.

"The... farm," the demon stuttered.

Oh god... did the demons find them? Denida's eyes met the demon's. "You won't remember this." He turned and bolted off in the direction he came from while the demon watched him go confusedly.

I must reach Robert and Dan before Lars and Whipboy! Denida didn't want to teleport and weaken his magic before fighting the demons. He stole a horse from the demons, setting it into a gallop. He tore through the fields.

Denida halted the horse after a few minutes, glaring back at from the hilltop. *I sure didn't get far at all... maybe I should use something to speed up the horse. A weak spell... it shouldn't tire me out and no one should be able to trace it...* He muttered a chant to make the horse gallop faster.

Denida let the spell subside as he approached the farm. He jumped off the horse as he arrived at the destroyed fence with several collapsed sections. *They're already here...* Denida scuttled from one hiding spot to the next, steadily sneaking toward the house. A posse rode past him, heading away from the farm.

Wonder who that was... Denida continued to the house.

"'A friend of Denida?' Did you know he used to go by the name 'Little Evil?'" Lars asked disgustedly. He stood behind Dan. With a hand clenching his hair, Lars forced Dan to arch his neck. "Such a shame, so many people had high hopes for him. He failed them and lost whatever talent he had."

Dan struggled to break free of the rope binding him to the porch's railing. "I already know all of this! He was Lucifer's apprentice; you think Lucifer would condone what you're doing?"

Lars chuckled. "We kept Denida alive for the Master... but times are changing; I can sense it within the Darkness!" He lifted the scarf around his neck. "- which is why I kept this ring."

Dan licked his lips.

"You recognize it; I can tell." Lars put his cowboy hat on. "Question is; what I should do with you? Rip out your heart like I did to his friend, Mick?" He leered at Dan with viciously grin.

"... Or maybe you should just deal with me!" Denida yelled from behind them.

Lars cracked his knuckles and turned to face Denida, who now stood not far from the porch. "Back for more? Your bruises seem to have healed well..."

"Magic helps... I'm back for my ring." Denida's black cloak waved in the air. Only his face was visible in the dark night.

"Magic," Lars muttered. He flicked his finger, vaporizing the rope binding Dan.

Dan tried to crawl away, but Lars grabbed his throat and lifted him off the ground.

"Surrender or you'll lose another friend." Lars raised his eyebrows.

"Wait; don't hurt Dan!" Denida lifted his arms. "It was just a weak healing spell! I'm nothing without the ring..."

Lars tightened his grip around Dan's neck. "What about Lucifer? Are you planning to summon the Dark Lord?"

Denida shook his head. "And get dragged back to Hell? No thanks!"

Lars scoffed, but let his grip loosen. "Come over here. I'll gladly take you instead of your friend."

Denida lowered his head and approached the house, branches cracking under each step. He stopped next to Lars, down the stairs from the porch.

Dan gaped nervously at Denida.

Lars released Dan and swung his fist at Denida, causing Denida to slump to the ground with a bloody nose.

Lars grabbed Denida's hand, which started to emit a swirl of Dark magic. "You think you can try *that*, again?" He kicked Denida repeatedly, his force increasing with each kick. The spite in Lars' eyes caused a dark aura to manifest around him.

"Stop!" Dan screamed over and over.

Lars spun around, charging at Dan, making him bury his head under his arms. "Stay quiet or else!"

Denida struggled to his feet.

"You want more?" Lars turned back with glee in his voice.

"We're not done yet." Denida let his cloak fall to the ground, revealing the necklace glittering in the night.

Lars rolled his eyes. "Even with the ring, you couldn't beat me! You want to keep trying anyway, 'Little Evil?'"

"The ring only reinforced my abilities, magic that I'd already harnessed. This is different."

Lars grinned and lifted his arms. "If you're sure, give it your best shot."

Denida winked. "In that case, allow me to ensure we both stay here until one of us is no more…" He touched his necklace.

Light emanated from his hand, burst into a cloud, and formed a circle around them, which blocked out Dan and the rest of their surroundings.

Lars frowned. "Light magic? I thought only Dark could shield us?"

"It's not light; it's the same type of magic the ring uses…"

"The Underworld powers!" Lars spat.

Likely more Henna's… wonder what happens next… Denida shook his head. "Enough dilly-dallying!" He charged at Lars.

Lars lunged toward Denida and thrust his arms forward. Murky red fireballs flew in Denida's direction, while holes of Darkness formed behind Lars.

Denida dodged to the side, avoiding the first wave of fireballs, but more followed him.

Dark figures encircled Denida, so he whirled around, creating a gust of wind to send them flying into the cone's walls, vaporizing them.

Denida turned to see if the gale had also struck Lars, who, to his amazement, charged out of nowhere and swept his legs.

Lars jumped on Denida and started to punch his face. Denida tried to grab ahold of Lars' arms, but they moved too fast.

"Think… you… can… beat… *me*," Lars mocked Denida with each blow. He paused as his eyes noticed Denida's unyielding confidence. "Were you telling the truth?" Lars lowered the fabric to reveal the pendant. He clenched it and tore it off Denida's neck, making the aura around Denida's body vanish.

Lars stood up and took a few steps back. "It really is a magic necklace… that's why you felt so sure of yourself!"

Denida moaned, trying with all his might to get back on his feet, but he felt weaker without the necklace.

Lars put on the necklace. A bright shade appeared around him. He flexed his fingers, examining them. "I feel stronger." He snickered and raised his arm to form a fist. The cone surrounding them shattered, startling Dan, who could suddenly see what had been happening under the cone's shroud.

Denida stormed at Lars.

Lars smiled and prodded his finger forward, sending Denida flying across the ground, into the barn.

Denida groaned and rose from the bales of hay he'd slammed into. His eyes found the window above the desk in the barn. He could see the house where Lars and Dan stood. A few revolvers still lay scattered on the table. He gritted his teeth, grabbed two, and trudged out, heading back to the house. *If I can just get him to agree to this…*

Lars lifted his clenched fist and Darkness enveloped it.

"Wait." Denida lifted his hands with the guns. "We are in a Western world, so why don't we see if you can beat me like they do here… with a duel!"

Lars rolled his eyes.

"You have my magic… but I'm a legendary Sheriff…"

Lars lowered his fist. "Your quickdraw was only speedy *because* of your magic. It won't work, now."

"… Then you've got nothing to lose, right? In case you were unaware, the Devil lost to me…wouldn't you like to defeat the sheriff who managed to take down Lucifer in a duel?"

Lars' eyes darkened as he stood, gazing at Denida's guns. "Give me one!"

Denida tossed one to the ground in front of Lars with a cunning smile on his lips.

Lars eagerly picked up the revolver, nearly dropping it at first. He adjusted his grip and aimed it at Denida.

"Duel," Denida reminded him with a raised eyebrow.

"How do you want to do this?"

"We stand ten steps apart…"

"I'll call it!" Lars tilted his head and moved into the center, in front of the house.

The two of them backed away, focusing on every small movement. Both of them took ten steps apart.

"… 8… 9… 10. Halt!" Lars yelled.

They readied their revolvers. Dan wrapped his arms around the pole he stood next to in anticipation.

"Dan, call it?" Denida didn't break his cold gaze locked on the world dead ahead.

"Me? I... can't-"

"If he can't-" Lars smirked.

"No!" Dan interrupted Lars. He took a step forward and wiped his tears away. "Um... now."

With divine speed, Lars spun around and fired. The dual blast echoed, startling him, making him drop the gun and step back.

Both bullets slammed into the barn, creating two tiny holes.

"What-" Lars sped to the spot where Denida had stood. There was nothing there, aside from a gun laying neatly on the grass. He peered around as he approached, observing no sign of Denida in the vicinity. He glared at the revolver, then at Dan, before reaching for the gun.

Denida appeared behind Lars and ripped the necklace from his neck. "No magic? I don't need the ring or the necklace for a basic cloaking spell..." He clenched his hand around the necklace and jabbed it forward, sending beams of light into Lars.

Lars staggered with each strike, eventually falling to his knees.

Denida placed the necklace on Lars' forehead.

Lars tried to grab it with his hand.

"Where is my ring?" Denida bared his teeth.

"I don't-"

Denida tore away Lars' hands away with the power of the necklace.

Wait... He put the necklace on Lars' head again and tore off his glove. *Still no ring.* He examined Lars' other hand, but with the same result.

Is Lars right?

"His neck!" Dan yelled.

Denida ripped open Lars' shirt, revealing the ring on a chain. He grabbed the ring, stepped back, and put the necklace over his head and slipped the ring on his finger. His aura changed immediately.

"Whip-"

Denida lifted his eyebrows and Lars' voice gave out.

Lars gasped, trying to speak, but no words surfaced.

"We can't have you doing that now, can we?" Denida winked, as he sauntered back to Lars.

Lars aimed the revolver at Denida. "Stay back!"

Denida just chuckled as he made a sideways gesture with his hand and the gun flew out of Lars' grip. "You killed *Mick*; it's time to pay the price."

Lars tried to scream, but no sound came out.

Denida grabbed Lars' throat. "Where's Whipboy?"

"He took-"

Denida loosened his grip. "Yes?"

Lars' eyes widened at the sound of his own words. "The Gate… he took Robert to the Gate, where we had you…"

Denida snarled.

"Whippy," Lars ripped his palm with his claw-like nails, making himself bleed. He clenched his fist. "Whippy, Whip-"

Denida ripped the heart from Lars' torso and squeezed it tightly. Blood soaked the grass as he stared into Lars' eyes,

Lars slumped to his knees, his eyes dimming into oblivion before he fell limp to the ground.

Denida threw the heart next to Lars and approached Dan. "Let's go…"

"Both of us?" Dan peeked at the gory mess that had been Lars.

Denida put his hand on Dan's shoulder. "They'll come here and find Lars… we can't stay."

Chapter 26- Heavani

Denida and Dan watched the cloud in front of them as it hovered above the Gate.

"You think Robert's alright?" Dan furrowed his brow.

I hope so... Denida shrugged. "All I know is that we have to finish this, whatever it takes. Whipboy's the last one!"

"I don't think I can help you fight Whipboy, but there must be something else I can do."

Denida nodded. "I'll need you to get Robert while I take care of Whipboy." He led the way to the hole in the Darkness they had escaped from earlier, but stopped abruptly.

Dan stumbled into Denida. "Hey, what are you doing?"

"It's gone," Denida said matter-of-factly.

Dan gazed at the Darkness and sure enough, the hole was no longer there. In fact, that particular weak spot was now stronger and more condensed than the rest of it. "What do we do now?"

"It's too thick." Denida turned around. "The only other way is through the front!"

"The front?" Dan rushed after him. "But I'm not a demon!"

"I've got this." Denida pulled his hood over his head and turned to Dan. He fastened the necklace around his neck, concealing it with Dan's clothing, before leading him into the Darkness.

They waited in line solemnly until the guards got to them.

Denida's eyes turned red and Darkness emanated from him. The necklace granted Dan an aura of magic, so the guards allowed them to pass through.

Demons swept past them and ran up the hill. Denida and Dan peered up at the mansion towering above them.

Whipboy marched down the hill, followed by demons.

Denida grabbed hold of Dan's arm and they became transparent.

"How can he be dead!" Whipboy stormed past them, screaming obscenities, but he suddenly stopped a few steps from where Denida stood. "We can't fail the Master; I should inform him…" He flicked his fingers. "*Little Evil* will likely come here, next; prepare!"

Talk to the Master… Lucifer. I must find out what he says to him… Denida squeezed Dan's arm firmly, making them resurface on the hill, overseeing the Darkness below. He turned to Dan. "I need you to watch what happens here while I check on something…"

"You're leaving?" Dan's voice creaked.

"You have a cloaking spell, so no one can see you…"

"But where are *you* going… what could possibly be more important than this?"

Denida lowered his head. "Assuring that all Hell doesn't break loose!" He smiled faintly before vanishing. He reappeared inside of Lucifer's chamber.

Lucifer's eyes widened. "Denny! How did you get in here?"

Denida gawked bewilderedly around the room. *Guess the necklace is still reinforcing the ring's power…* Denida sighed heavily. "Your tale?"

"Great!" Lucifer jumped up from his throne ecstatically, clapped his hands, and hurried over to his Well of Memory. "After the destruction of Earth, God sent Gabriel and me to hunt for Odin and everyone else we once knew from the time of Henna. There would be no exceptions!"

"It was war?"

Lucifer shook his head. "We had no idea where Valhalla was at the time. The force that threatened us was a mysterious, malicious entity. We knew nothing about it…"

"Then?

"Why don't I show you, instead…" Lucifer leered over the well as an image formed.

***

Lucifer chanted a spell and teleported to another place, only to set up another defensive spell. After he finished with it, he rubbed his forehead. *I wonder if Gabriel has finished his, too?*

He flew to where Gabriel prepared the other side of the protection. Gabriel had activated the spell, but Lucifer couldn't see him anywhere. *Where is he?* He surveyed the scene, searching for his old friend.

The only thing in the area was the old structure, which Henna had allegedly set up there long before they arrived. He sauntered over to it.

Gabriel sat near its center with his head resting next to the part made out of the same material as the dagger.

"What are you doing?"

"Hi, Luci," Gabriel said in a low voice. "I always find tranquility when I come here…" He sat up. "- we haven't seen Odin since before Earth was destroyed. Maybe he didn't create the force that's attacking us?"

Lucifer shrugged. "Who else could it be? It has real malevolent energy!"

"True." Gabriel rose to his feet. "Since you're done, let's return to Heaven."

They arrived back in Heaven and Peter, who stood watching the Pearly Gates as intently as always. He let them pass with nothing more than a simple nod of acknowledgement.

Lucifer turned to Peter. "Your job should be easier now that the protective shields are all up." He followed Gabriel, who ventured straight to God's chamber.

God stood watching the door with his hands folded in front of him. "Welcome back." He smirked.

Lucifer narrowed his eyes. "God? Is something going on?"

"Close the door behind you."

Close it? Before Lucifer could finish the thought, Gabriel already had.

"I believe the time has arrived. Since the world below us has been decimated, I should create something new." God raised his arms. "My greatest creation!"

"But you already created the angels," Gabriel frowned.

God raised a finger. "But they're not perfect... like Henna was."

"You want to create a *god*?" Lucifer raised his eyebrows.

"I want to create a perfect being, one I can control. Not a divine being, a little power yes, but not too much..."

Lucifer and Gabriel shared a wary glance.

God approached Lucifer and Gabriel and put his hand on Lucifer's shoulder, then Gabriel's. "You two-" He smiled at both of them. "- my two highest angels; you'll help me... won't you?"

"Sure," Lucifer smiled. "We set up the defensive spells encircling Heaven, so we can-"

God squeezed Lucifer's cheek. "Bye." He flicked his fingers.

Gabriel and Lucifer stood at the center of Heaven, staring at each other, baffled.

"What just happened?"

Gabriel patted Lucifer on the back. "Just how he is..." He sauntered past Lucifer.

When God instructed everyone to gather at the center of Heaven some time later, Gabriel took a break from gazing out into the distance. He had been in the new tower God had constructed to oversee anyone approaching. He'd called it 'an extra precaution in case Peter missed someone's approach.

"What's going on?" Gabriel asked Lucifer as they stood amongst the crowd.

As Lucifer shrugged in response, God appeared in front of them.

"Welcome, my friends!" God wore a wide smile. "Since a disaster destroyed all life on the planet below, we need to start anew!" He took a few significant steps back and folded his hands. A mist formed in front of him, increasing in density until he unfolded his hands. The mist dissipated, revealing a young woman in white, standing at the center.

"Henna?" Gabriel stormed through the crowd, followed by Lucifer.

She stroked Gabriel's cheek. "Sorry, dear friend, but my name is *Heavani.*"

"… Saint Heavani, my perfect creation," God gloated.

"You made her resemble Henna? How could *that* be *your* creation?" Gabriel bolted through the crowd back toward his tower.

Lucifer smiled faintly. "Sorry about that, Hen… Heavani, I mean." He sighed. "You just resemble someone we once knew very well…" He proceeded after Gabriel.

At the tower, he climbed the steps to the top, which took him at least an hour. He found Gabriel sitting at the top with his head buried in his lap.

"This… is… hard to… climb," Lucifer huffed.

"I used a spell at the bottom to make it instantaneous…"

Lucifer finished his ascent and doubled over. "I should've thought of that.!" He inhaled heavily and stood up straight, pointing. "Wow!" He gasped and gazed out with his mouth agape. "You really can see *everything* from here!" His eyes wandered around, stopping as his sight fell on Heaven. "- even all of Heaven below us…"

"You're here to tell me I shouldn't mention *Henna*, right?"

How does he know? "I… yes. God never wants us to talk about her, you know." Lucifer sat next to Gabriel. "But in a way, we kind of got her back."

Gabriel frowned. "Not really. Her eyes are different…"

***

Denida's eyes met Lucifer's for a moment, but neither of them uttered a word.

"*Master*," the voice of Whipboy sounded behind Denida.

Lucifer began sauntering over to the voice.

Denida jumped out in front of Lucifer, blocking his path. "Stopping, now? You're just getting to the relevant part... and you need to persuade me, *remember*? The people summoning you can wait!" He bared his teeth.

Lucifer stood still, watching Denida, as the voice calling out to him echoed through the room.

"Well? Are we done?"

Lucifer grunted and clenched his fist so tightly that his knuckles turned white. "Of course not." He smiled and returned to the well. Lucifer leaned over it, licking his lips. "God started to spend a lot of time teaching Heavani the right way of life… according to him. Gabriel and I continued patrolling, searching for any sign of Odin or Valhalla…"

* * *

Lucifer, Gabriel, and Peter stood side by side, focusing their strength as the Darkness penetrated the protective spells they'd set up. Sweat beaded on their foreheads, but their powers were barely enough to slow it down.

"Let's join our energy!" Lucifer yelled.

Peter and Gabriel sped to Lucifer's side. In the short moment it took them to approach him, the Darkness oozed closer. By the time they reached each other, it was only a few paces away. They reinforced Lucifer's magic with their combined might and the Darkness started to recede until it vanished from sight.

Lucifer bared his teeth. "We'd better check the spells!" He ventured over to the closest, but he rapidly turned away, disgruntled. "It seems fine."

"Same here," Gabriel remarked.

Don't they work anymore? "I better report this to God, then. You two stay and keep watch…"

Peter frowned. "I have to return to the Pearly Gates."

"I'll go to the tower; I can see if anything is approaching from there, while you go see God." Gabriel joined Lucifer.

They dispersed at the tower. Lucifer continued toward God's chamber.

"You must be ready to show them the way; you have the answer within you!" God pointed at Heavani's chest.

Lucifer cleared his throat. "I need to talk to you about the Dark-"

God clenched his fist, making the rest of Lucifer's words die down. "I'll be back." He smiled tenderly at Heavani, strolled over to Lucifer, and yanked him outside. "She's to be sheltered from that sort of evil! You are not to speak about any Darkness or anything involving our past in front of her! Am I clear?"

God's ferocity was so intense that it made Lucifer uneasy. He nodded swiftly.

"Now, what about the Darkness is so important that you interrupted me?"

"It almost reached us this time. The spells are no longer enough…"

God rolled his eyes. "What about the search for Odin or Valhalla… how is that going?"

"No luck. They must have some sort of concealment spell…"

"I better do what Henna did, then. I'll strengthen your and Gabriel's powers so that you can improve the spells…"

"Saint Peter, too. He's guarding the Pearly Gates, after all."

"Get Peter and Gabriel to meet us at the tower. I'll join you soon." God returned to Heavani.

Lucifer collected Peter and led him to the tower. "Wait." Lucifer paused and mumbled something. The stairs in front of them developed a strange fragrance. "It's ready."

"What is?" Peter frowned.

"A spell to speed up the ascent." Lucifer climbed the stairs with Peter close behind. After a few steps, they magically appeared on the top floor.

Gabriel stood watching over the horizon. He turned perplexedly when they entered. "Luci? Peter? Why are you here?"

"God wanted to meet the three of us… here." Lucifer smiled faintly.

"God?" Gabriel asked doubtfully.

"I'm here." God appeared out of the blue in the middle of the tower.

"What are we here for?" Peter asked. "The Gates aren't watching themselves, so it better be important!"

God chuckled. "A man with a cause! I brought the three of you here to grant you stronger powers."

"Stronger?" Gabriel's eyes narrowed. "Like Hen… I mean, like *she* did?"

"Not *that* strong, but stronger than you have now. You will be able to fight back against the Darkness!"

They gathered in a circle around God in the center of the room.

"Is it really safe? Won't Heavani notice something happening up here?" Lucifer turned to God, who met his eyes.

God shook his head. "I already ensured that any magic conducted up here is imperceptible from outside the tower."

"What about the stairwell?" Gabriel asked swiftly. "It's hard to climb without a permanent instant spell."

God rolled his eyes. "I'll take care of that… after this. If I may continue?" His eyes wandered throughout the room. "- if you don't have anything else?"

They all lowered their heads.

God lifted his arms. A white aura surrounded them, growing brighter and lighting the room until it was so intense that nothing else could be seen.

The warmth emanating from it made Lucifer feel more empowered.

The light vanished instantaneously, but the feeling of empowerment remained.

Gabriel, Peter, and Lucifer all raised their heads. Their eyes met before they turned to God, who stood with his arms lowered.

"You're ready to face whatever may come. Now, the stairway… Gabriel, show me." God and Gabriel paraded to the staircase.

Lucifer raised his eyebrows with a faint smile. "We should be more-"

Peter held up his hand. "Don't bother. I've got no interest." He marched past Lucifer to the stairs.

... And that's who's charged with keeping us safe; I somehow doubt he can...

"Luci!" Gabriel stepped through the door and waved at Lucifer. "God fixed it." He nodded toward a window. "Time for us to go and strengthen the protective spells around Heaven!"

Lucifer hurried after Gabriel. After a few steps, he was outside of the tower, but Gabriel was already on his way, so he had no time to pause to look at the tower. He hurried after Gabriel.

Lucifer strengthened each of his spells, making them more powerful. *That went smoothly. I wonder how Gabriel's doing...* He raised his head and suddenly teleported across the distance, finding himself right in front of Gabriel, which startled both of them.

"We're really-" Gabriel turned to the impending Darkness with wide eyes, watching it roll toward them even faster than it had before. "It's coming!" He sped toward Heaven, but paused when he noticed Lucifer wasn't following him. "Luci, come on!" Gabriel spun around, waving his hands frantically.

Lucifer still stood there, confidently sneering at the approaching cloud. "Don't worry; it won't reach us."

"What!" Gabriel screamed in disbelief. "We barely survived last time."

Lucifer peeked at Gabriel. "The difference this time is that we're prepared. *Think*! You feel the newfound strength in us too, don't you?"

Gabriel turned his eyes to the Darkness once more, swallowing deeply as he glanced back at the Pearly Gates, yet he didn't move. He nodded at Lucifer. "I trust you. Right or wrong, I'll stay with you." Gabriel trudged over and stood next to Lucifer, where he watched the Darkness approaching in utter silence.

The Darkness rapidly crept closer until it reached the first spell marker. Like a wall, the magic prevented it from progressing. It shifted back and forth, looking for an opening, but to no avail.

"You're right," Gabriel chuckled.

Lucifer stared at the Darkness menacingly. "Why are you here? Has Henna sent you?"

Gabriel shook his head. "It won't talk; it likely can't!"

If it's Henna, it should be able to...

The Darkness threw itself back toward him, only to ram the magic shield again with immense force before withdrawing completely.

"Told you." Gabriel threw up his hands. "Let's go back." He sauntered off toward Heaven.

Lucifer just stood frozen in place, taken aback. "I don't," he muttered.

Gabriel frowned. "What?"

Lucifer sighed before turning to face Gabriel. "I don't think Henna created this…"

***

Denida cleared his throat, which incurred a glare from Lucifer. "Something the matter?"

Denida shook his head. "It's just time for me to get back to Dan. I presume this is a suitable stopping point for now."

"You want to stop… got what you were after?"

Lucifer's stare burned into Denida's soul as if he knew. "I just… I need to take care of something. I'll hear the rest after."

Lucifer waved his hand. "We could be done already if not for all these breaks, but do as you need; I have been waiting for a millennia."

I will be back soon; I have an inkling I'd better be… Denida raised his eyebrows and nodded with a flicker of a smile. "You never told me what was up with that demon guarding your mansion."

Lucifer slammed his fists together. "Your friend awaits you, no?"

Denida lifted his hand. "You're right." *It worked.* "I'll finish that and be back in a jiffy." He sauntered away, vanishing into the air as he walked.

Chapter 27- Danyel

Lucifer stood in the corridor of his mansion with a foreboding cloud hovering above him. *Master…* He bowed his head before the Darkness. "Yes, I will," he muttered under his breath. Drops of sweat gathered on his forehead.

The cloud vanished suddenly, as if it had never been there at all.

Lucifer grumbled and entered his chamber, where he flicked his fingers, bringing forth his guard. "You wanted to talk?"

The guard chuckled. "I need to show you something…"

"Show me, then." Lucifer delighted at the prospect.

"Master, you won't regret it!"

Lucifer wrinkled his nose. "As you wish, but you'd better make it worth my while."

The guard teleported both of them to the center of Hell, where the new arrivals gathered.

Lucifer recognized the location from the screams of torment.

"I'll take it from here," the guard commanded a few demons tormenting one soul.

The young soul gazed at the guard with terrified eyes. "Please, no more!" He held up his shaking hands and his voice trembled.

"Tell us who you are," the guard asked.

"Who am I? I'm Jerry…"

"Where are you from?" The guard smirked at Lucifer expectantly. "Earth?"

The guard nodded. "And who do you serve?"

"Jack, the Scientist?"

Lucifer's eyes darkened. "He really is on *Earth*?"

Jerry became less panicky. "Damn right; I can tell you, how you-"

Lucifer charged forward. Darkness descended and flowed all around him and Jerry as he grabbed Jerry's head. The memories flared through Lucifer's mind. The more memories he witnessed, the redder his eyes burned.

"That little-" Lucifer Jerry's heart out and proceeded to tear him from limb to limb.

The guard chortled.

"You!" Lucifer yelled and grabbed his guard by the throat. They instantaneously reappeared back inside his chamber. "The… Scientist," Lucifer's voice trembled with rage as he uttered each word. "Want to redeem yourself with the Darkness? Now's your chance… *Danyel!*"

"Redeem myself?"

"You failed me with Denida… now you have to bring me Jack's *head*! Don't make me regret keeping you safe here until now!"

Danyel snickered. "It'll be my pleasure, but how?"

"Within his memories, I saw a familiar face, Claus'. He was released from Hell, but in exchange, he owes the Darkness…"

"Shall I keep my identity concealed?"

Lucifer shook his head. "Bring his soul to me by *whatever* means!" He leveled a bloody stare at Danyel.

***

Claus lifted his chained hands to his head to scratch his forehead as Susan frantically paced back and forth. *She needs to relax already.*

"I don't know how we'll get to Jack, now…" The Colonel patted Susan's shoulder and pulled up a chair for her. "But we'll find a way!"

Susan slumped into the chair with her hands resting at her side. She pointed at Claus. "He knows Dark magic; I always knew he was bad news!"

Claus tried to give her the most reassuring smile he could muster. "I just did what I have been doing all along, trying to *help you*!"

Susan threw her arms up. "I…" She lowered her head and sighed. "I guess you're right…" She stood and approached Claus. After a brief pause, she released him from his chains. "I'm still watching you… but I guess you've proven your worth."

Claus rubbed his wrists. "Thank you."

"Isn't this nice? But it doesn't get us any closer to Jack." Nina snorted.

The Colonel tapped his knuckles on the desk. "Maybe the time to involve Denny has arrived?"

"No!" Nina slammed her fist on the table, causing it to shake. "Claus, go outside for a minute; I need to talk to the Colonel."

"We can't just-"

Nina pounded the table again. "Don't start with me, Susan."

Claus smiled faintly as he rose and walked to the door. As he passed Susan, she avoided his eyes.

As soon as he stepped outside, the door closed behind him. He turned and put his ear to the door.

"Still the same Claus," a voice spoke behind him.

It can't be! He spun around with his eyes wide open. "How can you be alive?"

Danyel stood in front of him and raised his brows. "I don't die that easily."

"You escaped from my Underworlds, got killed in another Underworld, and then your soul was killed in Hell! All by Denida."

"Don't forget the time when Denida was *Little Evil* in Hell. I got away then, too!" Danyel snickered.

Claus peeked at the door nervously. "What brings you here, now?"

"The Scientist. Lucifer wants to avenge his betrayal!"

"Still don't see why *you* would come here…"

Fire appeared in Danyel's eyes. "You owe us."

Claus shook his head frantically. "I don't owe you or Lucifer anything! Just the Darkness."

"You honestly think the Dark Lord doesn't know about the deal you made with the Darkness? Lucifer *leads* the Darkness," Danyel winked.

Claus dashed outside, seeking cover amongst the trees. He kept running until he could go no farther. He stood doubled over, huffing and puffing, behind a tree.

"Think you can run from me?" Danyel appeared in a burst of flames.

Claus shook his head. "I wanted us to be a safe distance away so that they wouldn't overhear anything!"

"Well, here we are, now!" Danyel approached with each step crunching branches and leaves under his feet.

Claus stepped back, bumping into a tree. "What do you want to know? I'm not sure I can help you get close to the Scientist; we've failed every attempt so far."

Danyel put his arms around the tree, pinning Claus. "You won't fail with my plan. They trust you, now…"

"I guess…"

"Good." Danyel's eyes flared. "You'd better not raise suspicion, if you know what's good for you."

"But-"

Danyel threw Claus to the ground and a dark flame engulfed him. He lifted his arms above his head, where a hole formed. "Either that, or you shall return to Hell!"

Claus gazed in horror at the dark portal with the screams of Hell coming through. He clenched his jaw at the memory of how his worst nightmare felt so real there. "I'll help," Claus said without thinking. He immediately covered his mouth, gasping at what he just agreed to.

The cloud dissipated and Danyel reached out his hand. "Will you serve us?"

Claus sighed. "Susan will notice something's up…" He gazed down at himself.

Daniel gloated and snapped his fingers. A dark curtain ran across Claus' body.

"I will, if it means never returning to Hell," Claus bared his teeth and grabbed Danyel's hand.

"As you wish." Danyel chuckled.

Claus wandered back through the trees to the house. The Colonel and the others were still chatting in the room, so he continued over to the cars where they stored their firearms. *Time to prepare.* Claus started to sabotage each of them, removing and jamming the mechanisms so that they couldn't be used. When he finished, he squeezed his hands together. *Jack...*

An image of Jack appeared before him.

"I will hand Nina, Susan, and the rest of them over to you on a silver platter, if you let me go."

The figure of Jack said nothing. It just gazed back at him in silence.

"Did you hear me?"

"Know that if you betray me, you're dead!" Jack's eyes narrowed into a death stare.

Claus chortled. "I won't! See you soon..."

Claus unclenched his fists and the figure disappeared. He returned to the house.

The Commander left the room.

"Wait!" Claus yelled. "I've got an idea." He sprinted up to him.

The Commander walked back into the room with Claus. Susan turned to look away.

"What's your idea?" The Commander frowned.

Claus rubbed his hands together. "We should all strategize!" He raised his thumbs up and tilted them throughout the room.

Susan shook her head. "I should go patrol..."

Claus shook his head. "We need everyone here to come up with an idea!"

"He's right." The Commander held out a chair and smiled.

Claus winked at Susan and sat down in the chair.

"You can handle it; you *are* the one in charge and doesn't someone need to patrol?"

"I don't appreciate your defiant attitude. I'll let you off, just this once, but don't expect lenience in the future." The Commander gestured his hand for her to go.

Susan strode away. Nina sighed. "I'll go with her." She ran after Susan.

Too many key players aren't here... I wonder if it'll still work?

Gunshots sounded in the distance.

The Colonel shared a look with the Commander and they jumped up.

I guess it's too late...

The Colonel walked to the window and the Commander strolled to the door.

The Colonel moved the curtain aside to glance outside. "Demons…"

"Really, here?" Claus asked in as shocked a voice as he could manage.

"Just stay here!" The Colonel took out his sidearm and loaded it. "Where are the weapons?"

"In the cars." The Commander waved his hand for the rest of them to get ready.

"In that case-" The Colonel peeked at Claus. "You'd better come with us!"

"No!" Claus jumped up and started to retreat.

The Colonel and Commander both turned to Claus, mystified.

"Lady Nina and Susan are still out there... You go on ahead while I look for them. We should assure that they're safe." Claus scurried past them.

"Wait! Don't you need a gun?" the Colonel yelled, but Claus continued, pretending he didn't hear.

Claus ran down the corridor, stumbling into demons. He raised his hands. "I informed Jack of our location; let me lead you to our base!" He spun around, but a demon grabbed him and slammed him against the wall.

"Let him go!" Jack yelled. "I know him; he's the reason we're here." Jack smiled warmly. "Want to show me where they are?"

Claus nodded and pointed his hand down the corridor. He paused with his hand hanging in the air.

Down the corridor, he noticed the door he came from stood wide open.

"It's open? Are they gone?" Claus muttered.

"Gone?" Jack charged down the corridor and peeked inside.

Claus nervously followed him down the corridor, only to be jumped by Jack, who lifted him up against the wall.

"Is this a trick?" Jack's eyes flared. "- are you setting me up?"

"No!" Claus tightened his fists. A dark flare sent Jack hurtling into the wall, losing his grip on Claus. "I called you here for a reason!" He straightened his jacket. "They just must have heard you coming. They'll have gone to the cars to get their guns!"

"Guns?" Jack reached for his sidearm.

"But-" Claus lifted his finger. "I anticipated this, so I disabled them." He peeked at the demons, then back at Jack. "You're welcome," he gloated.

Jack stood up and glared into Claus' eyes without saying anything. Claus held his gaze until Jack turned away. "Take us to the cars…"

"It'll be my pleasure." Claus turned with the same cold eyes and marched outside.

Outside, the Colonel and the soldiers stood in formation with their weapons locked on Claus and Jack.

"Are you certain?" Jack whispered.

Claus ignored Jack, stepping out in between the demons and the soldiers. "Put down your guns, Colonel. It's over!"

The Colonel tightened his grip on his gun.

"Is that supposed to scare me?" Claus turned to the demon with a smirk before smirking at the soldiers. "Either shoot or surrender." He clapped his hands and turned to Jack. "Guess he won't; just charge-"

"Fire!" The Commander raised his machine gun and fired, but nothing happened. None of the soldiers' guns worked.

The Colonel dropped his gun and reached for his sidearm, but it flew from his hand and landed in front of Claus.

"Done?" Claus grinned.

"Kill all the soldiers without that gold UW on their lapels!" Jack commanded. "They may have some valuable intel."

The demons swarmed the soldiers and a battle ensued, but the demons swiftly overcame them, herding the soldiers they didn't kill into small cluster.

"Where are the girls?" Jack stepped up and glared intensely at the Colonel.

The Colonel turned his head away.

Jack squeezed his face and threw a punch. Blood dripped from the Colonel's lips. "Don't make me ask again!"

The Colonel peered at Jack, rolled his eyes, and then spat at Jack's foot.

"What the…" Jack stepped back, lifting his foot, appalled. His eyes flared viciously as he yanked the Colonel off the ground with his hand around his throat.

The Colonel tried his best to rip loose, but his hands had been tied tight behind his back.

A hawk flew in between them, causing Jack to let go, and the Colonel fell flat on the ground.

The hawk hovered in the air, flapping its wings, creating a whirlwind.

Claus raised his gun at the bird.

"You might not wanna do that," Jack smirked.

"Why not?"

The whirlwind gathered strength and the hawk transformed into the shape of a girl.

The sight stunned Claus, who stumbled and fell to the ground. "Mara, why are you here?"

"Close, but not exactly. The name's Maia…" She smiled coldly.

"Are you the same Maia Nina and I saw on the island?" The Colonel frowned.

Maia charged the Colonel and clenched her nails around his throat. Darkness covered her face. "Don't you dare mention that witch! She needs to pay for what she did to Morton…"

Jack smirked and approached Maia, resting his hand on her shoulder. "We'll find her; don't bother with the Colonel."

Maia spat in the Colonel's eye before releasing him. "I'm counting on it!"

Claus couldn't take his eyes off her. *It's so uncanny…*

"Jack, you know you cannot kill them until we catch them all!" Maia said demandingly. "Besides, I need my *revenge…*"

Jack turned to his demons. "Find Nina and Susan; they have to be nearby!" He squeezed his fist and threw it upward, causing Darkness to envelop the area around them.

"Too lazy to deal with us," the Colonel remarked.

Jack's eyes darkened. He lifted his foot.

"Jack!" Maia yelled. "Stand down!"

Jack grunted and stepped back.

Maia strolled over to the Colonel and wiped the blood from his face.

The Colonel coughed. "Thank you. Why are you with *them?*"

Maia pulled her hand away. "Don't mistake me saving you as a sign of compassion." She slapped his cheek with such a strong blow that blood spilled again. "- friend of Nina's!"

"Let's take them back," Jack ran back with his demons.

"What- no! What about Nina and Susan?"

Jack brushed Claus off. "They can wait; we should secure this group. Besides, there's no sign of them here…"

I need to find a way to keep him here for Danyel… Claus rubbed his forehead. "Jack, we need to talk *privately.*"

Jack frowned. "Can't it wait?"

"Maia can take them while we talk. It's something vital about *Denida!*"

Jack sighed. "If it's about him, fine. Maia, you're in charge!"

Maia nodded and transformed into a bird, flitting about to scan the area. The demons followed her with the soldiers.

Jack grunted and frowned at Claus. "What's so important about Denida? I've severed all my ties to the Underworlds."

Danyel manifested next to Claus. "Hello, *Scientist.* Long time, no see!" He winked.

"No see? Do I know you?" Jack clenched his fists.

Danyel lifted his hand and tapped his finger on his cheek. "I don't think I ever knew you, at least, not as well as Claus, here…"

"Okay? So, what did you-"

"I'm Danyel, leader of the Dark Angels!" Danyel smirked. "So how can you blame me for never taking the time to introduce myself to petty you? You were always too low-level for my time!"

Jack's forehead dripped with cold sweat. His eyes shifted to Claus, who stood smiling. Jack took a careful step back. "Maybe we ought to return to see Maia…"

Danyel shook his head. "You're going home with me."

Jack stopped and grasped Danyel's arm. "With *you*? The one who lost to Denida, not once, but several times!" He raised his eyebrows.

"Maybe so, but I still have a mission that will salvage my reputation!" Danyel raised his finger and pointed. "- I was told to get you!"

"By whom? Lucifer? The Darkness?" he mocked. "This is *my* world. Lucifer can't appear here; why do you think I came here? I control this world!" Jack lifted his arms and flames surrounded them. "Want to come at me? Go ahead and try."

Danyel chortled. A pentagram formed around him, only to flicker and vanish altogether, causing him to gasp. "How…"

"I told you," Jack grinned. "You're not in Hell- this world is *mine*."

"But I'm an archdemon, protected by Lucifer himself!"

"Advanced Dark magic can only be used in a world if the person who rules the Dark arts in that world permits it. In this case, that happens to be me!"

"More advanced…" Danyel's eyes broadened. He rushed back and grabbed Claus by the neck, throwing him to the ground in front of Jack. "He betrayed your trust!"

Jack sneered. "I never liked Claus. What's your point?"

"My point is that we found you through Jerry's soul."

Jack shrugged his shoulders. "I figured as much… I repeat; what's your point?"

"Your name precedes you. You betrayed the Dark Lord to work with the Archdemon Medusa. This is a world Denida doesn't frequent, so I want to join you… Master!" Danyel knelt. "Let me protect you from any demons Lucifer sends after you."

"You want to kill demons? Not afraid to?"

Danyel raised his head. "Me, *afraid?* I'm an archdemon who tricked the mighty 'Little Evil.'"

Jack extended his hand.

Claus crawled away, while Danyel grabbed Jack's hand to get up.

"Wait." Danyel scoped their surroundings. "Claus is gone!"

"Forget him," Jack threw up his arms. "As Lucifer once said, Claus is nothing but a mere pawn. Not important!"

As soon as Claus escaped from their immediate surroundings, he fled into the forest, where he crawled behind some brush, only to be thrown to the ground.

"I shouldn't have eased up on you!" Susan tightened her fingers on his throat. She held tight as his face turned pale.

Nina grabbed at Susan's arm. "He can help us get them back…"

Susan released him with a discontented grunt.

Claus held his throat, gasping for air. He could feel the malicious stare Susan fixed on him, burning his soul.

Chapter 28- Showdown with Whipboy

Denida appeared on the hilltop behind where Dan hid in some bushes, watching the entrance to the grounds around the Gate, where the demons gathered.

"They're getting ready," Denida said from behind Dan, who almost fell over.

Denida helped Dan back up. "I think it's best I take you back to Dynasty…"

Dan nodded. "Good, because I may have come up with an idea for the time machine."

"Good." Denida patted Dan's shoulder tenderly, grabbed him, and teleported them back to Dynasty's secret room.

"Wow." Dan sauntered through the room before turning to Denida. "But you're going back to the demons, aren't you?"

Denida mustered an inkling of a smile. "I'll need my necklace back." He held out his hand.

Dan removed the necklace. He paused with it in his hand, giving it another glance.

"Dan," Denida insisted.

Dan handed it over and Denida put in around his neck, changing his aura instantly.

"You're set, then." Dan nudged him forward and up the stairs. "I should have the time machine ready, soon!" He descended the stairs, slamming the door behind him.

Denida scratched his forehead. *At least he seems more spirited…*

"Denny, Sir. You're back at last?" The Butler eyed him, mesmerized.

Denida grimaced. "Not to stay, but Dan is. I'll be back soon." He stalked down the corridor.

Denida squeezed his hand to reappear on the hilltop overseeing the Darkness.

Guess, it's time… He paced down the hill to the entrance, which now swarmed with demons. He pushed through the crowd.

"Halt!" A guard held up his hand. "Lars is away; you can't come in, now."

Denida turned to the crowd of demons waiting for permission to enter. "But he'll never be back; he's dead." He turned back to the guard and removed his hood. "- "I killed him myself. After all, I *am* 'Little Evil.'"

The demons chattered and stepped back.

Denida stepped closer to the guard. "Why don't you let me through to see Whipboy?"

The guard's eyes flared. "You'd better leave… now, or else!"

Denida rolled his eyes. "You just had to have it the hard way…" He turned to the demons and transformed into his demonic form. The more he changed, the more the other demons reveled in fear.

"Charge!" Denida ordered in his demon voice and, in less than a heartbeat, all the demons rushed the guard, trampling him and breaking through the barrier.

Denida smirked as he sauntered inside. Two things stood out as being brighter than everything else; the Gate standing at the center, towering almost as high as the hilltop itself, and the top of the hill looked as though it reached the sky. Denida confidently turned and headed toward the hill.

Several demons ran down the hill toward him.

Denida clenched both fists, returning to his demonic appearance. His blood-red eyes shone mercilessly, and an aura of flames surrounded him. He surged toward the demons, lighting them all ablaze. He continued dashing up the hill, intense fire still emanating from his body and burning anyone who crossed his path, until he reached the mansion.

A crow flew into the Darkness above him. Denida frowned and stared at it. *How can it be in here?*

It circled a few times before suddenly flying out of the Darkness.

Denida shrugged and ventured inside.

At the end of the hall, Whipboy lashed his whip. "Welcome to your end, 'Little Evil.'"

The corridor lit up with a crimson glow. The whip slashed yet again and fire surrounded it.

It sliced Denida's cheek, but he didn't flinch.

The scar on his cheek flickered and healed instantly.

Whipboy tightened his hold on his whip. "Something's different about you…"

"Correct," Denida said. "Lars is gone because of this minute difference." He rubbed his hands together.

Whipboy slashed at the floor. "Doesn't matter, I'm not Lars!" He lifted his fist.

Demons burst into the corridor, encircling Whipboy.

"You think they'll keep you safe?" Denida chuckled.

"They're not here to keep me safe!" Whipboy yelled.

The demons all turned to face Whipboy and knelt before him.

What are they doing?

The demons began chanting in unison and a cloud formed above Whipboy.

Crap- they're strengthening him! Denida plowed toward them, but he only got halfway down the corridor before he had to slow down to carefully step over demonic bodies scattered in his path. He saw hearts with bite marks haphazardly discarded next to them. Denida could only take a few steps at a time, finding the number of corpses to be increasing with each passing second. *How many has he used?*

Whipboy teleported to Denida, standing face to face with him. "Enough to kill you." He lifted his finger.

What? Denida felt his throat being squeezed, but there were no hands around it; it was happening from within. He gasped for air and dropped to his knees.

"The end of the mighty Denida," Whipboy rejoiced scornfully. "Thought I would be as weak as Lars?" He stepped around him, savoring Denida's agony.

Denida tried to grasp his throat, but his hands were stopped by a powerful force.

"Give it up!" Whipboy gloated. "My barrier won't let any magical source near you. You're finished!" Under Denida's shirt, he noticed something sparkle, which made him shrug. He leaned in while Denida tried to reach his throat. Whipboy unbuttoned the shirt and a white flash burst out, knocking him off his feet and thrusting him into the wall.

Whipboy leapt to his feet, only to find Denida already standing.

"How?" Whipboy's voice trembled.

Denida stared at him and pulled his shirt to one side, revealing the necklace. "The ring isn't all I've got." The necklace under his shirt glimmered.

Whipboy took a few steps back.

"No one leaves." He extended his hand and clenched his fist tightly.

Fire shot up at the end of the corridor, crackling loudly and blocking the door.

Whipboy turned and ran to the elevator, pushing his hand forward as he ran. The elevator doors opened before he reached them. As soon as he entered it, the elevator started its ascent, not waiting for the doors to close.

He's running? Denida chased Whipboy. Demons attacked him from out of nowhere and pulled him to the floor, but he swiftly tore them asunder. As he reached the top floor, everything fell silent; he couldn't even hear a creak from his footsteps on the floor. The only light there emanated from glistening stars and the moon in the dim night sky. Denida's eyes traversed from one side of the room to the next, but nothing stood out. He stepped out of the elevator carefully. Darkness approached from his right, so he dropped to his knees, dodging the fiery whip.

Whipboy bared his teeth and slashed again. The whip's fire devoured the plant behind Denida.

Denida clenched his fist and muttered something, but nothing came. His eyes widened.

"Disappointed?" Whipboy slashed his whip, sweeping Denida's feet. "We prepared a barrier to block magic up here… lucky my whip doesn't require it. *Precautions,* I think you would call it?" He gloated and slashed his whip.

Denida groaned and rolled to the side, avoiding the next lash. He scurried behind some furniture.

Whipboy rushed after him, attacking with his whip, shattering the furniture Denida used for cover. Denida ran through the room, remaining mindful of his constant need for cover, trying to find an exit. *I'm not going to get out of here.* Denida brushed the thought aside and ran farther into the room determinedly.

"Come out, come out, wherever you are," Whipboy taunted and slashed his whip at a desk, slicing it in two. "Nothing can save you. now. You're doomed!"

"Never!" Denida lunged at Whipboy, tackling him. Denida didn't hesitate; he attempted to kick Whipboy.

Whipboy grabbed his ankle, and pulled it toward him, making Denida lose his footing. He punched Denida's face, then attacked so swiftly that Denida had trouble keeping up. He finished with a kick to Denida's groin.

Denida's eyes watered and he clenched his eyes shut. *Is it over?* He opened his eyes to see Whipboy grabbing his whip not far from him. He tried to crawl backward, but the pain proved too severe. He raised his hand. "Wai… wait; I can-"

"You can *die,* you mean." Whipboy rubbed the whip tenderly with his finger and slashed the floor, grumbling.

Denida closed his eyes and sighed. "Reficul, Reficul, Reficul…"

The room grew even darker and the murkiness thickened like a haze. There was still no sign of magic, but their surroundings filled to the brim with a dark sensation tangible enough to cut.

"What… did you… do?" Whipboy stared into the Darkness embracing the room, his voice barely audible.

"What's going on here?" A dark figure appeared behind Whipboy. The shadowy figure turned to Denida and its eyes grew fiery.

Whipboy stood with his eyes locked on Denida, sweat dripping from his forehead.

The being sniffed the air. "A magic barrier? And *you*, Whipboy, you didn't answer me."

Whipboy clenched his fist around the whip. He spun around and fell to his knees. "Master." He lowered his whip to the floor and lifted his hand above it. "I'm just repaying the service to the Darkness. Little Evil killed Lars," his voice brimmed with disdain and terror.

Lucifer leered down at him, his eyes still full of spite. "I have prepared him; he's *not* to be harmed." He peeked over at Denida, who groaned in agony, before his gaze returned to Whipboy. "- you failed me!"

Whipboy reached for his whip, but it disintegrated as soon as he touched it.

Darkness hovered above the floor, surrounding him.

"No one betrays me!" Lucifer placed his hand on Whipboy's face, causing him to start disintegrating into dust. The more Whipboy screamed in torment, the more Lucifer gloated in pleasure. When the Darkness finished devouring Whipboy, leaving only a pile of dust, the Devil turned to Denida. He closed his eyes and mumbled something. The magic barrier within the room lifted.

Denida crawled over, pausing to stare at the banister around the open floor. *Is that a sparrow?*

Outside, a bird rested on the railing, but it suddenly ascended into the clouds.

"I take it you're still trying to cleanse the Darkness from this world, too?" Lucifer frowned.

"And avenge what happened to Mick!"

"Mick?" Lucifer looked perplexed.

"Sheriff Mick…"

It was like a light lit up in Lucifer's eyes. "You mean your successor."

Denida grunted and rubbed his neck. "It's over now, anyway…" He continued out to the terrace, which was still veiled in Darkness. "Something doesn't feel right…"

The bird from before flew from above the clouds toward the Gate. It slowed down and sat down on the ground in front of it, where it transformed its shape into that of a human – with the same exact body of Whipboy.

The hell, how? Denida leaned forward and squinted his eyes to be sure he saw right.

Whipboy turned and raised his thumbs mockingly before he sped through the Gate.

"Whipboy… tricked… Lucifer," Denida muttered in disbelief.

Lucifer appeared next to Denida. "What?"

Denida pointed at the Gate. "Didn't you *just* kill him?"

Lucifer gazed at the Gate, where he witnessed Whipboy vanish. He spun around to face the room; his body encased in fire. "It wasn't a spell restricting magic- it was a concealment spell…"

"But the Gate," Denida turned to Lucifer.

"He's gone… to Earth, where I can't reach him… just like *Jack*!" The fire engulfed Lucifer.

Earth? Denida's insides turned at the mere thought of Whipboy being near Nina's human form, let alone his own. *I don't sense that she's in danger, at least…*

Lucifer turned and the fire around his body died down. He lifted his left arm. "Either way, you got what you wanted. This world is now free from the Darkness," he said with a rough voice.

A cloud of Darkness enveloped Lucifer, who vanished suddenly, causing light to return to the room.

Denida turned to see the Darkness surrounding the Gate lift. In its place, a bright sun bathed the landscape.

The ground under the light was barren; there was no sign of life, but Robert stumbled out of the building next to the Gate.

Denida squeezed his ring and appeared right next to the building. "Robert!" He rushed forward and pulled Robert into an embrace. "Is everything okay? They didn't hurt you?"

Robert shook his head. "They just locked me up in there…" He pointed at the building he had emerged from. "- but suddenly they were just… gone," his inflection rose with disbelief.

Denida rubbed his hands together. "The demons are no longer in this world…" He sauntered over to the Gate, which powered down because Whipboy had just used it.

Robert frowned. "Wasn't that on?"

"It needs to recharge after someone uses it."

"Someone went through it. Who would want to?"

Denida lowered his head. He stood there for a minute, licking his lips. His head hung before he raised it again. "Whipboy," he said disgustedly.

"Why didn't you follow with your ring thing?"

Denida arched his neck to gaze at the bright sun, squinting his good eye. "Can I trust you to establish some order here while I give chase in the next world?"

Robert patted Denida's shoulder and nodded before he rushed off and mounted the first hitched horse he came to.

Lucifer… Denida squeezed his ring, appearing in front of Lucifer's mansion. His eyes widened and he sauntered over to where the demon guarding the building always stood. This time, he was mysteriously absent. *Why isn't the guard here?* Denida scanned the grounds, but when he still failed to detect any trace of the guard, Denida continued inside, straight to the wide door to Lucifer's chamber.

"Lucifer!" he yelled.

Lucifer raised his head from where he stood next to the well. "I've been expecting you." He raised his arms in a welcoming gesture.

"No!" Denida shook his hand and dashed forward, grabbing the well tightly with both fists. "Where… did… Whipboy… go?"

Lucifer smirked and raised his finger. "I believe you already know the answer to that…"

"*Earth*, but that doesn't tell me anything; Earth is huge. But if he uses Dark magic there, you, as the Devil can track him!"

Lucifer shook his head, keeping his eyes locked on Denida's. "That won't work because the Scientist uses a lot of strong magic on Earth…"

Strong? Denida raised his eyebrows. "How-"

"He uses the fact-" Lucifer bared his teeth and his eyes flared up. "-that I can't set foot there to his advantage. He used Dark magic to build an empire!"

"Before you hunt him…" Lucifer leered over the well. "Shall we continue, seeing you're already here?"

But Nina? Denida squinted his eyes. "What about your guard- the demon who's always here; where is he?"

Lucifer clenched his fist. "None of your concern! Do you want me to continue or not?" He raised his voice aggressively.

Denida glared at the door and bit his lip. *Since I'm already here…* "Sure." Denida waved his hand and strolled over to the well. "What happened next?"

"'God' decided that I should patrol less, so he started asking Gabriel to make my rounds for me."

"He started to lose trust in you?"

"Far from," Lucifer gloated. "He trusted me more than anyone, which is why he took me off guard duty. He wanted me to watch something more important; his creation, *Heavani*…"

Chapter 29- The Change in Heaven

Lucifer couldn't shake his uneasiness; his fingers were jittery and he wasn't sure where to put them. "This is a bad idea; Gabriel isn't ready!"

God patted Lucifer on the shoulder. "He will be. This is more important." He smiled reassuringly.

"More important?" Lucifer raised his voice. "It's just your pet project! Odin and Henna are a threat to our very existence!"

God strolled across the room. "I like Gabriel, but I don't trust him like I trust you. Heavani is essential; she has to remain sheltered." He met Lucifer's eyes. "It has to be you! You'll help me, no?"

"Of course, you know I'll always follow you." Lucifer sighed and walked toward the tower that seemed to caress the sky.

Gabriel stood watching over the distance from the top of the tower, assuring no surprise attack could come.

"Hey, Gabe…" Lucifer waved. "Anything new?"

Gabriel shrugged. "The magic keeps the Darkness at bay." He lifted his finger over the horizon, pointing at a dark cloud sitting in the distance, which kept trying to move forward, but the magic barriers kept forcing it back.

Lucifer joined Gabriel, gazing at the horizon. "God wants… no, I mean…" He sighed heavily.

Gabriel frowned. "What is it?"

"Heavani, God's creation, has to be protected. He wants me to do it, so he wants you to patrol by yourself." Lucifer threw up his arms. "I can't join you on patrol anymore!"

Gabriel folded his hands. "If that's what he wants. He granted us more powers now; I can handle it, don't worry."

Lucifer nodded solemnly. "Let me accompany you before you set off…"

They trudged to the Pearly Gates in silence. After exchanging a complacent look, Lucifer watched Gabriel fly off.

Peter cleared his throat. After half a minute, he did it again.

"Something the matter?" Lucifer turned his head.

"Why aren't you going with him?"

Lucifer ran his fingers through his hair. "I have another task to attend to." He turned and headed back to Heaven.

Wonder where she is? His eyes fell on a patch of land now covered in trees and flowers. *Could it be? He did use Henna as a base, after all...* He strolled over to it and arched his neck to peer at the leaves in the tall trees before he ventured into the lush forest.

It feels like Earth before the destruction. Lucifer pushed through the thick branches, which made walking into the forest tricky. He could see a clearing ahead, so he ambled toward it. As soon as he escaped the branches and emerged into the clearing, he fell to his knees. "Free at last," he said ecstatically with his arms up.

Heavani giggled. "There's a path, you know?"

Lucifer straightened up. "I… know. I just-" He scratched his forehead. "I was searching for you, anyway. God instructed me to watch over you!"

"Babysit me," she smiled.

That smile… it's just like Henna's…

"Mr. Lucifer?"

Lucifer shook his head. "Just Lucifer. God only wants to keep you safe from any possible danger…"

"What Dangers?" Heavani handed a squirrel a nut and it scurried away with it.

"Dangers are all around, Ms. Heavani."

Heavani rose and lifted her finger. "If I'm not to call you Mister, you're not to call me Miss!"

"Saint Heavani then…"

She shook her head. "Nah- uh. We really do have long names, don't we?" She bit her lip and sauntered through the flowers. "I know," she suddenly jumped, waving her arms. "Luci for you and Heavani for me; that's easier!"

"Sure." Lucifer smiled awkwardly.

"Come on; join me!" She knocked on the bench with her knuckles.

Lucifer grunted, yet joined her. "What are you doing here?"

"I feel at ease, here. In here, away from everyone, nothing all around but the flowers…"

"You just sit here?"

"The creatures here keep me company; I feel at home with the fragrance of the flowers."

Lucifer lowered his head. *Just like Henna did in her garden…*

'Lucifer,' a voice rang in his head.

Yes?

'Saint Heavani; bring her to me.'

Lucifer sighed and stood. He turned to Heavani, who, to his surprise, rose with a smile.

"Let's go," she said.

"Go where?" Lucifer wrinkled.

"You were taking me to God, no?"

How did she know? Lucifer shrugged. "Yes." He turned and followed her out, this time following the path. *She's right; there's a path here.* As soon as they emerged from the woods, he recognized where they were and scooted in front of her. "Thank you. I better lead the rest of the way!"

"You are to protect me from the angels? Why would they hurt me?" Heavani asked behind him.

Lucifer ignored the question, increasing his pace. Soon they reached the main building in Heaven. Lucifer pushed the door open and stepped aside to let her enter.

God waited on his throne. "Thank you, Lucifer. Leave us. I'll call you when we're done."

Lucifer nodded and backed out. The door shut behind him. He peeked back at it.

What should I do while waiting... he'll just inform me when; maybe I should go there? He bit his lips and gazed up at the tower.

He strode to the tower and climbed it until he reached the top, where he watched the horizon, seeing a small figure in the distance near the magic outposts.

Gabriel's okay... Lucifer exhaled a sigh of relief and rested his elbows on the windowsill.

"Lucifer." God's voice rung behind him.

"Shad?" He turned.

God charged Lucifer, pushing him over the railing, but kept a tight grip on him, dangling him in the air. "Do not... use that name... ever! I told you that."

Lucifer ogled the ground far below him. Past that, he could see the planet, once plentiful, but now lifeless with debris circling it. "I meant God... it was just a slip of the tongue!"

God shook Lucifer. "I mean it; do *not* call me that. I won't repeat myself again..." He pulled Lucifer inside and let go of him.

Lucifer clutched at his throat. *He never would have done this before...*

"I'm not who I used to be; neither are you, *Azal.*" God spoke without sparing Lucifer a glance.

"Why have you come here? You never come here."

God turned. "I have to go; I must try to see for myself if Henna could have survived. After all, the dagger did endure… and I need to try to persuade Odin to leave us be!"

"Great!" Lucifer let go of his neck. "Want Gabriel to come, too?"

God rested his hand on Lucifer's shoulder. "He stays here. Same for you."

Lucifer frowned; he could not believe what he just heard. His mouth opened, but no words surfaced. *What can I say to that?*

"I need Gabriel to guard Heaven… and you need to watch over Heavani."

"Heavani? Why? How is that more important? She may act like Henna, but she's not; her eyes aren't even the same!"

God's hand clenched Lucifer's shoulder. "I know; I couldn't recreate the eyes for some reason, but she's important! Can I rely on you, my old friend?"

God glared at Lucifer in an intimidating manner, which made Lucifer feel uneasy. "Of course."

"Good boy." God patted Lucifer's head tenderly before he transformed into a flock of doves and flew out of the tower's window.

Lucifer looked out one last time before he descended the stairs.

He continued past the angels on his way to God's chamber, but no one was inside. *Where is-* Lucifer's eyes widened and he burst back outside and toward the clearing he found Heavani at before. He followed the path this time, slowing his pace so he could keep searching the area in between the trees as he walked through the woods surrounding Heavani's garden.

Nothing but trees… I don't even see any animals, either… When Lucifer reached the opening, he found a variety of pets gathered around the bench.

"Heavani?" Lucifer cautiously stepped out in the clearing. All of the animals scattered into the forest.

The one that remained there was a single cricket sitting in Heavani's hand.

"Hi Luci," Heavani gently put the cricket down on the bench. "God wants to see me already?"

"No, God left to tend to something. He requested that I watch you for a while…"

"Back to babysitting duty," she giggled.

Lucifer approached the bench, causing the cricket to scurry away. "I'm not babysitting! You're important, like *her*!"

Heavani's cheerful face froze. "*Her*, who's that?"

Lucifer rubbed his face and examined their surroundings. *I hope no one heard that…*

She took Lucifer's hand. "Tell me… please?"

Lucifer withdrew his hand and grabbed her other one. He led her out of the forest, sweeping by the angels. He didn't stop until they reached the tower.

"A tower?" Heavani frowned. "Why have you taken me-"

Lucifer put his hand over her mouth and tilted his head upward before gesturing her inside.

Heavani climbed the steps, suddenly reaching the top and turned around in disbelief. "Already?"

Lucifer signaled for her to continue.

She spun around and walked through the door as soon as she reached the landing. "It feels so different up here."

Lucifer glimpsed out at the horizon.

"Wow." Heavani joined Lucifer. "It's breathtaking." She peered out and down at the planet in shambles below. "What's that?" She pointed at it.

"Earth," Lucifer said under his breath.

"Earth? What happened to it?"

Lucifer sighed heavily and rubbed his forehead. "The ones Gabriel and I protect Heaven from, -" He tilted his head up toward the dark cloud, which seemed to hover at a safe distance.

Heavani gasped at the sight.

"- destroyed every living thing on that planet."

Heavani lifted her hand. "But why?"

"God, Gabriel, and I, come from a world… where we betrayed our queen… she wants revenge on us…"

"Queen?"

"Queen Henna… God based your appearance on hers… she used to like the small creatures and gardens in our world, just as you do here…"

"Dear," she muttered and fell to her knees. "Is it really safe to tell me this? Won't God be mad?"

"He's away," Lucifer smirked. "Besides, this is the one place he cannot hear or feel any magic without actually being present…"

Heavani's eyes widened. "God can't read your mind here?"

"Only if he's up here with you…"

She raised her eyebrows. "Interesting, but tell me more about who I was based off, please?"

"If you insist." Lucifer shrugged and sat down next to her.

***

Lucifer's eyes changed as he looked at Heavani in the well. The hatred turned to warmth, which Denida found peculiar. "Do you miss her?"

Lucifer raised his eyes from her image. "She's *my* Nina; I'm sure you can understand how that feels…" He closed his eyes. "It's been too long; I wish I could feel her tender touch…"

"The loss… at least you'll have her back."

Lucifer's eyes opened. "By whatever means, but I know the Darkness won't help me."

"You might have me," Denida smirked. "Let's continue. Did God succeed?"

Lucifer shook his head. "He never found our old world. Just like before, it was as if it had vanished without a trace…"

"Odin then?"

Lucifer rolled his eyes. "He met him… Odin gave him the same ultimatum… and even hinted that the Earth was destroyed because he wouldn't accept it."

"The Darkness trying to enter Heaven was Henna?"

"I think you had better see, rather than having me tell you…" Lucifer lowered his hand over the well and an image formed in the dark water.

***

Lucifer peeked at Gabriel. "God insisted."

"Alright, let's go." Gabriel followed Lucifer inside Heaven. "You think he actually found our old world?"

Lucifer rubbed his hands together. "Let's go talk to him; there's no point in speculating!"

They continued to God's chamber, not stopping to exchange greetings with the angels. When they finally arrived, Lucifer grabbed the door handle, but instead of pushing it open, he just stood there.

"Luci? What's the matter?"

Lucifer turned to Gabriel, who flinched nervously.

"He's changed," Lucifer muttered.

"God?"

Lucifer lowered his head. "Yes."

Gabriel waved his hand dismissively and patted his friend on the back before entering.

They found God strolling about the room, uneasy. He turned as soon as they entered the room. "You're late…"

"Did you-"

God slammed his fist into the wall. "Quiet! I called you here to hear me, not for me to hear you."

Gabriel stepped back and his eyes met Lucifer's.

"Our home is gone… I tried my best, but there was no trace of it at all."

Maybe… "A cloaking spell, perhaps?"

"Doesn't matter," God flipped his hand in dismissal. "I searched for Odin after trying everything…"

Lucifer smirked. "Got him to join us?"

"Odin will *never* join us," Gabriel remarked.

God nodded. "He not only told me he knew how *we* killed Henna, but also that *he* talked to her after... he insists that her spirit will linger here until she gets her revenge." He turned with a chilling stare. "That Darkness trying to enter Heaven isn't Odin; it's not even *her*."

Gabriel pushed past Lucifer. "Who then?" he demanded.

"The Darkness may have come from us; we created it when *we* killed Henna."

"Not possible, it's too strong," Lucifer insisted.

"I assure you, that's what he said." God put his hands around Lucifer, only to have Lucifer jerk free.

"No," Lucifer yelled. "I... I... It can't be!" He stormed out of the hall and jumped into the sky. Giant white wings formed on his back as he flew away, leaving Heaven's Pearly Gates.

He flew around Earth, when he noticed a hole in the debris encircling it. He headed down to the surface.

"Odin!" he screamed at the top of his lungs as he stood on the dead ground. "Come out; I know you can hear me!"

The clouds overhead became denser and started to thunder, growing in strength.

Something feels strange...

A chariot descended from the clouds, landing on Earth's surface, where Lucifer stood, mesmerized.

A man put the reins down and stepped off the chariot. "Azal, I take it?"

Lucifer squinted his eyes. "Do I know you?"

The man approached Lucifer. Each step sent a jolt through the ground. He had a hammer, hanging from his belt and his hair was as red as fire.

That hammer... Lucifer's eyes widened. "Odin's son?"

"Yes," the man commented. "Name's Thor; I was told to bring you."

"Bring me? Bring me where?"

Thor lifted his hands toward the chariot. "Our home, Valhalla. Father wishes to see you."

Lucifer wandered forward. "With *that*?" He lifted his hand with disbelief.

"Yes, it's the only way, I'm afraid... if you wish to see my father, that is."

Lucifer clenched his fist before climbing into the chariot. "My name's Lucifer, just so you know." Thor followed him and set off into the clouds. He surged through the sky with thundering clouds accompanying him.

Lucifer turned to examine their trail, seeing lightning flash behind them. *What a strange mode of transportation...*

They rose above the clouds. All Lucifer could see was dark space and stars lighting the sky in every direction.

"Thor, where exactly is your home… is it far?"

Thor took the reins in one hand and raised his other hand, pointing forward. "Valhalla is right there; we're getting close," he said cheerily.

Lucifer looked where Thor pointed, and a landscape appeared out of the darkness.

They descended into the atmosphere and touched down in a clearing between some trees.

"You sure do have a lot of greenery here…" Lucifer stepped off the chariot, examining his surroundings.

"Welcome, Azal!" Odin greeted him with open arms, stepping forward and pulling Lucifer into an embrace.

Lucifer shook loose. "Why am I here?"

"Am I wrong? Did you not wish to see me?" Odin folded his hands.

"That's-" Lucifer spun around.

Odin put his hand on Lucifer's shoulder.

Lucifer felt Odin's hand radiating with the same warmth God's had. "As I told your son, my name's Lucifer, now!"

Odin nodded and raised his scepter. "Alright, come with me." He led Lucifer in amongst the trees.

"I'm only here to ask you one simple-"

Odin lifted his scepter. "Shaddai, I know."

Lucifer skimmed with annoyance. "He goes by God now, like I go by Lucifer; you should respect that!"

"I know; you want to put the past behind you. The only problem is…" Odin slammed his scepter into the ground, making the trees around them vanish and colors appeared – flowers stretching as far as the eye could see.

"Hello, my sweet Azal."

That voice; it can't be! Lucifer spun around and froze, gaping. "Queen Henna! How is it possible? I saw you…"

Henna laid her warm hand on Lucifer's cheek. Her eyes shone with the rainbow colors that no one else had. "A soul can only die when the dagger dissolves *with* the body! My will shall linger here until it is fulfilled."

"Your… will? And that is?"

"You know the answer to that, Azal." Henna let go of his cheek and folded her arms.

Lucifer peeked at Odin, who stood behind Henna. "You won't get it; God will never let you enter Heaven because you destroyed Earth!"

Henna turned to Odin with a chuckle and he lifted his scepter. "I see." She turned to Lucifer with a smirk. "I did destroy Earth, but it was supposed to happen before Shaddai claimed it as his own. As for Heaven, I have no intention of entering it. My prediction will show himself; he'll be God's downfall in due time..."

"No." Lucifer lifted his hand. "The Darkness, which has been trying to enter Heaven, is real; I've been fighting it!"

"That it is..." Odin walked forward. "But it's not the queen."

"That's what you think," Lucifer mocked.

"The Darkness isn't mine; it's Shaddai's," Henna said calmly.

"Shaddai?" Lucifer shook his head. "Not possible-"

"Are you sure about that?" Henna sauntered around Lucifer. "It appeared after you made your home there, no? Has it ever wanted to go anywhere else, *but* Heaven?"

"No. It's been trying to enter Heaven from the time it appeared!" Henna stared intently.

"I'm telling you, it never tried anything but!"

"If it tried to enter Heaven while Shaddai was gone, then my mistake." Henna turned away.

When he was gone? Lucifer grew pale.

"Something the matter?" Odin asked.

"It didn't... try to enter while God was away... maybe it needed energy, or..."

"Or maybe it didn't know where he was."

Lucifer stared at Henna. "Why would it be him, anyway!"

Henna smiled at Odin before she continued. "It belongs with the hatred within his heart."

Lucifer wrinkled his forehead. "What hatred?"

"He always felt left out when Odin and others were selected; he wanted what I had- divinity. Killing me released the Darkness inside him. You see the change in him, don't you?"

"No, no, no..." Lucifer buried his head in his arms. Suddenly he could feel his surroundings shift, so he lifted his head, only to find himself standing next to the device in front of Heaven's Pearly Gates. He looked around, but he was alone.

There's only one way to check if this is true... He sped toward the Pearly Gates, racing past Peter, not stopping until he reached the tower. He hurried to climb it and rushed over to look into the distance.

He saw the Dark cloud in front of him, but it was no longer idle. It pushed against the magic outposts, just as it did every time God was in Heaven.

Henna might be right...

***

"Henna's still… alive?" Denida's voice trembled as he uttered the very name. "Or did God take care of that?"

Lucifer shook his head. "Physically, no… her spirit still lingers here; he can't kill her soul…"

Denida rolled his eyes. "A soul can be killed by removing the heart while they're still breathing… even I know that."

"Not with a goddess. Same goes for God. Odin, Gabriel, even me, we can only be slain by one means…"

Denida leered over the well and raised his eyebrows. "…Which is?"

Lucifer looked embarrassed, which Denida found strange.

"The daggers. The one that killed her or any of the seven others are the only things that can kill us all…"

"But God already tried to kill her with that?"

"Her hatred was so strong that her spirit lingered here…"

Denida nipped at his lip. "I need to go get Whipboy." His eyes grew dark. "- but I'll be back after!" He snapped his fingers and teleported to Earth.

Chapter 30- Looking for Nina

It's chilly here. Denida shivered, but continued through the downpour to the school as the kids scurried inside as fast as they could.

The soldiers around the school saluted Denida, not minding the pouring rain.

Denida pushed his wet hair back. "Where is the rest of the troop?"

"The Commander left with the Colonel, Sir," the soldier in front said.

What? I better get more men here, then... Denida grunted and teleported back to the Underworlds, where he appeared inside his office. *I need to remember how much the magic of the necklace strengthens my magic.* He sauntered over to the intercom to call his secretary.

She stopped in the doorway.

"Something wrong?"

She lowered her head, only to raise it and pointed at him. "You're… soaked!"

Denida waved his hand dismissively. "Not important; I need more soldiers sent to Earth, ASAP."

"Yes, sir. Anything else?"

Denida shook his head and leaned back in the chair. "You're-" He stopped in the middle of his sentence, his mouth hanging open. He stood and walked around the table, inspecting a picture frame on his desk. "Somebody's been in here!"

"I'll go get the soldiers!" The secretary ran out.

She knows something. Denida chased after her. "It's okay; just tell me who it was?"

She picked up the phone, her finger tapping the number. "The Colonel," she muttered.

I should have figured that... "Why was he in there?"

She shrugged. "The Colonel said he needed to leave you something."

Leave me? Denida shook his head, puzzled, and trudged back into his office. Inside, he sauntered around his desk and examined every nook and cranny of it. He continued to front, where he had noticed the picture was moved. Not seeing anything out of place, he headed to the bookcase.

After taking inventory of the shelf for several minutes, Denida lowered his head. *This is silly; of course, he didn't leave anything. It was an excuse!*

He sauntered back out to the secretary. "Please don't let anyone inside my office, unless I'm accompanying them."

"Of course. I just thought since it was the Colonel-"

Denida cleared his throat. "I understand, but it is vital!"

She nodded solemnly.

"Did you send more troops to Earth?"

The secretary nodded with a broad smile. "It's all set, Sir."

"Perfect." Denida closed the doors to his office from the outside. "I won't be back for a while." He waved as he stepped outside, where he clenched his fist tight, retuning to Earth.

Good, they're here. Denida wore a flicker of a smile and approached the new soldiers, who gathered outside the school.

"You're back, Sir?" The soldier from before greeted Denida. "We have more troops stationed here, now!"

"I know. Where exactly did the Colonel and Commander go?"

"After-" The soldier bit his lip. "I'm sorry, but they followed Lady Nina..."

Denida sighed. "Nina was here, but wasn't it only briefly? Why aren't they back, yet?"

The soldier stood with a look of confusion on his face.

She must be back in the Underworlds, right? I should check; I hope she's far away from Whipboy! He saluted the soldier. "Dismissed."

The snow had been falling at Dynasty, leaving a curtain of white coating the grounds. The Butler stood in the foyer, instructing some servants to clear the snow on the property.

Denida neared them, each step loudly crunching in the deep snow.

They turned toward the noise. The Butler hurried to finish his orders before he rushed forward. "You shouldn't be out here in the cold, my lord. Dan's still inside the chamber."

Denida shook his head and all the snow on him fell off. "I'm not here for Dan. Nina, she's here, right?"

"Let me get you some warm clothes," the Butler continued.

Denida's head pounded. "No!" he yelled. "Is she here or not?"

"It's chilly out here, Sir." The Butler rubbed his hands together. "I'll prepare you some warm tea." He hurried inside the building.

Denida's stomach turned. He dashed inside. "Tell me!"

"She never came back more than once since she went to Earth... Angel's been all alone..."

"Angel?" Denida frowned.

"Her... horse," the Butler muttered.

"Oh…" Denida scratched his head. *I should have remembered that! She's been on Earth all this time. How do I find her?* He shrugged. "Thanks, old friend." He sauntered back outside.

"Denny!" a voice called quietly into the blizzard before he could teleport back to Earth.

The blizzard raged, but out of it, a dark figure appeared.

As it approached, Denida recognized him. "Anneh!" Denida hurried forward. "You shouldn't be out in this weather. Come with me." He led him inside and urged him to sit in front of a giant fireplace. He sprinted to the Butler to get some hot chocolate. "You should be careful; it's freezing! What're you doing here, anyway? How did you even get on the grounds?"

Anneh sipped the warm drink. "The guards let me through when I told them I needed to see you, Denida…"

"But why?"

"It's been a while; I wondered if you united all the Underworlds?"

Denida sighed. "Not yet, I'm afraid."

"How come?" Anneh took another sip and put the cup down.

"Whipboy," Denida bared his teeth in revulsion.

"A boy with a whip?"

Denida rubbed his hair. "Whipboy's a demon, who escaped to Earth!"

"And why is this demon so important?"

Denida clenched his fist and inhaled slowly. "He almost killed me; we have to settle this before he hurts anyone else…"

"I see; he's in Dynasty?"

Denida shook his head. "I was just checking on something. He's somewhere on Earth…"

"Somewhere… did you lose him?"

Denida shrugged. "There's no way to find him…"

Anneh swallowed the rest of his hot chocolate and stood. "I need to get going. Don't you have some way of detecting the concentration of Dark magic or those who don't belong on Earth? That could help you find what you're after…" He buttoned his jacket and turned to the door, waving his hand. "Until we meet again." He stopped when he encountered Dan at the door.

"What's going on? I thought I heard familiar voices…" Dan's eyes fell on Anneh. "Sorry, I don't think we've met. How are you?" He extended his hand.

Anneh grabbed his hand and greeted Dan before turning his head. "I'd best be on my way…" He stepped past Dan and out the door.

Dan ran his hand through his hair. "Who's that?"

"A friend of Odin's. He's an old king, who's preparing to retire."

"But why's he here… with you." Dan shrugged.

"You said you might have something soon?" Denida smiled.

Dan shook his head. "Soon yes, but not yet."

Denida inhaled slowly before nodding in reply. "Alright. I'll check back later." He strolled outside, where he hailed one of the guards to prepare a car.

A soldier scratched his nose. "Are you sure that's a good idea with this heavy snow, Sir?"

"I have to check something vital at the UW Headquarters, so yes!"

The further they drove, the heavier the snow fell.

The driver glanced in the rearview mirror briefly, only to turn his sight back to the road. A few minutes later, he repeated the process, still not speaking.

"Something you wish to say?" Denida stared at the rearview mirror when the driver peered back again.

The driver bit his lip, then slowed the car to a standstill, parking at the side of the road before turning to Denida. "You have that magic, right? Why do you want to be taken somewhere now, in this heavy blizzard, when you can just use magic; what could possibly be so important?" He lowered his head, only to swiftly raise it again. "- I mean, what could make you want to do this, Sir?"

"I didn't want to bring attention to what I'll be doing…" *Besides, I may need all my magic to find him…*

"And that-"

Denida started to slowly tilt his head sideways. "Nothing which concerns you. If that's all, please just take me there." He leaned back in his seat and closed his eyes.

The driver set the car in motion and continued to their destination. Most of the snow had been cleared off the pavement in front of the headquarters. As soon as they parked, a soldier opened Denida's door and greeted him with a salute.

Denida nodded with a faint smile and raced inside the building. The receptionist stood up, but he gestured for her to stay sitting. He didn't pause to greet her, but ventured on through to the stairways and started his descent. At the bottom, he pushed the tight iron door open.

A guard was stationed within. "Sir, welcome to the cells. What brings you down here?"

Denida's eyes watered as he glanced down the corridor of cells. He squeezed his eyes shut. "Excuse me, I need to check something beyond the cells." He turned to proceed down the hallway, but each passing step grew smaller and slower until he stopped altogether with a red face and dimmer eyes.

He raised his head to glance at the cell door he had stopped at. The number 'five' was etched on it.

Denida wiped his eyes and grabbed the handle. He pushed it open. The cell was empty with nothing but a rust-colored spot of dry blood on the floor. Denida closed his eyes and inhaled heavily.

"It was pretty unreal what Michelle pulled off here, Sir." The guard from before stood behind Denida.

"It's in the past. Keep that cell locked!" Denida stormed down the corridor past the cells, continuing until he reached the end of the hallway. It was so dark; only a dim light reached this part of the corridor.

Denida felt the wall, searching for something. He stretched both his hands until they were wide apart. Eventually, he felt a small dent in the wall. *Found it!*

He pulled it aside, revealing a hidden entrance, leading to another dark room. Inside, a dim light emanated from an old machine.

Denida sighed heavily, but the dust made him cough, forcing him to wipe his eyes when he finished. He staggered over to the machine, wiping a coating of dust off the panel. Above him, a monitor showed a color-coded map of the Underworld, which depicted the prevalence of Dark Arts throughout the world.

It still works, but can this tech be used on Earth?

Gabriel appeared next to him in a white flash, which lit up the room in its entirety for a moment. "Afraid not, but aren't there other ways?"

"Other… ways?" Denida turned to Gabriel. "What are you talking about?"

Gabriel turned his attention to Denida. "Don't you have a magical connection to your 'soul mate?'"

"Of course, Nina knows magic… I can track it and find my sweet Nina!" Denida squeezed Gabriel's shoulder. "Thanks, you're always so helpful!"

The severe weather had subsided on Earth, but it remained overcast and the ground was muddy.

Denida rubbed his hands together. *Nina…* He arched his neck and sniffed. He turned and trudged to the side of the school where he glanced around for a second, before continuing through the mud into some greenery. After a few steps, he stopped and frowned.

I feel her in the other direction, too. Which one should I check first? Denida fiddled with his fingers.

A soldier saluted Denida. "Sir, want me to get Colonel Rogers?"

Denida approached the soldier. "No, just stay alert for any sign of the Colonel or Nina." He turned back and continued past the school, following the magic trail lingering in the air, his tongue touching his teeth in anticipation of finally reaching her, but that made him worry. *Is she okay?*

'*Bark, bark, bark,*' a man tried to control a set of dogs as an old woman sauntered past with her dog.

Denida approached to help the man keep the dogs under control. "Two people are better than one." He smiled at the man.

The woman hurried past with her small dog.

The man sighed. "I know. Thanks, Mister." He led Denida into a building, which appeared to be an animal shelter.

After he got the dogs settled in, he returned to Denida, wiping his head with a towel. "It's so stressful doing this by myself."

"Why don't you hire some help?"

"I *have* help… they just vanished." The man threw the towel over his shoulder and shook his head. "A brother and sister; the pets adored them. Especially Maia!"

"Maia?" Denida frowned. *That name sounds…*

The man nodded. "Maia and Morton were… *are* siblings, I mean."

Denida shrugged. "They should return with time."

The man shook. "I doubt it. Things changed since that blonde lady came by thinking Maia was… *Michelle*, I think the name was."

Michelle! Denida shot him a death stare, but then lowered his head. "Wait- the blond girl, who thought Maia was Michelle, did you happen to get her name?"

"Yeah, Nina, I think."

Denida rolled his eyes. *What the hell is going on here? Why didn't she tell me this?* "Do you know where they went?"

The man shrugged. "No idea; I just hope they return, soon…"

Dammit; so close, yet so far away! Denida jabbed his fist into the wall. "You're not useful, then." He charged out the door and headed back toward the school. As soon as he turned the corner, he froze in place.

Gabriel stood waving. "Hello, Denny."

"Why are you here? You always come for a reason…"

Gabriel stepped closer.

"Nina," Denida said and held up his hand. "You know something, don't you?"

"I always keep an eye on you… and Nina, too. I have to because my powers are not the same on Earth…"

"Fine, then," Denida grunted. "But you noticed something about Nina?"

"I explained who Maia and Morton were to her."

"And who are they? Nina thought Maia was Michelle?"

"For a good reason." Gabriel chuckled. "She looks exactly like her sister…"

Her sister… Denida rubbed his eyes. "Why would this matter, anyway?"

"Why do you think? It's Michelle's sister, and Nina hated Michelle, just as you do."

A tear welled up in Denida's eyes, but he swiftly turned away and shook his head. "She's dead; she has no siblings. Not now anyway, do you realize how long it's been since she was on Earth!"

"Her father was given a second chance of life. He found love again…"

"But how can she look like Michelle, let alone be alive still?"

Gabriel folded his hands. "You know how Hell operates slower than Earth, as well as the Underworlds?"

Denida bared his teeth. "Your point?"

"She came back to Earth and saw her father's new life. She was a trained demon now… with Dark magic."

"No… she didn't…" Denida felt afraid to hear the words Gabriel was about to say.

"She cursed Maia and Morton with eternal life and made Maia her spitting image… tormenting her father…"

"You and God allowed this to happen?"

Gabriel sighed. "Dark Arts are Lucifer's domain."

"You are Lucifer's friend; you're often in Hell!"

"Friend… not a demon." Gabriel smiled faintly.

I have to confirm Mara didn't survive before I continue here. Nina would be in danger; I may need to forget about uniting the Underworlds, if she is… Denida stared coldly. "Then, we'll ask Lucifer!" He grabbed Gabriel's hand and clenched his fist, teleporting them to Hell, inside Lucifer's chamber.

Lucifer ecstatically jumped from his throne. "Denny, nice-" His eyes fell on Gabriel, and he instantly dropped his arms, rubbing his wrist. "Gabriel and Denida; whatever bring you here?"

Gabriel looked at Lucifer, then at Denida. "What's going on, here?"

Lucifer shrugged. "I'm not sure why you're here…"

Gabriel stared at Denida, before sauntering through the room. "Just ask him."

"We have a question. Gabriel says you would know better than him."

Lucifer licked his lips. "About?"

"*Medusa!*" Denida clenched his fists, approaching Lucifer. "She cursed her siblings on Earth; you knew about that?"

"What a demon wishes to do to any of their family members doesn't concern me!"

Denida stomped across the floor heavily. "Yet, you didn't tell me, even after she *killed* my son?"

"Why would *you* care? You want to take more revenge on her?" Lucifer winked.

"Why wouldn't I?" Denida hissed. "If she did something so bad, you should have-"

"Stopped her?" Lucifer smirked. "I'm not getting rid of a useful demon.

You had to eventually... Denida stood staring at Lucifer, baring his teeth and clenching his fists. *I'm constantly reminded how bad the Darkness is...* "Let's go, Gabriel. I need to do something more important than this, here." He spun and trudged back to Gabriel.

Lucifer sneered and teleported in front of Gabriel. "You came to ask for information and think you can just leave after! You only get information in exchange for something..."

Denida glared at Lucifer's menacing look, before nodding solemnly.

Gabriel cleared his throat. "This is something I shouldn't hear." He stormed to the door, but he stopped as he reached it, and turned to Denida. "But I hope you don't choose the path of Darkness."

Lucifer chortled. "He always has to be the same old Gabriel..."

Denida stared at the well. "Speaking of which, what happened next?"

"Oh... Well, God had me continue watching Heavani... but I now knew the Darkness had come from my old friend's heart, and had been there all this time."

Denida squinted his eyes. "You never told him that you knew? Or Gabriel, for that matter?"

"He almost threw me off the tower!" Lucifer spat. "As for Gabriel, I considered it... allow me to show you, instead..."

Chapter 31- A Way to Continue

Lucifer sat on the floor of the tower, twiddling his thumbs.

"Luci?" Gabriel knelt to check Lucifer. "What's wrong; why are you being so distant lately?"

Lucifer got up. "Nothing's… up. I'm just-" He exhaled heavily. "God should be done with Saint Heavani soon; I better go check on them." He left the tower before Gabriel could say another word.

Lucifer wandered into the small clearing in the woods where Heavani often relaxed and sat on the bench in the center. The scent of the flowers wafted into the air. Small animals scurried out of the woods as soon as he sat down. A fox rubbed up against his leg. Lucifer picked it up and petted it gently.

"They've taken a liking to you," Heavani giggled.

Lucifer stood up and gently put the fox down. "That's just-"

She waved her hand dismissively. "Don't mind me."

"No, I should. I'm babysitting, remember?" Lucifer winked. Their eyes met briefly. "But God must be finished for today, I take it?"

"Yes," she muttered. A butterfly landed on her hand. She watched its every move for a minute before pushing her hand upward to make it fly away. "But I'm all yours now, *babysitter*!" She giggled.

Lucifer rolled his eyes. *That girl…*

"Luci?" Gabriel appeared on the path and waved at Heavani with a smile.

Lucifer hurried over to grab Gabriel and yanked him to the side. "What are you doing here?" Lucifer peeked at Heavani. "God wants me to protect her from meeting anyone he doesn't wish for her to know!"

"You left before we could finish our talk." Gabriel peered at Heavani. "She does look like Henna, *truly!*"

Lucifer shrugged. "There's nothing-"

Heavani joined them and greeted Gabriel. "Hi, I don't think I've met you personally. I'm Saint Heavani, but you can just call me Heavani."

Gabriel passed Lucifer and followed her to the bench. "Nice to meet you; I'm Gabriel."

She nodded. "I've heard a lot about you."

As soon as she sat down, animals scurried out from amongst the trees and joined them, encircling the bench.

Lucifer trudged closer to Heavani and Gabriel, but they were chatting casually. He licked his lips.

The fox that had rubbed up against Lucifer's leg before came up to him and he knelt to scratch behind the fox's ear, making it trill.

Gabriel stood up. "I should get to my patrol." He patted Lucifer on the shoulder before he left down the path.

"That was the friend you mentioned?" Heavani continued feeding the birds berries.

Lucifer nodded and approached Heavani with the fox accompanying him.

Heavani smiled tenderly at the fox. "He likes you. Did you ever tell-"

Lucifer dashed forward, accidentally knocking Heavani over with his hands over her mouth.

Heavani's eyes widened, full of puzzlement, staring straight into Lucifer's.

Lucifer shook his head and arched his neck. "Only upstairs; leave notes if you must," he whispered into her ear before crawling away and helping her to her feet. He shook his arms. "Sorry about that… bad balance. My mistake," he smiled.

"It's…" Heavani saw the fear in Lucifer's eyes. *'It's okay,'* she said in his thoughts while patting his shoulder reassuringly.

Lucifer grabbed Heavani's arm. "You should see how beautiful Heaven looks from above!" He hurried out of the forest, past the angels, ignoring their greetings, and continued straight to the tower at a steady pace. When they reached the top of the tower, Lucifer turned around to Heavani's pondering face. "You can't!" he began yelling, but her broad smile stopped him mid-sentence.

"What is it, Luci?"

How can she have such a sweet smile! Lucifer ventured away to watch the distance. "It's good that God taught you to talk with your thoughts, but he can read all our thoughts, here…"

"Not up here." She raised her finger with a smile.

"Exactly. If it's not everyday stuff, this is the only place we can talk about it, which is why you can leave me notes, in case there is anything…"

"Gabriel?" Heavani stood next to Lucifer with a curious stare.

Lucifer sighed. "I didn't tell him; I'm not sure I ever should."

"But isn't it best for Gabriel to know? He's an old friend of yours."

Lucifer lowered his head. "You don't understand; it would shatter what he thinks of God…" He raised his head to peek into the distance, where he could see Gabriel finishing his inspection of one of the magic outposts and strolling to the next. "How would he feel about protecting God if he knew the Darkness he protects Heaven from was a part of God?"

Heavani touched Lucifer's cheek and tilted his face to look straight into his eyes. "You're forgetting; he's protecting Heaven from the Darkness for more than just God. *You* and the other angels too!"

Lucifer leaned against the windowsill. "Want to see how Heaven looks like from up here?"

A bright glow appeared in Heavani's eyes.

Lucifer guided her to another room, which had a clear view of Heaven's expanse below them.

"Incredible!" She leaned out to peer down, turning her head for a clear view of the beauty all around them before turning to Lucifer. "You can see everything from up here!"

"It was always intended to be high enough that we could see everything in advance…" Lucifer flashed her a meek smile. "Let's go back down." He led Heavani through Heaven, passing by a giant lake on their peaceful walk.

Heavani ran forth and knelt next to the water. "It's so nice. Come and feel it!"

Lucifer grunted, but continued to her side. He stopped abruptly when God appeared in front of him.

"Lucifer! Where have you two been?" God asked with a high-pitched, demanding voice.

"Heavani wanted-"

"No!" God glanced at the lake Heavani sat next to. "Her name is *Saint Heavani*; use her full name." He grabbed Lucifer and thrusted him forward, sending him flying into the water, landing in the middle of the lake.

Heavani gasped. She jumped into the water, but God extended his arm, drawing her back toward him.

God picked her up. "No, he brought this on himself; he needs to keep you where I can see you!"

Lucifer crawled out of the lake, completely drenched.

"Hear this, Lucifer. Do *not* make me lose faith in you like I did with Henna! You will stay where I can see her at all times; if you don't…"

Heavani looked at Lucifer sadly.

"Come." God dragged Heavani with him.

Lucifer sighed and wiped the water from his face. *Would he do the same thing to me that he did to Henna?* He shut his eyes and clutched at his chest. The water soaking his skin and clothes dried as if it were never there. He trudged out to the Pearly Gates, where Peter stood on guard duty.

"What are you doing here?" Peter glared suspiciously.

"Waiting for Gabriel…"

"No!" Peter roared. "This is my spot; I'm watching Heaven. God has entrusted this to *me*."

"I'm just-"

Peter raised his fist and magic emanated around it. "Begone, now!"

Lucifer raised his hands and backed into Heaven.

He meandered aimlessly through Heaven, not knowing where to go for what felt like an eternity. He stopped as his eyes fell on the fox that always followed him in the distance. *What is it doing here?* He slogged forward, but as soon as he drew near, it scurried farther away.

Lucifer rolled his eyes. *I guess I have nothing better to do…* He chased the fox through Heaven, Lucifer was certain that it was going to the forest, but it continued past Heavani's garden, heading toward the tower.

The fox stopped and sat down a short distance away from the tower. *Here? Why has it stopped here?*

Heavani strode out of the tower and picked up the fox, kissed it on its head, and petted it tenderly while peeking at Lucifer. She put it back down and opened the door to the tower. The fox darted inside. She smiled at Lucifer and strolled away.

Lucifer frowned. He kept watching her as she passed him, avoiding eye contact. He shrugged and entered the tower, pursuing the fox.

The fox sat waiting at the top of the stairs. Lucifer reached down to pick it up, but it sped away into another room before he could reach it. In the next room, the fox jumped on a table and sat on a slip of paper.

What's that paper doing here? He noticed writing on the parchment. '*Lucifer.*' He grabbed the fox, put it down on the floor, and turned to pick up the paper.

As soon as he touched the paper, Heavani's voice echoed through the room and an image formed.

"Luci, I'm happy you came. I knew the fox would do the trick." Heavani grinned. "I'm sending this message to you with magic. It will be deleted after my words are spoken, so pay attention and know that we can reuse this paper for new messages, intended only for you and me!"

Lucifer felt a strange warmth from within.

"The magic," Heavani continued. "-is helpful up here where God can't hear. I can leave you notes and you can leave some for me if you wish!" She lowered her head. "I don't like… how he treated you… I'm sorry about that. You need someone to help you and be there for you. There's only one, as far as I know. *Gabriel!*" She raised her head with a sad look. "Please forgive me."

Heavani's image faded with the last word on the page. With the disappearance of the last letter, Lucifer smacked the sheet of paper down on the desk and ran out of the tower, sprinting as fast as he could to the Pearly Gates.

He reached it, panting to catch his breath. He lifted his arms to Peter, who peered, disgusted at the sight. "Gab...riel... is he-"

"Gabriel already left with Saint Heavani."

Lucifer gasped. *No, graces. The forest!* He spun around and flew through Heaven with his wings. He landed just outside the forest and raced through it, following the path. He could feel the cold sweat running down his forehead, but he didn't care.

He stopped abruptly when he reached Heavani's bench. *Nobody here, how can this be? She can't have gone somewhere else. Was Peter lying? She has nowhere-*

He spun around and hurried out of the forest as fast as he could. He kept glancing up at the tower as he ran. He raised his arms, the wings appeared, and he flew with a flash of light to the top of the tower, entering through the window looking out at Heaven.

Gabriel and Heavani watched him land.

Gabriel gazed sternly at Lucifer.

"She... told... you," Lucifer stuttered.

Gabriel charged forward and hugged Lucifer tightly. "Don't think you can't tell me something ever again!"

***

Denida licked his lips. "Did you inform Gabriel about Henna, too?"

"Yes. We had a long talk in the tower. I told Gabriel everything I knew... including how God started to show aggression..."

"But why didn't you and Gabriel leave Heaven?"

"I... I... never thought of doing that." Lucifer looked perplexed, almost embarrassed. "I guess for the other angels and Heavani. God was our longtime friend too, after all!"

"Yet, you knew the Darkness trying to enter Heaven originated from him!" Denida raised his voice.

"In retrospect, yes... but that's not how the story unfolded."

Thank god he's done. I really need to check on Nina... Denida tapped his foot. "I heard more. Now, can I go; I need to-"

"This isn't over, yet. Let's continue, so that you can get back to whatever you need to." Lucifer gloated.

Denida fiddled with his fingers. "Okay, just one more..."

"Gabriel kept a keen eye on God, so that he wouldn't lose his temper." Lucifer rubbed his hands. "Gabriel always liked playing the long game and he believed, *as he still does*, in the good that God can be. Heavani and I kept our routine in Heaven, where God still watched us, but we left messages for each other in the tower…

***

Lucifer climbed the tower and entered the main room, where the paper lay, as it always did. He knelt to pick it up and the fox jumped on top of him, fluttering its tail.

"Hey, Luci and… your fox is there with you, right?" An image of Heavani with the fox next to her leg appeared. She gracefully dropped to her knees to pet it. "He should have a name, you know. What should we call you?" She tapped the fox's nose.

The fox trilled close to Lucifer's leg. He felt a strange warmth from within. *What's this weird feeling?*

"Scout," Heavani rubbed the fox's head. "He's always scouting for us; Scout fits the bill."

Lucifer glanced at Scout, who wagged his tail.

Heavani sighed audibly and stood up straight. "God is still keeping a keen eye on you, but us keeping to our routines in Heaven and Gabriel talking you up is starting to help… I think."

Just like-

Heavani stomped her foot. "I know you'll say that Gabriel's stupid for believing in God's good side!"

You said it, not me…

"We saw the Darkness in him. Everyone has to have light in them, too; I believe Gabriel's right!"

Lucifer rolled his eyes.

"Give… Gabriel… time." Heavani's eyes became stern. The image faded.

Lucifer picked up the paper and gazed out at the horizon, fiddling with the paper.

"She's right, you know…" Gabriel stepped into the room.

Lucifer said nothing; he just continued toying with the parchment.

Gabriel strolled over to Lucifer and joined him at the window. "The Darkness wants to return, but you must remember, it hasn't yet… there's still time."

Lucifer spun around. "Are you sure about that? I saw Darkness in God when he almost killed Henna… when he almost killed *me*!"

"Throwing you off the tower won't do it; only Henna's daggers can kill us, you know that!"

Lucifer shrugged. "You didn't see his eyes; the scorn within them…"

Gabriel rested his hand on Lucifer's shoulder. "We're all old friends, Luci. Trust me; I know what I'm doing!"

Lucifer threw the paper into the room. It hung in the air while Lucifer glanced at Gabriel. "Heavani, I'll give Gabriel time!" As he spoke the words, text appeared on the paper. "But know this-" Lucifer lifted his finger at Gabriel. "Henna wants her revenge and the Darkness is out there. You and I need to seriously consider our future here…"

"We will." Gabriel folded his hands together. "- but I won't fail."

Lucifer and Gabriel descended the tower, accompanied by Scout. Scout suddenly sprinted off.

"Guess he couldn't wait for you," Gabriel chuckled.

"He's more Hea-" He peered upward. "- *Saint Heavani's* Scout."

Gabriel tapped Lucifer on the shoulder. "I'll see you; I need to run my checkups." He marched toward the Pearly Gates. Scout passed him and sped back to Lucifer.

Scout kept circling Lucifer, biting at the rope hanging from his waist. *He must want to show me something…* "I'm coming." Lucifer followed Scout.

Scout led him to the path inside the forest, but continued past the bench, venturing into the woods on the far side of the garden.

Oh no, not in there, again… Lucifer pulled the branches aside as he stepped into the overgrowth.

Scout had no problem navigating the forest, given that he was so tiny; he scurried under and around the branches effortlessly.

Heavani appeared, kneeling at a flowerbed in the middle of the forest.

Lucifer blinked. He couldn't believe his eyes. *Henna… no, Heavani!* "Hey, Hea-"

Heavani jumped up and put her hand over Lucifer's lips. She shook her head while keeping eye contact, pointed her finger downward, and squatted. She pushed some branches and underbrush aside and ran her fingers through the dirt to write. *'He can't see us because of the trees; he can only sense our presence.'*

Lucifer knelt beside her, wiped the ground, and wrote with his finger. *'Clever!'*

She giggled and raised her eyebrows. *'Where there's a will, there's a way,'* she jotted.

Lucifer shrugged and focused on the ground. *'As I said earlier, I'll trust Gabriel.'* He watched her as she looked up from reading it. He wiped the message. *'But… I doubt you'll be right!'*

She cleared the dirt. *'You'll see.'*

Lucifer rolled his eyes. *'Let's return before he gets suspicious.'* He stood.

Heavani followed him after smoothing out the dirt once more to erase the last traces of their messages.

They returned to the bench in the clearing where they usually met. As soon as Heavani sat down, animals started to envelop her.

Lucifer felt a strange sensation approaching. He spun around.

Henna stood in front of Lucifer, surrounded by a circle in the same colors as her eyes. She raised her arm and flicked her fingers. The cone around her grew and swallowed Lucifer and Heavani.

"Shaddai can't hear us, now. Who's this?" Henna marched past Lucifer to Heavani's side.

Heavani gasped. "It's like looking at myself!"

Lucifer cleared his throat. "This is… Queen Henna." He stepped in between the queen and Heavani with a stern look directed at Henna. "God… I mean, *Shaddai*… modeled Saint Heavani after you…"

"She's the queen you told me about? The one God and you…" Heavani grabbed Lucifer's hand.

Henna smiled. "I'm the one you heard about, yes."

"Why are you here?" Lucifer tightened his grip on Heavani's hand. "You showed up and know enough to block God from listening in on our conversation!"

"I've come to give you a chance to-"

"You came into Heaven… a place you swore you never wanted to enter!" Lucifer licked his lips. "I'm guessing you already tried with Gabriel, but failed."

Henna's rainbow eyes grew brighter. "Gabriel matters not. I'm giving you a chance-"

"A chance for what, to betray God?"

"To fulfill your destiny, Azal; you can be a god!"

"No!" Lucifer bared his teeth. "You're wrong if that's your *prophecy*."

Henna chuckled. "It's not, but I hoped you could prove me wrong." She turned to Heavani with a smile. "Nice to meet you, my dear, but you better get ready."

Lucifer pulled Heavani behind him. "You're not hurting her!"

"Me," Henna grinned. "Never, but I think God will want to see you two very soon, thanks to Gabriel…" She waved her hand and there was a flash of light. When Lucifer could see again, he saw that she'd disappeared along with the rainbow cone."

Lucifer rubbed his forehead.

"There you are," Peter nodded to Heavani. "God was not sure where you were amongst all these trees, so he sent me to find you."

"You," Lucifer scorned. "He usually just summons me by thought or sends Gabriel…"

"The trees." Peter lifted his head. "As for Gabriel, he's waiting with God already…" He gestured with his hand for him to follow. "… *unfortunately*," he muttered under his breath.

Lucifer licked his lips and followed behind Heavani.

Peter opened the door and waved his hand. "Go ahead."

Lucifer frowned. *"You're not coming, but Saint Heavani is?"*

Peter shrugged. "This is what God instructed me to do; bring Saint Heavani and you."

God never wants Heavani to see anything, yet now… I hope he hasn't discovered the note up in the tower…

Lucifer and Heavani entered God's chamber. The doors shut behind them instantly. God sat on his throne with Gabriel standing next to him. God jumped up and pulled Heavani into his embrace as soon as they entered the room.

Lucifer continued next to Gabriel. "Why are we-"

"Lucifer," God said ecstatically. "Gabriel found *something.*"

Lucifer coughed. "Saint Heavani…"

God stroked her back. "Saint Heavani needs to be ready… if the evil one, who looks just like her, were to come here." He led Heavani into another room with a broad smile.

Lucifer grabbed Gabriel's arm before venturing after them. "What did you find?"

'Come,' God's voice rang in Lucifer's head. He sighed and continued into the other room.

Gabriel sauntered past Lucifer and picked up a box, he brought over to God.

God turned to Lucifer. "You want to see this."

I have a terrible feeling; it's just as she said… Lucifer smiled and stood next to God.

Gabriel received a nod from God, so he put the box on the floor where they could all see it. He proceeded to open the box, revealing a dagger, just like the one God and Lucifer had used on Henna.

"How," Lucifer fell to his knees and touched the dagger. It had similar inscriptions and was made of the same familiar, unique material. *It's the same; the only difference is Henna's blood isn't there…*

God folded his hands and the knife slid from Lucifer's grasp into God's. "This is the *only* thing that can kill our kind, including the dangerous one who looks like you, Saint Heavani." He stared into Heavani's eyes.

"There *really* are seven of them?" Lucifer turned to Gabriel. "How did you find this?"

"It was lying next to one of the magic posts protecting Heaven…" Gabriel shrugged. "How or why, I have no idea!"

I do…

'And what would that be?' God spoke in Lucifer's thoughts.

"Henna wanted us to have it; she's playing us," Lucifer replied with a determined look.

***

Such hatred... I should not fall into that. Whipboy can wait; I should check on Robert to see if his world is in chaos... and I need to unite our world. I need to find Nina, too...

"I can see that you need to do something, don't you?" Lucifer smirked.

"Yes, but I'll-"

Lucifer slammed his fist into the well. "You go ahead, as I said. Remember, however, if you want me to stop interfering, you must see the rest of my story and help me!"

"Misery loves its company, Luci." Denida looked gravely at Lucifer before he turned away and paused. He clenched his fist that bore the ring and appeared back in the Wild West.

Chapter 32- A Rescue

Nina and Susan eyed the compound where the Colonel was being held captive. *I wish I could ask Denny for help. It would be so much easier, but he wouldn't allow me to kill Jack on my own...* Nina felt uneasy and rubbed her nose. "They might be holding the Colonel on the same island they kept us on."

Susan glanced across the sea to the island. "That's a *big* if!"

"Morton wasn't with Maia." Nina shrugged. "We need to check the island to find out why she's working with Jack..."

"That's right..." Susan threw a punch at Claus. "I'm not assuming you'll inform us about that!"

Claus squirmed. "I don't know!" he yelled. "I already told you, the demon just wanted to get Jack!"

Nina snuck a quick look at them. *Something about this doesn't add up...* "We should go to the island from the other side, so they won't notice us approaching." Nina pointed at a small boat, far enough away that it was hard to notice from the compound.

Nina approached the boat with Susan following behind, dragging Claus, who was tied up tight, his arms bound behind his back.

A middle-aged man, who had little hair left, stood working on the boat. Drenched in sweat, he paused his labor to wipe his face with a rag and sipped from a bottle. He squinted as he put it back down.

"This is private property you're on, Lady!"

"I know," Nina gave a sweet smile. "- but my friend and I were hoping you could help us."

The man spat into the ocean. "Why would I want to do that?"

"The island out there; we need to get out there for-"

"No!" The man turned away and focused on his work.

Nina and Susan exchanged a nervous stare.

"We can pay-"

The man slammed his fist into the boat's floorboard. "That island is privately owned... by *them*." He pointed at the fancy estate next to them. "There's no way I'm taking you there!"

Susan forced Claus to his knees. "Can we rent your boat?" she asked. "Then it won't pose any danger to you."

The man ogled her, then Claus. "I don't-"

Nina stepped closer. "We have to help our friend; he's on that island. This is the only way. Please!"

The man waved his hand. "Come on; I'll take you."

"You'll regret it," Claus chuckled.

Susan slapped Claus on top of his head and yanked him aboard the boat.

Nina smiled at the man. "We're ready, if you will, please?"

The man set the boat in motion. "We'll need to take the long way around, so they won't see us."

My thoughts exactly. It will take longer to reach Morton, but better safe than sorry. Nina nodded and glanced over at Claus and Susan before she turned away.

The boat sailed farther and circled the island before gradually approaching the far shore.

"I don't like this; I've got a bad feeling." Claus stared at Susan.

"Nobody cares what you think! We'll deal with whatever may come."

"Including *Maia*," Claus mocked.

Susan tightened her fist and grabbed Claus.

"Susan, not now!" Nina yelled. "Besides, after what he did to Daniel, you're not killing him without me."

"Lucky... you," Susan muttered as she loosened her grip. "Someday... someday..."

Claus snorted.

"We're here!" The man helped Nina to the shore.

"Come on," Nina commanded.

"What, us?" Susan shook her head. "It's not a good idea to let him on that island!"

"We don't have a choice." Nina bared her teeth. "If we encounter something, we need someone who can use black magic!"

Claus grinned. "Shall we, Suzy?"

Susan grunted. "Don't call me that; it's Susan!" She pulled him off the boat with her.

"I'll be waiting here." The man reclaimed his spot at the helm.

Nina led the rest of them to the spot she had stayed at with Morton and Maia.

"It's strange... I can't feel anything when I try to find him with magic." Claus frowned.

"It's not strange." Nina waved her hand. "The magic barrier."

"If there's a magic barrier here, why the hell am I coming?" Claus raised his voice.

Nina turned to Claus. "You're here as a prisoner, no? *You betrayed us!* Who would be a better decoy if we encounter Jack?" She raised her eyebrows.

Susan grinned and pushed Claus forward.

Nina paused abruptly and lifted her hand. "I know this place; we're close." She loaded her gun before continuing into the woods beyond the shore. Within a few minutes, she reached the camp.

Everything was silent. Nina listened carefully, but couldn't hear a single sound. Looking down, she flinched at the sight of bloodstains scattered throughout the camp.

"What... is... this," Nina stuttered, but she couldn't stop herself; she had to find the cause. *Maia's alive... and Morton can't die; he's immortal!* Despite what she knew, she couldn't shake the feeling that she would discover something terrible here.

She reached the table where they kept the drugs. It had been knocked over and the white powder was scattered across the ground. A human leg stuck out from under the table.

Nina gasped and rushed to move the table, revealing Morton, pale and lifeless, lying on the ground. "No, no, no. How?" She pulled him out, finding that he was cold and stiff. "This can't be; he's immortal!" Nina yelled.

Susan stopped. "So that's why..."

"No, it isn't!" Nina screamed. "Medusa cursed him; he can't die."

"Well, he sure looks dead," Claus smirked.

Nina charged Claus and struck him with such force that he fell to the dirt. "You kidnapped Daniel and now you're mocking Morton's death!"

Claus bared his teeth. "Got your panties in a bunch? I didn't even do this, but you had to know something was up when you saw Maia."

Nina fell to her knees and continued punching Claus, who was defenseless with his hands still tied.

Susan grabbed Nina under her arms to pull her back. "Enough, Nina! There are plenty of reasons to hate Claus, but this isn't one of them."

Nina shook herself free and shot Susan a condemning stare. "I didn't think anything was wrong! There's no way he could have died."

Claus coughed and sat up. "Are you sure about that?"

"Yes!" Nina kicked at the dirt next to Claus. "They tried to kill themselves in myriad ways."

Claus shrugged his shoulders. "Before or after Medusa died?"

Susan cleared her throat. "The Colonel and the others aren't here," Susan broke the silence.

Nina nodded.

"Let's go to the compound to rescue our friends," Susan said.

"No, no, no." Claus tried to crawl away.

Susan grabbed Claus. "Remember what we need you for," Susan winked.

Nina marched through the trees to the tunnel. When they were a few paces off, she suddenly hid amongst some bushes, signaling for Susan and Claus to follow suit. "There are guards," she hissed and turned to Susan.

In front of them, several guards watched the tunnel. The area around it had been cleared since the last time Nina was there, so the tunnel was easily visible.

One of the guards rubbed his eye. "It's hot; are they really sure Lady Nina will return?"

The guard next to him flicked his fingers. "Yes, but you can make the rounds to see if there are any signs of them, seeing as it's too difficult for you to stand here," he chortled.

"No!" The first guard yelled and grabbed his gun. "I can do it; anyone who comes will regret it."

Nina lowered her head. *How are we going to get past them?*

Susan glared at Nina and held up a dagger. "We need to give them a reason to check on something."

"Something?" Nina stared at her blankly.

Susan sighed and jabbed the knife into the ground.

Claus licked his lips and tilted his hand toward it, while Susan crawled the short distance to Nina. Claus wrapped his hand around it as Susan reached Nina. He cut his rope, not taking his sight off the two girls.

"Is Claus falling for it?" Susan whispered.

Nina's eyes widened. She tilted her head to look at Claus, who smiled innocently at her. "What are… you playing at?" she muttered to Susan.

The rope tore with a snap.

Nina spun toward the sound and lifted her gun.

Susan grabbed it from her and aimed at Claus. "Give me the pleasure!"

Claus rolled to the side evasively and dashed toward the guards, waving his hands. "They're here!" he screamed.

Susan and Nina ran from behind the bush, planning to ambush the guards from the other direction while the guards were focused on Claus. They lifted their firearms and gunned the guards down.

Claus spun around and ran into the trees.

Susan aimed and fired after him. "Dammit," she hissed.

"Susan; forget about him. We have a limited amount of time before they notice the guards are down!" Nina examined the bodies and removed their earpieces. She took one and handed the other to Susan.

Susan grunted.

"They'll come and check on the guards and find Claus; he won't get away."

Susan grabbed the earpiece and followed Nina into the tunnel.

Susan and Nina stood on each side of the door leading out. They stole a look outside to see if the entrance was clear.

"Wait," Susan extended her arm. "Someone will notice us!"

Nina rolled her eyes. "Which is why we'll be careful to avoid letting them see us."

"But I have a better idea; we dress up like them. We can even use the guards' outfits." Susan winked.

That could work… "If they didn't find them yet…"

Susan shook her head. "Not possible!" She tapped her ear. "We would have heard about it."

Nina cracked her knuckles. "Then let's do it!" She ran back through the tunnel with Susan.

They rushed to put on the guards' uniforms and hide their bodies in the shrubs, away from prying eyes.

Nina blinked. "This had better work."

"Where's everyone?" A guard emerged from the tunnel with another one in tow.

Nina held her finger near her gun's trigger.

"You should stay at the entrance… at least one of you!" The guard waved his hand. "Go on back to the compound; it's our shift."

Susan patted Nina on the shoulder and walked into the tunnel. Nina followed, giving the two guards a glance as she passed them.

This time, they trudged out onto the grounds of Jack's compound without worrying about who would notice them. The Darkness lay even thicker on the ground making it hard to breathe.

Where are they keeping them, I wonder? Nina focused on the main building. *Jack would know…*

Susan pulled Nina back. "Don't go there!"

"He'll know," Nina murmured.

"Who, Jack, or is it Danyel, you mean? Not to forget about Maia, who for some reason, joined them!"

"Must be because of her brother's death…"

"Exactly!" Susan roared, making the other guards turn their heads. She waved with a smile and took Nina under her arm to the side. "Something, which shouldn't be possible," she whispered. "We must be careful now that we're finally here; he wouldn't hold them this close to his compound."

"True, but where then?" Nina turned 360 degrees, scanning the area for anything that stood out. Her eyes stopped on one specific, heavily guarded building. "Maybe in there!"

Susan faced the building. "There's a lot of guards there…"

"Just wait here." Nina vanished from sight, but continued toward the building.

She ambled into the crowd of guards inconspicuously and slipped inside as someone exited the building.

"I don't know where they are!" the Colonel yelled from the center of the room.

"Really?" Maia leered at him, smiling deviously. "Are you sure about that?"

"You're not who Nina-"

Maia grabbed the Colonel by the throat and slammed his head into the wall. "Do *not* mention her name!" Her eyes were as dark as coal.

"Please… don't," he stuttered.

Maia released her grip.

The Colonel clutched his throat. "You are as malicious as your sister!"

Maia stared at him coldly. "If my sister Mara saw Nina kill our brother, she would have done the same to her!"

The Colonel and the Commander both gasped.

"That's not possible," the Colonel insisted.

"No?" Maia leaned in close to the Colonel's face, so close he could feel her breath. "I saw it myself. She stabbed him with the one thing that can kill a soul eternally; *the holy dagger!*"

The Colonel cleared his throat. "He's immortal, like you are…"

Suddenly Nina felt a coldness behind her. "Immortality doesn't mean anything if you're stabbed by the dagger," Danyel said behind Nina.

"Holy… dagger?" The Colonel's voice screeched.

"You wouldn't know; you might have liked to know… it could have killed Lucifer…" Danyel chuckled, then tilted his head a little to the side. "*Interesting…*" He moseyed about the room. "There aren't too many in existence… yet she had one!"

"Not many?" Maia frowned. "Just produce another, so Nina can get what she deserves!"

"We can't," Danyel sneered and threw his arms around Nina and squeezed tight.

The magic around Nina failed, revealing her.

"Nina!" Maia charged her, but she bumped into an invisible forcefield, blocking her.

"No, sorry," Danyel gloated. "Hello again, Nina… it's been a long time. If you're here, so is Susan!" He flung Nina into the wall and spun toward the exit.

"Wait!" Maia screamed. "Let me through!" She slammed and kicked the barrier.

Danyel stopped. "The magic barrier is there for a reason; to prevent her from using magic as well as to keep you from touching her!" He continued out the door without looking back.

"Lady Nina has been captured!" Danyel yelled, raising his arms, rejoicing.

The guards watching the entrance all applauded.

Danyel rubbed his hands together and clucked his tongue.

"Sir, is something wrong?" a guard asked, puzzled.

"Susan's still here, somewhere," he met the guard's gaze. "- close by!"

"We should find her, then!" The guard used his earpiece to request reinforcements.

"Yes, find her!" Danyel returned to the building.

Nina tried to crawl backward, but she couldn't get out of the invisible dome. She stared in fright as Danyel approached.

"Where's your friend?" Danyel asked. "You would be smart to tell me!" He watched Maia. "- or should I let her have her way with you?"

"I didn't… hurt Morton. I never knew about any knives!" Nina shivered.

Danyel turned his sight on Nina and helped her sit up. "You okay?"
He's asking if I'm okay? Nina nodded doubtfully.

"Good, because, you see; I don't really care if you did, but she wants revenge! Whether you killed him or not, you are going to provide me with the info about Susan!"

Nina shook her head, jumped to her feet, and charged toward the door, extending her arm, hoping to create magic around her fingertips, but she slammed into the barrier before she reached the door.

"Tick, tock," Danyel gloated. "There's no escape!"

The door slammed open in front of Nina. She raised her head with anticipation.

A set of troops rushed in. "Sir, we've got a problem!"

"Big enough to bother me?" Danyel shook his hand. "Go inform Jack!"

"But it's about *Susan*," a guard insisted.

"Susan?" Danyel marched up to the guards. "What is it?"

"The island. We discovered two dead guards on the other side of the tunnel… their uniforms were gone."

"Of course!" Danyel smirked at Nina. "I was wondering where you got that uniform!" He teleported behind Maia, where he put his arms around her. "I'm gonna go catch another girl. You watch them while I'm gone. If Nina's dead when I return, I'll bring you more pain than your sister ever could!" He knocked her on the head gently with a wicked grin and left to search with the soldiers, slamming the door behind him.

Nina tilted her head and her eyes met with Maia's. A cold chill ran down her spine.

Maia grumbled and glared at the Colonel, who refused to look her in the eyes, which caused her to march up to him and grab his cheek tight and turn to Nina. "I can't hurt you, but I can hurt the ones you care about!"

The Colonel's agonizing scream made Nina squinch her eyes tightly.

Chapter 33- A New Gate

Denida scratched his forehead. The midday sun drenched his forehead with sweat as he approached Robert's farm. Inside it was as empty as outside in the baking sun.

Denida searched the house and found no one present. He sat down on the bed after inspecting several of the rooms. *No one's here...* He turned his head toward the front door, stood, and walked out.

In front of the house, a horse was tied to a post while it sipped some water.

"What..." Denida scoped his surroundings, but there were no signs of anyone, so he circled the horse and checked its satchel.

'Click.'

Denida lifted his hands and saw a man standing with a gun raised, aimed at his head.

"Step back from my horse," the man commanded and tilted the gun to the side.

Denida lifted his arms higher and backed away. "Who are you?"

"Funny, I was about to ask you the same question!" The man revealed a sheriff's badge on his chest. "I'm the law, here to fetch something for the owner. You?"

"You know where Robert is, then?"

The Sheriff holstered his gun on his belt. "Sheriff Robert has many fans..." He waved his hand. "You may as well not stay here if you know what's good for you; he won't be back for a long time." He tied a bag to the satchel and mounted his horse.

"Wait," Denida extended his arm. "I'm not just another of Robert's fans."

But it was too late; the Sheriff had already ridden away.

Denida gritted his teeth. *There's only one way if he won't show me...* He muttered a spell, causing him to vanish from sight and reappear on the Sheriff's horse, sitting right behind the lawman, staying invisible.

The Sheriff slowed his horse and glanced back. "Strange, I thought I felt something..." He shook his head and continued forward.

Denida enjoyed the landscape as they passed the fields and mountains. He remembered some of the places from his youth, there.

Wait... this is... He turned his head to focus on their destination.

Ahead of them, the Gate towered into the sky without any Darkness surrounding it. Instead of demons, people gathered out in the open, talking and laughing and making the land surrounding the Gate noticeably less quiet than it had been the last time Denida was here.

The Sheriff nodded and waved at the lawmen standing watch. He rode on, past the Gate, onwards up the hill to the estate, where he dismounted and hitched his horse to a post. He took the bag with him into the house.

Denida climbed down and trailed behind him. Inside the building, it was anything but quiet. The ruckus was so deafening that he couldn't hear himself think.

The Sheriff strolled up to a guard watching the elevator. "Robert is expecting me!" The guard nodded and led him into the elevator, where they started their ascent.

Denida clenched his fist and brought his lips to the ring, making his spirit hover in the elevator, while his body stayed put. His lips stayed on the ring until the Sheriff left the elevator, at which point, Denida raised his head from the ring, causing his body to meet up with his spirit on the upper level.

The Sheriff marched directly up to Robert and handed him the bag.

I finally found him! Denida became visible and walked into the room.

The Sheriff and the rest of the men around Robert raised their guns at Denida.

"No!" Robert bolted forward. "Don't shoot; this is the former Sheriff Denida, who helped get rid of the demons."

The Sheriff lowered his head.

Denida stood with his arms raised and winked at them as they lowered their guns.

"We're establishing order." Robert tilted his head and stepped out on the balcony. "You saw the ruckus down there; they're all prepared to start life anew."

Denida's eyes scanned the room. "That's fast work. You've already accrued a lot of followers."

"My name precedes me, apparently," Robert chuckled.

Denida scratched his forehead. "Maybe you're more capable as a leader than a Sheriff, then."

Robert frowned. "Nah, it's just a coincidence."

"To get people to follow you is leadership, Ro..." *Is this what Anneh was trying to get me to see?*

"It's only tempo-"

"Temporary?" Denida smirked. "It was the same in my world. After the Dark Angels fell, I led it *temporarily,* except *temporary* never ended. We can't deny our destinies, Robert..."

Robert peered across the room.

"They need someone strong to prevent the demons from returning."

"But me?" Robert shook his head.

"I can help you; I am here to unite all the Underworlds again. This is the last world I have left…"

Robert put his hand on Denida's shoulder. "Not anymore. Before Dan left, he prepared some weird device, which sends an odd image from your world."

Denida flicked his finger. "Good to hear you finally have one. We tried to get through Heaven and Hell with a robot before, but it didn't go too well."

"A robot?" Robert lifted his brows.

Denida waved his hand dismissively and grabbed Robert's hand. "I'm glad to hear that this world has achieved peace. I'm excited to hear about how the world evolves." He shook Robert's hand.

Robert headed back inside.

The Sheriff took off his hat, cleared his throat, and stepped out onto the balcony.

Denida nipped at his upper lip. "Something I can help you with?"

"I just want to say I'm sorry… I didn't-"

"Don't worry about it!" Denida slapped the Sheriff's shoulder before following Robert inside. "I should go. Take care and do let me know how it goes."

Robert smiled. "Yes, I'll look forward to working with you."

The ground shook suddenly, sending the furniture hurtling across the room.

An earthquake? Denida ran over to stand under the archway to the balcony with Robert, who'd chosen the same spot.

Robert watched as the others scattered to seek shelter from everything flying about. He turned his head to the other side, his eyes widening as he stepped out into the balcony.

What's he doing? Denida tried to grab him. "Get in here!" he yelled.

"The… the-" Robert turned with wide eyes to Denida. "The ground…" He turned back and ventured farther out on the balcony.

"Yes, it's shaking, so get back here!" Denida screamed. *Can't let something happen to him.* Denida stroked his ring, causing a magic cone to surround him, and then hurried to follow Robert. He stopped abruptly. *How can this be?*

The ground had crumbled next to the house, creating a giant, gaping hole. A second Gate, significantly larger than the one standing not far off, rose out of the crater. The shaking suddenly stopped, and the dust began to settle.

"What… is… *that?*" Robert stuttered.

The Sheriff joined them on the balcony and gulped at the sight.

Denida extended his hand. "Let's go."

Robert nodded and grabbed ahold of Denida's hand.

Denida and Robert teleported down to the strange, new Gate, over three times the size of the other Gates, both in height and width. They split up and strode around it. When they met on the other side, their eyes were as broad as when they first started.

"Keep watch; I'll go check if it has a device like the other Gates."

Robert tightened his grip on his gun. "You really think this is the same? It looks bigger and where does it lead to? The first leads into this world…" He peered down the hill at the other Gate. "- and that one leads away…"

"I… don't… know…" Denida sighed heavily and approached it with tiny steps. He glanced around restlessly, as if expecting something to charge at him.

As he reached the center of the Gate, he knelt to touch it. The main unit's material was the same as on the other Gates.

"It's safe; come," Denida signaled to Robert, who ran up to him.

Denida examined the main device closely. "An engraving…" He ran his finger over it. There was another emblem under the inscription, comprised of symbols, which reminded Denida of the dagger Lucifer had shown him.

"Know what it is?" Robert holstered his gun.

Denida rubbed his hands together. "I know someone who may; keep it under surveillance until I return, please?"

"Sure, but whom?"

Denida had already started to march off. He teleported to Hell, where he appeared outside of Lucifer's mansion. He walked toward the front door, but stopped after a few steps.

Wait, maybe I should try to find that dagger? Denida lifted his ring to his lips and muttered something. A cone surfaced around him.

Inside, he paused again and looked around the dark corridor, toward where the two rows of doors lined the hall. He crept down the corridor on tiptoes, squeezing his necklace tightly, feeling for any hints regarding which door he should try. As he passed by the doors, no response came from it. He clenched his fist tighter. *Why doesn't it work…*

The door to Lucifer's chamber burst open and a set of demons hustled out.

Lucifer marched behind them. "You better get both of them for me!" he hollered. His body was encased with flames, when he turned back to his chamber without noticing Denida.

I'm not going to find the dagger; Lucifer hid it too well… The cone around Denida dissipated and he walked into Lucifer's chamber.

"Luci?" His eyes wandered around the empty room. *Didn't he go in here?*

Light shone from a back room.

What's that? Denida took a cautious step. An image of Heavani had been etched into the wall, but he couldn't see anything else in the dim light.

Lucifer appeared and slammed the door shut. *"Never* go in there!"

The fury in Lucifer's eyes was darker than Denida had ever witnessed before, so he nodded rapidly.

Lucifer yanked him over to the Well of Memory.

"Wait." Denida lifted his hand. "I'm not here for that."

The water inside the well caught ablaze instantly.

"After everything I've done to help you with the Underworlds, are you sure you dare say you don't want to hear more?" The Darkness in Lucifer's eyes flared.

Denida peered at the door to the room where he saw Heavani's image.

"Now, *Denida*," Lucifer growled irritably. He approached Denida. "Either you listen to the rest of my story or there's no chance of a deal!"

"But-"

"Don't press your luck; my patience has almost run out!"

Denida shrugged. "In that case, let's continue; it's in both our best interests. For you; Heavani, for me; the safety of my loved ones!"

Lucifer ran his hand over the flames, making them die down before meeting Denida's eyes. "God instructed Gabriel to bring any holy daggers he found to him immediately. He kept one on him; the other he took…"

Denida frowned. "But, you have the one used on Henna?"

"God was sure that dagger worked, so he wanted to keep it close to Heavani at all times!"

"He gave it to you? I thought he didn't trust you."

Lucifer ran his hand across his face. "I didn't think so either, but Gabriel must have persuaded him to trust me…"

***

Lucifer sat in the tower, holding the dagger and examining it. He rubbed the bloodstain, which had soaked into the dagger, becoming a part of it.

Gabriel stood next to him, tapping on the windowsill with his finger, peering out and keeping watch over the horizon.

"Henna set us up to find the dagger, yet if she knew we would… as she predicted God's downfall… did she also foresee us killing her?"

Gabriel scratched his cheek. "That's an interesting question."

Lucifer stood and concealed the dagger under his rope. "You think you'll ever find any of the other daggers?"

Gabriel lowered his head. "You said it yourself; Henna wanted us to find that one. She'll never let us find another unless it serves her…"

"Yes, but if she lets us find more on purpose, *why*! What's her goal? To have us kill her again?" Lucifer threw up his arms in distress.

"Just keep Heavani safe, and I'll focus on keeping Heaven safe."

Lucifer strolled around Heaven chatting with the other angels, while he waited for God to finish with Heavani. He could not shake the feeling deep down that Henna's intent was evil. He sat down next to the lake at the center of Heaven.

It's nice here… but I'm not going swimming this time! Lucifer smirked to himself.

Scout rubbed up against Lucifer's leg, which made him scratch behind its ear.

Lucifer lay down in the grass and Scout crawled on top of Lucifer, lying cozily on his stomach. Lucifer closed his eyes and inhaled deeply. *So peaceful…*

A tickling sensation on his nose woke Lucifer. He raised his hand to flick it away, but nothing was there. Shortly afterward, it returned but when he tried to scratch it again, he still didn't feel anything there. Lucifer sat up, waving his hands in all directions.

Heavani sat grinning in front of him. "Aren't you a shining morning star?"

Lucifer grumbled and rubbed his eyes. Scout sat next to Heavani, gazing at him. As soon as he got back on his feet, Heavani was already on her way to the forest with Scout. Lucifer raced to catch up with them.

Scout waited for Lucifer on the path. When he approached, the fox led him into the woods, where Heavani sat leaning up against a tree trunk.

Lucifer paused for a second, just taking in the sight with a soft smile, before kneeling beside her. He sat in silence. After a few minutes passed, he jotted a message in the dirt, *'Did it go well with God?'*

Heavani nodded and reached over to wipe away the writing in the dirt. *'How are you? You were napping with Scout at the lake?'* She peered back at Lucifer, who swallowed and cleared the message.

'I just-" He stopped, sighed, and ran his hand over the dirt again. *'The dagger and Henna,'* he wrote after a short break.

Heavani wiped the ground clean. *'It'll be okay; we won't allow her to win!'* She put her hand on top of his and smiled when Lucifer's gaze met hers. Nothing else mattered for that brief moment.

Scout lightly scratched their hands with his paw, causing them to scuttle back, as if suddenly remembering their places as a saint and her guardian.

Lucifer cleared his throat. "We should… get out of the forest before God wants to see you." He hurried to help her.

When they emerged on the path, they could hear a ruckus coming from the Pearly Gates.

"Let's go check that out!" Heavani sprinted forward, not waiting for him to object.

Lucifer glanced back into the woods before running after her with Scout following.

Heavani suddenly stopped at the Gate and gasped.

Henna stood next to Odin and waved. "Hello again, my dear."

Lucifer grabbed the dagger.

Odin turned to Henna with worried eyes, clenching his fists and closed his eyes.

Lucifer charged past Heavani, barreling toward to Henna, but as soon as he reached her, she vanished, only to reappear next to Heavani.

Odin shot Lucifer a displeased look, before he turned his sight to Sleipnir.

"Sorry, no luck." Henna stroked Heavani's cheek. "You're so pretty, my dear."

Lucifer bared his teeth. "You made sure we found the dagger. Didn't you want us to have it so that we can kill you?"

Henna raised her eyebrows. "That's the conclusion you reached?" she snickered. "I'm already dead, but I'll be here as long as you three are still around."

Lucifer tightened his grip. "Okay…" He took a few steps, decreasing the distance between him and Henna. "What do you want… why have you come, here?"

Henna folded her arms. "I wanted to give you one last chance…"

"Last? You're leaving?" Lucifer stepped closer.

"Soon, it shall be too late…"

"Oh, why is that," Lucifer snickered. His voice brimmed with the evident contempt.

She tilted her head and winked at Odin.

"Why?" Lucifer demanded, screaming at the top of his lungs.

"Soon, nothing will ever be the same again. Everything will-"

Lucifer jabbed the dagger deep into Henna. He used all the force he could muster to dig it as far into her chest as could, yet no blood appeared this time.

"… and so it begins…" Henna smiled tenderly with her rainbow color eyes. She held onto Lucifer's hands. "We shall meet when the time comes, my child." Henna shut her eyes and vanished in a cloud with Odin, as if she had never been there at all, leaving Lucifer holding the dagger in the air.

"We should inform God about her appearance here," Peter glared at Lucifer before marching past Heavani.

"What… wait!" Heavani chased after him, but Peter was too fast for her, so she rushed back to Lucifer. "Luci… this… isn't good!" Her hands shook rapidly.

"I know." Lucifer grabbed her hand and pulled her into an embrace. He flew across Heaven to God's chamber, where they arrived just after Peter.

God stared at him furiously.

"I tried to stab her with the dagger, but it didn't faze her." Lucifer shrugged. "No blood, either!"

God charged forward and extended his hand. "Give me the dagger!"

What? Lucifer gasped.

"Now," God commanded.

Lucifer handed God the dagger.

God turned to Peter. "Bring Gabriel to me when he returns!"

Peter nodded and sprinted out.

Lucifer peered, puzzled. "What's going on?"

God laid the dagger on a table beside his throne, next to the other one he had kept for himself. "We need to find and *kill* all of them!"

Lucifer licked his lips and his eyes met Heavani's. "I don't-"

"Not you!" God spun around. "You are to stay here and keep Heavani safe."

"But you took the holy dagger?"

"Gabriel and Peter need it to kill them; if she comes here, she won't find you."

"Of course, she will. She always has." Lucifer stepped closer.

"She won't feel you in the tower and you *will* stay there with Heavani at all times!"

"You are seeing Henna-"

God shook his head slowly. "I'm going with Gabriel and Peter!" He stared into Lucifer's eyes. '*If you need to reach me, call Shaddai three times,*' he spoke exclusively to Lucifer's thoughts.

Lucifer propped himself up with his elbows on the windowsill in the tower. He watched as Gabriel, God, and Peter took off in search of Henna and the other gods.

"They won't find her!" Lucifer shook his head.

Heavani joined him to watch their departure. "Don't think so?"

"The way she said it…"

Heavani hugged Lucifer, but he stepped away. "Don't worry; I'm fine. I need to keep a watchful eye!" He leaned over the windowsill to look out at the horizon.

"We can talk about anything, you know. God *actually* wants us up here this time!"

"… to keep you safe." Lucifer tightened his grip on the windowsill.

"From whom? You said Henna's gone…"

Lucifer threw up his arm. "Valid point, but what else am I supposed to do? You must stay safe, even if there's only a fraction of a risk!"

"You could talk to me," she grinned.

Lucifer smiled and sat down next to her. "Of course; what do you want to talk about?"

"What about the story God, you, and Gabriel share?"

Lucifer gaped. He closed his mouth without saying anything and lowered his head. "I shouldn't; God would be angry if I told you the details…"

Heavani lifted his head with her finger and smiled. "I can keep it to myself."

Not a good idea… Lucifer clasped his hands together. He turned to her, ready to say no, but her sweet, tender smile and innocent eyes stared into his, as if she saw right through him. Lucifer became lost in her precious eyes and he told her the story… the full story of where they came from and everything which happened along the way. She listened intently to every detail and absorbed every word he spoke. He punctuated his tale with a heavy sigh. "You know the rest…"

Heavani rested her hand on his. "Thank you for telling me."

I hope it wasn't a mistake…

"It wasn't," Heavani said lowly.

Lucifer glanced over at Heavani.

Heavani and Lucifer gazed deeply into each other's eyes.

Scout trilled and rubbed up against Heavani, but she didn't waver. They both kept staring into each other's eyes. It felt like time had paused and all that mattered was each other.

They slowly leaned in close to each other, as if it were the most natural of movements. Their fingertips touched lightly.

Lucifer glanced down at her hand, intertwined their fingers, and returned his eyes to hers.

It feels so right. He tilted his head close to hers, so close that he could feel her warm breath. He paused, his and her head standing still for what felt like an eternity.

Heavani clenched his hands tightly and pulled him in. Her lips met his in a wet embrace.

***

"Wait!" Denida stomped his foot as the image faded. "You're stopping now? What happened next? Heavani and you? What about God; did he find Henna?"

Lucifer's gaze turned cold. "God didn't. No one saw her again… ever!"

"Ev… er," Denida muttered in disbelief. "But-"

"They came back empty-handed. Odin never returned to Heaven after that day… as for Heavani and I, I'm sure you can imagine what happened next…" Lucifer's eyes filled with elation.

Chapter 34- Wanting to Hear More

Denida stepped from the hallway into the reception area and approached his secretary. "I do *not* wish to be disturbed." He walked into his office and slammed the door behind him. Denida sighed as he surveyed the room and made a beeline for the bar cabinet. He rummaged through it and yanked out the strongest liquor he could find. Denida threw himself into his chair and swallowed as much of the bottle as he could before stopping with a huff. *This is too insane; is Henna out there, somewhere?* He raked his hair back before letting his head slump into his arms.

'Knock, knock.'

"I said I didn't want to be interrupted!" Denida yelled, not even raising his head.

"Blame me; I insisted on needing to see you." Anneh winked.

Denida lifted his head and rubbed his forehead. "Why?"

"The Underworlds have-"

"Leave us." Denida waved his hand.

After the secretary closed the door, Denida turned to face Anneh. "Yes, I've united the Underworlds, as you suggested..."

"Do you see now what I meant about leadership?"

Denida nodded reluctantly. "You said the world you lead is a planet? Which one?"

Anneh crossed his arms. "You wouldn't know it by name, so why don't I show you?"

Denida shook his head. "I need to-"

"It won't take long," Anneh said swiftly. "You'll like it!"

Denida extended his arm. "Fine, take me to your world." He laid his hand in Anneh's.

As soon as he did, they appeared in a bright new world. Denida squinted his eyes and held his hand up to his forehead while peering up. "That's strong," he said.

"Despite the suns, it's a cool world." Anneh closed his eyes and smiled. "It was my home..."

"Suns?" Denida frowned.

Anneh pointed his finger upward at two suns in the sky.

Denida squinted his eyes as he glared at the sky, noticing the two suns with a sense of deja vu. Finally, he looked down and followed Anneh, as he led him through his world, peeping at all the people who passed them. None of them said anything; they all just met his eyes with a somber smile. A strange sensation came over him as Anneh led him onto a path leading into a small forest.

Denida nipped his upper lip and turned back.

"This way!" Anneh hollered. Next to an old, wide tree trunk, wider than the Gates themselves, he paused, waiting. "It feels strange here, I know."

Anneh pointed at a fallen log in front of them. "Why don't we take a breather?"

Denida sat down next to Anneh.

"They know I want to retire; that's why my people are so distant."

Denida flicked his finger. "Make sense. You like it here? Are you sure you want to let me lead your world?"

Anneh lifted his head toward an even bigger set of trees towering around a building. "My castle garden; it's my home, but yes. The time is ripe, now!"

Denida squinted his eyes. It was like he could suddenly make out a vast castle bathing in the sunlight, as clear as day. He frowned. "Was that there before?"

"It might not have been ready for you to see; it appears when you are ready…"

Denida licked his lips. "You're friends with Odin... has he ever been here?"

"Odin hasn't been here for a long time…"

Odin… of course! Denida spun around. "I'm really sorry; I have to see Odin about something vital. I completely forgot about it!"

"Always a busy bee," Anneh chuckled. "Go on. Just come back when you're ready."

"But I don't know how to get here?"

"You will." Anneh pointed at Denida's chest. "You'll know where it is when you search within."

Most be the same as Valhalla, then… "If you say so." Denida stood. As soon as he was on his feet, he teleported to Valhalla, which took even him by surprise.

Chatter sounded from the crowd, fingers pointed at him, but Denida ignored them and entered the Great Hall, where Odin sat on his throne while people mingled, socializing and eating. As soon as he entered, a hawk flew past him and landed on Odin's shoulder. No one even acknowledged it, like it was a common occurrence.

The people stopped eating and turned to face Denida, clearing a path to Odin.

"Denida, what brings ye forth?"

"Henna-" Denida bared his teeth.

The mumbling resumed and Odin jumped to his feet. His scepter appeared in front of him. He banged the scepter into the ground, ending the chatter instantly.

"What do you know?" Odin's eyes were vacant like two black holes.

"Where is she? Is she still here?"

Odin stood as silent as a rock.

"Will you tell me one thing?"

Odin clenched his fingers around the scepter. "Not that."

"The last time you were in Heaven, when Lucifer stabbed her with the holy dagger…"

Odin slammed the scepter into the ground, causing it to rumble.

Denida stood alone with Odin. His audience vanished from sight.

"What do you know about the mighty queen?"

"Mighty queen? Is that what you call her?" Denida fought hard against giving into laughter.

Odin scratched his scepter with his nails. "She is! Everything started with her… and will end with her."

"I thought no one had seen her since Lucifer stabbed her with the holy dagger at the Pearly Gates?"

"No one from Heaven," Odin gloated. "She has been coming here often! She only stopped appearing for *them* because their downfall began with a chain of events, which Azal, who you know as Lucifer, initiated when he attacked her…"

Denida surveyed the surroundings in silence. "Why don't you introduce us, then? Let me meet your queen…"

"I don't need to and you have overstayed your welcome, for now. Don't you need to find some demons on Earth?" Odin slammed his scepter into the ground and everything around Denida disappeared. He found himself standing outside the school on Earth.

He refuses to answer me! Forget about Whipboy; Nina has the Colonel and Commander, so she'll be fine. Right now, I need to hear the rest from Lucifer! Denida clenched his fist so tight his knuckles turned pale. The ring teleported him to Hell, just as he wanted. He stormed inside and slammed open the doors to Lucifer's chamber. His eyes glowed crimson.

Lucifer glared at Denida with a soft smile. "Denida, welcome-"

"Yeah, yeah; your story?" Denida continued over to the well. "You and Heavani made out; what happened next!"

Lucifer slammed his fist on his chair. "You're forgetting how big a deal it was. It wasn't just making out behind a gym!"

Denida swallowed. "Not what I meant, sorry."

Lucifer sauntered toward Denida. "But, how nice of you to make time!" Lucifer smirked. "Realized you can't protect everyone on Earth without *my* help?"

Denida hastily shook his hands. "I just wanted to know the rest-"

Lucifer clenched his fist. Fire encased it. "Just know you don't wish to press your luck... *Denida!*"

Denida glared at the flames and nodded. "I'll remember that! What happened with Queen Henna? Odin? God... what happened to them all?"

Lucifer grinned cunningly and appeared in front of the well. "Heavani and I kept our involvement between us; the forest was our secret meeting spot!"

"... Secrets always come out." Denida raised a brow. "Is this your tale of when it did?"

Lucifer ignored Denida's question. "We knew the danger, but we didn't care. The more we continued, the more infatuated we became with each other..."

The water in the well bubbled and an image started to form.

"God trusted me again; upon his return, he gave me the dagger to keep Heavani safe."

***

Lucifer lay in the woods with Heavani in his embrace. He stroked her arm tenderly and gazed deep into her eyes. "It's so easy to get lost in your eyes..." he whispered.

Heavani blushed. "Don't say stuff like that," she whispered.

'*No?*' Lucifer jotted in the dirt.

Heavani swiftly wiped the ground, only to have Lucifer reach for her hand. He intertwined his fingers with hers and they shared a deep gaze before they kissed.

Scout jumped on top of them, startling them both.

Someone's coming! Lucifer hurried out to the path, accompanied by Scout. He glanced up and down the trail to see who was there, but no one appeared at first. After a short moment, steps could be heard approaching from one end.

Lucifer rubbed his palms together.

"Hi, Luci." Gabriel waved as he appeared in the distance.

It's just him...

Gabriel frowned. "What?"

Lucifer shook his hand. "It's nothing. What's up... why are you here?"

Gabriel smiled. "This is where you bring Heavani, isn't it? Where is she, anyway?"

"She... she's," Lucifer stuttered, his hands all jittery.

"I'm in here." Heavani came out from the trees. "Lots of critters in there."

"… And flowers." Lucifer raised his hand.

"Critters… flowers…" Gabriel scrutinized them before turning away. "The Darkness trying to enter Heaven has continued to grow in strength."

Lucifer frowned. "Continued?"

Gabriel sat down on the bench and dropped his head between his hands. "As I told you before, it has been growing more aggressive ever since you stabbed Henna."

"Why are you telling us this?"

Gabriel stared into Lucifer's eyes. "God instructed me to tell you… Luci." He stood and repeated his glance at Lucifer before turning away.

Heavani reached for Lucifer's hand, but he withdrew it.

"No." He yanked her back in under the trees, where he knelt, pulling her down beside him. '*Something concerns me… Gabriel wanted to tell me something,*' he jotted down.

Heavani shook her head and wiped the ground. She began to write. '*You're just-*'

Lucifer grabbed her hand. "I know him," he whispered, his eyes intense.

"The… tower," she muttered.

Lucifer nodded and kissed her tenderly.

Lucifer watched Gabriel entering the tower. *Heavani might be right, yet I can't leave her unattended. God was adamant about that!*

"Take me to see God; I have something to discuss with him." Heavani winked at Lucifer.

"No, I-"

"Please, Luci?" Heavani laid her hand on Lucifer's shoulder.

Lucifer couldn't resist her request, so he led her to God. As she probably had expected, God told Lucifer to leave them be. Lucifer exited God's chamber, arching his neck to look up at the tower. *Fine!* He expanded his wings and took flight. As soon as he touched down in the tower, he noticed that Gabriel had been expecting him. Gabriel stood awaiting him.

"What did you want to say?" Lucifer licked his lips.

"We should leave!"

"Leave?" Lucifer felt his insides twist into an aching knot. "Leave Heaven, you mean? What about everyone? *Heavani?*"

Gabriel sighed profoundly and opened his mouth, but no words surfaced. He strolled through the room. "I know it's a bad idea… but the Darkness *will* get through. It might not be tomorrow, but someday… someday soon it will!"

Lucifer bared his teeth. "I'm not leaving *her*… there are other angels too, unless you have forgotten?"

Gabriel rubbed his eyes. "Why are you so worried about Heavani?"

"I'm guarding her…"

Gabriel shrugged. "But you're right, we should have hope…"

Hope? Lucifer gawked out at the distance. Just as Gabriel described, the Darkness was broader and more condensed, now. It charged forward, passing one magical barrier, before the other barriers repelled it and forced it back.

Lucifer peered at Gabriel and he turned his head away without saying anything. "God's calling; he's done with Heavani." He swept out the window and flew down to Heaven with Gabriel watching him leave.

God and Heavani stood chatting inside of his chamber. Lucifer cleared his throat, which made God signal for Lucifer to approach. "Saint Heavani is growing concerned about the Darkness approaching. Help make her understand that we have it under control, Luci!"

Lucifer closed his eyes, wishing he had stayed with Gabriel.

"Luci," God repeated with a frigid stare.

Lucifer cleared his throat yet again. "Yes… it's-"

"Wrong!" Gabriel hollered and stormed forward. "It's growing stronger. We need to take more precautions, or else…"

God gasped.

Gabriel bowed to God. "I'm sorry, but if we don't, it'll enter Heaven in no time!"

A deafening silence followed.

"Dagger," Lucifer muttered, but it was so quiet that they all turned to face him.

"What about it," God asked.

Lucifer glanced at Heavani, then at God. "Henna's dagger is made of powerful magic, even more potent than yours! It shielded Heaven when the meteor struck Earth…"

God grinned. "That's true. It could work!"

Lucifer took out the dagger and extended it to God.

"No," God insisted. "Use that as a last resort to keep Heavani safe. I'll use the other one!"

Lucifer moped. "But how can you use it?"

"Let me handle that," God smirked. "Go take care of Heavani while Gabriel and I set it up!"

Lucifer accompanied Heavani outside without a word.

Heavani kept peeping at Lucifer. Each time, she turned away without speaking. Eventually, she stroked his hand. "Are you sure this is a good idea?"

"Yes," Lucifer hissed. "You must be safe, whatever it takes!"

Scout dashed over from where he sat waiting for them and brushed up against Heavani's leg.

While Heavani followed Scout to the forest, Lucifer glared back. *I've got a bad feeling about this. I shouldn't have voiced my idea...* He spun and followed, staying behind them with his head down.

"Luci?" Heavani paused and turned to face him. Her face appeared as worried as her voice sounded. Scout sat next to her feet, gawking at Lucifer. Heavani hugged Lucifer and stroked his hair gently. "Don't worry; I'm sure it'll be okay." She smiled softly and leaned in to kiss him.

"Lucifer and Heavani, God wants you to-" Gabriel gasped and stopped mid-step at the sight of Lucifer and Heavani kissing. "What's going on here?"

Lucifer charged forward and shoved Gabriel off the path into the woods, pinning him down at first before he lifted his hands. "Please listen to me first."

Heavani joined them and held Lucifer's arm.

Gabriel rubbed his forehead. "I've got a feeling I won't like your story..."

Heavani tightened her grip. "Why are you here, by the way?"

"God..." Gabriel shook his wrist. "- wanted you to wait with Lucifer in the tower while we set up the spell... but what did I just see?"

Lucifer and Heavani shared a deep stare without saying anything.

Lucifer sighed. "We-"

"No!" Gabriel yelled.

"- love..."

Gabriel pulled at his hair. "No, this can't... let me take you to the tower..." He yanked Lucifer and Heavani with him.

When they entered the tower, Gabriel swiftly spun around and threw a punch that struck Lucifer's gut. "Curses, what are you thinking!"

Heavani ran to his aid, but Lucifer signaled for her to stay back.

"I can't answer that; it's just what we feel..." Lucifer shrugged.

"How you *feel*?" Gabriel glanced at Heavani with wide eyes. "Not you, too?"

She nodded. "I would do anything for Luci; he's always in my thoughts."

Gabriel squinted his eyes and turned back to Lucifer. "When I saw you earlier while she was in the forest?"

Lucifer staggered, holding his stomach, but nodded.

"Are you ignoring the danger? Despite what you may feel, if God *ever* finds out... you know what I mean, Lucifer!" Gabriel shot Lucifer a stern glance.

"We're careful! You'll help keep the secret, I hope?"

The gaze between them intensified until Gabriel broke it. "I'll always help you, Luci. I just think it's a bad decision..." He shook his head. "I need to get back to God; we're going to use that strange device outside Heaven."

Lucifer was at a loss for words. "What…"

"The machine Henna created before we even came here… a piece of it is made from the same material as the holy daggers. God thinks we can use its magic to safeguard Heaven!"

"Is it that powerful?" Heavani hugged Lucifer from behind.

"It's the only thing that can kill us all, so yes, it holds powerful magic!" Gabriel flew down to Heaven.

Lucifer licked his lips without uttering a word. *Kill us all, huh?* He approached the window to gaze out at the horizon.

"Luci…" Heavani grabbed Lucifer's robe, stopping him. She lifted her other hand with white light around it, forming an image in front of it.

The image showed the large building outside of Heaven with Gabriel approaching it, accompanied only by God.

Gabriel knelt next to the strange device and ran his hand over it. "Found it!" he suddenly shouted after a few minutes.

God rushed to Gabriel's side, where he reached for what Gabriel still had his hand on, but he stopped before making contact with it. "This is the same material… I can sense it without even touching it."

Gabriel moved out of the way, as God folded his hands and mumbled something. His hands began to emanate the same white light encircling Heavani's.

Lucifer peeked at Heavani momentarily before turning his attention back to the image.

God flinched and the white glow encircling his hands faded. Still, God continued and it returned, appearing a little stronger, until God unfolded his hands and dropped them to his side. "I can't get anywhere!"

"Maybe… attack it from another angle?" Gabriel frowned.

God rolled his eyes and turned to glare at the Darkness trying to enter. One of his hands rubbed against the dagger, which he drew from its sheath. "This lets me use its power to protect us." He jabbed it into the structure, which it penetrated as if it were butter, blending with it. He clenched his fist around the dagger's shaft. "I think I can do it, now!" He winked at Gabriel and proceeded to mutter his spell.

A bright light shot out of the device.

"Oh… God." Heavani gasped. Her hand trembled, ending the image. With her eyes fixed on the horizon, she lifted a shaking hand to point.

Lucifer stepped forward and approached the window, where he could see the same weird light enveloping Heaven, causing the Darkness to withdraw into the distance.

***

As the image faded, Denida chuckled and raised his head. "Need a break? Did you regret trusting Gabriel?"

Lucifer cleared his throat. "You needed to find someone on Earth, no?"

"Whipboy, yes, but he can wait." Denida met Lucifer's dark eyes with determination. *My Nina should be okay...* "Please continue!"

"Adamant," Lucifer smiled faintly. "Gabriel kept our secret safe and the light protected Heaven. The Darkness just hovered in the far-off distance..."

"But," Denida insisted.

"*But* nothing lasts forever. God was starting to suspect us, and it didn't help that others, such as Saint Peter, started to, as well..." Lucifer turned his eyes to the image forming in the well.

Chapter 35- Susan and Claus

Susan marched through the front door to the main building like she belonged there. The other guards saluted her. She kept her head down, yet maintained a menacing hardness in her eyes for when the other guards peeped at her cautiously.

As the guards' suspicions intensified, she became confident that she was on the right path to Jack.

A guard rushed by her from behind. "Susan is dressed as one of us!" he screamed.

"Lock up the house," Susan stepped forward.

The other guards turned to her with skeptical eyes.

"Good idea," the guard ran back toward the entrance.

Now, backup can't come. Nice! Susan couldn't help but find that small success amusing. She continued past the remaining guards, who didn't look at her so cautiously anymore, after her command.

After a few minutes of walking through several rooms, she reached a section of the house that had more guards than her HQ back in the Underworlds.

"Attention!" Susan commanded.

All the guards saluted her, except for one dissenter, who stepped forward. "What the hell do you think you're doing?" He scratched his bald head. "Who are you, anyway? I don't remember you." He turned to the rest of the guards. "Do any of you know her?"

They chattered a moment, then spun around, aiming their guns at her.

Susan maintained her cold stare. "I'm with *Danyel.*"

The guards lowered their guns and looked puzzled at the bald guard. "Can she be?" one of them asked.

The bald guard, who stood a few steps away from Susan, cracked his knuckles and charged forward.

Susan ducked, barely evading his attack. "Wait!" she hollered, holding up her hands, but the guard grabbed them.

Susan stepped back.

The guard drew a knife and waved it back and forth as he sped toward her, pursuing her each time she eluded him. The other guards joined in the chase, finally cornering her.

Susan tried to catch the guard's hand to disarm him, but he was too quick.

I need a way to even the odds against me... Susan looked at a desk, but the bald guard swept her legs and rushed forward to stab her. She grabbed his wrists to hold him off.

"No, you don't!" The bald guard pushed harder.

The knife moved closer to her.

Susan tried a scissor hold on the bald guard, but the other guards pulled her off him and hauled the bald guard away from her.

Another guard ran forward and pushed her up against the wall, while the others pulled the bald guard back to his feet.

"Let go of me," the bald guard tightened his grip on the knife and charged Susan yet again.

Jack stepped out of a door with a frosty glare. "What's going on, here?" The guard froze and put the knife behind his back.

"Nothing, Sir; we're just taking care of an intruder," He smiled nervously and pointed at Susan.

Jack gazed at Susan. "You're an intruder?"

Susan swallowed and stared around the room. "I'm a new arrival; I need to deliver a message from Danyel..."

"Danyel," Jack hissed and turned to the guard with the knife. "She's with Danyel, but you didn't bring her to me?"

"She... let her go," the guard commanded the others to release her.

Jack led Susan into his private chamber. "I'm sorry about them, but they aren't allowed in here. What did Danyel send you to say?"

Susan raised her eyebrows. "We caught Nina; she came here with Susan!"

"Great!" Jack rejoiced and stepped behind a counter, which had a dagger sparkling on it.

Susan shrugged. "Not exactly; Susan's still missing."

Jack raised his finger. "Of course, do you know how you'll find her or shall I use the holy dagger?" He lifted the dagger, brandishing it. He had an unholy spark in his eyes.

"Holy dagger, you sure it works?" Susan asked dubiously.

"Of course!" Jack smirked. "I extracted some of its power to kill Morton."

"Extracted?" Susan frowned.

"… So the dagger wouldn't get destroyed when I killed him with it." Jack raised the dagger above his head. "It completely obliterates any soul, but destroys itself in the process. By using only a fraction of its power, I was able to kill him without losing it!"

"Are you sure it worked, then?"

Jack stabbed the dagger into the desk and leaned in close. "Why don't I show you, instead?"

"Show?"

"Morton was Maia's brother. Nina left them together on the island." Jack smirked. "Of course, I would've done the same. "You see, Mara resented her father and cursed Maia to look just like her, so that she could torment their father. The same Darkness resides inside Maia!"

Darkness? "But she… joined us?" Susan felt uneasy.

Jack lifted his hand above his head and clenched his fist. Darkness swallowed it and an image formed on the ceiling.

***

Jack strolled down the tunnel with two guards accompanying him on either side. He trudged out of the passageway and signaled for one of them to remain on guard duty, while the other one followed him. They strolled farther across the island, toward the camp.

Maia sat on a rock, trying to ignite the campfire, while Morton appeared to be passed out next to a table with white cocaine powder scattered on top of it.

So, Nina did leave them behind. "Maia!" Jack leered over her. "Nina escaped…" He shot a glare at Morton. "- yet it seems she didn't take either of you with her!"

Maia continued adjusting the firewood and reached for a piece of flint. "Are you here to set *us* free?"

"Us?" Jack mocked. "You really want that worthless brother of yours holding you back?"

Maia pushed the logs aside and stood. "I'm not leaving without Morton. *Nothing* will ever change that!"

Jack shrugged. "Nina left; you-"

Maia hurled the flint at Jack's face and slammed him into a tree, squeezing his throat.

Jack's guard pulled out his sidearm and fired, hitting the ground right next to Maia.

Maia released Jack and fled toward the trees.

The guard aimed, trying to hit her legs, but she reached cover before the shots could connect.

Jack trudged up to the guard, stroking his throat. "You couldn't even hit her?" He pushed the guard's arm down and snatched the gun from him.

"I didn't want to kill her, only disable her. She is your prisoner, Sir."

"A gun can't kill her," Jack hissed and pushed the guard back to the tunnel, where the other one awaited their return.

The guard at the tunnel saluted Jack. "Sir."

Jack nodded and turned to the guard who'd let him down. "Failure is never tolerated!" He lifted the gun up to the disgraced guard's eye and pulled the trigger, causing the other guard to flinch. Jack handed the gun to the guard watching the tunnel. "Get rid of him; I need to attend to something!"

Jack marched through the forest with a cloud of Darkness forming behind him. *Yes, you're right. Her powers could be useful...* Jack paused and clenched his eyes. Slowly, his body began to change until he looked exactly like Nina. He reached for a gun holstered on his belt. Jack drew it and examined his reflection in the metallic muzzle with a solemn nod. *This can work!*

A sparkle shone within Jack's eyes as he concealed the weapon and stepped into the camp. He smirked down at Morton, who still slumbered under the effects of his drug cocktail. "Wake up!" He kicked Morton's side.

Morton let out a loud groan and glared at Jack. "What do you want, Nina?"

Jack chuckled and held out his hand. A holy dagger magically appeared in it. "I want to end you."

"Morton!" Maia sprinted through the trees, screaming.

Morton shrugged, now standing. "What's up with her?"

Jack smirked at Maia. "Hello, Maia."

"Nina, what are you doing? I thought you left..."

Jack winked and thrusted the dagger into Morton's heart, making his face turn white. Morton fell backward, knocking over the table. The cocaine that had coated the table's surface dusted the ground like a macabre snowfall.

Maia sprinted to Morton, holding his head up. "He can't have died; it's not possible! How-"

"A magic dagger," Jack gloated and picked up a log of firewood. He slammed it into her temple, knocking her out. *First step, done...* Jack closed his eyes and mumbled a chant, causing him to revert to his own form. He retrieved the dagger from Morton's chest.

Jack stroked his finger across Maia's face, making her wake with a shock.

"Jack! Where's Nina?" Her eyes shone dark as coal.

"I only just found you... and..." Jack's eyes turned to the body she hunched over. "- what's left of your brother..."

Maia jumped up. "She has to pay," she hissed.

Jack smiled vividly. "I can help you get revenge, but you have to help me first by welcoming the Darkness that resides within you..."

"Why?" Maia bared her teeth. "Maybe I should just kill you and chase her down, myself!"

"Nina wants me dead… she will try again, soon. When she does, I can help you get her." Jack smiled crookedly.

"We wouldn't be here if it weren't for you! There's no reason to trust you, especially after

what you did to Morton and me…"

Jack shrugged. "Good point, except it benefits me too, if you get rid of Nina for me."

"And why should I care if it benefits you?" Maia hissed.

"Because you'll get your revenge on Nina and anyone else who's wronged you. You will

become so much stronger."

"Stronger?" Maia gritted her teeth. "I'll join you, for now, but if you hurt me again, I'll make you regret it!"

***

Jack cleared his throat. "Morton was weak, so I didn't need to use all of its strength to kill him, luckily!"

"I see… but magic like that isn't needed, now," Susan giggled. "I happen to know Susan's dressed as a soldier."

"A soldier?" Jack put down the dagger and approached her.

Susan nodded. "Like me. It would be bad if Susan came here, so I made sure no one can enter this compound. There won't be anyone coming to save you, *Scientist*." She spat on the ground and stepped closer.

Jack rubbed his hands. "You're Susan, I presume. Quite gutsy, coming here all alone! Could I interest you in joining me?"

Susan wrinkled her nose in disgust. "I would *never* join you! Nina wanted to kill you, but she is detained, so I guess I'll just have to do it for her."

Jack chuckled. "Do you think you can? I'm untouchable, here. I've got Maia and the former leader of the Dark Angels, Danyel, working for me," he smirked.

"Danyel? I thought he was dead. How is he here?"

A smirk appeared on Jack's face. "Lucifer kept him alive, but he betrayed Lucifer just to join me!"

"What do you think Denida's going to do when he finds out what you're up to, here? And worse, just wait until he finds out that Danyel's alive… and here, of all places!"

"He won't do anything, because you won't get a chance to tell him!"

"That's what you think!" Susan reached for the dagger.

Jack extended his arm and clenched his fist tight. His knuckles whitened, the room grew dark, and a heavy weight fell on her.

As the Dark cloud filled the room, her feeling of unease grew. "Crap…"

Jack chortled and strolled to the other side of the room, where he leaned over a table. "Since you're from the Underworlds, I'll enjoy telling you this."

"Tell me… what?" Susan cringed as she spoke those words, feeling her insides turn.

"Lucifer can never come here. I can rule-"

"How has no one ratted you out to Lucifer yet?"

"Ha-ha!" Jack laughed loudly. "Because I am the ultimate evil here, thanks to that!" He pointed up.

Susan arched her neck to glance at the Darkness, which hovered above them.

"Michelle," Jack said abruptly.

Susan forgot about the cloud and turned to Jack immediately. "What about her?" Her eyes filled with disdain.

"She was empowered by the same Darkness as Lucifer… so am I." Jack smirked; his eyes full of glee.

"No!" Susan shook her head rapidly. "Not possible."

"No?" Jack asked. "Then let me show you. Action before words!" He folded his hands together and the cloud hovering under the ceiling enveloped him. A face formed in the densest part of the cloud, directly above Jack's head.

'*Susan hunted Medusa; bring us retribution,*' a deep voice inside the cloud rang out.

"Yes, Master." Jack cheered. "It shall be my pleasure." He stepped forward.

Susan charged him and punched his chest.

Jack didn't appear to feel it. He grabbed Susan's throat and lifted her off the ground.

Susan kicked as frantically as she could, but he didn't respond. She clenched her fists tight, but her arms suddenly felt limp and dropped to her sides.

Jack laughed, tossing her aside. He turned to the cloud and fell to his knees. "All done, Master."

'*Not yet… bring me her heart,*' the deep voice said.

Jack stood up and turned, but Susan was not lying limply, anymore. She had approached him, holding a chair, which she slammed over his head. He collapsed to the ground, but swiftly reached out to grab ahold of her. Before he could make contact, she sped away. "Dammit," Jack hissed and forced himself up, chasing her. "There is no escape, my dear."

The cloud spread throughout the room, inspecting every piece of furniture she could use for cover, before returning to its initial position near the center of the room.

Jack bared his teeth. "She must have left the room!" He flicked his fingers and stormed out with the cloud following.

Susan dropped from the stone curtain rod she hung from, rubbed her face, and hurried to the door, slamming it open.

"My, my." Danyel raised his brow. "I was coming to announce that we hadn't found you, yet here you are… served to me on a silver platter."

"Not you…" Susan stepped back.

Jack ran into the room and paused. "Danyel." He glanced around the room with wide eyes. "You've got her... take her to wherever you're detaining Nina!"

"But why is she-"

"That was an order!" Jack raised his voice. "Do it, now."

Danyel yanked Susan with him and she glanced back, only to see Jack's triumphant grin.

The Colonel sat chained to a chair with blood running down his forehead. Susan could barely recognize him with all the blood and bruises on his face.

Maia hunched over him. "Want me to give you more?" She turned to Danyel. Her eyes sparkled with the same maniacal glee Susan remembered from Michelle's. Danyel smirked as he threw Susan into the room with Nina. "Having fun with him?"

Maia groaned. Her eyes fell on Susan and saw Nina helping her up. "You want to keep her from me, too?"

Danyel's eyes darkened. "You have enough fun with the other soldiers, no?"

Maia stared at them, then at the Colonel, before she turned back to Danyel with bleaker eyes. She slammed her fist down on a table. "When I joined, Jack assured me I could get my revenge for what *she* did to Morton!"

Danyel approached her, closing the gap between them. "Do you know who *I am*?"

"I don't care," Maia hissed.

"Allow me to introduce myself, regardless. I was a high demon of the old school, just like your sister. And like your sister, I betrayed *Lucifer*, so I fear nothing. Do *not* cross me!" His eyes locked on hers.

Maia returned a cold stare. For the next few minutes, they eyed each other in silence.

Susan crawled over to Nina. "We need to get out of here," she whispered.

"We can't; there's a magic barrier preventing us from leaving," Nina said under her breath, while her eyes stayed fixed on Danyel and Maia.

Susan glanced at the Colonel, who smiled faintly, though Susan almost didn't notice it under all the blood and bruises. "Is he okay? What's Maia doing to him?"

Nina sighed. "She thinks that will make me tell her how *I killed Morton.* The only problem is that I can't tell her about something I didn't do!"

Susan licked her lips. "The Scientist knows Dark magic. He has help from the same Darkness that helped Medusa…"

Maia broke her intense staring match with Danyel. "What did you say?" She ran toward Nina, but before she reached them, she slammed into the cone. She bared her teeth. "You mentioned Michelle's magic?"

Susan frowned. "Yeah, the Scientist can also use magic here because the Darkness empowers him…"

Maia peeked back at Danyel. "What's she talking about?" She approached him. "Darkness… you said you were a demon in Hell, so you must know what that is!"

"*The Darkness,*" Danyel said gleefully. "- is what controls everything; Lucifer, Jack, even your sister. Its power is immense, even bigger than the Devil himself!"

"What does it want?"

"Want?" Danyel gave a perplexed look.

Maia spat while keeping her vicious stare on Nina. "Nothing ever comes for free… what does it want from Jack or my sister, for that matter?"

Nina stepped to the edge of the cone, right in front of Maia. "I can answer that; the Darkness aided her in her plan to kill the Devil, to try to replace him with Denny!" She peered at Danyel. "He would know; he was in Hell with Denny!"

"Really?" Maia turned her vicious stare back to Danyel.

Danyel clenched his fist. "Medusa died by Denida's hand, not mine! Besides, you hated her, didn't you?"

Nina scratched her forehead. "Maybe that's why Morton died... Medusa's curse ended with her death!"

"No," Maia hissed. "He died because you!"

Dagger? Susan's eyes widened and she jumped up, pulling Nina away from the edge of the cone.

"You can't save her!" Maia screamed. "She's living on borrowed time! I need to see Jack." She stormed out.

Nina sighed and ran her fingers through her long hair. "What are you doing? She can't reach me."

"You need to hear this," Susan whispered.

Danyel stepped closer to the Colonel, raising his head to look into his eyes. "How long has it been? I so wanted to get my hands on the mighty Colonel!"

"The dagger," Susan continued with a low voice. "Jack used it to kill Morton." She sighed. "I'm sorry, but we need Denny... really bad."

"I… know," Nina muttered. "There's a way to get him here; I should have done it a while ago."

The Colonel met Nina's glance. His eyes lit up and he spat in Danyel's eye. Danyel smacked him across the face with so much force that more blood splattered on the floor.

Susan bared her teeth and rushed forth, only to crash into the cone. "Do it to someone who can fight back!" she yelled.

Danyel smirked. "You're nothing to me. The Colonel was there when they overthrew me... you weren't!"

Susan hurried back to Nina. "Are you sure you can call Denida?" Susan whispered, staring at Nina, who barely even nodded. "How... with magic?"

"Denny and I have a connection; he will know when I'm in danger. I've been deliberately preventing him from feeling it…"

"Do it, now!" Susan clenched her fist.

"We're on Earth," Nina shrugged. "It might take some time to reach him, but he'll know... and he'll come…"

***

Claus ran his hand across his forehead, drenching his hand in sweat. Drawing in a deep breath, he quickened his pace, running through the forest. He stayed on the trail he remembered following with Susan and Nina when they first came, but the familiarity didn't ease his concern that he was being pursued. *Susan hates me... a lot! There's also the possibility that the Scientist's troops might discover me.* The bushes in front of him rustled, making him halt suddenly and clenched his fist. Darkness surrounded his hand.

A squirrel scurried past him.

Jesus! Claus exhaled a sigh of relief and swiped away his sweat. *I need to get away from this accursed island!* He unclenched his fist and continued through the bushes, increasing his pace.

The boat still bobbed in the shallow water near the shore where they'd left it, but there didn't appear to be anyone around. Mystified, Claus slowly scanned the area, his eyes settling on the boat. When he didn't see anything threatening, he climbed aboard the boat.

The owner of the boat emerged from the boat's cabin, starling Claus, and frowned at the sight of him. "Where are your friends?" His eyes focused on Claus' hands. "- and why aren't you tied up anymore?" He bit his lip.

Claus wiped the sweat from his forehead before it reached his eyes. "It went bad; they're both dead. We need to leave before the demons find us!"

"Hurry up, then... untie the boat!" The man's eyes filled with dread and he pointed at the line fastening the boat to the pier.

Claus turned to the line and extended his arm, burning through it. "Done," he smirked.

The man had already reached the bridge and started the motor, not giving Claus a glance. The boat raced away, this time going straight to the opposite shore.

"Wait! Shouldn't you take the same route as before so that they don't see us?"

"No!" the man screamed. "They killed your friends and are after you… we're calling the cops as soon as we get to shore!"

Claus peered at the shore, his eyes closing as he exhaled. *I must kill him when we dock the boat before he can call…*

The boat reached land shortly after that. The man secured the boat and sprinted toward the building near the pier. "Follow me; I've got a cellphone in the house!"

The house… what a perfect place to get rid of you. Claus' eyes glowed as he neared the little house. It reminded Claus of the cottage in the forest next to Dynasty, where Denida caught him. *An ironic place to end someone…*

Not waiting for Claus to catch up, the man hustled into the cottage and Claus increased his pace.

Glass shattered in the building, Claus paused and glared back at the boat. *They couldn't be here already, could they?* The boat was still fastened to the dock, so Claus made his way toward the cabin, albeit carefully, with slow, small steps. He watched his immediate surroundings while he approached, fiddling with his fingers anxiously.

He hesitated when he reached the door, turning to glance back at the boat once more. He clenched his fist and spun around, pushing the door open.

The door sprang back in his face. Claus staggered and reached for his nose. "What the…" In an instant, his trepidation morphed into fury and he burst through the door. "Who's here?" he hollered.

"I am," a voice echoed and a whip slashed the ground, leaving a blue flame behind.

Claus' eyes shut at the sight of it. He backed out of the cottage with his hands raised over his head.

The man with the whip chased him. "I sense Darkness in you… *I like it.* My name's Whipboy."

"Whip…boy," Claus stuttered. "Why are you here?"

"I escaped Denida and the Devil in my world. Came through the Gate. I tracked the trail of Darkness and it has led me here…"

Claus lowered his arms and rubbed his hands together. *This could work…* "I can-"

"Not you!" Whipboy slashed his whip in the grass, leaving a black line on the greenery. "You're too weak. The Darkness here can't be you."

Claus shifted his feet. "True, but I can take you to see whomever you're looking for, in exchange for a finder's fee…"

Whipboy frowned. "Which is?"

"An assurance that you would back me up if I ever need it. You're a powerful one, after all."

"If you can bring me what I want, we have a deal!" Whipboy clenched his fingers around the whip.

Claus chuckled. "Follow me; we need to go to," he stopped mid-sentence. *We won't need to go to the island. We can just go to the front of the estate…*

Whipboy slashed his whip. It coiled around Claus' throat. "Not until you tell me if we have a deal?"

Claus tried to wrestle free, but a Dark forcefield prevented him from even touching it, so he lifted his finger and pointed at the mansion standing in the distance. "Yes… it's… up… there," he gasped.

Whipboy loosened his whip. Claus swiftly backed away and coughed, his hands on his neck. He grumbled, then turned to lead the way to the mansion. "You killed the man in the cottage, right?"

"Of course," Whipboy chortled.

The guards watching the entrance to the compound aimed their guns at the sight of them approaching, focusing on Whipboy and the whip he carried.

Claus lifted his arms. "Don't get your panties in a bunch. Jack knows me; let us through!"

The guards shifted their guns, pointing them at Claus instead. "Leave!"

"You don't want me to leave." The white within Claus' eyes vanished, replaced by a dark shade. The Darkness thickened in his eyes and he started to lift his fist, when Whipboy lashed out at the guards with his whip, setting them on fire.

"Let's go." Whipboy casually marched past them as they rolled and writhed on the ground, trying to smother the flames.

Claus returned to his old self and hurried to catch up with Whipboy, who was halfway to the mansion. "How did you know where we were going?"

"That's where the Darkness is at its strongest," He pointed at the mansion. "- or am I wrong?"

"No, but I'm leading!" Claus stepped in front of Whipboy and marched to the mansion, which had a significant number of guards watching it.

"No one is allowed in," one of them said.

Must be a captain, judging by the gold on his uniform. "We have a reason."

The Captain shook his head. "Denied! That's what Susan said to deceive everyone to get in!"

Deceived? Claus' eyes narrowed in puzzlement. "We're not working with Nina and Susan, so let us through."

"We know that; they're both apprehended," The Captain laughed. "- but still, no."

Claus bared his teeth and approached the Captain.

"What? I told you to leave," the Captain reiterated.

Claus shook his head slowly while sizing up the guards in front of him. He glared into the Captain's eyes with Darkness filling his own.

The Captain flinched, yanking a rifle from one of the other guards and turning it on Claus.

Whipboy charged forward, but stopped as Claus lifted his hand.

Darkness leaked from Claus' gaze. "You don't wish to oppose me; you want to let us through."

"I… want to… let you through," the Captain stuttered, turning to the other guards, who backed away. "Let them through."

Claus sauntered through the crowd. He held the door for Whipboy, before turning his gaze back to the Captain's horrified eyes. "You may now kill yourself for doubting me!" He slammed the door shut and locked it from within.

A deafening gunshot sounded from outside.

Claus sniggered as he caught up with Whipboy. They continued farther into the estate, following the sense the Darkness left in the air. It was so thick that even Claus could feel it.

When the air felt so thick that it could be sliced with a butter knife, Whipboy stopped and turned to face Claus. "It's here; I can sense it!"

Claus nodded solemnly and scanned the room, spotting a set of doors. He charged forward and slammed the doors open. "Jack!" he screamed.

Jack appeared right in front of Claus and grabbed his throat. "What are you doing here?"

"The… demon!" Claus screeched and pointed his shaking hand at Whipboy.

Jack glanced at Whipboy. "Him?" he asked mockingly.

"Yes, me!" Whipboy's whip blazed with a murky red flame. He lifted it and slashed a few strokes in the air, leaving a dark scar of letters as if it cut the air. He smirked. "Still here?" He slashed the ground, setting the dark writing aflame.

A dark cloud arose from the text and settled over Jack. Startled, he loosened his grip on Claus' neck and dropped to his knees. He shielded his face from the cloud by burying his head in his arms. After a minute, it vanished as swiftly as it had appeared. Jack opened his eyes to see Whipboy and Claus standing side by side in front of him.

"I sense real Darkness here," Whipboy said. "Could it have really chosen you?"

Jack narrowed his eyes and stood up. "I control this world. Who are you? That was real Dark magic! Did Lucifer send you to get me?"

Whipboy laughed. "I escaped from the Dark Lord... and Denida."

"Interesting," Jack grinned. "Then join me in ruling this world... where Lucifer can never set foot." He extended his hand.

"Only if Claus joins us, too."

Jack peered at Claus. "If that's what it takes to get a demon escaping Lucifer to join me, then so be it. Welcome to Earth!"

Chapter 36- Rebellion

Lucifer waited outside of God's chamber for Heavani to finish. He chitchatted with the angels who passed by, yet that didn't ease his boredom. The wait to see Heavani again was unbearable. *That sweet smile, that pretty voice... no, there's too many things to pick just one to focus on. She's too perfect!* He sat down and rubbed his forehead. Scout was lying curled into a ball next to him.

The giant door leading into God's chamber opened, which made Lucifer spin around, eyes filled with anticipation, but only Gabriel emerged.

Gabriel folded his hands and sat next to Lucifer. "You might want to work on not making that face; it looks too obvious..."

My face; what's he- Lucifer lowered his head. "You... have a point," he mumbled.

"Good." Gabriel squeezed Lucifer's shoulder. "I need to go do my rounds. God instructed-"

"Wait." Lucifer frowned. "Wasn't Heavani in there? Why are you here?"

Gabriel looked at the fox sitting next to Lucifer.

Lucifer smiled and tenderly petted him. "This is Scout!"

Gabriel arched his head into the sky. "God wanted something to change for Heavani, but I need to *scout* out the ones I have to deal with!" He spun around and marched away.

Lucifer frowned and petted Scout. *Why was he giving Scout such a stare?* His eyes grew wide. *Scout out the ones... he couldn't mean...* He lifted Scout into his arms and set flight to the tower, where he put him down and fed him some nuts before flying back down. As soon as he returned, he found God standing outside his chamber, wearing an annoyed expression.

"I told you to always stay near Heavani! Are you going to be a problem again?" God raised his voice with each word.

Lucifer lowered his head in shame. "I won't; it was only-"

"Only? Where were you?" God lifted Lucifer's chin with his hand. "You came from the tower! What were you doing there?"

"I had to check on something, but I'm here to watch her, now!"

"Really? Then come." God waved his arm and in an instant, he, Lucifer, and Heavani all appeared in the tower.

Heavani became as pale as her white magic.

God surveyed the room until his eyes came to rest on something that caught his attention. With unbreakable focus, he stepped toward it. He held up his hand and clenched his fist. Scout glowed as everything else faded from sight. God lifted Scout up and turned to Lucifer. "I told Gabriel to remove this fox from Heaven and you deliberately hid him?"

"I…"

"You should have let him do as I'd asked. Now, you leave me no other choice, but to once again show you why you should obey!"

Heavani charged forward, but God lifted a finger, freezing her in place.

"Such a sweet creature." God winked.

"No… no… you wouldn't…" Lucifer shook his head. His heart beat faster than when he was with Heavani, but this time, it wasn't for a good reason.

"Yes, but you brought this upon yourself." God snapped Scout's neck and let him slide from his grip to the floor.

Lucifer watched Scout's limp body fall for what felt like an eternity. He raised his head in disbelief at God. "How… could… you…"

"It wasn't me; you made me do this." God spun around. "This is your last chance, Luci." He vanished from the tower, ending the spell that kept Heavani frozen. She dropped to her knees next to Lucifer.

Lucifer slammed his fist into the ground, his eyes watery. "There's only one way to end this… God has to die…"

"No," Heavani shook her head at Lucifer. "We-"

"Don't you see? It will be us, next! If he ever finds out about us, we're dead, just like… *Scout!*"

"We can persuade-"

"No!" Lucifer screamed. "Queen Henna died… because *he* wanted her gone. Shaddai was always bad to the bone. Wishing he'll turn good is just asking for trouble." He yanked the dagger out of its sheath. "Henna's blood is still on here; this *is* the only way!" Lucifer jabbed the blade into the floor.

* * *

"You wanted…" Denida swallowed. "- him dead?"

"Do you believe he would have spared me? Peter was already starting to suspect us!"

Denida sighed heavily. "Peter's still alive, though. Are you going to tell me he refuses to die, just like Queen Henna?"

Lucifer shut his eyes. "Are you sure you're ready to hear this?"

Denida slammed his fist down. "Show me!"

Lucifer folded his hands together. "I knew there would be only one way, only one chance. I gathered support around Heaven. The angels and I kept it between us... we didn't even tell my old friend, Gabriel..."

***

'*I've got a bad feeling about this,*' Heavani jotted on the ground and peered over at Lucifer.

He stroked her cheek tenderly. "I've got this," he whispered and kissed her softly. '*We won't have to meet in secret, anymore!*' he wrote and led her out of the bushes.

Lucifer nodded to a few angels awaiting them on the path. "Take her to the tower." He turned to another group of angels standing behind him, who acted a little jittery. He pulled out the dagger and jammed it into the dirt, creating a cone around them. "We need to do this fast before God detects the magic. Distract the other angels and focus on keeping Saint Peter away at all costs!"

"What about Gabriel?"

Lucifer closed his eyes. "He has to stay away too, but we shouldn't hurt any of them." He lifted the dagger from the ground, dispelling the cone.

Lucifer trudged toward God's chamber, while the other angels scattered to complete their own tasks. When Lucifer reached the door, he paused for a second. He put his hand up to his mouth and clenched it as tight as he could. *There is no other way; I must...* Lucifer reached for the door, but it was pulled open before he could even touch it.

God stood in front of him. "Hello, Luci. What's up?"

Lucifer licked his lips. "Are you going somewhere?"

"I have this strange sensation that something's not quite right, like something ominous is coming..."

Lucifer walked inside. "What created the Darkness trying to enter Heaven?"

"Henna created it to get us all, including you. I already told you that. Why do you ask?" God followed Lucifer into the room.

"Strange." Lucifer lifted his finger. "It never tried to enter when you left Heaven. Any idea why that might be?" He shut the doors behind him. "Furthermore, I don't sense any maliciousness toward me." He approached God. "Want to try again... *Shaddai*?"

"I told you to *never* call me that again!" God raised his voice.

"Or what?" Lucifer stepped closer. "What will you do to me? What you did to Queen Henna? Would you do that if I told you that I already explained everything to Heavani, including why she looks so much like Henna?"

"You soiled my creation?" God's eyes turned dark.

Lucifer stepped in front of God and smirked without a word.

"Tell me! If you don't, I'll-"

"Fine," Lucifer gloated. "Not only has your special creation been told everything, but she's been having a secret romance... with me!"

"What!" God's eyes filled with fury. "You're going to suffer if you-"

"No, I won't, because I intend to make you suffer instead." Lucifer drew the dagger and lunged forward, but God teleported farther into the room.

God's face turned white. "What are you doing? Drop that knife before you do something you'll regret."

Lucifer's fingers wrapped around the dagger's shaft. "Isn't it already too late? You want to kill me now like you did with Henna; the only problem is that *I'm ready for you!*"

"This is different," God insisted.

"I doubt it!" Lucifer lifted the dagger above his head. "Maybe this is what she predicted; you are meeting your end by my hand."

God licked his lips. "No, I won't; you will."

"It's fitting, you know. You're dying by the dagger you used to kill her," Lucifer sneered.

"Henna always knew about our destinies. Mine doesn't involve me dying; I'm to rule over everyone else!" God gloated.

"It's not just me anymore; Heavani knows and half of Heaven agrees that it's best to end your reign once and for all!"

God snorted. "What about Gabriel?"

Lucifer lowered his head. "He'll understand after..."

"Clever timing, seeing as he's away... but Peter isn't!" God chortled.

No, he doesn't! Lucifer charged God with the dagger, but God reappeared behind Lucifer.

"You want to keep playing this game?" God folded his hands.

I'm not getting anywhere... Lucifer's eyes fell on the dagger in his hand. He stabbed it into the floor, sending a shock of energy throughout the room.

God's eyes turned wide with dread. He sprinted to the door.

Lucifer yanked the dagger from the floor and manifested in front of God.

God flinched. His eyes turned to his hands as he flicked his fingers, but nothing happened. As Lucifer approached him, he kept trying.

"Something doesn't work, perhaps?" Lucifer gloated.

"Azal, you-"

"Azal? Like you, I've got a new name, now!" Lucifer tightened his grip on the shaft and thrust it forward. It pierced God and he fell to his knees.

God's eyes teared up, as he reached for the dagger, but Lucifer held on tightly and leered at him wickedly.

Peter opened the door behind them, ending the magic seal in the air that the dagger had created.

God threw his arms forward, throwing both the dagger and Lucifer across the room. The dagger struck the wall next to Lucifer and became lodged in it.

Peter's eyes widened. "Sorry, am I interrupting something?"

God sped to the door. "Lucifer tried to kill me!" He stopped and glanced down at his wound when he reached Peter. "You always disliked him, no? Now's your chance to finish him off!" He extended his hand and a holy dagger appeared in Peter's. "That is the only thing that can kill him."

Peter curled his fingers around it with a gleeful smile. "Yes, my Lord."

God strode outside, slamming the door behind him.

"Lucifer… how I have wanted to do this." Peter smirked as he carefully stepped into the dark room. "You should have stabbed all the way through; I won't make your mistake." He turned to the door, when a rumble echoed from the other side.

Lucifer charged, but Peter spun around and met Lucifer's dagger with his own. "Guess my other angels will be here soon," Lucifer gloated.

Peter bared his teeth and slashed at Lucifer with more strength than before, making Lucifer jump back.

"Is this all there is to the mighty *Lucifer*? I'm so filled with disappointment." Peter mocked.

The two daggers sliced through the air, lighting the room with each clash. Lucifer barely kept up with Peter's attacks.

Peter stepped back and threw his hand forward. Everything in front of him was thrown aside. Lucifer lost his grip on the dagger, which flew across the room and landed far away.

Lucifer scurried after it.

Peter raised his dagger, pulling Lucifer's toward his.

Lucifer changed direction, but it flew so fast that he couldn't catch up. It stopped at Peter's foot.

Peter swiftly picked it up in his other hand and smiled pleasantly, as he rubbed the two blades against each other with a grating, metallic sound. "Are you anticipating what's about to happen as eagerly as I am?"

The glee Lucifer saw in Peter's eyes scared him to his core. "I…" He turned to scan the room, hoping to find something he could use to fight back, but there was nothing in the room other than God's throne at the center.

"There's no escape for you!" Peter stepped closer, still clinking the daggers against each other. He lifted Lucifer's above his head. "This is the one you had. Poetic for it to be the one that kills you." He tightened his fingers around it and lunged it forward.

"Stop!" God held up his hand, causing time to pause for Peter.

Gabriel dashed past God, who stood in the opening of the door. He ran straight to Lucifer. "Luci?" He dropped to his knees and grabbed Lucifer's head. When Lucifer remained unresponsive, Gabriel slapped his cheek, breaking the terrified concentration on his friend's face.

"Gabriel?"

Gabriel nodded with a soft smile. "What have you been doing?"

"He betrayed us, Gabriel!" God hollered with a cold voice and snapped his fingers, which ended time being frozen for Peter, who looked around in shock after striking the air where Lucifer had been.

God's expression brimmed with disgust. "Your rebellion failed." He snapped his fingers and everyone reappeared outside, where bodies of dead angels were being stacked atop each other.

Lucifer recognized some of the faces of his followers amongst the dead.

"Your rebellion has been quashed! But you know what this means?" God squinted his eyes at the crowd of angels, all with terror-stricken expressions. "They're dead, all thanks to you!" He tightened his fist and pointed at the angels who reached for their throats, faces red, until they slumped to the ground.

"But," Gabriel gasped.

God waved his hand dismissively. "I'll make some new ones after Lucifer has been dealt with!"

"Dealt with? You're going to kill me after everything I did for you!" Lucifer bared his teeth. "That Darkness is *yours*, not ours." Lucifer almost broke through the magic, which kept him under control.

Gabriel clenched his fist. "No!" he screamed, punching Lucifer's face hard, knocking him down. Then, as if that only fed his anger, Gabriel kicked Lucifer repeatedly.

God put his hand on Gabriel's shoulder.

Gabriel spat on Lucifer. "You deserve to die!"

God turned and took the holy dagger he had used on Henna and handed it to Gabriel. "Go deal with him; kill him wherever you see fit!"

"Wait!" Peter hurried over to God. "Is that a good idea? They're friends who-"

God folded his hands. "I trust him more than anyone; it will be fine."

Gabriel stowed the dagger under his cloth, nodded, and yanked Lucifer with him, dragging him past the Pearly Gates, bringing him so far away there was nothing but clouds all around them. Eventually, he stopped and turned around to face Lucifer. He pulled out the dagger from under his shirt and played with the blade in silence.

Lucifer raised his head. "Promise you'll keep Heavani safe for me!"

"Heavani?" Gabriel asked appalled. "You are you going to die and all you can think about is *Heavani*?"

Lucifer lowered his head and stared into the white cloud. "You don't understand. This white layer we walk on is the same light she has lit within me. She's all that matters!"

Gabriel dropped to his knees and laid the dagger in Lucifer's hands. "Let's go."

Lucifer met Gabriel's determined eyes with his own. "No, I won't leave Heavani to die!"

Gabriel sighed heavily. "Alright, I'll make sure she stays safe; you have my word!"

"How?" Lucifer demanded.

"She's God's first, his purest creation. Deep down, he'll want to keep her safe. I'll remind him…"

Lucifer staggered to his feet. "But the dagger won't have my blood on it."

"You keep it. It will keep you safe. I'll say I needed to use all its power to kill you, which destroyed it…"

Lucifer licked his lips. "That might work, like your punches did; you didn't have to hit that hard."

Gabriel shrugged. "It worked, didn't it?"

They shared a momentarily chuckle and hugged each other tightly before Gabriel turned back toward Heaven. After a few steps, he paused. "I'm guessing I won't need to tell you this; you can't return, here… *ever*."

"No, you don't."

Gabriel vanished from sight, leaving Lucifer to stand in the middle of the cloud all by himself. He could not return to Heaven nor Earth, since God might sense him there.

Where can I go, then? I can't go home. There's nowhere left… His knees felt like liquid and he collapsed onto the cloud. Lucifer didn't bother to get up for what felt like an eternity.

Eventually, he stood and wandered onward, knowing he couldn't sit there forever. After a short while, he passed by the barrier he had set up to protect Heaven. Lucifer felt misty-eyed, seeing the mark he had set up, but there was nothing to do now, but continue to where there was no chance of God ever finding him. The farther he travelled, the more the air thickened around him. Eventually, it was so dense that he couldn't see his own hands.

The Darkness trying to enter Heaven! "Give it up; I can't give you God- Shaddai, whatever you want to call him. I can never go back!" he screamed at the top of his lungs. "But if you want to kill me, don't let me stop you!" The Darkness spun around him before concentrating in front of him to take the shape of an individual. It looked uncannily like Shaddai, and yet completely different with its barren, soulless eyes.

'Lucifer, he threw you out, but I can help you,' the Darkness said.

"I don't need help," Lucifer laughed bitterly. "If you won't finish me, I'll do it myself!" He ripped the dagger from under his shirt and held it to his throat.

'Saint Heavani,' the voice said.

Lucifer lowered the dagger and turned his head. "How do you know about her?"

'I know everything; I'm the part of God he won't accept. I may be able to help you get her back.'

"Really?" Lucifer frowned. "How? What do you want for it?"

'One simple answer to both your questions; God dead.'

Lucifer sheathed the knife and nodded. "You've got a deal, but how?"

'Follow me.' The shape disappeared as it enveloped Lucifer, whose eyes grew as dark and cold as the entity itself.

* * *

"…And that's my tale. Will you help me free Heavani, since the Darkness hasn't been able to?" Lucifer frowned with bloodshot eyes.

Denida shrugged. "What happened next?"

Lucifer shook his head. "That does not involve Heavani; it doesn't concern you."

Denida rubbed his eyes. "Really?" he yelled. "If I'm supposed to help-"

"I told you my story of Heavani and me. You want me to leave you alone? Your family? This is how you do it!"

He's playing me. I need to know… wait! There's one other person who can tell me. Denida's eyes lit up. "Dan needs me back in the Underworlds. Ta-ta!" He waved with his fingers before he clenched his fist and teleported to a cottage in a clearing in the forest, away from curious eyes, but still on the grounds of Dynasty.

"Gabriel," Denida chanted, holding his hands together, waiting for him to appear.

"You called?" Gabriel appeared out of a flash of light and smiled tenderly.

"Yes… we need to talk."

Gabriel scratched his forehead. "What about?"

"Lucifer."

Chapter 37- Gabriel's Side

Gabriel rolled his eyes. "You should know enough about Luci, by now…"

Denida bared his teeth. "Not about him, specifically. More precisely, what happened after you helped him escape Heaven, following the botched attempt to kill God with the dagger?"

Gabriel's eyes widened. "The… dagger… what?"

"The holy dagger Lucifer tried to kill him with?" Denida frowned.

"How… do you know about that?" Gabriel's voice became lower with each word. He approached. "Lucifer, right? Why'd he tell you about that?"

Denida shook his head. "Not just telling me, he's been showing me! He wanted me to see that he had no control over what happened to Daniel…"

Gabriel rubbed his face. "Why are you asking me, then... couldn't he just show you the rest?"

"He couldn't… or *wouldn't* show me what happened after he fled Heaven or how he ended up in Hell, nor anything regarding Heavani's stay within the tower…" Denida rubbed his face. "How did he fail? He had so many angels supporting his cause."

Gabriel bit his lip. "That's… I had a feeling I needed to return to Heaven."

"God wanted you back?"

Gabriel shrugged. "Maybe, I don't know. When I returned to Heaven, Peter was fighting off some angels, so I hurried to assist. God had given Lucifer, Peter, and me stronger powers, so it was easy…"

"You killed all of them?"

Gabriel shook his head. "Not all… there were more inside of Heaven, so Peter rushed to God's chamber before I knew what was happening. It took me longer, since several angels ambushed me. When I finally reached it… why don't I just show you, instead? You're used to seeing it with Luci, right?" He gazed at Denida sorrowfully.

Denida wrinkled his forehead. "How? Lucifer used the water in a Well of Memory to show me. Do you have one, too?"

Gabriel chuckled. "I don't need one." The greenery around them changed into the same exact image that Denida had seen of Heaven. A young Gabriel huffed and puffed as he pushed through a mob of angels charging at him. In front of him, God sat on the steps outside of his chamber.

"Where's Peter?" Gabriel asked wearily.

God raised his head, revealing eyes full of glee. "He's finishing the job!"

"The... job?" Gabriel stuttered.

"Lucifer tried to *kill me!*" The scorn in God's voice sent a chill down Gabriel's spine.

"Wait; you mean he's finishing Lucifer!" Gabriel stormed forward.

God stood in front of Gabriel, blocking the way. "I'm sorry, Gabe." He laid his hand on Gabriel's shoulder.

God's hand felt warm. "He's our friend! He's been with us since the beginning!" Gabriel raised his voice.

"He changed," God rebutted coldly.

Gabriel shut his eyes. "He's not as powerful as you; do you not want him to see how he has failed?"

God raised his eyebrow. "Maybe-"

A row of angels charged forward, attacking them in droves.

Denida peered over at the older version of Gabriel. "Lucifer showed you that the Darkness came from God, yet you helped protect God!"

"I believed... I still believe that he can change in time..."

"Still?" Denida scratched his head. "You still believe it, even *now?*"

"Lucifer should have thought about it more; what he did was wrong..."

Denida nipped his lips, then turned to face God and the young Gabriel yet again. God had brought Lucifer to his knees in front of the other angels, who were piled atop each other, just as Denida remembered seeing in Lucifer's Well of Memory. *Everything Lucifer showed me happened!*

God waved his hand, dismissively. "I'll make some new ones after Lucifer has been dealt with!"

"Dealt with? You're going to kill me after everything I did for you!" Lucifer snarled. "That Darkness is yours-"

Denida spun to face the older Gabriel. "I saw this... this exact scene! Lucifer showed me how you struck him!"

Gabriel lowered his head. "It was the only way; I knew what God would do if I didn't... It was the only choice I had."

"I've already seen the rest." Denida spat on the ground.

Gabriel closed his eyes and everything surrounding them faded back to Dynasty. "Then, you know everything, now..."

Denida clenched his fist. "Not all of it. What happened after you left Lucifer outside Heaven?"

"When I returned to Heaven, I assured God that Lucifer was no more, that killing him destroyed the dagger…"

"Like you told Lucifer you would…"

"I see; you already knew that, too." Gabriel leaned up against a tree. "God didn't care about the dagger. Lucifer's death was enough, but it also meant that he didn't wish to waste the last dagger. God told me he was going to repopulate Heaven with new angels and we were never to talk about it again." Gabriel sighed heavily. "God took Heavani and me to the tower, where he set up a protective spell… using the remaining dagger's power, even knowing it was already weak from protecting Heaven. After that, he abandoned Heavani in the tower."

Denida rubbed his hands together. "Did-"

"He informed her, '*you failed me.*' The look in his eyes has stayed with me ever since… God passed me, saying '*you deal with her; I don't ever want to hear her name again.*'"

Denida squinted his eyes. "But she had a son?"

Gabriel nodded. "I discovered she was pregnant soon after that. God didn't want to hear any talk of her, but I did manage to bring it up after Daniel, Lucifer and Heavani's son, was born… he didn't care; he wanted to stick with the tale about Lucifer being the evil angel who got jealous and tried to seize control of Heaven for himself."

Denida rolled his eyes. "That still doesn't answer how you got so involved with him in Hell, let alone how he got there?"

Gabriel glared at Denida thoughtfully. "Why don't I show you; you know part of this story. After God created his angels, his sight turned to Earth, where he created the humans. He wanted them somewhere more contained, so he found a secluded spot, an Underworld, where he set them loose."

Denida shrugged. "Why not on Earth?"

"Other Gods had already started there, like Zeus, and Odin, whom God still detested."

Denida flinched. "The humans… what happened to-"

"Yes, Adam and Eve," Gabriel remarked swiftly.

"Adam… and… Eve," Denida stuttered, unsure if he heard right, but Gabriel nodded. "Is that the story from the myths then?"

"Almost…" Gabriel lifted his hand and their surroundings changed as if they had been teleported into the past again.

Denida looked around, noticing a man, not wearing much, and a woman sitting next to him, but he was more shocked at what was behind them. A younger Gabriel stood next to a younger version of God. He spun around to see if Gabriel was still next to him.

Gabriel smiled reassuringly. "They still can't see us; we're only watching what played out in the past…"

"This looks great, Gabriel; well done." God patted the young Gabriel on his shoulder before turning away. A wide snake slithered around his feet. God stomped his feet to squash it, but it slid past his strike each time. It crawled in front of God, where it transformed into Lucifer.

"Hi, Shaddai," Lucifer smirked, his voice full of disdain.

God almost fell backward. He snuck a quick look at Gabriel before turning his attention back to Lucifer. "You're alive?"

"I'm more than alive; I'll be your nemesis. Wherever you go, I'll be there and I'll be the one who kills you, in time."

God chuckled. "*You*? With what help? The dagger? I presume you still have that, seeing as you're alive, but it won't be enough. The dagger won't keep you safe. It failed you once; it'll fail you next time, too."

"I don't have it with me. I'm not here to kill you today, only ruin your schemes and reveal my presence…"

God's eyes lit up. "So, you don't have any protection?"

"I do; I have the one thing you dread." Lucifer lifted his arms into the sky and Darkness enveloped him. "Do you remember this? The power that wants you dead?"

God stepped back.

"It is what empowers me!" Lucifer changed form and slithered over to the two humans.

God yanked Gabriel close to him and flew away.

The surroundings of Denida and the older Gabriel changed to that of in front of the Pearly Gates, where God set Gabriel down.

"What are you doing?" Gabriel yelled. "We just can't leave Lucifer alone with them!"

God rubbed his hands together. "What can Lucifer really do?"

"Well, he's alive and with the Darkness!"

"Good point… how is it Lucifer's still alive? You told me he was *dead*!"

Gabriel's cheeks turned bright red. "I… he was… is my friend…"

"You're saying you never did it?" God's eyes turned menacing as he approached Gabriel. "He's here, *alive* because of you!" His voice echoed around them. God's menacing eyes flickered, making him pause. "Something's wrong with the humans…"

In front of them, an image formed of Eve glancing around nervously and sliding behind a tree, where she unfolded her arms, revealing an apple. She took a deep bite of it. Her eyes glowed brighter the more she ate of it. It didn't take long before she had devoured the entire morsel.

She clenched her fist and spun around, striking the tree she was leaning up against. To her amazement, the force split the tree in half.

"She shouldn't have done that!" God clenched his fist.

The snake from before slid up the trunk next to Eve. "Do you see it, now... the power God has kept from you?"

Eve examined her hand. "I do. You're right..."

"No!" God let out a roar, which echoed throughout Heaven. He yanked Gabriel closer. "Throw them to Earth with the rest of the barbaric humans Odin has there!"

"Them? But it was only Eve."

"Both," God insisted. "I don't trust Lucifer not to mess with Adam, too. Do this for me and I might let your previous transgression slide..." He stomped into Heaven, leaving Gabriel alone.

Gabriel peered at the image of Eve and the serpent. "I must have faith that God will forgive Luci," he said under his breath.

Denida glared at the Pearly Gates.

"This way," the older Gabriel rested his hand on Denida's shoulder and everything around them changed to show where Eve now resided in the Underworlds.

Eve yanked Adam over to a giant tree, taller than anything else in the garden, where she picked an apple and handed it to Adam. "Try it."

Adam gaped at the apple, then back at her. "I don't think-"

"I do." Eve grinned and spun around, lifting both her arms, creating a bright aura around her. "We can be just as strong as God!"

Adam licked his lips, glared at the apple, and took a large bite.

A flash of light crashed into the ground on the far side of the massive tree. When the glow subsided, the younger Gabriel appeared in its stead.

Gabriel clapped his hands, making the sky dark and filling it with clouds. "You made a mistake; you should not have taken a bite from the apple," The young Gabriel gazed back and forth from Adam to Eve. "- neither of you."

Eve squeezed Adam's hand tight. "We know the truth!"

"The truth is that you failed the Lord." Gabriel waved his hand, causing the two to vanish.

"Fulfilling God's orders, I see." The serpent lifted its head from the grass and transformed into Lucifer.

"I'm just sending them to Earth." Gabriel sighed. "I told you never to return."

"I'm not in Heaven. Besides, I had to for Heavani-"

Gabriel closed his eyes and inhaled deeply. "Stop! She's fine in Heaven. God kept her locked up with me watching her. You didn't need to return."

"That's not a life. Is she okay?"

Gabriel lowered his head. "They're fine... both Heavani and Daniel..."

"Daniel?"

Gabriel turned his head. "Your son."

Lucifer gasped. "My... my... son..." He raised his head and met Gabriel's. "God won't let me see them! You'll tell me how they are doing, right?"

Gabriel shifted uneasily on his feet. "I... don't," he muttered. "Where would I even bring such news?"

"I have a place," Lucifer gloated. "A place with the Darkness. It has become one with me!" He flicked his finger. "Only you can enter; remember this." He folded his hands and vanished with a burst of fire.

"Shaddai, Shaddai, Shaddai," Gabriel chanted swiftly, causing God to appear in front of him.

"I sent them to Earth, but Lucifer appeared. The Darkness didn't stop coming because of us; it's with Lucifer, strengthening him... using him."

God's eyes lit up. "Which means it left us!"

"Lucifer says he has a place where the Darkness resides. He said only I can go see him..."

God squinted his eyes. "Really? Why?"

"We could-"

"Wait." God flicked his fingers. "The Darkness is with him?"

Gabriel shrugged. "I guess. But what I meant-"

"Go see him, but inform me of whatever you find." God wrapped his arm around Gabriel's shoulders. "Don't fail me again; you're my *only* hope."

Gabriel gasped and nodded swiftly.

Their surroundings changed back to that of the forest next to Dynasty.

"What?" Denida turned to Gabriel. "What about what happened next?"

"Next, I went to the place, which later became known as Hell. I told God about it..."

"Heavani?"

Gabriel sighed. "The Darkness has control over Lucifer; it's been using him to meet their goal... to kill God."

Denida frowned. "You're stalling, then? You can't keep doing this forever!"

"What else can I do? Let the Darkness kill God? Let God kill Lucifer? This way, they stay alive until the day they can forgive..."

Denida shook his head. "You have too much faith in them. It's been too long for that to ever happen for either of them..."

"We were all friends once; in time, we shall be again."

That backroom in Hell... Denida sighed heavily, then smiled at Gabriel. "Thanks for telling me this. I must go..."

"Wait," Gabriel rushed in front of him. "Where are you going?"

"God… Lucifer… Henna… you have been playing this cosmic feud causing us all to suffer!" Denida met Gabriel's eyes with a chilly stare. "I'm going to see Lucifer."

Gabriel drew in a deep breath.

"Denny!" Dan burst through the trees. "I thought I saw you… I finally succeeded!"

Succeeded? He can't possibly mean… the time machine.

Dan stood with glee in his eyes, the same as he had when he first turned on the Gates a long time ago.

Denida turned to Gabriel. "I need to-" To his surprise, Gabriel was nowhere to be found.

"Need to?" Dan frowned.

"Nothing, come on." Denida hurried through the forest to return to the main building. After a few steps, he stopped. *Something doesn't feel right; what could it be…* He frowned and suddenly, his eyes widened. *Lucifer, it must be him!* Denida laid his hand on Dan's shoulder. "I'll meet you at your lab; I have to take care of something."

"Again?" Dan sounded unimpressed.

Denida spun around, ignoring his old friend's comment. He disappeared into the air and reappeared in Hell. He took a deep breath while checking his surroundings. *The castle must have moved again.*

"'Little Evil,' what an honor." A demon knelt next to him.

"I'm not… get back on your feet; I'm just here to see the Dark Lord."

The demon lifted his head, bearing a wicked grin. "I know where the castle moved to. Want me to take you there?"

Denida clenched his fist, only to glance around. *It might be the fastest way.* "Alright, lead the way."

The demon sprang to his feet and led Denida through Hell. "We should reach it swiftly."

Denida peered at the familiar gathering area for new arrivals and the demons starting to torture them, as a sadistic means of welcoming them to Hell. "Is his guard back?"

"Guard?" The demon stopped and turned back, confused. "Oh, you mean *Danyel.*"

"Dan… yel? Not…" He stopped in disbelief. "Isn't he dead?"

The demon's eyes widened in terror. "Forget… what… I… said," he stuttered.

Denida's eyes darkened into a murky red and he clenched his fist, making his entire body light up with flames. "Finish your sentence! What did you mean?"

"No… nothing, Master."

Denida closed his eyes. "Take me to Lucifer!"

The demon bolted forward. The air thickened and gradually became denser, until the demon stopped and pointed ahead. "It's up there."

Denida squinted his eyes, but he couldn't make out anything other than a thick mist in front of him. "Are you sure?"

The demon nodded. "Can't you feel it? Us regular demons don't dare to enter that!"

The Darkness; of course, they wouldn't dare. Would be against Lucifer's will... "Thanks for bringing me here." Denida ventured into the mist. *Maybe the ring would have been faster, after all.* He squeezed his fist, but the ring insisted it was close. Malicious intent filled the air, as it had when he was a youth in Hell. After a few more steps, Lucifer's mansion appeared in front of him. He sighed and looked around. He approached the demon on watch.

The demon crossed his arms, forming a dark shield. "The Dark Lord isn't accepting visitors."

Denida nipped at his lip. "...Danyel..." His eyes fixed on the demon standing watch.

"I'm filling in for him."

Denida stepped back. *Filling in... he really was the demon, here...* He rushed toward the entrance.

The guard demon appeared in front of him and lifted his hand. "I *said* he's not accepting visitors."

"He'll accept me." Denida's eyes darkened and he waved his arm to the side, but the demon's shield protected him, which only infuriated Denida more. He stepped back and lifted his fist, clenched it tight, making the ring flicker, and, in the next second, the demon froze, only able to move his eyes. Denida walked past him confidently.

Inside, in the dim light, he charged straight to Lucifer's chamber and slammed the doors open. Nobody was there. Denida rubbed his cheek and stormed through the room to the back room, where he had seen a flicker of Heavani on the wall.

The walls were adorned with murals of Heavani. In the center of the room, Lucifer sat holding a cloth, burying his face in it, tears rolling down his cheek.

Denida's rage had built as he learned more about Lucifer's past, but it softened at the sight of the Devil looking so vulnerable. "Luci, I'm here to inform you that I'll help."

Lucifer lifted his head, his face full of joy.

"But there is a condition." Denida's eyes were cold as ice.

"Yes?" Lucifer's eyes widened, full of hope.

Denida inhaled deeply. "This feud of yours has made ripples far and wide. If I do this, you have to guarantee the Darkness will leave the Underworlds and my loved ones alone!"

"You have my word!" Lucifer smiled.

"Secondly, the truth… is Danyel alive? If so, *how?*"

Lucifer put the cloth down carefully. "He is, but I sent him after *Jack, the Scientist,* but he never returned. Like Medusa, I fear he betrayed me."

"I asked how!" Denida bared his teeth, the fury returning to his eyes.

"When you and your son first came to Hell, I wanted to set you back on your dark path by making you kill Danyel. However, the Danyel you killed wasn't the real Danyel…"

Denida's clenched his fists. "Why not?"

"I still needed him. Why would I sacrifice him just for that?" Lucifer mocked Denida with a smile.

Denida moved in close to Lucifer and stared into his eyes. "I'm only bringing Heavani here to ensure my family's safety and to ensure that the Darkness no longer has any sway, but *Danyel*? You can consider him collateral damage for real, this time!" He turned and started to walk out.

"Wait!" Lucifer yelled and strode over to the wall, where he took out a cloth and unfolded it, revealing the holy dagger, which had an old stain of blood tarnishing its blade. "This can kill God. If you need to…" He handed it to Denida.

Denida glared at it for a second, then lifted his eyes to Lucifer. "You want me to take this?"

Lucifer nodded. "You may need it to bring Heavani home…"

Denida reached for the dagger.

Lucifer maintained his tight grip on its shaft. "Fail me and you'll pay… mark my words!"

"My family's safety depends on it, too; I won't fail you."

"Good." Lucifer relinquished the dagger.

Chapter 38- Maia's Moment of Truth

Maia surged through the main building, not slowing down for anything. Eventually, she reached the doors to Jack's personal chambers, now with several guards standing in front, keeping watch.

"Halt!" A bald man commanded and stepped forward.

The other guards spread out in front of the door.

Maia snarled, then lifted her arms. Fire embraced her while she clenched her fist and her eyes burst red. The guards in front of her vaporized. She slammed the door open. "Jack!" she yelled.

Jack appeared from another room. "Maia? Why are you bothering me? Is something wrong with the captives?"

Maia stepped past Jack into his private chamber. She stopped as her eyes fell on the dagger. She spun around. "Why do you have the dagger?"

"Who cares?" Jack yanked her out of the room and closed the door behind them.

"I do." Maia shot him an icy stare. "Susan said you killed Morton! Is that true?"

Jack grunted. "She would say anything to you to aid Nina. Don't mind her."

"Yet, you have the dagger, which was used to stab Morton."

Jack shrugged. "We found it on him and it's too dangerous to leave out in the open." He scratched his head. "- or do you actually believe her? Do you want to set Nina free?"

"No, no, of course not," Maia said swiftly.

"Good." Jack smiled reassuringly. "Then, you can *leave*!" He strolled back into the room.

Maia transformed into a hawk and flew out the window and down to the ground, where she changed back into her human form. She returned to where Nina and the others were imprisoned.

"You're wrong!" Maia stepped up to the cone and glared at Susan.

"Really?" Susan didn't move. "Whatever you wish to believe. Just ask yourself this; what would Nina have to gain by killing Morton?"

"*Vengeance!*" Maia kicked the cone.

"No!" Nina was about to stand.

Susan swiftly dragged Nina back down. "She'd want revenge on Jack, *not* your brother. Plus, Jack had something to gain from killing him…"

Maia's eyes met with Danyel's and she saw how blank they were. "What would he have gained?" she asked, not moving her gaze from Danyel.

Susan stood. "What else? You're Mara's sister. You have her curse, the *evil* she left behind." She sighed. "She can never atone for it, but you can. The question is, will you?"

Danyel walked into the cone and grabbed Susan by the throat, lifting her off the ground. "You'd better behave." He flung her to the floor. She fell on Nina, who was already getting up to help.

Maia rubbed her fingers against each other.

"Maia!" Danyel stopped a few steps from her and glared into her eyes. "The Colonel needs some of your loving care." He chuckled.

"Of course." She sauntered past him and approached the Colonel. She jabbed her finger into a wound, which had started to heal, causing him to emit an agonized scream.

Danyel laughed and turned to the door. "I'll leave the torment to you. I'll be back!" he hollered.

Susan lowered her hand from her throat. "Don't be like your sister. You can still-"

A whip struck the floor, lighting up the room with the fire surrounding it, revealing the trapped soldiers. "Time to shut up if you know what's good for you." Whipboy took huge steps forward, dragging his whip on the floor behind him.

Susan withdrew slowly to Nina's side.

Maia watched Whipboy slowly approaching the cone, letting the whip follow his trail, making a screeching noise as it slid across the floor like a fiery snake, ready to strike.

Whipboy stopped in front of the cone with a smirk. "Nina, you've certainly aged well!"

"Who the hell are you?"

"I am the guy holding you captive. What matters to you though, is the fact that you're lucky that I didn't kill Denida when I had the chance!"

"What are you talking about?"

Whipboy glared at the Colonel. "I met him in my home world and saw an old picture of you. I really should let Maia have at you!"

Maia turned with a joyous smile.

Whipboy chuckled. "But I can't do that; Jack is the master and that's not his will!"

Nina bared her teeth. "It's not over, yet! Denida will come."

"Oh really," Whipboy mocked. "Here? The place with so much Darkness? Where all his enemies have gathered."

Nina clenched her fist. "We have more soldiers here than you have guards!"

"You mean the ones watching Denida's human side, right? You think they'll come for you, as well?" Whipboy slashed his whip, lighting up the room. The fire glinted in his eyes. "Denida won't be coming to save you!"

"He will; trust me." Nina tried to smile, but it never surfaced.

Maia grabbed the Colonel's face and leaned in close. "What do you say... think she's right?" she asked in a low voice.

"I wouldn't-"

Maia put her hand on top of the Colonel's mouth and gazed determinedly into his eyes. "I have to know," she whispered.

The Colonel glared over at Nina and back to Maia, then closed his eyes and nodded.

Maia slammed his head backward, knocking him out. Furiously, she turned to Whipboy. "Watch them. I need to go see Danyel."

"It'll be my pleasure," Whipboy lifted his whip and turned his attention to the back room, where the Commander and his troops were imprisoned.

Maia stomped toward the exit, but her eyes met with Nina's for a short glance. '*I hope your friend is right,*' she said to her thoughts before she stepped outside. *I hope I'm not making a mistake... I have to avenge Morton by getting revenge on anyone responsible for his death...* She swiftly spun around and transformed into a hawk, which beat its wings before taking flight out across the island and farther.

She hovered around the school. *Nina was right about one thing; there are more soldiers around, now. Maybe I should see if this 'Denida' appears. I could check on the pets while I wait...* She descended next to the dog shelter and transformed back into her human form. From where she landed, Maia could watch the dogs playing outside. Upon noticing her, the dogs scurried toward the enclosure's fence with their tails wagging, which brought a smile to Maia's lips for the first time in a long time

They're still happy to see me, despite what I've become! Maybe she's right that it's not too late... Maia sauntered to the pen to pet them.

The tails wagging swiftly stopped and the dogs scurried back toward the building, whimpering and cowering.

Maia frowned and felt a stabbing pain at the sight of their fear and knelt to try to desperately call them back.

They growled and scratched on the building's wall, trying to get inside.

They used to love me... Have I changed?

"What's going on out here!" Maia's old boss exited the building. "Well, look who decided to show up! Like I told that guy, I had my doubts that you'd come back!" He waved at her. "- but here you are, glad to have you return, at last!" He frowned and his eyes turned to the dogs. "Wait, why are they cowering and where's Morton? Something's off about you!"

Maia inhaled yearningly with a stare at the dogs. "Something did change… Morton's dead." She bared her teeth and stood up.

The dogs next to her former boss scurried behind his leg, whimpering. He petted them, but kept his gaze fixed on Maia. "I see; well, they sure aren't comfortable with you, now…"

Maia shrugged. "I'm afraid I'm carrying a little anger because of his death. I'm sorry to scare the dogs... but, you mentioned some guy?"

"Oh!" Her boss nodded. "He was nice, but he left when I mentioned that Nina-woman you met; he seemed to know her, too."

Maia ran her hands through her hair. "Nina's husband?"

"Could be." Her boss led the dogs into their enclosures.

Maia stayed back and watched longingly while her old boss brought the dogs in. *I wish they wouldn't be so afraid… I've missed them so...*

"Not sure what's gotten into them, really. They used to love you."

"That's why I'm not here to stay." Maia closed her eyes. "I need to fix myself, first."

"It would seem so!" Her former boss raised his voice. "I really need the help and you can't even do that, now. You left me and my business high and dry."

Maia sighed. "I can never return; I'm sorry."

"Never?" he asked in disbelief.

"Everything has changed." Maia sighed.

"Then, why did you bother coming back?"

"I just wanted to see the dogs before…"

Her former boss shook his head. "Before what?"

Maia gazed at the dogs one last time, then turned back to the owner. "Doing what I must." She marched out the door.

She cracked her knuckles outside and headed toward the school. Tears fell from Maia's eyes as she trudged away. Her former boss watched her from the window, so she increased her pace, abandoning the place that reminded her of Morton more than she liked. She turned the corner, glaring back to check if he still stood there.

'Click'

Maia spun around. A soldier aimed his gun at her. "Freeze; I know who you are and what you can do!" he yelled.

She raised her fists.

The soldier fired a shot into the ground. "Don't even try it! You won't get away, this time."

This time?

Several soldiers sped up and raised their guns at her.

Maia rolled her eyes. "Isn't this a little much?"

"You know Dark magic," the guard closest to her asserted.

Maia shrugged. "That's true, but still…"

"No buts; we're not giving you a chance to hurt the humans!"

The soldiers surrounded Maia on all sides.

"Denida," Maia said. "I'm here to see him; he's your boss, isn't he?"

"Oh, you will." The first guard said. "He surely wants to see you!"

Maia frowned. A dart lodged itself in her neck. She reached for it, but the tranquilizing effect had already begun. She fell to her knees. "Mara," she heard the voice of her accursed sister right before everything turned black.

***

Maia batted her eyelids, trying to open them. She wanted to rub them, but her hands wouldn't move. Eventually, she managed to force her eyes open. She'd been tied to a bed with an armed guard standing watch over her.

"She's awake!" the guard screamed, tilting his head back.

She squinted her eyes and surveyed the room, which looked like a barracks.

"Morning, *Mara*." Another guard entered the room. He wore a uniform with several medals adorning it, clearly a man of importance. "I'm Colonel Rogers. How did you manage to survive, let alone come to Earth?"

Mara? She couldn't help but laugh so hard that her sides hurt. "I'm not Mara; I'm Maia."

"Mara, Michelle, Medusa, or Maia… all names for the same individual. We all know *what you are!*"

For God's sake! She yanked at her arms. "You think, but you don't *know*. I'm not Mara! I'm her damned sister!"

"Sister?" Colonel Rogers looked at his fellow guards, who all shrugged. "Yet, you look and sound *exactly* like Sergeant Michelle!"

"She put a curse on us, which is why I look so similar to her!"

Rogers laughed heartily. "Really, and who's 'us?'" He waved his arm across the room. "You're the only one here!"

"Morton… my bro-" Maia shed a lonesome tear. "He was killed."

"Why are you here, then?"

"I need to see Denida."

Colonel Rogers peered around the room at the other soldiers, then turned to Maia. "Don't you worry; you will. It shall be my personal pleasure to bring him here myself, *Mara!*"

Maia rolled her eyes. "I told you; I'm not-"

"I don't buy it!" Rogers snapped his fingers and spun around. "Watch her while I go get Lord Denida."

"Sir, do you want us to get the robot to send a feed to the Underworlds?" the first soldier asked.

Rogers clenched his fist. "Do it. It might be better to show her." He turned to Maia while several of the soldiers rushed out of the room.

"So, you're the infamous Mara who killed Lord Denida's son; you don't seem that special, but maybe that is due to the seal we put on your magic?"

"Seal?" Maia frowned and tried to transform into the hawk, but she couldn't call it forth. She found herself unable to tap into even a fraction of her powers. Her eyes filled with dread.

The soldiers marched in. One of them carried a device in his hands. He put it down in the center of the room, next to Colonel Rogers. He saluted the Colonel. "Here you go, Sir!"

Colonel Rogers knelt to turn the device on. "Colonel Rogers calling the Underworld. Anyone present?" He grunted when its screen remained blank.

A private appeared on the screen and saluted him. "Yes, Colonel. What can we help you with?"

"I need to deliver a message to Lord Denida."

The private lowered his head, then back up. "That won't be possible, Sir. Lord Denida isn't here, but I can take a message and deliver it for you, if you'd like."

Colonel Rogers rolled his eyes. "No, thank you. I'll do this another way, then." He shut off the device and skimmed the soldiers. "You take care of Mara; I'll go back to the Underworlds and get Lord Denida myself!"

"It would be faster if you brought me with you." Maia chuckled.

"Denied," Rogers snapped and headed for the door.

"Wait!" Maia yelled. "You can't leave me like this. I came here to help *them*."

Rogers paused and turned to face her. "Them? Who's them?"

Maia cleared her throat and hope returned to her eyes. "The other Colonel, his Commander, all of his men, not to forget Susan and-" She breathed in sharply.

"And?" Rogers cracked his knuckles.

Maia ran her tongue over her lips before she continued. "They have Nina, too..."

"Nina?" Rogers frowned. "Why would I give a rat's ass about some girl!"

"Sir!" A soldier saluted the Colonel. "Maybe she means... Lady Nina?"

Rogers nodded and dismissed him, his head as red as a tomato when his face returned to Maia. "Are you referring to *Lady Nina*?"

"Of course," Maia gloated. "That's why I need to see Denida!"

Rogers rubbed his hands together. "Who's keeping her? Your brother? You claimed you're Mara's sister... is she the one holding them?"

"Of course not. Mara's dead, remember?"

"She's supposed to be… If it's not her, then who is it?" Rogers grabbed her by the throat.

"Danyel… Whipboy… Jack," Maia stuttered.

Rogers tightened his grip. "Danyel's dead. You're lying about this, just like you're lying about not being Mara!"

"No! He's the second-in-command, just under Jack, himself!" Maia bared her teeth. "And I already told you; I'm not Mara!"

"Who's Jack?" Rogers frowned.

"I think…" Maia squinted her eyes. "- Nina mentioned his other name was '*The Scientist*?'"

"He's there too… where? Tell me!" Rogers jostled her.

Mara coughed, then raised her head with a defiant stare. "I'm not telling you anything without Denida here!"

"Tell me!"

"Never!" she spat defiantly, her eyes flickering red with fury. "Denida only!"

Rogers released her and slammed his fist into the wall. "Fine," he hissed under his breath. "Then, you have no choice but to remain here, whether you like it or not!"

"While you go get him?" Maia gloated.

Rogers met Maia's eyes and frowned.

"Watch her!" Rogers commanded as he stormed out the room.

Goodie! I hope this isn't a mistake; Denida can help me find out if Nina is innocent. Maia shut her eyes and sighed.

Chapter 39- The Time Machine

Denida strode through Dynasty's front doors.

The Butler greeted him with a welcoming smile. "Long time, no see. What brings you back?"

Denida felt the warmth emanating from the dagger Lucifer gave him. "Not now!" He waved his hand, then rushed to the secret door, where he proceeded down the steps. "Dan!" he hollered.

Dan stood up next to a desk with a perplexed look on his face.

"The time machine, you said you got it to work?"

Dan nodded. "I did. When we were in the Western world, I came up with this idea that I might be able to use magic from the device and figured out how I could extract-"

"Even if you explain it, I doubt I'll understand it!" Denida rubbed his hands together. "I just want to know if it works."

"Yes, I already conducted a test, but are you sure this is a good idea? Changing the past could alter everything that happened after…"

"Medusa killed my son. Why should I care what changes? Nina and I can have him back!" Denida hissed.

Dan coughed. "We still need to find out where and when to go…"

"Not a problem, I know exactly where she kept Daniel. We go there before the confrontation that led to her killing him!" Denida glanced at Dan sternly.

Dan handed a device to Denida. "When we're ready to return, press this." He set the time machine in motion. Just like with the Gates, it turned on with the same buzzing sound.

In a split second, they teleported from the room to the garden outside the building that Denida remembered with nothing but sorrow.

Denida turned his eyes through garden, exhaling deeply. "That's where Daniel…" He arched his neck to peer up at the giant magical cone, which surrounded the grounds. "The magic barrier is already in place…" His eyes fell on the house. He could see his son through the window, filling his heart with warmth. Denida flicked his fingers, causing both Dan and himself to become invisible. "We have a cloaking spell active. Let's go!" He sped toward the house and walked through its walls. He appeared inside the living room, where Daniel sat between an old couple at a table with the Scientist standing watch from across the room.

Daniel glanced at the old couple at the table. "I finished my story."

"Not yet, but I'll write you the final chapter," a familiar voice sounded, filling Denida with fury.

Medusa chuckled, then ambled out.

Denida charged in pursuit with Dan right behind him.

Medusa continued past the cone and up the road. She turned into another farmhouse not far away.

Denida increased his pace to catch up to her, but she had already entered the house.

"Denny," Dan gasped between breaths. "You shouldn't-"

"No?" Denida swiftly spun around. "Why do you think I wanted to come here? To come and pet her? No, I came to *kill* her."

"It will change everything; nothing will be the same if you go through with it."

Denida reached for Lucifer's dagger. "That's the point. She needs to die… *now!*" He spun back around and trudged inside the building.

A dark aura emanated from the room opposite the door.

"Master!" Medusa knelt. "I've got everything set up with Denida like you asked."

'Not good enough, yet…' it sounded above Medusa in the cloud.

Denida turned to Dan perplexedly. "I know that voice," he mumbled.

Dan shrugged. "I would presume so; it's the Darkness…"

"Is it?" Denida stared confusedly at the cloud.

'He hasn't returned to Hell to take Lucifer's place,' the cloud said.

"I have a plan," Medusa spoke rapidly. "Daniel, Denida's son. We can-"

'Kill him,' the cloud commanded.

"No… no, we should use him to persuade Denida to join us in exchange for Daniel's safety…"

'You dare to oppose the will of the Darkness? You wouldn't be where you are without us!'

Medusa shook her head with wide eyes. "I just meant that there's a better way…"

The Darkness lifted her up by the throat.

The same image Denida saw of the younger, lifeless God from Lucifer's flashback appeared. *Maybe it is the Darkness after all…*

'Do not oppose us, Mara. We can easily replace you with someone else,' it rang from the Darkness.

Medusa gagged, trying with all her might to use magic to break free. Suddenly, the Darkness released her throat, but it still intensified, turning a deeper shade of black. The face formed in front of her. *'Or do you want to lose your heart, now? Just say so!'* The face emanated a Dark, vicious intent.

"I'll do… what… you… ask," Medusa stuttered.

Dan tore the dagger from Denida's hand and ran outside.

Denida, feeling shocked from what he had just seen, coupled with Dan's theft, hesitated for a moment before chasing after him. "Give it back!" he shouted when they had exited the building.

Dan held it behind his back and lifted his other hand. "Just hear me out…"

"Hear *what?*" Denida hissed. "We already went over this! You know why we're here."

"I know, but thinking about it… do you remember how Claus screwed everything up when he changed the timeline? This will go just as badly; I know it!"

"I… don't… care." Denida trudged toward Dan and eyed him before reaching for the dagger.

Dan clenched both his hands around the dagger. "No, I said!"

Denida tried to wrestle it from Dan.

"I will do as the Darkness commands. It didn't need to send you!" Medusa opened the door and spun around, holding the door open.

The Darkness sent someone? I thought it wanted to replace Lucifer… Denida watched the door, intrigued.

"Good." Henna appeared in the doorway with her rainbow eyes. "Just remember that Denida *has* to witness you killing Daniel."

Denida felt his heart in his throat before it shattered into a million pieces. *Henna, here… how… why? Why does she care about Daniel?* He stood frozen, watching them.

"I'll show you Daniel." Medusa fiddled with her hair.

"Not needed… I shall see Daniel after you kill him. Don't fail the Darkness!" Henna rested her hand on Medusa's shoulder before strolling away.

"Oh… my… you're right." He met Dan's gaze. "Killing Medusa won't change it. Henna is behind everything." He lowered his head.

"Henna?" Dan asked with a strange expression on his face. "Who's Henna… that woman with those rainbow eyes?"

Denida bit his lip and stared in the direction she'd gone. *It's hopeless…*

"Who have I seen with eyes like that?" Dan mused. "I know there was someone else-"

"There's nothing left, here." Denida took out the device. *I'm sorry, Nina...* He pressed a button, sending them back to the present in the exact spot they left from.

"Thank heavens it worked," Dan exhaled. "Ah, wait! I remember, now. The guy who helped before had eyes exactly like hers!"

"Eyes? What, who?" Denida turned confused.

"That guy with the strange rainbow eyes in the Wild Western world."

Rainbow? Queen Henna's rainbow eyes flashed through Denida's mind. "What guy?"

"Henry," Dan said matter-of-factly.

Hen...ry? Hen... na? Can it be? A guy, but Henna's female? Denida's gut turned. "How did you meet Henry? How did he help you?"

"I found him when I needed to extract that material from the Gate's main unit. He made that necklace for you."

Denida rubbed his hands together. *It can't be, can it? Wait... Wild West... the Gate.* He pulled out the dagger and expected it, then shielded it behind his shirt. "We need to go back to the Wild West world; follow me."

"Again?" Dan shook his head, then shrugged. "Okay then..."

Denida embraced Dan. Within a second, they vanished and reappeared back in the Wild Western world, just beyond the grounds of the mansion Robert took over from the demons' reign. The new Gate towered higher into the sky than the building atop the hill.

"Back again," Dan smiled faintly.

Denida grunted and strolled forward. The grounds had more guards patrolling now than the last time he was there.

The soldiers saluted and let them approach the new Gate on the grounds.

"That's humongous!" Dan arched his neck, ogling the giant Gate. "The others pale in comparison."

"They do, but we can't activate it, which is why I brought you here..." Denida pulled Dan toward the house on the hill.

Dan couldn't help but glance back at the marvelous Gate. He finally turned his full focus to Denida and increased his pace to catch up. "How do you need my help with that? Where did it come from?"

Denida shrugged. "It just popped up from somewhere underground..." He scratched his forehead. "- and you said something about knowing how to work with the main unit's material, right? So, I was hoping you could help with this one, too."

Robert met them with a smile when they reached the estate on the hilltop. "Denny and Dan! Whatever brings you back?"

"The Gate." Denida pulled out his dagger. "I brought some of the material that controls the Gate. I think Dan might be able to extract some of it to power it on."

Robert's eyes fixed on the dagger. "That's… exactly the same shape as the key on the Gate."

Denida peered down at the dagger. *It's a holy dagger created by Henna… who also created the Gates. Just maybe…* "Dan, let's go see the Gate."

The Gate was surrounded by a plethora of guards.

Robert dismissed them. "There hasn't been any activity here since the quake that revealed it." He tilted his cowboy hat.

Denida carefully stepped closer to the main parts of the Gate. Just as Robert had said, the keyhole was the same shape as the dagger. Denida inserted it, but it didn't fit right; there was a noticeable gap around the bottom of the hilt.

He turned to Dan. "You got the old Gates to work… do you have any ideas?"

"I can take a look." Dan stepped forward, removed the dagger from the keyhole, and inspected it.

"Keep him safe; it's vital that he finds out what is behind that Gate," Denida whispered into Robert's ear before he patted Robert's shoulder and waved. "I'll be back." He teleported to the front office at his headquarters, where his secretary sat at her desk. A soldier jumped up and saluted Denida.

"Sir, this is Colonel Rogers. He says he's here on urgent business," Denida's secretary remarked.

"Rogers? Do I know that name?" Denida wrinkled his forehead.

"I'm stationed on Earth while the Colonel and the Commander are absent, Sir!"

Denida groaned. "Fine, it must be important, then. Follow me; I need to check on the status of the Underworld in my absence…"

Rogers hurried after Denida.

"What can I help you with?"

Rogers clenched his fist around his beret. "It's… um…."

"Speak up! What is it?"

"Medusa, Sir." Rogers' voice sounded a little rough.

She can't be alive too, like Danyel… can she? Denida raised his head from his drawer. "Me… dusa? *Michelle*? What about her?" His eyes grew cold at the mere thought of her. He had seen her in the past and now, he never wanted to again. *But alive; she better not have escaped!*

"We caught this girl, Mara, who says she's Maia… Medusa's sister, yet she looks and sounds identical to Medusa."

Denida slammed the drawer shut. "You *caught* her? Where? Do you still have her?"

Rogers nodded. "She came to us, searching for you. She said she wouldn't talk to anyone, but you. We have her contained on Earth…"

"Show me," Denida demanded and laid his arm over Rogers' shoulders. They disappeared and suddenly reappeared on Earth.

Rogers looked around, baffled. "How…"

"I used my magic." Denida lifted his arm. "Where is she?"

Rogers led Denida over to a small shed filled with gardening tools and toys. Soldiers surrounded the shed and others crammed in so tight that they had to leave to make space for Denida and Rogers.

Maia lay on the bed, surrounded by soldiers. She turned her head and smiled. "Rogers, welcome back. Did you reach Denida?"

That is too uncanny; it must be Mara! Denida stepped forward, staring at her.

"Are you Denida? If you are, I need to speak with you. If you aren't, I'm not telling you anything I haven't told these guards!" Maia hollered.

"Leave us!" Denida flicked his fingers and everyone withdrew from the cottage.

"You must be a bigshot, getting everyone to leave, even Rogers," Maia smirked.

Denida strolled around the room. "You want to speak… to Denida, right? I will decide… if you do."

Maia yanked against her restraints. "I already told you, I'm not speaking to anyone, but Denida… bring him here or you'll learn nothing from me!"

"Why?" Denida knelt next to her face. "What do you need to see *Denida* about?"

"It's none of-"

Denida put his hand with the glove over her moth. "I decide," he growled. "Either you tell me why or you will *never* meet him!"

"The Colonel, Commander, Susan, and Nina, Denida's wife, are being held captive. I need to show him where they are so that we can free them!"

"Really?" Denida snorted. "And who has them?"

"I'll only answer that because you're not assuming I'm my sister, like the other ones did." Maia remarked. "That Scientist guy and his cohorts took them hostage."

"Cohorts? Names would help…"

Maia shut her eyes tight. "That guy with the whip… Whipboy, I think. And there's another demon, the most vicious guy I ever met. He's supposed to be a big deal or something. I think his name was Danyel?"

Denida grabbed her head and held it tight as he drew closer, his eyes turning murky red. "How do you know about them? Are you lying to me?"

"Why would I? I want to see Denida," she snorted.

Denida let go of her head and stood up. He slowly started to remove his glove. "You don't need to convince me to let you see him. You already *have*!" As soon as the glove was off, the ring flickered and Maia's restraints vanished. "You will take me to see Danyel, but don't make me regret this."

Maia's eyes widened. "You're Denida?"

Denida put his glove back on and nodded.

"Then, I need to ask you something!" Maia approached Denida. "Could Nina have killed my brother with a holy dagger?"

Denida gasped. "There's a holy dagger, here? Where?"

"Jack has it, but is it possible?"

Denida clenched his fist. "Nina doesn't know what a holy dagger can do, let alone where she could have found one..."

Maia grunted. "I'll take you to them, but they have Dark magic, there."

"So do I. My first priority is saving Nina and the others!"

"If Nina didn't do it, then Jack killed my brother. I can't just-"

"We'll deal with them after we free everyone. I have a score to settle with Danyel, myself..." Denida stared at Maia. "Your resemblance is really uncanny, but I'll help you, if you help me; you've got my word."

Maia's eyes lit up. "Thank you."

Denida sighed deeply. *This must be why I've had a bad feeling; it wasn't Lucifer, after all...*

Chapter 40- Help Comes

Denida and Maia arrived near Jack's compound in the pouring rain. She led him into the cottage near the dock next to the compound and shut the door behind them, so that the rain wouldn't reach them.

"We can stay-" Maia gasped when she noticed the blood on the walls behind Denida.

Denida turned to see what had startled her. His eyes widened, then followed the trail with his hand around his glove, ready rip it loose. The further he strolled into the cottage, the ghastlier the trail became until it finally ended in front of a man sprawled out in a gory mess on the ground, his heart ripped from the body. Denida scratched his forehead. "This is bad…" His eye fell on a mark on the floor, which he knelt to examine. *A burn mark like from…* He turned to Maia with a vicious glare. "This is Whipboy's work; Nina had better be alright!"

"Yes, like I already told you, she's a prisoner, but Danyel's been protecting her with some magic cone or something." Maia smiled gloatingly.

"You say that, but I can sense Dark magic in you, which means that you can't be trusted!"

Maia sighed heavily. "Nina helped me, yet I mistakenly thought she was the one who killed Morton. She insisted that you, Denida, would come to her aid. When the Colonel proved to be just as optimistic, I began searching…"

Denida tightened his fists. "How do we get in undetected? The compound is crawling with guards."

Maia sauntered over to the window and pointed out at the water. "There's an island out there with a tunnel leading to the compound, which has fewer guards… that was where Morton died…"

"I'm sorry about your brother…"

"He and I always wanted to rest, to find peace from our sister's damned curse!" Maia slammed her fist into the wall.

"I can grant you peace after this, if you wish."

Maia raised her head, surprised, and met his eyes.

"I have the power to set you free from it," Denida reiterated.

Maia cracked her knuckles. "Come; I'll take you to the boat." She guided him outside. It was still raining, but had let up considerably, with only a few sparse drops falling. She hurried to the docked speedboat and jumped aboard. "Get on!" she hollered, not pausing to look back.

Denida stepped onto the boat. "This is the way?"

"Yes." Maia flicked her fingers, causing the boat to rip loose from the dock. She stepped up to the helm and turned the key in the ignition and pushed the boat's shifter forward, setting the boat into motion with a jolt.

Denida stared straight ahead as the boat sped toward the island. Maia, for some reason, piloted the boat around the far end of the island before approaching it. Denida cleared his throat. "The guards won't notice us on the island?"

"No, it's just where we're entering. Danyel and Whipboy are watching the captives."

"We can't just charge in. We need another tactic to free them…" Denida rubbed his forehead. "You said Danyel *and* Whipboy?"

Maia halted the boat and inspected the wharf, managing to dock the boat with just a slight hesitation. "Yes, they're both watching them."

Denida smirked. "Can you get Whipboy to the island, undetected?"

"Why?" Maia looked at him quizzically.

"Humor me, Maia. I've got a plan."

Maia shrugged, and descended from the boat to the island, where they traversed the brush. She led him through meager woodlands, avoiding marked paths. "We have troops making rounds on the island, now."

"Not a problem." Denida clenched his fist and disappeared, then returned. "I was trained in the Dark Arts, too. Just bring him to me and make sure no one sees you doing it…" He vanished again. Maia transformed into a hawk and flew off.

Denida sauntered around the island, staying on the path since the guards couldn't see him, anyway. After a while, his instincts kicked in and led him to a small wooded area near the beach, where he saw a campsite. He felt compelled to examine it and discovered a corpse beside a table. Denida knelt to examine the body and noticed a stab wound. Slowly, he lowered his fingertips so that they were hovering just above the gash. *There's an energy here that feels eerily similar to my ring's… could this be Maia's brother?*

'*Morton*,' the ring whispered to him.

Denida stood up, yet his eyes remained transfixed on the body. *I must bury him to give him peace…* He lifted his hand above his head and tightened his fist.

The ground under Morton caved in, burying him underground. The table and everything else around Morton's remains joined him in the crevice. As soon as the remnants of the tragedy were buried, the ground closed back up. Denida folded his hands and kissed his ring. *Rest well, Morton…*

"What is it that you want to show me?" Whipboy's voice approached in the distance.

"My brother, Morton," Maia burst through the trees and stopped suddenly with a gasp. "He's gone!"

"He is?" Whipboy charged past her, dragging his whip along the ground. "Maybe 'the Scientist' removed him?"

"He didn't; I did." Denida appeared where Morton had been. "He can rest, now."

"Denida!" Whipboy slashed his whip.

Denida teleported behind Whipboy. "Your strike didn't land."

"I can change that!" Whipboy cracked the whip through the air. Denida drew his head back, dodging it. Whipboy's eyes flared and he slashed the whip again. Every time Denida avoided an attack, Whipboy's haste intensified. "Maia!" he yelled, but Maia remained silent. He let his whip fall to the ground and retreated until he stood next to her. "Why aren't you helping me?" His eyes shone with fury.

"Why did you want me to bring him here, Denida?" Maia stared disgustedly at Whipboy.

"I have to settle a score with this coward. Plus, when he doesn't return, Danyel will wonder what happened, which would pose an opening for us!"

"You're helping him?" Whipboy spat, then turned to Denida. "Well, that isn't going to happen!" He cracked his whip, setting it ablaze. He slashed it in the air, creating a trail of crackling fire in its wake. Denida didn't move a muscle.

"It doesn't faze you anymore, does it?" Whipboy snickered and bared his teeth. He rotated his whip in a circle like a cowboy maneuvering a lasso, building momentum before slashing to the left, where it coiled tightly around Maia. The fire emanated from it blazed brightly. "But she might be!"

"You can't kill her; only the holy dagger can," Denida gloated.

"Really?" Whipboy smirked. "That can be arranged."

"Enough of this," Denida raised his hand.

"Don't even think about it!" Whipboy tightened his whip around Maia, making her squirm.

Denida loosened his fist and lowered it. "What do you hope to accomplish, here? You can't kill me by torturing her…"

"Nor can you kill me!" Whipboy gloated. "Misery loves company, Denida. But I don't love it, so I'm going to summon some friends to help me; I think you know them, too."

Color drained from Denida's face and he felt a twinge. *Danyel…*

"Denny! How nice to see you."

Denida tilted his head to the voice. His heart stilled for a second upon seeing the face of the person he'd hoped had really died, in spite of his knowledge to the contrary, but here Danyel was, in the flesh, standing in front of him. He raised his hand, but Danyel grabbed it tightly.

"My, my, what a peculiar ring you have." He ripped it loose and put it on his own hand, smiling at it with admiration. "I like this, especially since it is what made you so *strong!*" He snapped Denida's fingers.

Two demons surrounded Denida, gagging him, and tied his arms behind his back.

"You came to see Nina, I presume? I'm not callous." He chuckled and turned to Whipboy. "Let's bring them to the other prisoners... *both* of them!"

The demons led Denida and Maia back to the main compound with a substantial magic barrier enshrouding them, preventing them from using their magic. Upon being shoved into the building to join the others, the demons yanked Denida and Maia into the cone.

Nina hurried to embrace Denida. "Denny, are you okay?"

Denida tried to smile, but could barely even force his lip to twitch.

"I'm sorry I didn't ask you for help sooner." Nina squeezed him tightly, shedding a single tear.

"Feeling at a loss for words, Denny? Your wife really missed you!" Danyel crowed and turned to Whipboy. "I trust you can watch them while I go inform Jack of our precious company." He spun around and ventured out.

Denida arched his neck. *A magic barrier...* "Whippy!" he hollered. "I'm giving you one last chance to walk away."

"Last?" He laughed. "You're locked up; there's no escape!"

"Are you sure about that? I don't quit..."

The Colonel raised his bruised head to peek in the direction of Denida's voice.

Susan sauntered over. "Do you have a plan?" she whispered and stared with hopeful eyes.

Denida stood up and straightened his jacket. "These barriers prevent us from using Dark Arts."

Whipboy ran his whip across the floor. "Wrong! The primary purpose is to block Dark magic, but the barrier also blocks Light magic, which even I know you are capable of using!"

Denida furrowed his brow. "But I don't *just* know Light and Dark; the ring has its own magic, which doesn't fit either of those categories."

"Danyel has your ring, so do you have a point other than requesting another beating?"

Denida let a smile surface on his face. "I do." He unbuttoned his shirt to reveal his sparkling necklace.

"Crap; I forgot about that one!" He flicked his whip in the air, making it fiery.

"No." Denida snapped his fingers and the whip vaporized. "Guess we should call you something else, now," he chortled.

"I can replace it just as fast!" Whipboy lifted his arm into the air and a new whip materialized.

"You don't belong in this world." Denida clenched his fists. "The time for your death is long overdue. Fortunately for me, you're just a demon." His body blazed with a blue flame and he charged forward.

Whipboy spun around and jumped behind the Colonel. "Approach me and he dies!" he screamed.

Denida paused and held up his hands. "Don't do something you'll regret."

"I won't if you stay put; we'll just wait here for Danyel to return…"

Denida met the Colonel's eyes. He saw the fire he remembered from the Colonel and he exhaled with a small chant, which loosened the Colonel's restraints.

Denida stepped forward, which made Whipboy crack his whip on the floor. "Don't even think about it!"

The Colonel ripped loose from his restraints and struck Whipboy in the gut, which made him drop his whip. The Colonel continued kicking and hitting him, gasping from the exertion, but wearing a wide grin on his face.

Whipboy swept the Colonel's leg and crawled toward his whip.

Denida tightened his fist, making the whip vanish. He pushed his hand forward, creating a cone above Whipboy.

Whipboy shook his hand, trying desperately to summon his whip, but the cone prevented him from using the required Dark magic.

Denida chuckled. "Only magic that is neither Dark nor Light can work in there." He stepped into the cone.

Whipboy chanted and struck the edge of the cone.

Denida jabbed his hand forward. Whipboy grabbed it and hit Denida in the face with his other hand. Denida headbutted Whipboy, knocking him to the ground. Whipboy quickly struggled to sit up, but Denida rammed his hand inside of the demon's body.

Whipboy watched with frightened eyes as Denida felt the heart and smiled broadly at Whipboy, who clutched Denida's arm.

Denida tightened his grip around the heart, making Whipboy release him, then ripped it from his chest.

Whipboy coughed up blood. "There's… more… of… us… you… won't…. esca-" His limp body fell back to the floor.

Denida flicked his fingers, shattering the magic cones in the room, including the one encasing Nina and Maia. "We need to leave before Danyel returns."

"How?" Maia stood at the door, peeking out. "There are demons keeping watch out there."

Susan supported the Colonel and guided the other captives to the door.

"We need a diversion." Denida turned to Maia. "We'll meet at the boat. Do the demons know you betrayed them?"

Maia's eyes widened. "You're right; they don't. I'll meet you there." She marched out the door and approached the demons. "Follow me." She waved at the demons and they hurried after her in a second.

Denida and the others took the chance to flee.

***

"What is it you want to show me?" Jack growled irritably. Surely, everyone knew better than to interrupt him, but Danyel insisted on its importance.

Danyel smirked as he stopped at the door to the cells. "You'll love it; mark my words!"

Jack scanned the area. "Where're the demons who should be on guard duty?"

"They're probably watching *Denida*." Danyel raised his eyebrow.

"Den… ida?"

"Yeah, we've finally caught him. We have-"

Jack shoved past him, ripped the door open, and charged inside. "I knew it… we're doomed!"

"What?" Danyel joined him gloatingly, but his face froze at the sight of the empty cell. "How can this be?"

"How can it *not* be?" Jack backhanded him.

"I took his magic ring." Danyel raised his hand to exhibit it.

What an idiot! "He beat you in the Underworld without magic and you're telling me you just left him here?"

"With Whip-"

"Whipboy!" Jack yelled. "Whipboy is here because he fled from Denida in the Wild West world!"

"Where is he, anyway?" Danyel strolled through the room, but stopped after a few steps. "Whipboy's dead…"

'He must die,' the Darkness whispered into Jack's ear.

Jack slammed Danyel into the wall. "Either you bring him to me dead or the Darkness shall devour your very soul! Use Claus or Maia if you need to!"

Danyel cleared his throat. "Maia helped him get here; she's working with him, now…"

Am I surrounded by incompetence? Jack's eyes flared with Darkness. "I hope taking Denida's ring weakened him or we're all dead. Find him!" He released Danyel and bolted out of the room. Darkness followed him as he ran back to the house. As soon as Jack entered, he ordered several guards to accompany him to his private chambers. He confidently strode through the mob of guards, who fell in line to follow him as he passed. He grabbed the dagger from the table he'd left it on. *If he comes for me, I'll finish him myself!*

"Sir?" Claus knocked on the door. "You wanted to see me?"

"Denida!"

Claus rubbed his eyes. "What about him?"

Jack threw up his arms. "He's here. He set all the prisoners free."

"What?" Claus raised his voice. "We have to stop him before they get a chance to get away!"

"Danyel's trying... but he captured Denida and didn't kill him."

Claus slammed his fist on the table. "I'm not going back to prison! He has to *die* before he returns to the Underworld... they will be slower since they have to keep everyone together."

Jack rolled his eyes. "We can't... Whipboy's dead. Maia helped him. Danyel failed us..."

"I think I know where they are, then." Claus spun around and ran out of the office.

Maybe so... Jack jabbed the dagger into the table. *If not, I'm prepared either way!*

Chapter 41- Confrontation

Denida scrambled through the tunnel with everyone as fast as they could, while also supporting the Colonel, but even with their help, the Colonel walked slowly.

Nina stopped and peeked back, nipping at her lip.

Denida noticed her hesitation, so he approached and gently grabbed her hand. "Is it Jack?"

"We can't just leave him here!"

"Yes, we can. We have to get the Colonel and everyone else off the island. I promised Maia I would help her avenge her brother, too…" Denida snuck a glance at Nina.

"This way," Claus' voice echoed from the mouth of the tunnel.

Denida approached Claus.

"No!" Nina reached for Denida's arm. "You said it yourself; we have to get the Colonel to safety."

She's right. Denida tightened his fist around his necklace, creating an illusion of the empty tunnel. "Let's go," he muttered and assisted the others with the Colonel.

As they exited the tunnel on the island side, a hawk appeared hovering overhead.

Denida licked his lips. *Dark magic…* He took a step back.

The hawk swooped down. When it reached the ground, it transformed into Maia. "Come, I'll take you to the boat. I saw a shortcut from above." She led them through the shrubs, arriving quickly at the boat.

The Commander and Susan boarded with the Colonel.

Nina stayed next to Denida with her arms folded.

"Come on!" Susan hollered at them.

Nina and Denida shared a glance, peering deeply into each other's eyes.

Nina grunted and turned to look at the boat.

Denida reached for Nina's hand, but she pulled back.

"We're staying. Return the Colonel to the Underworlds; that's an order!" Denida put his other hand on his necklace and the boat ripped loose from the pier.

"We're still here," Maia shrugged. "They'll come soon, you know?"

"I'm counting on it! I saw Claus leading them through the tunnel." Denida winked.

"Claus?" Maia's eyes widened. "He knows about the boat!"

'*Creek*,' it sounded behind them. They spun around to the sound, yet nothing appeared. They all stood mute for a moment.

Nina frowned. "Maybe it was just-"

Denida put his hand on her arm, not moving his eyes from the trees. "Maia, take a look from above…"

Maia transformed into the hawk and soared into the sky.

Soldiers emerged from the shrubbery around them, bearing guns. Claus led the platoon with a wide smile on his face.

Danyel sauntered out in front of them, smirking. "You didn't get far, did you?"

"Danyel…" Denida bared his teeth.

Danyel admired his hand, rubbing at Denida's ring. "It sure does suit me… shame we didn't have this when we were the Dark Angels in Hell. Killing *Ignacio* would have been so much easier!" He met Denida's glare with a chuckle. "Jack will be overjoyed when we capture you, but I presume everyone else escaped?"

"Yes," Denida hissed. "- and they'll be back with reinforcements from the Underworld!"

"Really?" Danyel mocked. "Claus, find the escapees on the other bank and *kill* them."

"It'll be my pleasure." Claus nodded before a Dark cloud surrounded him, enabling him to fly across the water.

"Darkness?" Denida frowned.

"He already learned some Dark magic, but I thought he might need a little assistance." Danyel approached Denida and Nina.

"You… you," Denida stuttered.

"Yes, I taught him more. He will destroy your friends before they reach the Underworld Gate." Danyel turned his sight to Nina. "You're together again, I see… such a shame it won't last."

Armed men grabbed Nina and Denida by the arms and wrapped a ribbon around their hands.

Denida's skin crawled as the ribbon touched his skin.

"You don't like it? Tough luck! It prevents you from using any type of magic." Danyel glanced at the ring on his finger. "Including the magic of the ring… just in case!" He waved his hand and the men dragged them behind Danyel. "It's kind of funny how Lucifer ripped you from your body on Earth, yet you finally come back here, only to die by my hand… *permanently!*"

***

We must hurry before they follow us! The Colonel pushed himself forward.

Susan jumped off the boat and frowned.

"Come on," the Colonel waved and marched past her. A rumble shook the ground, so he turned back to look at the water. A cold gust of wind blew past him, swirling and forming a Dark cloud in front of the group. The Colonel staggered nervously. *It's not…*

The cloud vanished, revealing Claus standing with a smirk on his face. "Are you cowards running away or will you fight me?" He raised his finger to his lips. "Wait… that's right; you don't have any weapons, do you?"

Susan stepped in front of the Colonel. "You don't have any soldiers, either!"

Claus shrugged. "I don't need them. I'm not here to bring you back."

Susan scratched her cheek. "You're here to help us flee?"

Claus shook his head gloatingly. "Want to try again?"

"Kill… us," the Colonel stuttered.

The smile on Claus' face widened. "… finally, bingo!" Fire flared in his eyes.

"Claus!" The Colonel yanked himself free and staggered closer. "You… don't… want-"

"Oh, I do." Claus bared his teeth.

Susan hurried to the Colonel. "Sir, no!"

"Yes," the Colonel hissed. "Denida…" He stood with sweat pouring down his face and his legs barely supporting him. "He once told me… to trust you. There was a time he had you, trustworthy by his side… only… *you!*"

Susan and the Commander exchanged a nervous glance. Susan tilted her head toward the bushes and the Commander nodded in reply.

Claus raised his hand and tightened it in a swift motion, pulling the Colonel nearer to him with a gust of Dark wind. Claus gripped the Colonel's throat. "Lying to me won't help you!" His other hand blazed as he lifted it.

"Why would I lie if I already know you'll rip my heart out?"

The flame around Claus' hand flickered.

"He's my nemesis!" Claus shouted.

"Yet, he made a deal with the Devil to free you from Hell…"

The flame subsided and Claus struck the Colonel in the gut, causing him to groan in agony. "What deal? The Devil intended to free me from the start, for a price!"

"You've been free for months! Denida owed the Devil a favor in exchange for your freedom and he paid it in full."

"The... Devil?" Claus stepped back. "What favor!"

The Colonel sighed and rubbed his throat. "The Devil knew Medusa had to die and he wanted it because she intended to take his place. Her complete death was exchanged for your freedom!" He peered at Susan. "And you know who killed her, no?"

Susan nodded.

Claus shook his head. "Denida's not good. He was trained in Hell!"

"Like you?" The Colonel raised his eyebrows. "At least he escaped and acknowledges that he made a mistake in letting Lucifer have you, which he corrected."

"I can't just let you go. Danyel will know!"

"Danyel? The one facing Denida?" the Colonel gloated.

"We've got Denida surrounded!"

"Oh? That has always worked so well, hasn't it?"

A loud bang sounded as Claus clapped his hands. "Not this time; it's over. We've got his ring now!"

His ring? The Colonel chuckled. "He never relied exclusively on that. When we beat Danyel in the Underworlds, we succeeded by outsmarting him... not with magic. He's still the same person he was back then, just with the added benefit of magic..."

"No," Claus scowled. "He won't be able to do that, here; Danyel's magic is too strong."

"Michelle," Susan hissed. "He got his revenge on her, didn't he? She was an archdemon, feared by the Devil himself!"

"That's-"

"Unrelated?" Susan stepped forward. "A one-time case?" She glanced out at the water. "Mark my words; he will win again."

Claus pushed the Colonel aside and trudged forward. "You're wrong. Danyel and Jack both are smarter!"

"Really? Jack, too? Isn't he only here because he fled Denida?" Susan grinned.

Claus tapped his foot.

"You know deep down what you want to do," the Colonel remarked.

"I can't... they would-"

"Deep down, you know the Devil will never allow Jack, Danyel, or even *you* to betray him... even if Denida fails, others shall come to settle the score..." The Colonel met his eyes with a chilling stare, until Claus broke it off.

"Right… it's just a matter of time," Claus muttered, then snapped his fingers. "But not if I'm not here… away from Danyel and you, where Lucifer never can get me!" He marched past them.

"Alone, there will be no one to protect you from the Devil!" Susan yelled.

Claus paused, not uttering a word, then spun around. "What do you want me to do? Help you so that you can lock me up again?"

"That won't happen if you help us this time; you have our word." Susan exhaled heavily.

Claus grunted. "I just have to lead you back to the Underworlds, correct?"

"Yes, bring us home." The Colonel extended his hand.

***

Danyel sent two guards to lead Nina back to the cone within the cells and took control of leading Denida. He dismissed the rest of his guards at the mansion.

Interesting. "You want to have some alone time with me?" Denida smirked.

"Jack will want to see you without distractions!" Danyel yanked him through the house, continuing to Jack's private chambers, where there weren't any guards.

Denida looked around as they walked. "This sure brings me back, doesn't it, Danyel? You never had any guards near your private chambers, either."

Danyel snuck a vicious glare, then increased his pace, not saying anything. As soon as he reached the room, he forced Denida to his knees. "Jack, we've arrived."

Denida sniffed and frowned. *Am I sensing the Darkness?*

Jack came into view with a Dark cloud encircling him.

"You've got the Darkness supporting you!"

Jack knelt and the Dark cloud extended in front of him, where it changed into a shape Denida recognized, that of the younger version of God, but devoid of any soul.

'*Welcome, Denida,*' sounded from the figure.

Denida shrugged. "Darkness of Shaddai, I presume?"

The cloud flickered a little, but swiftly reformed to the face of Shaddai.

'*You're well-informed. I'm also the one who can grant you your son back from the other realm!*'

Denida rubbed his fingers together. "Maybe so, but you're also the one that persuaded Medusa to kill my son in the first place!" He stared with eyes as dark as the cloud.

The cloud's old face of Shaddai chuckled. *'If you want him back, only we can accomplish that…'*

"Really?" Denida started clapping his hands, which were still bound at the wrists, in mock excitement, before suddenly stopping with a frown. "Oh wait… I do have another way. By using the magic Queen Henna created, you can make a time machine… and guess what; I *did*!" Denida gloated. "Do you have any more aces? I'm not as weak as Lucifer. You'll never manipulate me into joining you."

'Kill him!' it screeched before the Dark cloud vaporized.

Jack stood up. "The mighty Denida… the one who was trained to succeed Lucifer. Legends do put you high on a pedestal. *Killed an archdemon,* how I'm going to enjoy this…" He turned to Danyel. "Bring me his wife."

Danyel bowed before he spun around and strolled out of the room.

"Alone at last." Jack sauntered around Denida. "When I helped Claus keep you from returning, even when I assisted Medusa with keeping your son, I always wondered if the day would come… and here it is!" He shook his head. "I don't see why everybody is so nervous about you. Maybe the powerful ring you held?"

"I'm also in awe of how you managed to survive until now."

"I must just be that good," Jack winked.

"No, I think it's pure luck," Denida grunted.

"I've got the Darkness supporting me, now. Earth is mine," Jack hissed.

"Medusa had the Darkness' support and *still* failed… but you already know all about that."

Jack grabbed Denida by the throat and yanked him into another room, where he threw him on the floor. He grabbed a dagger off a desk. "See this? It has the same magic as the Gates do, this powerful magic you insist on…" He jabbed it into the floor just between Denida's legs.

"Do you know what else I learned?" Jack leered at him. "It can kill any soul *permanently!*" He swung the dagger in front of Denida's face. "Even without the Darkness, I'm untouchable!"

Denida nipped at his upper lip. "How exactly did you come across a holy dagger?"

"The Darkness showed me where I could find one on Earth."

The Darkness? I thought only Henna knew where they were. Is she plotting what the Darkness does? Denida didn't know how he should respond to that, so he just gasped.

"The mighty Denida, frightened!"

"Not exactly." Denida chuckled. "Danyel has my ring, yes. But I learned Dark magic before I even had it. Even better, I don't even need the ring to amplify my magic because I've got something else…"

"Nothing can stop me from doing this!" Jack attempted to stab Denida with the dagger, but a barrier intercepted the blow before it made contact with Denida's leg. "What?" Jack stepped back.

'*The necklace,*' a voice hissed from the Darkness hovering in the ceiling.

Jack fell to his knees, grabbing the necklace, tearing it from Denida, and throwing it away into a corner. "Why don't we try this again?" He bared his teeth and stabbed with the dagger.

It tore through Denida's leg like butter, the magic cutting into his very soul.

Jack twisted the blade, rejoicing in it.

I must... endure! Denida bit his tongue and tried to reach for the dagger, but the magic prevented him.

Jack's eyes flared as the Darkness enveloped them. His hand leaked Darkness as he outstretched it toward Denida's chest.

Denida could feel the Darkness pressing down on him and oozing underneath his skin to his core, trying to enter his soul.

Jack laid his hand on Denida's skin. He ran his hand through the blood on Denida's leg and laughed, raising the dagger over his head, but before he could jab it down, a hawk flew through the window, scattering blades of shattered glass throughout the room.

The hawk attacked Jack with its talons, making him throw his arms up, trying to shield his face and strike the bird, but it kept pecking and scratching him and avoiding his jabs.

Denida forced himself to fight against his pain and slid toward the necklace on the floor while Jack was occupied.

Jack floated above the floor, lifted by the Darkness. "Maia," he hissed. "I know it's you. Time for you to join your brother and sister!"

The hawk flapped its wings, creating a gust of wind.

Jack waved his hand to the side, causing the wind to die down, and Maia stood in her human form. He shook the dagger from side to side. "I can't wait to see if you will whimper like your brother."

"That's what you think." Maia flicked her fingers and Denida's restraints burst.

"She won't!" Denida hollered. He stood drenched in sweat, yet leaning against the wall, the necklace bathed in the light filtering in through the window.

Jack lunged to stab Maia, but before he reached her, the dagger flew from his grip and landed in Denida's outstretched hand. He drew it close to his face. "I think not!" Denida approached, waving the dagger.

Jack's eyes nervously followed the dagger's every move. He clapped his hands and the Darkness surrounded him in a dense cloud, creating a thicker cone than Denida had ever seen before.

Denida stopped in front of the newly formed cone, shared a gaze with Maia, then turned and pierced the cone with the dagger. The Darkness scattered and bolted out through the window, leaving Jack standing in a state of shock.

"The dagger has stronger magic than the Darkness. Of course, it would flee." Denida put the dagger under his shirt and stepped into the area the cone had covered. "You're all alone, now. How does it feel?" Denida raised his brow. "A little disconcerting, perhaps?"

The air behind Denida grew chilly and dark. He spun around. "Someone's coming…"

Maia and Denida turned to the door and Jack seized the opportunity to chant a cloaking spell before tiptoeing across the room.

The door burst open and Danyel entered with several guards, who had Nina in restraints. They pushed her to her knees.

"Maia, what an honor," Danyel gloated, but his face froze quickly as he looked across the room. "Where's Jack?"

"Right he-" Denida turned and pointed to where Jack had been, his mouth hanging open mid-sentence.

Danyel grunted. "You don't-" He paused and tilted his head to the side. "Really… I see… how interesting," he muttered and raised his arm, vaguely pointing at Maia and Denida. "Get them!" he commanded the guards.

The guards charged forward, encircling them. Denida bared his teeth in a reply. "You think you can surround us? Maybe Jack forgot to mention one thing!" He pushed his shirt to the side, revealing his necklace. "I may not have the ring, but I still have this."

Danyel chortled and teleported next to Nina, whom he lifted off the ground with a grip around her neck. "And I have your wife… your *soul mate*. Are you going to tell me you want her to die like Daniel did?"

"No," Denida insisted.

"The necklace, then," Danyel hissed.

"The dagger, too!" Jack dissipated his cloaking spell and appeared behind Danyel.

Maia slowly stepped back while the guards encircled her. She lifted her arms and clenched her fists. "Stay back or else!"

When they continued approaching, Maia raised her fists above her head. Fire flowed around them, starting with a low flicker, but it didn't take long before it became a hot blue flame oozing through her fingers.

Fire enveloped the guards who tried to beat it out. The attempts to suffocate it only made it burn hotter.

"I feel hot," one of them suddenly glanced down at his bare arm, which burned as if he had been out in the sun for too long. The same blistering skin appeared on every inch of his body as well as the other guards'.

"Is this Dark magic?" Jack turned.

Danyel shrugged. "Nothing I've ever seen…"

The guards moaned in agony as the fire attacked their insides until they succumbed and fell limp to the ground, burning until there was nothing but ashes left.

Denida's eyes widened. "I remember… when Medusa died, she turned to ash, too…"

Danyel grunted. "Must be advanced magic, then…" He bit his lip. "Lucifer taught you too, Denny? Funny how much you learned, yet he had you completely fooled!"

Denida shook his head and glanced at Maia, who was lowering her arms.

"He had you so convinced that you killed me and that he sent Claus to kidnap Daniel… until it went wrong… who knows what else…"

Denida's eyes narrowed. "Forget about taking Nina to safety; you need to die!"

Danyel rolled his eyes. "It won't be me, like in Hell. You escaped, but you should have died with the rest of them. Now, I get a second chance to finish the job," he chortled.

Ignacio… Intense hatred raged within as Denida thought of the five friends he lost in Hell that night. "Ignacio insisted you would eventually turn… but like you said… it's time to even the score!"

Denida and Danyel stared at each other for what felt like an eternity.

"Danyel, stop!" Jack commanded. "We need him in case Lucifer tries anything else."

Danyel straightened up. "I have something to settle, like you do with Maia."

Jack shook his head. "She wants to settle it, but I don't!"

"You'll have to." Denida turned to Maia. "Catch!" He pulled out the holy dagger and tossed it to her.

Maia snatched the dagger out of the air.

"He killed Morton with that. It's only right that he dies by it… by *your* hand." Denida turned to Jack, nipping his upper lip. "You will need to leave us." He snapped his fingers and Jack, Nina, and Maia vanished from the room.

"He'll be back. We better hurry," Danyel winked.

Denida drew in a deep breath, laid both hands on his necklace, and muttered a chant. The room filled with a strange aroma. "We won't be interrupted, now."

"You still have magic." Danyel furrowed his brow. "So do I… but maybe we should finish this more physically. Humans like to beat each other to death and since we are on Earth…"

"Like in Hell," Denida said with a frigid, unemotional voice.

"Where we were interrupted on that fateful night."

Denida's eyes darkened. "We won't be this time!"

"It would bring back memories from before all this. I want nothing more than to beat you to a pulp."

Denida knelt and laid his hand flat on the floor. "Then, let's disable magic."

"Let's!" Danyel slammed both his hands on the floor. A pentagram appeared on the floor, encircling both of them. Danyel took off the ring and put it down at the center of the pentagram. "Your necklace!"

Denida solemnly removed his necklace and put it down next to the ring.

The pentagram lit up with a blue flame, which followed the drawing on the floor, until it reached the ring and necklace, where it flared up into a vivid, white flame.

Danyel and Denida peered at each other through the flame. The scorn in their eyes grew with each passing second.

Danyel jumped up and charged Denida at the same moment that Denida attacked. They smacked into each other above the flames, only to swiftly trade punches.

Denida slid to the floor, where he rolled and swept Danyel off his feet. He swiftly grabbed a candle holder and removed the candle, revealing a sharp stick and jabbed it at Danyel's face, but Danyel grabbed Denida's hand. The candlestick slipped, tearing at their hands, creating bloody gashes from their palms to their fingers.

"No," Danyel grunted, clutched the candle holder, and attempted to bash Denida with all his strength. When it was halfway to its mark, Danyel started to gain some traction, but it slipped from their hands again and clattered to the floor.

Denida crawled toward it.

Danyel jumped after Denida, then scanned the room frantically. "That can work!" He turned to run over to a sculpture and pulled a spear free, but it was stuck, so he yanked harder until it gave in. He spun around, only to find an empty spot.

Danyel scoped the room. He clenched his fists around the spear. "Come out, come out, wherever you are. It's time to die!"

The silence grew thicker as Danyel rubbed his lips and lunged in front of some furniture across the room. "Denida!" Danyel called out, his voice cracking.

'Thump.' Danyel charged to the other side of the room, only to find a wooden box. "What the?" He picked it up and investigated it.

Denida tiptoed up behind Danyel. "Now, you know how it felt," Denida hissed and struck Danyel as hard as he could with the candlestick.

Danyel dropped his weapon and fell to the floor, but he reached for the spear.

Denida dropped the stick and threw himself on top of Danyel. He reached for Danyel's arms, holding him back so that Danyel couldn't reach the spear.

Danyel spun around and kneed Denida, kicking him until Denida loosened his grip. Danyel crawled after the spear. He grabbed it and turned sharply, and jabbed it into Denida's side.

Denida's teeth clattered as pain seared through him. He fell to the floor, trying to tighten his grip on the spear.

Danyel responded by shoving it in deeper, making Denida stop trying to reach it, biting his fist in agony. Danyel crowed and twisted the spear in the wound, reveling in Denida's pain. He knelt next to Denida's face and smiled. "Lucifer always nurtured such high hopes for you, but I've always been disgusted!" He shook his head. "Maybe I should have just killed you then, so they all would have seen how *worthless* you truly are!" Danyel tore the spear free and threw it to the floor. He flipped Denida over and slapped his cheek. "If you really do have any powers, it's time for someone else to have them." He tore open Denida's shirt so forcefully that the buttons dropped to the floor.

"Any last words?" Danyel raised his eyebrows.

Denida coughed and sniffed, then raised his head to stare at Danyel. With a small, confident smile, he spat blood into Danyel's eyes.

Danyel wiped it off. "Does that make you feel good? What makes *me* feel good is knowing you and your wife die here, just like your son!" He thrust his hand forward, but when it reached Denida, it stopped abruptly, like he couldn't penetrate Denida's skin.

"What!" Danyel raised his voice.

"You thought killing me would be that easy?" Denida smirked.

"I did," Danyel hissed. "I forgot that magic doesn't work here, but you have a wound I can use!" Danyel spun Denida around to his stomach and jabbed his hand into the wound in Denida's side.

Denida tried to crawl away, but the pain made him weaker. He started seeing his friends from Hell appearing one at a time. *Pedro... Jan... Mia... Nicklas... Ignacio...* His vision changed to the memory of Danyel tearing out Ignacio's heart. "No!" he screamed.

"Yes," Danyel rejoiced, his tongue licking his lips, as he coiled his fingers around Denida's beating heart.

Denida pushed his arms up with newfound strength, as if he had been injected with power, causing Danyel to lose his grip around the heart. "I'm not dying without avenging them!" he yelled.

Danyel struck Denida's gut and Denida punched back, splitting Danyel's cheek. The demon paused in shock.

Denida snatched up the spear and used it to trip Danyel. They crashed to the floor as Denida stabbed the spear into the demon's stomach.

Danyel roared in agony and grabbed Denida's wound with one hand, while the other tried to grab ahold of the spear. While he tried to control it, he continued to push his hand into Denida's wound and twist it around.

Denida tightened his fingers around the spear and shoved it deeper using his body weight to support the blow. Danyel gave up on the wound and clutched at the spear. Denida's weight forced it through Danyel and into the floor. Denida perched his neck on the spear's handle and spat in Danyel's face.

Denida staggered toward the pentagram. Danyel tightened his fist around the spear and pulled as hard as he could, but he couldn't make it budge.

Denida trudged toward the white flame and reached for the items, but a force prevented him from reaching the objects under its shroud. No matter what angle he tried, his hand always froze before his fingers could make contact. *Why can't I touch it?* Denida sighed and glanced at Danyel. *Maybe...* He stepped toward Danyel. "Looks like one of us has to die... and it's not going to be me."

Danyel swallowed as Denida approached him, limping, each step screeched on the floorboard.

Denida moaned as he knelt next to Danyel, who was still trying to push the spear out of his wound.

"No!" Danyel yelled. "You've... done enough... to me."

"Not yet," Denida bared his teeth and fell to his knees, ignoring the pain coursing through his body. He ripped the spear out and tossed it aside, thrusting his hand deep into Danyel's wound, until he reached Danyel's still-beating heart.

Danyel's eyes widened in panic.

"Yes," Denida gloated. "You deserve the same death you gave to our friends..." Denida tightened his jaw, then grabbed onto the heart and ripped it from Danyel's body.

Danyel clutched Denida's arm before it was entirely out. "No, I can help you–"

"Help?" Denida mocked. "The only help I want from you is your *death*!" He smacked his other fist into Danyel's wound.

Danyel groaned and lost his grip.

Time for your last breath, Danyel… Denida ripped the heart free and crawled back to where Danyel couldn't reach him. He gazed deeply into Danyel's eyes, then closed his own and slammed the heart on the floor with a gory splash.

Danyel's fingers stiffened and his body became lifeless.

Chapter 42- Settling the Score

Nina and Maia stood opposite Jack. Silence filled the air. Jack could hear the wind blowing and the squirrels chattering in the grass, but no one spoke a word.

"You won't succeed," Jack said, ending the silence.

Maia spat on the ground. "Is that what you said to Morton before you killed him?"

Jack turned to the building. *A magic barrier…* He licked his lips before turning back to them. "You really think you can kill me now, sister of *Mara*? And you, wife of Denida, you're *nothing* compared to me!" He lifted his arm and Darkness spiraled around it. "Enough playtime!" Jack swung his arm back and forth, sending forth a wave of dark energy, which enveloped both Nina and Maia in a thick mist, knocking them both out.

Jack lowered his arm, which made the dark cloud vanish. He tilted his head to a group of approaching guards. "Take them to the island and kill them. I've had enough of their antics," he ordered disgustedly. Jack rubbed his hands and turned back to the building. *I wonder if Danyel has killed Denida, yet…*

Inside of the building, there was no sign of Danyel nor Denida, so Jack took his time meandering to the upper floor. He could only stall for so long. Eventually, he arrived just outside of his chambers. He stopped, terror paralyzing him and keeping him from entering.

It's so quiet… the fighting must've stopped. Jack pushed his arms forward and the door sprang open with a bang. "Danyel?" He cautiously meandered into the room.

Denida knelt over a giant pentagram on the floor, slipping the necklace over his head. The infamous ring glinted on his finger. Jack looked through the room for Danyel. His mouth dropped at the sight of Danyel's lifeless body next to his squashed heart. *How can this be?*

"Jack, how nice of you to come." Denida glared up with a smile.

Jack shook his head. "You can't have won… this isn't possible!"

Denida placed his finger over his lips. "Oh, but it is… didn't you have a score to settle?"

"I don't need to!" Jack thrust both his arms forward. The door flung wide open and the Darkness concentrated in an intense fog, shielding him from sight. He turned and approached the door, which slammed shut before he reached it.

"Going somewhere?" Denida clenched his fist in front of his face, weakening the fog.

Jack bared his teeth. "You really want to do this? I'll finish the job Danyel began!" He charged Denida, who opened his fist, ending the fog instantly. Jack jumped back.

Denida raised his brow and waved his fist to the side. Jack smashed into the wall. Denida sauntered forward slowly. "I won't fight you. Maia needs to settle the score. Nina seems to be holding a grudge for some reason too, so no!" He stopped and squinted his eyes. "Where are they, by the way?" He rested his ring on Jack's forehead.

'The island,' his ring whispered.

"I see…" Denida stared at the island in the distance. "Maia helped me and Nina's in danger. He turned around and winked at Jack. "So, what you did might be a blessing in disguise!" He grabbed ahold of Jack and threw him with an immense wave of magic.

They suddenly appeared outside with trees all around them. Jack scoped their surroundings with worried eyes.

"I've used the necklace to put a shield on this island. Neither you, Nina, nor Maia can leave until the score is settled… I gave Maia my word!" Denida stood with his necklace sparkling in the sun.

I could kill her…

Denida chuckled. *'That's funny! Thanks for the joke. It's amusing that you actually think you can. Nina is determined like no other and you played a role in Morton's death,'* Denida spoke in Jack's thoughts. He turned his eyes on the forest.

"True, I did play a role in Morton's death, but Nina is pissy with me because she thinks I had a hand in Daniel's death, too."

"Daniel?" Denida frowned.

"Yes, and you know as well as I do, that I already fled Medusa. It was all her doing and she tried to kill me too, remember?"

Nina and Maia marched out from amongst the trees, their eyes dark as coal.

Denida gazed at Nina, then Jack and shook his head.

"Wait!" Denida strolled up to Nina with a tender gaze and put his arms around her shoulders.

"No!" Nina hissed. "Jack has to die for what *he* did to Daniel."

Denida flinched. "No, Nina. Daniel's gone. Claus kidnapped him and *Mara* killed him, not Jack. They've paid their dues. Please, do what's right…"

Nina ignored Denida and turned to Maia. "Shall we?" She tilted her head.

Maia nodded and clenched her fists.

"Well, I tried, but my word is my bond! You will have to pay for what you did to Morton; it's been nice knowing you, Jack…" Denida inhaled deeply and shrugged before he teleported away.

This isn't good! Jack jumped to his feet and ran into the trees to the left, but the girls followed shortly behind him.

***

Denida appeared outside of Heaven, but instead of approaching, he stayed still, watching Saint Peter guarding the entry, letting some in, but rejecting others.

He won't let me in…

"Denny?" Jesus' voice sounded behind him.

Denida turned around with a smile and waved.

Michael stood next to Jesus with the same tender smile Denida remembered. "You can follow us back to Heaven. We've finished our exploring for today."

Denida scratched his head, then followed them toward the Pearly Gates.

It didn't take more than a few steps before Peter noticed Denida and his eyes bulged. He stepped forward. "He's not-"

"Peter." Gabriel appeared and raised his hand. "God welcomes you, Denny." He widened his arms in an embrace. "The Lord's expecting you."

Denida glared at Jesus. "What for?"

"He shall inform you in person." Gabriel guided him through the Pearly Gates. Peter trailed Denida with his eyes, which were clearly filled with dismay.

Gabriel cleared his throat. "Why have you come here? You were asking about our past and now you are here? With God wanting to see you?" He paused and spun around. "I have this strange feeling something bad is about to occur…"

"Destiny has brought me here, Gabe!" Denida squeezed Gabriel's shoulder.

Gabriel lowered his head and sighed. "That's what I'm afraid of…" He continued inside of God's chamber.

God stood at the center of the room, waiting for them. "Thank you, Gabriel. You can leave us." He strolled over to Denida and shook his hand. "Nice gloves you have on."

Denida peeked at his hand, realizing it was the one with the ring under his glove. He withdrew his hand and rubbed his face. "You wanted to see me?"

"Yes, come." God led Denida farther into the room, where magic oozed off the ground. He stopped behind it and extended his hand into the stream of magic.

An image formed of Medusa killing Daniel.

Denida shifted his eyes to God, instead. *He sure looks like the form the Darkness takes...* He shook his head. "Please stop; I don't want to see this. I've already experienced it," he complained.

"But you haven't seen this!" God tilted his hand, making the image change to show Lucifer and Medusa next to each other. "The Dark Lord wanted this, but I am God, so I have the power to reverse it!"

More like Henna... "Reverse?" Denida raised his voice. "You can't change the past... and you *shouldn't*!" He ground his teeth. "Why were you waiting for me? Were you expecting me?"

God moved his hand away from the stream, ending the image. "Yes, I felt you coming. *Destiny*, I think you called it?"

Denida rubbed his forehead. "Let me think about it... but, why would you help me? I'm prophesied to destroy you."

"I want to give you a chance to escape the Darkness, which made you suffer!" God patted Denida on the back. "Spend some time here. The light might be the answer you need..."

He doesn't want me on Lucifer's side... Denida returned God's cold stare. "Peter wouldn't like me staying here-"

"He shall accept it from now on. You can come and go as you please. Let me know when you've decided." God returned to his throne.

Denida suddenly found himself outside of God's chamber. He arched his neck to gaze at the tower, rising high above. *Let's do this. There's no going back, now!* He marched toward it, passing by a multitude of angels. When he reached the tower, he paused and spun around, noticing Peter entering God's chamber. Since nobody else was around, Denida ventured inside the tower.

Heavani sat sipping tea, as she always did, with her son Daniel by her side, peering out the window at Heaven below. "So, the time has come?" She took another sip.

"You know why I've come?" Denida frowned.

"I always knew you'd be the one to bring us together, again..."

Denida slid into a chair next to her. "Will it go well?"

She tapped her finger on her cup. "I wish I knew, but that part always eludes me..."

"What are you two babbling on about?" Daniel stared at him in revulsion.

He looks exactly like Lucifer did when he was young...

Heavani grabbed Daniel's hand and squeezed it tightly. "He's going to reunite us with your father!"

"How?" Daniel demanded. "That's not possible with the magic barrier up here, let alone outside of Heaven. What is he going to do, just walk us out!"

"No, of course not," Heavani tried to reassure Daniel.

Denida tilted his head. "Actually, he's right. We are going to just walk out." He unbuttoned his shirt and smiled. "- with the aid of this necklace's magic!"

Daniel shrugged. "What's that?"

"It has the same magic as the Gates do. It's more advanced than Light or Dark magic!" Denida tilted his ring with his fingers. *I need to figure out why Peter stopped by to see God...* "But not yet, we'll just make everyone suspicious. Just get ready because we'll be going, soon!"

Outside, Denida strode to God's chamber, his mind pondering what was coming. *It's now or never!*

"Denny!" Jesus burst through the crowd of angels with his hands waving. "We finally found you." He huffed and wiped the sweat off his forehead.

"We... whose we?"

"Michael." Jesus pointed at Michael, who gracefully emerged from the crowd.

Denida licked his upper lip. "We should go catch up with your dad. It's been a while." He rested his arm around Jesus' back and guided him forward.

Peter exited God's chamber as they arrived at the entrance. His eyes glared at Denida irritably. "You'll have to excuse me; I need to watch the Pearly Gates." He pushed past them.

Denida watched him wander toward his post. Peter peeked back and met Denida's stare.

"Come on," Jesus yanked Denida inside the chamber with him. "Father, look who's here!" he called.

God clenched his fist in front of Denida, wearing a broad smile. "Always nice to see you, Denny!"

Denida returned the same smile, arching his neck. "How does Heaven look from up there, high above, looking down on Heaven?"

"You wish to see it?" God shook his head. "That's not-"

"Why won't you show him?" Jesus held a bewildered look.

God glared at Jesus and frowned, then smiled at Denida. "Anything for... Denida!"

Denida and Jesus approached the throne.

God stepped in front of Jesus. "Only one person, though."

Denida paused. "Why not Jesus first?"

"It's too high up for him. It will traumatize him!"

"It sounds intriguing, then." Denida sat down on the throne and it hovered above Heaven. Denida could only see to the edge of Heaven, but could see everything inside its boundaries. He squinted his eyes and peered at the tower. Just like everything outside of Heaven, he could not see inside its walls. *Lucifer's right!*

When he returned to the ground, Jesus was nowhere to be seen.

Denida looked around confusedly. "Where's Jesus?"

"He had to go. Did you enjoy the view from *my* throne?"

Denida nodded. "It was very… thoughtful."

God frowned. "Since you know how to shield your thoughts, you'll need to clarify what you mean by that."

Denida chuckled. "I learned a lot about Heaven from that, nothing more."

"I see. Learning is good. Did you find out if you want me to bring your son back?"

Denida nipped his lip. "He's dead!"

God tilted his head. "Yet, I'm God!"

Denida shrugged his shoulders. "You are and I might have taken you up on that offer once, but I realize now, that we shouldn't alter the past." He gazed into God's eyes. "I'm sorry, but I don't want to owe you or Lucifer anything… goodbye, *Shaddai*!" He spun around and strode out, leaving God with white knuckles.

Denida ran his hand through his hair and sped toward the tower.

Heavani stood hugging Daniel when Denida arrived on the top floor. "We can't leave because of the magic barrier. It keeps us here."

Denida clapped his hands together. "I know about that, but I can change it. I told you that!" His ring and necklace lit up, enshrouding the room in a bright aura, which encircled the three of them. He lowered his head to the ring and whispered a small chant.

A cloaking spell appeared around Denida and extended to cover Heavani and Daniel.

Denida walked back down the steps. Heavani trailed carefully until they reached the door to the tower. She hesitantly laid her foot outside on Heaven's cloud and gasped, speeding up to reach Denida.

When Denida stepped out of the tower, birds flew from the trees in the forest, but no one seemed to notice them.

So far, so good… "Let's go!" Denida ran his thumb across his ring and proceeded with cautious steps across Heaven, eventually passing God's chamber.

Heavani stopped suddenly. "God!" She raised her hand to point dead ahead.

"Granddad…" Daniel sped toward God and Heavani gasped.

Denida threw his arms around Daniel as God passed him. "No, stay still," he hissed.

God stood opposite Gabriel and Peter and tilted his head to gaze in Denida's direction. He stepped closer to the escapees, putting himself within arm's reach of Heavani.

"God!" Gabriel yelled. "You said something was up?"

"Yes, I can feel something brewing in the air." God stared in Heavani's direction. "Stay alert!" He waved his arm through the air. Heavani shifted, barely evading it.

"Maybe it's because you wanted to let Denida in," Peter moaned.

God turned away from staring, turning his full attention to Peter. "Wrong, but this is my will. You either follow it or I remove you from Heaven, like I did Lucifer…"

Peter grunted and returned to the Pearly Gates.

"Are you sure this is a good idea?" Gabriel scratched his forehead.

"There's only one person who can bring bad stuff here… and you know whom."

Gabriel's eyes grew misty. "We were friends, once. You still can-"

"No." God lifted his hand. "We're not talking any further about this." He marched toward his chamber, but stopped after a few steps and thrust his hand forward, wiggling his fingers wildly. "Something's here!"

Gabriel moved closer and Heavani stepped back, fidgety.

Denida rushed to her side and covered her mouth with his hand. "Relax, if he could see us, we would already know," he whispered.

God kept peeking back and forth until his eyes stopped, peering straight at Daniel.

Denida stomped his foot on the ground, catching everyone's attention. He lifted his hand to his lips. *'Stay silent.'*

Gabriel wandered over to where Denida stomped the dirt, which had made a dent in the soil. Gabriel scrutinized it. "What could have made this?"

God nodded. "Just some animals. Come with me!" He turned and strolled away.

"But-" Gabriel didn't take his eyes off the dirt.

"Gabriel!" God hollered. "Don't make me tell you again!"

Gabriel rushed after God.

"Let's get out of here!" Denida led Heavani forward. *Wait, where's Daniel?* Denida stopped and peered back. Daniel still stood, glaring after God. Denida hurried back after Daniel.

"Daniel, we need to go!" Denida took Daniel's arm and led him to Heavani, where he gave her Daniel's hand. "Make sure he stays close; we have to stay together!" He grabbed her other hand. "Heavani, is there any other way out, other than through the Pearly Gates?"

Heavani closed her eyes and shook her head.

"Then, there's no other choice." Denida approached the Pearly Gates, where Peter stood watch. Despite the magic cloak, he still felt uneasy, so he took cautious steps while staring around intently.

Peter spun around. "Is somebody there?" He squinted his eyes and wandered over, stopping right in front of Denida.

Denida's eyes darkened as he observed Peter.

Heavani carefully pushed herself and Daniel past the two of them and through the gates. She waved at Denida, but noticed that he was still staring into Peter's eyes.

Denida had his hand lifted near Peter's chest.

'You can't, ripping out his heart would reveal that you're here and it won't be enough to kill him, anyway. You would need a holy dagger,' Heavani spoke to Denida's thoughts.

Denida tightened his fist, then sauntered past Peter. "You can say that, and you're technically right, but someday..." he whispered as he sauntered past Heavani.

When they reached the Gate outside of Heaven, Denida stopped and turned to Heavani and Daniel. "The time has come for me to take the two of you to Lucifer... are you both sure this is what you want?" He glimpsed sternly at Heavani, then at Daniel. "Once I take you to Hell, there'll be no undoing it..."

Heavani stroked Daniel's hair. "I was torn from Luci; there's nothing I want more than to see him again!"

Denida turned to Daniel. "And you? You've never met your father!"

Daniel shrugged. "I'm a little nervous, but I know Mother really wants to, so let's go..."

Denida lifted his arm and formed a cone around the three of them, teleporting them to Hell.

"It's very dark, here," Heavani looked around them, yet her eyes were full of joy. "Where's Lucifer?"

Denida stroked his ring with his thumb and nodded. "It's this way." He led them through Hell. The demons they passed watched them, but jumped out of the way as soon as Denida approached.

Daniel looked repulsed by them, but like the demons, he didn't utter a word. "Wow," he suddenly blurted out at the sight of Lucifer's mansion.

"No entry!" The demon guarding the door put his hand on Heavani, but he swiftly withdrew it with a tormented scream. "What *are* you?"

"They're with me!" Denida's eyes flared red.

"Of course, 'Little Evil.'" The demon nodded and backed off.

Heavani hurried inside, her eyes searching hopefully.

Denida opened a set of doors.

The screeching noise of the wide doors made Lucifer lift his head. "Denida, what are-" Lucifer's eyes widened and he jumped to his feet.

Heavani and Lucifer slowly stepped closer, like they were afraid that what they were seeing might not be real. When they could see each other fully, they stood staring into each other's eyes, then rushed toward each other, meeting in a tight embrace. Lucifer lifted Heavani off the ground and showered her with kisses.

Daniel strolled into the chamber and started to examine every item in the room.

"You actually did what the Darkness couldn't!" Lucifer said with the utter joy in his voice that Denida had never heard outside of the flashbacks.

"A deal's a deal!" Denida winked.

"There's a shrine dedicated to Mom!" Daniel yelled, scowling.

Lucifer chuckled. "All I had for a long time, but not anymore. She was the only thing I thought about!" He smiled at Heavani, then kissed her tenderly.

Daniel examined the spot where the holy dagger had been. "Interesting; it's gone…"

It? Denida shrugged. "Daniel, meet your dad, Lucifer!" He pointed in between them.

Daniel shook Lucifer's hand. "Nice to know you."

Chapter 43- In Pursuit

We have to get him! Maia rubbed the sweat from her eyes as she ran through the forest with Nina in hot pursuit.

Jack darted to the spot where Morton lay buried, picked up a plank next to the collapsed table, then spun around to face Nina and Maia as they emerged from the woods.

Nina halted with her hands raised. "Don't do something stupid, Jack. There's no escape!"

Jack bared his teeth and tilted the plank.

Maia withdrew into the trees while Jack stayed focused on Nina. She tiptoed around the clearing, keeping her eyes fixed on Jack.

"You can run, but we'll just follow…" Nina shook her head.

"We?" Jack scoped and waved the plank around. "Where did Maia go?"

"I ran ahead of her. She'll be here in time," Nina said soothingly.

Jack turned his plank toward Nina. "What you're saying is; I could just kill you now, since you're alone!"

"You're welcome to try." Nina tightened her fists.

Jack slammed the plank into the tree next to him. "I might just do that." Glee glinted in his eyes.

"Not this time!" Maia burst through the trees.

Jack spun around and slammed Maia with the plank, breaking it in two.

Nina kicked Jack in the back, making his focus shift from Maia to her. Nina swiftly followed with another kick to his stomach, but Jack grabbed her leg and twisted her foot. She lost her balance and fell.

Jack glanced back and saw Maia getting up and charging him. He threw what was left of the plank toward her and ran away.

Maia rushed to Nina's side.

"No," Nina waved her arms. "After Jack!" She rocketed in pursuit with Maia. They finally caught up to him where the boat had been anchored.

Jack sat on the pier with his head buried in his lap. He lifted his head as Nina accidentally stepped on a branch. "He's right!" He got up and spun around. "Your husband set a real barrier here, but I'm not afraid." He approached them. "Neither of you can use magic here; it's sealed on this island." He smirked.

"Only one way then, isn't there?"

Jack winked. "Don't you see; we're stuck on this accursed island until someone dies, so I might as well up the ante and *kill* you both!"

"We'll see about that. I don't need magic to kill you!" Maia charged forward.

Jack jumped to the side and shoved her into the water.

Nina jumped into the water and swam to help Maia.

"Denida planned it well, throwing me here, where I can kill you both *myself*!" Jack sauntered around the beach, where he turned. "There's only one thing your husband forgot."

Nina pushed Maia up on the pier and dragged herself up to join her.

"I placed this here as a precaution." Jack pushed some bushes to the side, revealing a wooden box. He entered a code on a padlock and ripped it open when it clicked.

"Why do I have a bad feeling about this?" Nina glanced at Maia.

"No, it's two against one. Let's just finish this!" Maia trudged forward.

"But I have a little friend!" Jack pulled out a shotgun and aimed it at Maia.

Maia continued forward, speeding up, baring her teeth. Jack pulled the trigger and the blast sent her flying into the water.

"No," Nina gasped and ran to the edge of pier, but the only sight that met her was Maia's lifeless body floating in the water.

Jack tilted the barrel in Nina's direction. She jumped straight into the water on the other side of the pier. Jack ran onto the dock, tilting his weapon left and right, searching for her.

Nina plodded to the shore at a snail's pace as she waded through the water.

Jack lifted his rifle and pulled the trigger. *'Click,'* but nothing happened. Jack opened the gun and found it empty. He cursed under his breath and ran to the box, reloaded his gun, and pocketed some extra ammunition. He slammed the box shut and sprinted toward Nina.

When Jack reached the shore, Nina was gone, but several footprints in the sand led into the woods. "You can't escape me!" he screamed. Jack lifted his gun and proceeded in hot pursuit. Amongst the trees, he turned in a circle, scoping the area with panicky haste.

Nina appeared behind him and smashed a log over Jack's head, making him trip and lose his grip on his rifle. She continued hammering at Jack.

Jack put his arms over his head to block her blows, then spun around and swept her leg, knocking her off her feet. Jumping to his feet, he dashed toward the rifle.

Nina leapt on Jack's back, sending them both into a bush.

Jack jabbed at her and grabbed her throat, his hands tightening while her face paled. She tried to wrestle free. Jack strengthened his grip in response to her struggling.

Nina put all her energy into her left arm and punched Jack's side. His grip loosened and she dropped to her knees and crawled away.

'Chung, chung.' Jack raised the gun and shot into the air, causing the birds to scatter overhead. "I already told you; there's no escape!" He put his hand on her head and lifted it up while holding the shotgun near her face. "Got anything to say… you know what?" He moved her around on her back. "- I want to look at the horror in your eyes as you breathe your last breath!"

"Is that how it was for Morton?" Maia kicked Jack in the groin from behind.

Jack reached for his groin, his eyes watery.

Maia followed up with a circle kick, knocking him off his feet. "I'm immortal, in case you forgot!" She helped Nina to her feet.

Nina put her hand on her throat and sighed. "Denny was right, before. I was upset about Daniel… I couldn't target Claus, as he was already imprisoned, nor Mara, who was already dead. Jack was the only one left for me to blame, but he wasn't personally responsible for my son's death." Nina drew in a deep breath and looked at Maia. "He may not have killed Daniel, but he did murder your brother. This is your fight, Maia. You deserve to end it!"

"It will be-"

Jack charged, smashing his rifle into Maia's skull, then swung at Nina, but she caught it. Jack yanked at the rifle, but when he was unable to free it from Nina's grasp, he pushed forward, knocking Nina into a tree.

While Nina and Jack wrestled over the gun, Maia stood back up. "Enough!" she hissed and withdrew the holy dagger, the blade sparkling in the light.

The glint from the knife caught Jack's attention and he choked with dread. He smacked the butt of the gun into Maia's stomach, then fled, dodging back and forth as he ran.

"Are you okay?" Maia paused to check on Nina.

Nina nodded. "Yes, but he's unarmed now!" She lifted the rifle above her head.

Maia looked at her doubtfully. "If you think he doesn't have more weapons hidden somewhere, I'm sure you'll be disappointed!"

Nina stayed behind Maia with the shotgun at the ready. She glared at Maia, who only grinned, not concerned at all. "What if he has another one of those daggers?"

"Doubt it!" Maia waved her hand dismissively. "If he does, then at least I can finally attain peace." She peeked back at Nina and her eyes narrowed. "- but I need to avenge Morton, first!"

"That's… like *me...* " Nina ran her hand through her hair. "It's not good to live like that."

"I was cursed by my sister and this-" Maia raised the dagger in front of her face. "- can grant me the peace I've longed for, but Morton and I were supposed to always be there for each other. I *will* settle this!" Maia's voice cracked and her eyes filled with tears.

Nina reached over to hug Maia, but she froze in place before she reached her, standing completely still, as if she saw a ghost.

What's with her? "Nina?" She turned to see what Nina's eyes were fixed on.

Jack stood in front of them with two guards by his side. "Guess what I found in the tunnel; guns and guards!" He gestured toward them and the guard next to him fired a warning shot, striking the ground in front of Nina.

"You can't die, Maia, so I can't hurt you, but I can hurt Nina!" Jack pointed his finger at Nina and the guards aimed their guns. "Want me to finish her off or will you return the dagger you stole from me?"

Maia tightened her fingers around the dagger and glared at Nina. "You're going to kill us, anyway!"

"If you give me the dagger, I promise to only kill you," Jack smirked.

"I have no reason to trust you!"

Jack bared his teeth. "No? Well then, I can just kill you both!"

Maia glared at Nina. *I can't let her die after everything she's done for me…* "Fine, then she leaves and I die." Maia pointed the dagger's edge toward Jack. "Give me your word!"

"Of course, you've got it."

"Wait, you can't," Nina objected.

"You said it yourself… revenge is not the way to live. At least this way, I can see Morton, again…" Maia threw the dagger on the ground.

One of the guards stepped to pick it up, while the other one still stood with his gun aimed at Nina's head. The first one handed it over to his boss.

Jack examined the dagger, then ordered the guard next to him. "Kill her."

"No!" Maia jumped in front of Nina, taking the gunshots for her. "Go," she insisted. "I'll be fine!"

Nina swayed to the side and ducked in amongst the trees, avoiding the blazing guns.

Jack rushed forward and kicked Maia in the back. "You idiot!" He knelt and put the dagger to her throat. "You have been bad news from the very beginning."

"You should not have lied!" Maia spat in Jack's face.

"Grab her!" Jack ordered and the two guards dragged her up and twisted her arms behind her.

"You do know what this does?" Jack raised the dagger. It glinted in front of her. "It kills the soul, so there's no meeting Morton after you die!"

"No… no…" Maia shook her head.

"Yes." He lifted the dagger, but an arrow penetrated his shirt and fastened it to the tree behind him. Jack gasped and turned in the direction it came from.

Soldiers with the Underworld symbol on their shirts stood around several soldiers with bows at the ready.

"Charge!" Susan ran forward with her own machine gun raised. Jack's guards that held Maia released her and returned fire, but with all the soldiers Susan brought, they swiftly fell next to Maia.

Jack pulled the arrow from the tree, glanced at Maia, and sprinted into the forest.

When Susan reached Maia, she waved at her fellow soldiers to continue the chase, but she stopped. "Are you alright? Where's Nina?"

Maia lifted her arm. "Same direction that Jack went…"

Susan clenched her fist. "We had better hurry, then!" She dashed after the soldiers with Maia following her.

***

Nina paused to catch her breath. *I should be safe… wait. I wonder if Jack's box had more weapons!* She resumed running to the pier on the far end of the island. She stopped where she remembered Jack opening the box, but couldn't find it. *No, it must be here; it was right next to the pier!* After searching frantically through the brush, she tripped over the box.

Nina tore it open and rummaged through the spare ammunition, revealing a bowie knife. *Bingo! Not as big as his holy dagger, but better than nothing…*

"Nina, what a pleasant surprise!" Jack smirked from between the trees, sweat pouring down his forehead. "Just what the doctor ordered!" He thrust his holy dagger forward, but Nina pushed it aside with her blade.

"I won't be that easy, especially after what you did to Maia!" Nina slashed at him with the dagger, forcing him back to the side. Jack came after her again and Nina defended herself, desperately trying to find an opening. She ducked behind a tree. *His knife's blade is too big to keep up with!*

"You're just prolonging the inevitable! This is a holy dagger. Your knife can't compete!" Jack shouted in scorn.

"You're right!" Nina gripped the blade, flinging it at Jack. The hilt hit him in the face.

"Crap! I'm not bleeding, am I?" He lifted his hands up the where it hit.

Nina seized the moment and rushed Jack, tackling him to the ground. She tried to wrestle the holy dagger free.

Jack struggled to push the dagger toward her, but she fought back by using her knees to slam his stomach. He endured and gradually started making progress in getting the dagger closer to Nina, despite her fighting back with all her might.

"Die!" Jack screamed in her face. The tip of the knife reached her skin. Suddenly her grip on the dagger loosened as it penetrated her skin with a glowing wound. *Sorry, Denida.*

An army boot slammed into Jack's hand, sending the dagger spinning away.

"No!" Jack reached for the knife, but Susan punched him and he spat a tooth onto the ground.

"It's over, *Scientist*!" The disgust in Susan's commanding voice sounded clearly.

"Ma'am!" A soldier handed the dagger to Susan.

Jack wiped the blood from his mouth and looked at Susan. "Wait, I can help! I control Earth."

Maia helped Nina up, keeping her eyes fixed on Jack.

Soldiers escorted Nina a safe distance away from Jack.

Maia grabbed the dagger from Susan's hand and slammed it into Jack's chest. His body glowed. Jack gasped, opened his mouth, and the light vanished as he and the dagger disintegrated into ash.

Susan rubbed her forehead. "Well, I guess that's that…"

Nina inhaled deeply, then exhaled slowly. *It's over… but Daniel's still gone.* She glanced over at Maia. *Same with Morton. Now, we must grieve our losses.* She sat next to Maia and put her hand on Maia's shoulder. "I'm sorry, I know how empty it feels without the one you love…"

Chapter 44- Henna

Denida stood inside his office, sipping a drink. "It's finally over?" He turned to the Commander, who stood watch over Claus, sitting in a chair in between several solders.

"He led us back safely, yes." The Commander glanced at Claus.

"And John?"

"The Colonel is recovering. He should be back soon…"

Denida shrugged. "What am I supposed to do with you then, Claus? I must decide before I return to Earth…"

"I…" Claus sighed heavily. "I realize I did some bad stuff, too; hopefully you can forgive me."

Denida grunted. "Stay here with the soldiers. I need to talk to you, Commander." He strolled out with the Commander, who looked at him perplexedly.

"Sir?" The Commander frowned.

"When everything on Earth is settled, I want a magic barrier covering Earth. We must ensure that magic cannot be used on Earth, so that this doesn't happen ever again!"

"Yes, Sir!" The Commander saluted Denida. "I'll send the Colonel your way when he returns." He marched out of the front office.

"…Denida…" a voice sounded with a low screechy voice.

Denida turned to the voice. "Loki, right? The one from Odin's world!"

"That's me." Loki giggled with the same low voice.

"What can I do for you? Is something wrong with Odin… do I need to go to Valhalla?"

Loki grinned yet again. "No, Odin knows not where I am."

Denida squinted his eyes. "Then?"

"Odin has always been faithful to the queen, which is bad. You should not fall for it, too. I want to caution you…"

"Que- You mean Henna?" Denida's demeanor became more serious. "But I've never met her!"

"Oh, but you have… just not as a queen… you are being played. She's been watching… as someone else!" Loki laughed again. "Think, if you are as smart as they say…" He clenched his fist and held it in front of his face with one last chuckle. "Besides, isn't there a Gate you want to go to?"

Denida sighed. "We have not found a way to enter…"

"Oh? Was it not the shape of the holy dagger and…" Loki tapped his finger on top of Denida's glove with the ring underneath. "Something else that fits, maybe…" He lifted his arms. They transformed into wings and he flew away like a bat.

Claus tapped his foot nervously as the soldiers kept an intense watch on him.

"Leave us!" Denida surged through the door, let the soldiers out of the room, and closed the door behind them.

"Denny… I mean Denida?" Claus shifted in his chair.

"I know where I'm taking you!" Denida sat on the chair next to Claus. "You saved my friends, but still hurt a lot of people who can never trust you again, including Nina. I will leave you in another Underworld, where you can start anew!"

"Another?"

"The Wild West, led by Sheriff Robert, but if you disappoint me, there won't be another chance." Denida held out his hand.

Claus smiled and accepted Denida's hand. "Alright, thank you."

Denida shook it, then took ahold of Claus' hand. "No magic from you ever again!"

Claus nodded rapidly.

Denida closed his eyes tightly and they teleported to the Wild Western world, where they appeared inside a town.

Claus' eyes widened in amazement as he marveled at his surroundings. "This is… very different."

Denida put his hand on Claus' shoulder. "I hope I'm not making a mistake. Take care, Claus." He turned around and rubbed his glove, feeling his ring. After a few steps, he vanished and reappeared in front of the giant Gate.

"Denny!" Robert waved from in front of the Gate, where he stood next to Dan.

Dan approached Denida. "You're back. Do you have the ring with you?

Denida lifted his hand. "Always. Why do you ask?"

"I know this is crazy, but the gap in the insertion of the Gate is about the size of the dagger *with* the ring, so just maybe…"

Didn't Loki hint at something with my ring, too? Denida's eyes widened. "Maybe that's not as crazy as you think…"

Denida flashed Robert a smile, then tilted his head back.

Robert ran up to Denida. "Is something wrong?"

"I left an old friend in your world. Can I trust you to keep an eye on him for me?" Denida whispered.

Robert tilted his hat. "You've got it!"

"Glad to hear it." He turned to Dan. "Can you leave us? I need to test something with Dan."

Robert signaled to his lawmen. "Until next time, Denny." They marched away.

"Sorry, Denny. I wanted to try to extract some material from the Gate, but Robert couldn't find *Henry* to help me do it..." Dan's eyes looked like a sad puppy's. "But maybe with your ring?"

Henry? Denida clenched his fist. "We can do it without *him*!" Denida turned to Dan and extended his hand. "Let me see that dagger!"

Dan handed it to him.

Denida set the knife into the lock, just as they had tried before. Once again, he could see that the knife fit for the most part, except for the gap at the lower end of the shaft. He took the dagger back out and examined the bottom of the shaft. *It really does look like the ring fits there... and Loki hinted that it might be.*

Denida jabbed the blade into the dirt, then removed his glove and pulled off his ring. His finger maintained the mark of where the ring had been, which he stroked. After a moment of resignation, he placed the ring into the small indent at the bottom of the shaft. It slid right on.

Dan gasped. "That's-"

"Wait." Denida held up his finger and put the knife back into the Gate's keyhole. It now fit perfectly.

The Gate lit up with a bright silvery color, the passageway in the Gate active.

"How... how did..." Dan stuttered, waving his hands vividly. "We should-"

"Wait here in case something goes wrong."

"You can't just enter it. We don't know where it-"

"Yeah, yeah," Denida waved his hand dismissively and strode through the Gate. The silvery light encased him fully as he stepped through. When the light subsided, he found himself in a place with many individuals sauntering about. Some wore clothes from the Roman Empire, while others were glad in Western gear, and others still had clothes from the present day.

This place doesn't make any sense!

"You don't belong here."

Denida spun around to the voice. The person who stood before him couldn't be real. "What?" was all he could think of saying.

"This is the last Underworld, where the souls who died reside..."

So that's how the President of the Underworlds can be here!

"It is," the President remarked.

"You don't... fully die? I thought once a soul dies, it's gone for good."

"We do die. We can only leave this realm if our will is extremely determined to remain behind. You may know whom I am referring to..."

"Queen Henna was here?"

"*Is*, you mean," the President stated harshly. "She leads our world..."

"Here?" Denida's gut turned.

The President nodded. "Since you're here, I want you to meet someone..." The President guided Denida through the crowd of people and down a dimly lit path.

"This place looks-"

"You'll see..." The President waved his hand for him to join him as he entered the building.

Denida turned to look where he came from. *Fine*. He followed the President inside.

Within the building stood a man in the middle of the room, but the light behind him forced Denida to squint and hold his hand up to make out the figure.

"Don't recognize your old friend?" The man stepped into the light.

"Oh my... *Ignacio!*" Denida ran forward to examine him closer, but the joy he felt in his heart was short-lived. "Danyel has paid the price..."

Ignacio nodded solemnly. "I know. He already came by."

Denida frowned. "Then why did you want to see me?"

Ignacio took Denida's hand. "To let you know that it's okay to let us go."

"Us?"

Ignacio tilted his head to the other side of the room.

Denida turned his head.

"Hi, Dad." Daniel smiled innocently.

Denida gasped and fell to his knees. "Daniel?"

Daniel put his hand on his father's cheek, which Denida caressed tenderly. "You have to come back with me!"

"That's not possible." The President stepped forward. "We're on a different plane than the rest of the Underworlds. You can only visit with the dagger stained with Henna's blood and the Ring of the Underworlds..."

"But... but..." Denida's eyes welled up. "I finally have him back."

"She only wanted you to see..." Daniel said melancholically.

"She?" Denida shook his head.

"Henna," the President remarked.

"I don't even know her," Denida hissed.

"Are you sure about that?" The President shrugged. "She has several supporters still following her in your world, such as Odin. Have you not met anyone in Valhalla who reminds you of her?"

In Valhalla, I've only met that old guy, Anneh… Denida shook and a cold chill went down his back. "A…n… n… e… h… wait; h… e… n… n… a, King Anneh… Queen Henna?"

"Gender is irrelevant to her…"

Denida gasped and ran his hands through his hair. "How could I not see this?" He looked at the President with fury in his eyes. "Why?" he yelled.

"She expects you to carry out her prophecy. She's putting all the pieces in place…"

"No," Denida stormed out. "She's not going to win this time!"

As he passed through the giant Gate, it shut off.

Dan stood up from the rock he'd been sitting on, awaiting Denida's return. "Hi, welcome-"

Denida ignored him and yanked the dagger from the device, put the ring back on his finger, stuck the blade in the waist of his pants, and spun around to face Dan.

"Nobody goes near that Gate until I come back. If anyone tries, *kill them!*"

"What-" Dan's mouth hung open. "What was inside? Where did it lead to?"

Denida raised his finger and his eyes glowed with fire. "I repeat; no one!" He clenched his fist and teleported away.

As soon as he rematerialized, he squinted and lifted his hand to cast some shade over his eyes. *That sun is so intense! Aren't there any clouds?* He arched his neck but fell backward from the shock. Two suns hung opposite each other, one to the west and the other to the east.

Of course, this is Henna's world, why didn't I notice! He spun around, looking at the people passing by, but just as before, they kept their eyes on the ground, avoiding eye contact.

Denida stepped in front of one of them, but he just smoothly readjusted his path to wander around him. Denida grabbed the guy's head and tilted it upward.

The person's face stared back at him with rainbow-colored eyes. The guy raised his hands and pointed toward a castle standing in the distance before it vanished from sight with all the other people sauntering about.

The castle from Lucifer's memories! Denida stood mesmerized at the sight of it. As he approached, he noticed it wasn't comprised of glass, but rather, the same material as the Gates. Yet, something about it more *uniquely.*

The trek to the castle stayed as devoid of life as the castle itself. Each step inside reverberated with echoes throughout its great rooms and empty corridors.

"Welcome, Denida." Anneh appeared, folding his hands together.

"Still playing this role?" Denida snickered.

"Do you prefer this, maybe?" Anneh lifted his arm above his head and the face transformed into Henna's with the distinct rainbow eyes.

"You're revealing that willingly?"

"Why wouldn't I?" Henna smiled mesmerizingly. "You have been to the last Underworld, no?"

"What are you hoping to gain? Why did you show yourself as 'Anneh' and offer me an opportunity to take over your world?"

Henna glided next to him. Her feet floated with a silvery shade. "This world needs a new start. That's why I sent you the necklace, too…" She lifted her hand and an image appeared of Dan receiving the necklace.

"You?" Denida stepped back. "Why?"

"You need to fulfill your prophecy, Denny. It's not complete, yet."

"Wrong," Denida objected. "Lucifer got-"

"Azal, you mean…" Henna smiled gloatingly. "Lucifer's tale isn't over, yet. Daniel was your son's name? The same as Lucifer's. Death follows it…"

Denida shrugged. "That's-"

"The destiny I foresaw shall occur. I see which one shall play out now."

Denida's eyes wandered about the empty room. "And that is?"

"Death shall befall everyone." Henna smiled innocently.

Denida shook his head. "You need to let it go. There has been enough suffering…"

"You know what happened. They must pay!" Henna's rainbow eyes darkened.

Denida ran has hands through his hair, feeling small drops of sweat from the heat the two suns created. "No!" His scream echoed through the castle. He tore the dagger out from under his shirt.

"This ends, now!" Denida charged forward. Henna vanished just before he reached her, only to appear where Denida started from.

"Really?" Henna folded her arms. "You are only here because I willed it. I led you here to fulfill the duty I foresaw, nothing else."

Denida slashed at her. Again, she teleported across the room.

"You think that can kill me? I already died in this world. There's only one way to extinguish me, now…"

"We'll see about that!" Denida teleported forward and flung the dagger into her stomach. "Got you!"

Henna smiled and snapped her fingers. A force threw him backward into the wall of the strange material. "I already told you."

Denida exhaled deeply. His eyes fell on the dagger, which Henna picked up.

"Besides, don't you need *this* to repay Maia?" Henna extended her hand. "Go ahead." She winked.

Denida reached for it cautiously, expecting her to make a move before he took it, but nothing came. He retrieved the dagger and examined it. "Why?"

"As they say in your world, *everything happens for a reason.*"

"You don't belong here!" Denida waved the dagger.

"Maybe so, but as long as Shaddai, Gabriel, and Lucifer remain, so will I!" She met Denida's eyes and her rainbow colors stilled for a second.

Denida could not stop thinking of Heavani, who looked so similar to her. *Heavani, Daniel, and Lucifer are finally back together…*

"Shame they won't stay together." Henna lifted her eyebrows.

What? Denida burst to her side. "What do you mean by that?"

Henna giggled and shook her hand. An image appeared on the ceiling, depicting Denida using the cloaking spell to escape Heaven and standing in the very spot where God had nearly discovered them. "It's nice that you got away, seeing as Shaddai can see through all magic when a cone isn't shielding it, especially in Heaven…"

Denida gasped and he turned to Henna. "But… but…"

Henna pointed at God, staring directly at Daniel, who was shielded by Henna's magic. "Wonder what he said to his grandson. Daniel seemed interested in following him, no?"

"What are you getting at?"

"Shaddai cares only about 'Shaddai.' He will never accept Lucifer, let alone allow him to have her. Two birds with one stone, perhaps?" Henna frowned.

"She got out of Heaven. If Daniel wants to go back, he would have said so. I asked him before I took them!"

"Misery loves company," Henna patted Denida's shoulder and suddenly, Denida stood at Dynasty, but a tremendous feeling of unease came over him, making him unsure of what he just experienced.

I have to go to Hell! Denida smacked his fist into his hand and teleported.

Chapter 45- The Perfect Family

Denida appeared at the center of Hell and hurried to the mansion, which stood encased by Darkness, as always, but within the castle, it was completely different. The chambers brimmed with greenery. The corridors, which had been dark, now shone brilliantly with light. *The Darkness can't like how he drove it from here and changed everything so much...*

He ran into Lucifer's main room.

Gabriel sat on the throne in an empty room. His head lay on his arm, but when the door opened, he peered up. "Denida..."

"Where are they?"

Gabriel shook his head. "You shouldn't have brought them here!"

Denida licked his lips. "I asked where!" Denida screamed. "I have a really bad feeling."

Gabriel grunted. "About this going wrong?" he mocked. "I could have told you that, but you all made your own choices."

Denida huffed impatiently and walked into the backroom of Lucifer's chamber, where he'd seen the Heavani ornaments Lucifer had stored, but it was empty, now. He rushed back and shook Gabriel. "Remember Henna? Your bad queen."

"You shouldn't know more about her..."

Denida chuckled. "I know *everything* about her. I've even met her!"

"You know Henna?" Gabriel asked doubtfully.

"What she said about her predictions worries me; *'shame they won't stay together.'*" Denida's eyes had dread within them.

"I can't help you..."

***

"I will not fail you." Daniel lowered his head. "They will never hurt you, again!"

'*Good,*' a voice echoed out of the cloud above him. '*Go finish it.*'

"Yes, Granddad." Daniel gawked at the cloud.

The cloud above Daniel dissipated, so he cleared his throat and wandered away.

Heavani lay next to Lucifer, who put a wet towel over her forehead.

"Something wrong?" Daniel asked, sounding not concerned at all.

"Your mom isn't feeling well… she just needs some rest."

That's what he thinks!

Lucifer glanced at Daniel quizzically. He rose and approached his son, his eyes watching Daniel's every move. "Why did you think that?"

Daniel gasped. "You can read my thoughts?"

"The Darkness has that ability…"

Daniel waved his hands dismissively. "It's nothing important. I'm just skeptical."

"Have you forgotten who I am? I'm the Dark Lord. I lead Hell… I can tell when someone is lying!"

Daniel stared at his mother, lying in agony, then turned back to his father. "You really think God just let us stroll out?"

"What do you mean by that?"

"Just saying," Daniel shrugged.

Lucifer slammed Daniel into the wall. "What are you not telling me?"

"Luci," Heavani slowly reached out her hand, but swiftly drew it back as a heavy cough came.

Lucifer swept to her side. "What do you need?"

Daniel gazed with the same black eyes his father bore as he sauntered away.

"He's… just… a kid," she stuttered while coughing.

"I will behave." Lucifer held her hand and caressed it tenderly.

Daniel turned a corner and rested against a tree. He took a deep breath, then exhaled slowly.

"Daniel, I found you!" Denida strode toward him rapidly. "Where are Lucifer and Heavani?"

Daniel tilted his head toward where he'd come from.

"Lucifer!" Denida ran over to him, yanking Daniel with him, and dropped to his knees opposite Lucifer, next to Heavani. "What's the matter? Why's she looking so ill?" His hands jittered.

"We're not sure. She just started-"

"God," Denida hissed. "He could see us leaving…" He turned to Daniel. "What did God say to you?"

"That we'll regret leaving." Daniel approached on his father's side. "Because she can never leave Heaven without activating the curse!"

"Curse? What curse?" Lucifer rolled his eyes and turned his focus back to Heavani.

"Why do you think she's ill? The longer Mom's away from Heaven, the sicker she'll become."

Lucifer's eyes flared. "He played you. It's what Shaddai always does!"

"Really? Daniel laughed hoarsely. "How come he showed me where this is, then!" He pulled out a holy dagger, which glinted with a silvery glow.

"The holy dagger? Is this what she meant?" Denida jumped over Heavani and pulled out his own holy dagger. "No, she won't be right, this time! Daniel, put the knife down…"

"Relax! God didn't give this to me to use on Mom." Daniel sneered. "It's to kill *him*!" He turned to glare at Lucifer in disgust. He ran his tongue across his upper lip. "It's time."

Heavani rubbed her throat, starting to gag. Her eyes were bloodshot. "Lu… ci…" Her hand waved around. Lucifer grabbed it and held it tightly, but her hand crumbled into grey ash that dripped from his hand.

"No!" Lucifer screamed as she crumbled into ashes. He fell into the pile, sobbing while digging through it. "Heavani…"

"Time to die," Daniel smirked and swung his dagger downward, but Denida met the blade with his own. Lucifer, absorbed in his grief, didn't move a muscle.

Denida bared his teeth and put his weight on the dagger and pushed Daniel back into another room. He took a step back, holding his dagger up at the ready. "You knew this was going to happen?"

"What if I did?" Daniel sniggered.

"She was your *mom*. She…" Denida clenched his grip tighter on the blade. "Henna was right!" He flung his blade forward, but Daniel countered the blow.

Daniel's dagger lit up with each strike. It didn't take long before the room glowed brightly from the two dazzling blades.

Denida jumped to the side. "You can't win. You were locked up in a tower…"

"I was, yet I am the Devil's son, not just a petty apprentice!"

Denida grunted, then switched the dagger to the hand with his ring and used its power to charge at an inhuman speed.

Daniel, caught by surprise, was slammed into a tree.

"Enough!" Lucifer rushed into the room with his body encased in fire. He tightened his fist and Denida vanished, leaving only Lucifer and Daniel.

Daniel lowered the dagger and grinned. "Thanks, Dad."

Lucifer's flames subsided and he extended his hand. "Let me have the dagger?"

Daniel waved the dagger above his head, then smiled. "Of course." He approached and lay it in his fathers' hand and clenched his fingers around it. He peered into Lucifer's eyes and pushed it into Lucifer's stomach.

Lucifer fell to his knees as soon as the tip pierced his skin. He gasped in shock.

"Shaddai says '*goodnight.*'" Daniel pushed Lucifer down to the floor.

"Shad… dai?" Lucifer ripped the dagger from his stomach in rage and stuck it into a wall. Darkness surrounded him and kept deepening.

Crap, I didn't push it deep enough! Daniel stumbled backward in shock at the sudden Darkness.

Behind Lucifer, the image of the younger God appeared. '*God only sent him here to take Heavani from you, yet again…*'

"No!" Daniel waved his hands. "Granddad promised he would make me an angel like Gabriel if I saved us all from the vicious evil *you* and Mom do."

'*See? God only told him his side of the story. There's only one way.*' The dark cloud floated around to his other ear. '*Do what he did to Heavani…*'

Lucifer increased in size and switched to his demonic form. "Yes!" He threw down his giant hand, but Daniel rolled to the side and raced to the dagger.

Lucifer didn't hesitate. He slammed his hand on the floor in such a rage that all of Hell shook. Lucifer tightened his fist around Daniel as he lifted him up and started to squeeze the life from his body.

Daniel jabbed the dagger down, but Lucifer's rage made him impenetrable. No matter what he tried, Daniel couldn't even scratch his father. He struggled to breathe as he felt his strength dwindling. In desperation, Daniel lifted the dagger over his head as high as he could reach. Silvery light shone from it, then from him. A blast of light broke Lucifer's grip and sent him flying back across the room.

Daniel fell to the floor, but the dagger was still in his hand. *What was that?* He peered at the blade in his hand, mesmerized.

Behind Daniel, hordes of demons charged him. He thrust the dagger forward. Each slash was lethal, but there were too many of them, even with the holy dagger. He spun around and bolted into the room where his mom had vaporized into dust.

Daniel rolled on the floor to avoid a sudden attack from Lucifer and dropped the dagger.

Daniel glared. *He's back to his normal size. It's now or never!*

Lucifer flicked his fingers and the demons vanished.

Daniel grabbed the dagger next to him and slashed at Lucifer.

Lucifer jumped back, but when Daniel struck yet again, he grabbed his son's arm and tried to take control of the dagger. But Daniel fought back, determined, pushing forward to try to reach Lucifer.

The dagger slid from both their hands and flew across the room to land in Denida's hand. "Miss me?" He slid the dagger into his belt. "Surprised you're still alive!"

"You're not welcome here, Denida!" Lucifer yanked Daniel forward and pushed his head down into Heavani's ashes.

Daniel tried to wrestle free, but it was hard with his head buried in the silvery ash.

"Luci!" Denida yelled. "Stop toying with him. Just finish it!"

Lucifer released him and kicked him in the gut repeatedly before he turned to Denida. "Maybe 'Little Evil' has a point." He ventured over to Denida and held out his hand. "You freed them from God, so I'll be taking my dagger back." He glared at Denida menacingly. "Now!"

"It was destroyed when I killed Danyel. You remember him, don't you? He's the one you *protected*."

"Then, give me the one you just took! It's the only way our deal still stands!" Fire surrounded Lucifer and his eyes brimmed with rage.

"I'm sure I'm going to regret this, but it's for my family." Denida handed the dagger to Lucifer.

Lucifer grabbed it and smirked widely. "... And for mine!" He bared his teeth and spun around, only to witness Daniel sprinting away. Lucifer gave chase with the dagger drawn and ready. Demons appeared by his side. They roared through room after room, stopping when they reached a dead end. "Find him," he ordered his demons, who spread out searching.

The Darkness appeared above Lucifer. *'We can't let him get away.'*

"We won't fail!" Lucifer hissed.

Daniel glared at Gabriel. "Are we okay to stand here?"

Gabriel sighed at the sight of Lucifer and the Darkness. He stood still, shielding Daniel with his wings.

"Lucifer can't see us with my magic," Gabriel tapped the dagger he had sheathed in his belt and closed his eyes. "God wants me to take you back. Are you sure you wish to go?"

Daniel's eyes widened. "You've got a dagger, too. We can finish the job, still!" He reached for the one in Gabriel's belt.

Gabriel grabbed Daniel's hands. "No, it is God's. Besides, you think you can achieve that with everyone chasing you? Including your dad with his own dagger?"

Daniel sighed and lowered his head. "You're right. Let's go..."

Gabriel nodded solemnly and soared into the sky, flew over Heaven, and swept into the tower through its window. When his feet touched the floor, he unfolded his wings.

"I'm back here. Why?" Daniel bared his teeth at Gabriel. "God said I would be free!"

"That was only if you succeeded!" God sat on a chair, biting into an apple. "- you didn't. Lucifer is still alive."

"But Mom -"

"Heavani dying wasn't your doing."

"But I helped," Daniel insisted.

God handed the half-eaten apple to Gabriel. "But you didn't help enough. You think taking pride in your own mother's death helps?" God mocked him. "Besides, I was never going to let you, a son of *Azal,* out *there.* Roam freely in Heaven? Don't make me laugh." God patted the top of Daniel's head.

Daniel shook his hands. "Gabriel brought me back because you wanted to save me from Lucifer!"

God smirked at Gabriel. "Gabriel knows what happens to those who oppose me."

Gabriel clenched his fist on the windowsill. "I need to check on Peter."

God waved his hand. "Perfect."

Gabriel kept his eyes focused on Daniel, even as he flew away from the tower.

"Then you're just leaving me here like you did with Mom? I thought we had a deal!"

God closed his eyes. "Did you see the Darkness?"

"Yeah, it was amazing how it looks like a younger you."

"Want to know why?" God's eyes glared brightly.

Daniel shrugged.

"The Darkness is the version of me that lies in my heart. It was created inside of me in the dawn of days." God rubbed Daniel's cheek. "Yet, I still have it within me. I always will." He opened his hand and a holy dagger appeared on his palm. His eyes turned as black as coal and he thrust it into Daniel.

The pain coursed through him, but the dagger also made his body tingle, as if he were falling apart from the inside out. He glanced at his hand as it turned to the same silvery ash as Heavani's. *No, he didn't-*

Epilogue

Denida and the Colonel marched together to where Nina and Maia sat, Denida stopped just before reaching them. "How is it going?"

"Slow work, Sir. We've never created such a large barrier before, but we will succeed."

"I'm counting on you."

"Yes, Sir." The Colonel saluted and marched away.

Denida continued forward.

Nina met him halfway. "You were right," she whispered with her eyes fixed on the ground. "- about Jack. I let Maia..."

Denida kissed and hugged her tightly. "It's okay. I found something that may help you..."

"What?" Nina gazed at Denida, a frown furrowing her forehead.

Denida put a finger over his lip. "You'll see."

Denida smiled at Maia. "I'll come see you after, if you still want me grant you peace..." He took Nina's hand and smiled before they vanished and reappeared in front of the giant Gate.

Dan gasped at the sight of Nina and Denida approaching the Gate. "No, it's not a good idea!" He ran toward them.

Denida ignored him. He removed his ring and put it on the shaft of the dagger he'd reserved for the Gate and inserted it in the keyhole, which instantly made the Gate light up.

"Why is it so tall? If Dan is against it..." Nina stepped back.

"*Daniel*. You said you wanted closure, so come." Denida stretched his arm out.

Nina glared at Dan. "Sorry." She took Denida's hand.

Denida led her toward the Gate. Dan ran after. "Stop this! You said-"

Denida stopped and rolled his eyes, then muttered something and flicked his fingers. Dan grew drowsy and slumped to the ground.

Nina breathed deeply as she stood in front of the Gate.

"Don't worry. I've been through it once, already."

Nina shook her head. "Shouldn't we talk about how we move forward now, rather than go on a new adventure?"

"This is not-" Denida sighed, took Nina's hand, and kissed it tenderly. "We'll do it, as we always do- together, but you need to see this, first!"

Nina nodded, took Denida's hand, and walked through the Gate. Nina looked around confusedly at the many people strolling around in their dated outfits from various eras in this strange world.

Denida held her hand and led her through the crowd.

"Why are we here?" Nina clicked her tongue.

Denida smiled and nodded, then entered a building. "President, is he here?"

"Mom?" a low voice sounded from across the room.

Nina spun around with her mouth hanging open. "You can't be… Daniel?"

Daniel waved. "Hi, Mom-"

Nina ran up to Daniel and squeezed him as tightly as she could muster. "How can you be here?"

"This is the realm where souls who die permanently go… I brought you here to say goodbye before…" Denida rubbed his eyes. "I destroy the dagger by using it on Maia…"

Daniel knelt next to Nina. "I'm okay and what happened to me is not your fault. You need to stay alive with Dad."

Nina shook her head, then pinched Daniel's cheek. "You're right. I know you are…"

"But?" Daniel stared at Nina.

"It's just… hard," Nina sighed.

"I know you can do it." Daniel winked. "I've got an awesome Mom, after all!"

Denida stayed next to the President, leaving Nina alone with their son. "Where is Henna? Is she ever here?"

The President groaned. "Sometimes, but she comes and goes. We're not privy to her whereabouts. Why do you ask?" He gawked, puzzled.

Denida shrugged. "Nothing," he waved his hand.

Daniel sauntered over with Nina's hand in his. He stopped in front of Denida and put Nina's hand in Denida's and smiled softly. "Bye." He vanished and they appeared outside of the Gate.

Nina hugged Denida tightly with moisture in her eyes seeping onto his shoulder. She kissed him softly. "Thank you for showing me that. Please, go do what you need to, then come back to me. Say goodbye to Maia for me, and thank her for everything. too."

Denida nodded solemnly and took the dagger from the keyhole, removing the ring. He chuckled, eyeing Dan. Instead of waking him up, he just lifted his ring to his lips and whispered, "Dynasty." They immediately teleported back to their home world. Denida swiftly teleported himself farther to Earth.

Maia sat next to a lake, running her fingers through the water, creating ripples.

"Hello again." Denida knelt next to her. "I'm back. Have you decided if you want to go through with it?"

"I have the same view as before. Mara's curse is in me. Her viciousness appeared in me. I need to die to end it..."

"In that case. Nina wanted to say goodbye and thanks for everything..." Denida took out the dagger. "Your death will destroy this." He handed her the dagger.

"Destroy? Why? Jack had the one he used on Morton!"

Denida shook his head. "This dagger vaporizes with the person."

Maia shook her head. "Morton didn't vaporize and he was dead for sure!"

"Maybe the curse-"

"No," Maia insisted. "Jack shot me and it didn't kill me!"

"The Darkness can release the curse. Jack forgot you had it." Henna sat down beside Maia. "Morton's dead. He's in my world with the other dead souls... Denny's been there, so he can tell you."

Maia tilted her head at Denida, then at Henna. "How is he?"

"Why don't you go see for yourself?" Henna winked at Maia.

"You're right." Maia clenched both her hands around the shaft and thrust it into her stomach. The blood gushed out, but her eyes lit up. "I feel... tingling."

Shortly after her words, the blade started to dissolve into silvery ash along with her body, but her face didn't change from the peaceful smile until the wind blew the ash away.

Denida rubbed his hands against each other and peeked over at the ash on the ground. His eyes met Henna's smile. "Goodbye," he hissed.

"Bye? But we're only getting started, Denny."

"No!" Denida sprang up. "No more about this feud ever again. I've got Lucifer's-"

"Azal? You think he determines what I do? It's destined!"

Denida ignored her and stalked away.

Henna appeared beside him. "You're the one who's destined to set everything right! Have you forgotten the *legend*?"

Denida arched his neck. "You don't belong here. Whether I'm the one from your legend or not, we are done!"

Henna chuckled. "Perhaps, but someday, the time will be ripe. Destiny has ordained it. I'll be waiting you know where." She vanished from sight.

I wonder if my deal with Lucifer was part of her plan all along. Denida shook his head. *Enough of this! I can finally see my beautiful girl, instead of all this nonsense.*

He shrugged when he arrived at Dynasty. The warm air blowing reminded him of the gardens both Heavani and Henna adored. *It's finally Spring... time for a new beginning...* His eyes fell on the Butler, who greeted him with a smile.

Denida approached him. "Where's Lady Nina?"

"Not at the estate. She went to see her human form."

Why would she go to Earth... and how did I miss her? Denida smiled somberly, then teleported to Earth.

Nina sat on a bench, staring at her human side.

"Nina?" Denida joined her on the bench.

She sighed, not taking her eyes off her human counterpart. "I hope she will be okay and not end up as bad as..." She shifted her eyes to Denida. "The sad fate that met Maia."

"I'm sure she-" Denida gasped as he saw his own human side emerging from the school, his hair all crispy white.

The boy walked across the playground and stopped next to Nina's human form.

Their eyes widened. Nina grabbed and squeezed Denida's hand.

Denida kissed her hand, not taking his eyes off the humans, who walked away hand in hand. "Together at long last."

"Maybe things will look as bright as the shade of your human's hair in the future..."

Denida gazed into Nina's eyes as if nothing the world had to offer mattered and met her lips, finally feeling like he came home.